Forgotten Memories

"Can you believe that I'd forgotten how beautiful you are?" Rhys said as he set the wine aside and rounded the bed toward Juliana. He stopped inches away, reaching up to draw one of her jeweled pins from her hair.

A cursed trembling began in Juliana's body as Rhys removed the pins one by one until her hair tumbled down about her shoulders. His wine-scented breath feathered over her face, summoning up long-buried memories—of the way his mouth had once covered hers, teasing and possessing.

She stiffened, fighting the memories. This wasn't the Rhys who'd taken her with care on their wedding night. This was the Rhys who believed her a schemer and a liar. And she would *not* let him seduce her.

Rhys lifted her hair, letting it fall over his hands. "I'd also forgotten how soft your hair is." He stroked her hair back over her shoulder.

He took a gulp of wine, then set the glass down hard on the table. "Take off your clothes," he said tersely.

"No! N-not until you leave."

To her chagrin, he laughed, a mocking, hard laugh. "Perhaps I didn't make myself clear earlier. You're my wife now, and I'm not leaving, Not ever again. . . ."

STORMSWEPT

Deborah Martin

A TOPAZ BOOK

To my husband, Rene,
the man with whom I've weathered many a storm.
Thanks for eleven wonderful years.

TOPAZ
Published by the Penguin Group
Penguin Books USA Inc., 375 Hudson Street,
New York, New York 10014, U.S.A.
Penguin Books Ltd, 27 Wrights Lane,
London W8 5TZ, England
Penguin Books Australia Ltd, Ringwood,
Victoria, Australia
Penguin Books Canada Ltd, 10 Alcorn Avenue,
Toronto, Ontario, Canada M4V 3B2
Penguin Books (N.Z.) Ltd, 182–190 Wairau Road,
Auckland 10, New Zealand

Penguin Books Ltd, Registered Offices:
Harmondsworth, Middlesex, England

First published by Topaz, an imprint of Dutton Signet,
a division of Penguin Books USA Inc.

First Printing, September, 1995
10 9 8 7 6 5 4 3 2 1

 REGISTERED TRADEMARK—MARCA REGISTRADA

Printed in the United States of America

Prologue

Carmarthen, Wales
June 1783

In the shadows the Welshman stood, his keen eyes trained on the brightly lit mansion. He'd learned the hard way to avoid the light ... to watch, wait, and plan rather than attack. He'd taught himself to use cunning over brute strength and never to tip his hand to the enemy.

But tonight called for a different strategy—stealth, yes, but some daring as well, even brashness.

Once, long ago, he'd been brash, relishing the light, using it to preach his ideas. Once he'd sought noble goals—liberty, freedom, and justice for his beloved Wales.

Not tonight, however. Tonight he sought justice for himself. And that was more obtainable.

He eyed the wall he'd scaled so long ago. Laughter and music trickled out to where he stood, but it didn't deter him. He threw the rope and grappling hook over, pulling until it caught on the wall's stone lip.

Years ago he hadn't used a rope. Love had sent him grasping for a tree branch, then up and over, like a wanton fool.

Love. What a farce. Lust, more like, of the kind only a green lad would call love.

He braced his feet against the brick, then climbed swiftly hand over hand, pausing at the top to switch the rope over and climb down. Once he reached the bottom, he left the rope where it was. He didn't think he'd need it later, but one never knew.

Glancing around the garden to make certain no one had seen him, he removed his cloak and left it behind the nearest hedge. He inspected his formal attire—the gray silk waistcoat with its gold braid edging and the stark black cutaway with matching breeches—all carefully chosen for this night. He brushed a few specks of dirt off his sleeves and straightened his snowy neckcloth.

Then he walked toward the light.

Leaning over the balustrade that ran along the second floor of Northcliffe Hall, Juliana St. Albans paused to observe the guests milling below. Here and there bobbed a white-wigged male head with powdered hair tortured into unnatural sausage curls and ringlets. And the women wore elaborate coiffures beyond any Juliana had seen. A particularly bizarre one sailed into view, with a miniature ship floating in a sea of foamy hair that rose almost two feet above the haughty woman who wore it. Stifling a laugh, Juliana drew her gaze elsewhere before she followed her perverse urge to toss her handkerchief down atop the ship.

She knew few of the guests whom her family had invited. Only the cream of Carmarthen society was in attendance. The other guests were English nobility who'd come for the festivities. A twenty-course feast had been prepared, champagne and wine were flowing freely, and a very expensive, nine-piece orchestra had been engaged to play music by Handel and Arne.

Darcy ought to be pleased, she thought as she caught sight of his large frame near the entrance door. And indeed he looked inordinately pleased with the crowd and their obvious astonishment at this display of ostentation.

It was the first time since Father's death two years ago that the St. Albans family had possessed the wherewithal to purchase such extravagance, and Darcy hadn't hesitated to provide it on this important occasion.

Her engagement party.

She sighed. She could have managed without the elaborate celebration, but whatever Darcy St. Albans, the Earl of Northcliffe, wanted, he got. And he'd wanted to impress everyone with his newly gained wealth.

She scanned the room until she found her other brother, Overton. Unlike Darcy, he was scowling, looking as if he'd rather be almost anywhere than here—

especially if the anywhere was hunting or fishing or trading wild stories with his rapscallion friends. She smothered a laugh. The two of them were so very different.

Still, they both approved of her fiancé. Stephen Wyndham, Marquess of Devon, was English to the core, which mattered a great deal to them. Darcy in particular had taken to the man instantly. The two men had already entered into a mining project together, and Darcy had great plans for future joint investments. Indeed, he'd been delighted to find the marquess to be the kind of ambitious and determined man who would go far in business and politics. Not unlike himself.

Not unlike Darcy. Oh, bother, that didn't sound good at all. Darcy always tried to bully her into doing what he wished.

Suddenly, Stephen entered from the drawing room and was surrounded by well-wishers. At the sight of him, she felt the tightness in her chest subside. No, for all his ambition, Stephen was kind to her, even gentle. He was nothing like Darcy.

He was more like Rhys.

Dear heaven, where did that come from? she thought. She squeezed her eyes shut and tried to wipe all wayward thoughts of Rhys Vaughan from her mind. Instead, a tall, lean orator with eyes blue as the Celtic sea shimmered into focus in her mind.

After six years, she told herself bitterly, she should be able to evict the man from her thoughts. Especially now that she knew he was dead.

Yet guilt nagged at her. *I'm not betraying him by doing this,* she told herself. *I'm not!*

She had a right to be happy. She wasn't getting any younger. At twenty-four, she was practically on the shelf. Fortunately, Stephen didn't care about her advanced years. He claimed to love her, and he was certainly willing to make her his marchioness. And, more important, give her children.

Children. She colored. She well knew how children were made, even if six years had passed since she'd engaged in such behavior. Six years since Rhys had vanished after spending one glorious night. . . .

Ruthlessly, she stifled that memory. Thinking about another man at her engagement party was absolutely unacceptable. Stephen loved her, whereas Rhys . . . Rhys couldn't have loved her, no matter what he'd claimed. If he had, she'd have received some word from him in the years before he'd died. If he had, he'd be here and she wouldn't be marrying another man. She wouldn't be in the sticky position of having to "revive" her virginity.

Her former maid, Lettice, had sent her to old Brywn for advice on that particular procedure. The old Welsh-woman had guffawed and said that after six years Juliana was liable to be "tight as a glove" anyway. Then she'd advised Juliana to sprinkle pig's blood on the sheets when the time came.

Yet Juliana still worried. What if Stephen caught on to the trick? What if she didn't play her role well enough to fool him about her experience? It would take some doing to act as naive with him as she'd been with Rhys when he'd first lain atop her and . . .

Another blush stained her cheeks. "Oh, bother." She lifted her skirts and stalked toward the stairs. She wouldn't spend another moment thinking about a man who was either dead or too dense to remember where he'd left her. It was disloyal to fill her head with thoughts of anyone but Stephen on this night.

As she descended the wide staircase, first one and then another of the guests looked up until all eyes were on her. The attention made her squirm, especially when Stephen turned his ardent gaze on her and smiled. The crowd smiled, too, their eyes dark with secret knowledge. It gave her a headache.

They looked at her as if she weren't in on the secret, as if she floated in a fuzzy state of complete naiveté. She could almost hear every woman's secret thought—*You'll see. 'Tis quite a surprise, being bedded.* She could almost hear every man's secret wish to have a virgin bride in his bed.

Even my fiancé, she thought as Stephen's gaze drifted to her low décolletage. She stiffened, then chastened herself for it. Stephen was to be her husband. Of course he found her desirable. She wouldn't want it any other way. After all, she certainly couldn't have children unless he did.

Still . . .

She felt his gaze hot upon her, on her exposed shoulders and the soft swells of her breasts, and wondered why it made her vaguely uncomfortable.

When she reached his side, he crooked his arm and she clutched at it, forcibly squelching her traitorous thoughts.

"The beauty has arrived at last," he murmured with a smile.

She relaxed. This was, after all, only Stephen, who always did his best to make her feel at ease. It was with genuine fondness that she smiled back at him and murmured, "Good evening, my lord. You're looking very handsome this evening."

He started to say something, but others began to crowd around them, offering congratulations. Some had questions about the wedding and Stephen answered every time, even when the questions were addressed to her. She frowned. It was one of Stephen's few irritating qualities, his tendency to speak for her. Of course he was merely saving her the effort of answering, but occasionally she wondered if he might be indifferent to her opinions.

Unlike Rhys . . .

Oh, stop it! she told herself.

Suddenly, Stephen placed his hand over hers and squeezed, signaling that someone had addressed her who apparently hadn't been satisfied to let him answer for her.

"I'm sorry," she murmured. "What did you ask?"

Lady Eldor frowned, crinkling the papery skin about her beady eyes. "I suppose you won't live at Llynwydd any longer, eh?" She tapped Juliana's hand with her fan, as if contemplating where to smack her if Juliana gave the wrong answer.

"No, of course not." She could only hope her voice sounded more firm than she felt.

Stephen took it from there. "Llynwydd belongs to Juliana, so of course we'll repair there from time to time. But we shall spend most of our time at Wyndham Castle in Devonshire, shan't we, my love?"

With Stephen's expectant gaze on her, Juliana fixed a bright smile to her face. "Certainly. And I am so looking forward to exploring Stephen's estate."

"Indeed," said Lady Eldor. "I'm sure Wyndham Castle shall be a more enjoyable place to live. And no doubt easier to manage than Llynwydd, since you won't have to deal with stupid and incompetent Welsh servants."

Juliana bristled. "I don't hire stupid servants. Furthermore, the Welsh are neither stupid nor incompetent."

Squeezing his fiancée's hand almost painfully, Stephen hastened to add, "Juliana's been fortunate in her choice of servants, but I'm sure she'll find mine more agreeable. You'll be happy to know that they're all thoroughly English."

As Lady Eldor merely sniffed and moved off to relate Juliana's comments to her friends, Juliana bit the inside of her lip to keep from correcting Stephen.

In truth, Wyndham Castle was a Norman monstrosity filled with surly servants capable of cowing the bravest lady who sought to manage them. The thought of taking on that task worried her more than managing Llynwydd ever had. Thoroughly English indeed! If the servants at Wyndham Castle were indicative of the English nation as a whole, then England was in sad straits.

"Is my sister waxing poetic about the Welsh again?" came a voice behind Juliana. It was Darcy, scowling at her.

Stephen flashed Juliana an indulgent smile. "You know Juliana. She defends everyone."

Darcy stared at her, a question in his eyes, and she stared back impudently. Let him think what he wanted. Her feelings about the Welsh were not his concern. Nor was her past with Rhys.

Her brother sighed. "In any case, I came to ask if either of you know that fellow over there by the window. He's been glaring at the two of you ever since Juliana came downstairs. He looks familiar, but I can't place him."

When Juliana turned to see whom he meant, Darcy added, "Too late now. He walked off while we were talking. I'll point him out later. Handsome fellow, but I don't like the looks of him. He's got a hard face, and he never smiles. Not a congenial sort at all." Darcy glanced at Stephen. "Hope he's not one of *your* friends."

"Oh, I doubt it." Stephen scanned the room. "That doesn't sound like any of them. No doubt he's some acquaintance of your wife's."

The two men continued talking for some time about mutual friends, while Juliana's mind wandered. She wished she'd seen the man Darcy had spoken of. The attention she was getting from Stephen's friends was enough to put her on edge without having some stranger watching her.

All this attention was irritating. As mistress of Llynwydd, the estate her father had given her, she'd led a solitary life. But her life would be solitary no more, for Stephen had already told her that as mistress of Wyndham Castle, she'd be doing a great deal of entertaining.

She hated entertaining. She much preferred the challenge of managing Llynwydd. Running the place had been her only joy for several years, even though her parents and their English friends had thought it scandalous that a woman should live away from home and manage an estate alone.

Fortunately, the Welsh tenants and staff hadn't cared who ran Llynwydd as long as it ran smoothly and didn't trouble them. And once it was run efficiently, the estate had begun to gain in profits, which had silenced her family's objections.

A pity she had to leave it all behind.

A servant stepped into the drawing room then and announced that dinner was served, but Juliana scarcely noticed, her mind focused on the estate located two hours' ride north of the St. Albans estate and Carmarthen.

Indeed, as supper was served and all gasped at the artistry of a gilded suckling pig, Juliana could think only of vaulted halls, the rose garden she'd worked so hard to cultivate, and the Welsh landscape paintings and furniture she'd traveled far and near to acquire.

She sighed. Now Llynwydd was to be her occasional home only. It was enough to make her reconsider her decision to marry.

After all, she couldn't yet claim to love Stephen. She felt a great deal of affection for him, of course, and she respected him. In time, she would no doubt learn to love him. But it did bother her that she didn't love him now. Indeed, marriages that weren't based on love could be disastrous. Darcy's marriage amply illustrated that.

She glanced over at her sister-in-law, Elizabeth, and

tensed. The woman wore her usual carved-ice expression, which never cracked, not even in the presence of her husband. Darcy's reasons for marrying the young heiress had been thoroughly mercenary. But were Juliana's reasons for marrying Stephen any different?

Yes, she told herself firmly. 'Twas one matter to marry for money, but quite another to marry for companionship. Even Llynwydd was lonely at night in the dead of the cold winter. She was tired of being alone. She wanted a husband and children.

Besides, she liked Stephen. She truly did. They'd do nicely together.

Before she knew it, the meal had passed, and Darcy had risen to begin the evening's toasts. He turned to her, his broad, serious features softening before he faced their guests.

"Welcome, my friends, to this celebration," he said in stentorian tones. "You honor me by your attendance at an occasion of such importance to me and my family." He paused, a wide grin crossing his face despite his efforts to appear solemn. "A year ago, this fine gentleman, the Marquess of Devon, came to court my sister, Juliana. And as luck would have it, they found favor in each other's eyes."

A shadow passed over his face. "Although my father died before he'd had the chance to meet Lord Devon, I know he would have approved of his lordship. Lord Devon is one of the most respectable, intelligent, and engaging men I've ever known."

Darcy stood a little straighter, looking almost military in demeanor. "So tonight, my friends, I'm pleased to announce on behalf of my mother and my late father, the betrothal of my sister to this honorable man."

He held up his glass, his face flushing with pleasure. "A toast! To Lady Juliana and her husband-to-be, Stephen Wyndham, the Marquess of Devon! May their joy be unbounded!"

All of the guests raised their glasses, preparing to cheer, but before a sound could be uttered, another voice rang out loudly from the other end of the hall. "I protest that toast!"

Darcy paused, incredulous, even as the other guests hesitated with their arms suspended in the air as if held by invisible wires. And Juliana's heart dropped into her stomach.

She searched for the man who'd spoken and found him at the other end of the ballroom. He was impressive, standing tall and lean in immaculate evening clothes. Was this the man Darcy had spoken of earlier? She couldn't make out his features at this distance, for he stood in the shadows, but what she could see chilled her.

He was dressed more soberly than her guests, and his entire bearing bespoke arrogance. The gasps of those around him had as little effect as she imagined arrows would, for he carried himself forward with the invincibility of a battleship.

He snatched a glass suddenly from one of the guest's hands as he passed. "In fact, I would propose another toast entirely."

Something in his voice tweaked her buried memories. *It cannot be*, she thought. His accent wasn't right. And as he came closer, she could tell he wore the expensive clothing of a lord, not the modest garb of a radical. What's more, he was too big, too self-assured, and entirely too imposing to be . . .

But try as she could to deny it, her fear became a certainty as he strolled slowly up the long row of tables toward the head table. Speechlessly, she stared at the broad shoulders, the curly black hair cropped at the chin and framing an arresting and painfully familiar face. She rose, not realizing that she did, disbelieving the evidence of her own eyes.

Darcy seemed to regain his wits. "What preposterous rudeness is this? I don't know you, sir, and I'm certain you weren't invited here. Pray you, leave at once, before I have my footmen throw you out!" He signaled one of the servants, who nodded and hastened toward the stranger.

With a sinister clang, the man withdrew his sword. His was no dress sword, worn by the pretty gentlemen of London to affect a pretend masculinity. His weapon had a lethal look that made the summoned footmen fall back.

Sure of his audience now, the man spoke directly to her brother. "There seems to have been a mistake." He had finally reached the front of the room and stood not six feet from the head table. "If anyone should have been invited, 'tis I. But then, I'm sure you treacherous blackguards thought yourselves well rid of me." He scanned the head table, including every one of its members in his scathing glance. "Otherwise, you wouldn't be engaging in this farce."

Coloring from head to toe, Juliana stared mutely at the man's face. Her pulse raced madly. *'Twas impossible, simply impossible!*

Stephen jumped to his feet at her side. " 'Treacherous blackguards'! 'Farce'! I'll call you out for that, sir!"

The man chuckled, his dark face lit with a frightening amusement. "Ah, but you have it all wrong, Lord Devon. I should call *you* out. Ask Juliana."

Stephen shot her a questioning look, but Juliana took no notice as the man before her fixed his gaze on her, searing her. Blue eyes, she thought dimly as her throat began to tighten and her knees to shake. Dear heaven, only one man had those blue eyes.

"You should have told him, Juliana," he said in clipped tones. Disapproval warred with fury in the lines of his face, making her breath catch in her throat. " 'Tis an important thing to leave out of any discussion about betrothal."

"It c-can't be tr-true ..." she whispered, stumbling over the words.

His eyes narrowed. "What can't be true? That I've returned? That I've come to reclaim my lands ... my inheritance ... you? Oh, yes, love, it most certainly can be true. And is."

At his words, the entire company was thrown into confusion, except for her brothers, who bristled and looked as if they'd commit murder any moment.

Though the man's voice was laced with bitterness, she felt no answering anger, just a rapidly numbing shock. It was like seeing a corpse rise from the grave, yet the man before her was no corpse.

"Rhys ..." she whispered, clasping her chair for support as her knees began to buckle in earnest.

Rhys stared at her, lips unsmiling and expression cold as the frostiest winter. Then he lifted his glass in a toast. "To Juliana, my darling wife. I've come to take you home."

And for the first time in her entire life, Juliana fainted.

PART I

Carmarthen, Wales
July 1777

"If you marry a green youth,
  you will cut the sprouting corn;
  and you may find that the harvest
  is too stormy to be borne."
  —Anonymous,
    "Stanzas for the Harp"

Chapter One

"As sweet is your pose
As a riverbank rose
Or a posy where lily or lavender blows."
—Huw Morus,
"Praise of a Girl."

"Is that him? Rhys Vaughan? The man who's giving the lecture?" Juliana St. Albans whispered to her lady's maid, Lettice Johnes, who sat beside her. Juliana gestured to where a serious-faced young man stood stiff and silent at the front of the crowded room.

Amidst the clamoring Welsh radicals called the Sons of Wales, he didn't fit in. He wasn't like the others sitting in the basement of Gentlemen's Bookshop in Carmarthen, who were rabid with enthusiasm. "That can't be him," she added. "He looks too quiet."

"Too quiet?" the slender, ruddy-cheeked Welshwoman murmured. "Too quiet for what? Or did you think he'd look like his father, the squire—a hard-drinking, hard-boasting gambler?"

"I wasn't sure what to think." She swept her gaze around the room. "None of this is what I expected." In her naiveté, she'd thought to find earnest young men discussing politics in earnest voices ... not this rabble of hotheads.

"I don't suppose you want to go home now?"

Lettice sounded so hopeful that Juliana had to smile. "Not a bit. After I went to all the trouble of following you here and dressing like a poor Welsh servant, I'm certainly not going to leave."

"I should never have told Morgan I'd attend," Lettice grumbled. "And I shouldn't have let you stay once you showed up. Morgan won't be happy when he finds out."

"It's not your fault I'm here. If anything, it's Morgan's. He's always so heedless of his surroundings when he courts you beneath my window. I couldn't help but overhear him mention the meeting." *And Rhys Vaughan's part in it*, she thought, although she dared not say that.

Lettice sighed. "Still, if any of the Sons of Wales realize an Englishwoman is present during their secret meeting, you'll be in a pack of trouble and I'll never forgive myself for letting you stay. There were few enough women invited, and certainly no English men or women. If they guess who you are, they'll think you're a spy."

"They won't guess who I am." At least, she hoped they wouldn't. She was wearing her simplest gown, and a mobcap covered her telltale red hair, so that no one would connect her with the English earl's redheaded daughter. As soon as Juliana had arrived, Lettice had given her a shawl, which helped Juliana blend in with the crowd and definitely enhanced her attempts to look like a Welsh servant. Still . . .

"If your father were to find out you were here consorting with 'those dirty Welsh,' he'd give you a thrashing," Lettice persisted in a harsher whisper, trying to strike the fear of God into her mistress. "You'd best leave before you get into trouble."

Juliana lifted her chin with determination. She hated the way Lettice sometimes tried to tell her what to do. Lettice's wealthy family had lost everything when the maid was young, so her background made her inclined to treat Juliana like an equal rather than a mistress. Most of the time Juliana didn't care, but today she didn't like it one bit.

She acts as if I'm a child who doesn't know her own mind, she thought peevishly. *But I'm a fully grown woman.*

Why, at eighteen, some women were already marrying, bearing children, and running households. Surely eighteen was old enough to attend a late-night meeting of Welsh radicals.

"Will you stop haranguing me if I promise not to get caught?" Juliana grumbled.

Lettice shot her an arch glance. "I tell you, this meeting won't be the sort of thing you like—all that 'romantic' Welsh poetry and history. It'll be a lot of rough men shouting and waving their arms and talking of politics."

"They're not shouting now." Not exactly, although they were awfully rowdy.

"They will be once Rhys Vaughan starts to speak his piece."

Juliana followed the direction of Lettice's nod to where the squire's son stood beside a burly shopkeeper, waiting for nine o'clock when the meeting was to begin. The people in the audience, most of them men, were scowling at him and making sarcastic comments behind their hands as the squire's son strove to ignore them.

"Why are they so hostile to him?" Juliana whispered to Lettice.

"His father wasn't the radical that he is, you know. Squire Vaughan loved to talk of how the English would save Wales, so needless to say, this crowd is suspicious of his son. After all, Rhys Vaughan has been away a long time—at the university and then on the Grand Tour. They don't know what to believe about him. They think he must have his father's blood in him."

"But that's not fair," she protested in a whisper. "Children don't always take after their parents."

"Aye, that's true enough. Heaven knows you're nothing like yours."

Juliana watched as a man made a rude gesture in Mr. Vaughan's direction. "They're being awful. Surely they realize that no man would come speak to them unless he was on their side."

Lettice flashed her a speculative glance. "You're terribly interested in the squire's son, aren't you?"

Juliana stared blindly ahead. Lettice was far too perceptive sometimes. "Not at all."

"You came to see *him*, didn't you?"

"Of course." Juliana tried to sound nonchalant. "I wanted to hear his lecture. He's going to be speaking about the Welsh language, isn't he?"

Lettice chuckled. "Aye, but don't tell me you came to hear that, because I won't believe it." When Juliana started to protest, Lettice held up her hand. "I know you're fluent in Welsh, and I know how much you love Welsh poetry. But you came to get a look at that squire's son up there. You might as well admit it."

Fingering Lettice's shawl, Juliana sat there mute as a swan.

"You came to see him because curiosity got the better of you. After everything you've heard about the Vaughans and what your father did to them, you wanted to see what the son was like, didn't you? So what do you think of the man whose inheritance your father stole?"

Juliana stiffened, then glanced around to see if anyone had heard. "Father didn't steal Llynwydd." But her low-voiced words lacked conviction, and she knew it. "Squire Vaughan was a profligate man who gambled away his estate. He lost his home through his own carelessness. He shouldn't have played cards at such high stakes if he hadn't been prepared to lose."

"Perhaps. And perhaps your father shouldn't have agreed to such high stakes in the first place. A man's estate is his life." She leaned closer to Juliana, her voice the merest whisper. "You know, some claim the squire was drunk when he made that bet. And some claim your father cheated in his eagerness to get a fine estate to use as your dowry."

Juliana frowned. She hadn't heard the gossip. No one would have repeated such scurrilous nonsense to her. Surely Father hadn't done anything unfair in acquiring Llynwydd, had he?

"I don't care what the gossips say. Father won that estate fairly."

"Then why did he deed it to you, his daughter? Fathers don't generally give their daughters ownership of their dowry properties, especially when the family's finances are strained. I think he did it because he wants to protect Llynwydd from anyone who might challenge his claim."

"That's not why he did it," she said softly, but didn't elaborate. She should never have told Lettice in the first place that her father had deeded Llynwydd over to her, and she was certainly not going to reveal why. Father had only been trying to protect her. He knew how obsessive Darcy had become about increasing the family fortunes. Father had worried that if something happened to him, Darcy would take Llynwydd for himself, instead of letting it stand as her dowry. So he'd made it legally hers—her inheritance.

But in the process, the squire's young son had been deprived of his own inheritance. "Father didn't do anything wrong," she said, trying to convince herself. "All the same, I'm sorry the squire's son lost his inheritance."

"Aye, and lost his father, too," Lettice said calmly, staring straight ahead.

His father. That bit of gossip Juliana *had* heard. The squire had killed himself after losing his estate.

The ever-present guilt clutched at Juliana once more. No matter how much she told herself she wasn't responsible for what Father had done to get a dowry for her, she still felt guilt at being his daughter. It wasn't that she didn't love Father. She did. Yet he was so single-minded in his ambitions, so determined to make a little England in Wales.

And he did hate the Welsh. Juliana could still remember her early childhood, when the St. Albanses had owned three estates and spent most of their time at the one in Devonshire. Gradually, Father's poor investments had necessitated the sale of their two English estates, until Northcliffe Hall in Wales had been the only estate he could afford to maintain in the style to which he'd grown accustomed.

She'd been happy with the change. She'd always loved Carmarthen, with its wild hills, ancient oak of Merlin, and the ruins of a castle near the rushing Towy River. When her family had taken up permanent residence at Northcliffe Hall, she'd soaked up everything about the Welsh and their history and customs. But she'd kept her passion secret from her father. And her brothers.

She thought woefully of the carved oak dower chest in her bedchamber where she hid her books beneath piles of embroidered linens. She had never fit in with her family. Never.

And now Father had ensured that she'd forever be part of the shameful act he'd committed two months ago when he'd "won" the Vaughan estate Llynwydd to use as her dowry. Couldn't she do something to make it right, to assuage the unwanted guilt?

She'd followed Lettice to the meeting because she'd hoped to find Mr. Vaughan as much a profligate as his father, someone she couldn't possibly pity. If she'd found him an irresponsible ne'er-do-well, she wouldn't have felt nearly as much guilt.

But Rhys Vaughan didn't look like a ne'er-do-well. If anything, he looked too serious for his age.

Not to mention, far too handsome. Tall and lanky, Mr. Vaughan had features that appealed to her instantly—a wide, unblemished brow, a determined but generous mouth, and the strong jaw of a man of character. He didn't look much older than she, perhaps twenty-two or so, yet he lacked the ungainly awkwardness of other young men. He didn't fidget or wipe clammy hands on his clothing, or shift from foot to foot like an impatient heron. He simply stood there in complete solemnity, remote and perfect.

His appearance confused her. On the one hand, his regal reserve and arrogant stance obviously came from good breeding. Like her brothers he stood straight and confident. His neat clothing wasn't too extravagant, but certainly finer than anything worn by the men in his audience.

Yet he wore no wig. How shocking in someone of his class! He kept his lustrous black hair tied back in a queue, like a common Welsh laborer.

And his eyes! There wasn't a whit of reserve in them. They were all passion and fire ... blue and wild and fierce, like the crashing waters of the Welsh sea.

Suddenly, he seemed to feel her gaze on him, and he stared back. She caught her breath, unable to look away. His eyes probed her, and she panicked, certain he could see right through her flimsy disguise. Nervously, she dragged the homespun shawl more closely about her shoulders. Then he gave her the barest half-smile, and she relaxed.

When his gaze left her, she let out the breath she'd been holding. No one she'd ever met quite compared to him. Certainly not the few English noblemen she knew. They were cold and dispassionate, even when they smiled at her. There was a lack of energy about them. Yet this man ... even from where he stood, she felt him thrum with a power he kept carefully restrained, like a compressed spring.

He was like King Arthur. Arthur had been Welsh, too, a scholar and not a warrior. She could almost envision this fervent squire's son admonishing his knights to ride forth and uphold the ideals of the realm.

Oh, bother! she told herself in a fit of peevishness as she jerked her gaze from him. *As usual, you're making everything romantic. Rhys Vaughan is not an Arthur, and certainly not a king.*

"Well, there he is, the devil," Lettice muttered under her breath as she glanced back at the entrance to the basement. Juliana followed the direction of Lettice's gaze and shrank into her dark corner. Morgan Pennant was coming down the row toward them, stepping over the people crowded tightly together.

Lettice's latest sweetheart was a handsome printer in his thirties who always smelled of ink and paper and who wooed her often in the garden beneath Juliana's window. Men generally trailed after Lettice like dogs at the heels of their master, but only Mr. Pennant had captured Lettice's affections. Unfortunately, his involvement with the Sons of Wales had forced Lettice to keep her courtship a secret from the Northcliffe household, afraid that her employer wouldn't approve. But the maid hadn't been able to keep it from Juliana's curious eyes.

As Mr. Pennant sat down beside Lettice, he laid a proprietary hand on hers, then leaned forward to see who her companion was. When he caught sight of Juliana, his smile faded, and he shot Lettice a quizzical glance. "What's she doing here? 'Tisn't a place for a young English girl, and you know it."

Juliana glared at him.

"I couldn't help it," Lettice snapped. "She followed me. She heard you invite me, and she took it in her head to come, too. You know how she is. She likes to learn about Welsh matters, and you did say Rhys would be talking about reviving the Welsh language." Lettice shrugged. "Once she was here, I couldn't send her home alone, could I?"

"I still don't like it," Mr. Pennant grumbled.

Lettice patted his hand. "You needn't fear that she'll speak of it to anyone."

"I know." Mr. Pennant sighed and glanced over at Juliana, who was trying to look as innocent as possible. "Oh, devil take it, I don't suppose it matters. I'm more concerned for her safety than anything." He paused and looked toward the front of the room. "And you mustn't let Rhys know who she is."

"Certainly not," Lettice retorted.

Juliana followed the direction of Mr. Pennant's gaze to Mr. Vaughan, who was consulting with the florid-faced shopkeeper at the front of the room. When they were finished, the shopkeeper rose. But as he stepped forward to the podium, the crowd's gabbling increased rather than decreased.

The shopkeeper cleared his throat and began to speak in-Welsh. "Today we are privileged to have with us Mr. Rhys Vaughan, son of our own Squire Vaughan."

"Aye," called someone from the crowd, "the *great* Squire Vaughan." The sarcastic tone drew laughter from the crowd.

The shopkeeper went on as if nothing had happened, stating Mr. Vaughan's affiliation with the Gwyneddigion Society, a well-known London group supporting Welsh causes, and with numerous French radicals, but the crowd grew only more hostile.

Juliana couldn't keep her eyes off Rhys Vaughan, whose face had hardened. Her sympathy went to him instantly, and when he scanned the crowd, a dark scowl beetling his forehead, she waited until his eyes met hers again, then flashed him an encouraging smile. His eyes widened with surprise, then became unnervingly direct.

As she continued to smile at him, some of the sternness left his features. He kept his eyes trained on her face until the shopkeeper was finished. Only then did he jerk his gaze from her and take his place behind the podium. He laid out his notes and drew a deep breath. "Good day. I'm very pleased to be here."

Low, angry mutters punctuated the tense silence in the room. He dropped his head to his notes, then lifted it, his expression grim as he surveyed the room, finally stopping at her. Once more, she gave him her best reassuring smile.

He stared at her, then drew his shoulders up and broadened his gaze to include everyone. "I am a man without a country," he intoned in slightly accented Welsh. Rich and resonant as rumbling thunder in the mountains, his voice raised goose bumps on her skin. He nodded to one of the scowling men. "As are you"—

he nodded to another man—"and you"—he nodded to someone in the back of the room—"and you."

Glancing at her, he went on. "And why are we without a country?" He paused. "Not because England holds us captive to strange laws, although that is our burden. And not even because the cloak of the English church sits poorly on our shoulders, although that is also our burden. Nay, we're without a country because our language has been stolen from us."

As he warmed to his subject, a fervent energy lit his face. He held up a sheaf of legal papers, then shook them furiously. "When you go to sell your cattle, what language is your bill of sale written in?"

While he waited for an answer, she held her breath. At last a man in the front called out, almost impudently, "English."

He smiled, a cold, mysterious smile. "Aye. And when you choose a book of verse from the lending library, what language is it written in, more often than not?"

"English!" cried a few men in unison. They'd begun to sense his sincerity. Looks of concentration replaced their scowls.

"That's right." His smile faded and his voice hardened. "And when you stand before the Court of Quarter Sessions to defend yourself for breaking one of *their* laws, what language do they use to condemn you?"

"English!" several shouted.

He nodded, waiting for the noise to subside. "English. Neither our mother tongue nor the tongue of our forefathers, but a bastard language thrust upon us against our will."

He scanned the room once more, his gaze stopping here and there on expectant faces. "Perhaps you wonder why I speak of language at a political meeting. Perhaps you think it doesn't matter what the squires and the judges speak as long as good, honest Welsh is still spoken in the streets."

He dropped his voice to a thrumming. "Yet how many Welsh in Carmarthen no longer speak their native tongue?" Leaning forward, he said in confidential tones, "I myself was sent to London, first to Eton and then to Oxford, because my father believed the English were our saviors and would give us a say in their government as long as we followed *their* rules and spoke *their* language."

He slammed his fist down on the podium. "By thunder, he was wrong! I tell you he was wrong, and he died because he believed in the English!"

Juliana caught the ring of pain in his voice and winced. But she wouldn't shrink from the words of this fierce-eyed Welshman. He spoke the truth, even if it was painful to hear.

"My father died," Mr. Vaughan went on in a voice soft as a whisper, "because he'd lost his country . . . and his language." Every man in the room hung on his words, emotion glistening in their eyes. "And when he wrote his dying words, do you know what language he wrote them in?"

"English," came the murmur from the crowd, following the ebb and flow of his voice as if they were one with him.

"Aye. English." He gripped the edges of the podium as a shining, fervent light glittered in his eyes. "How long before the Welsh tongue is a quaint memory, like the fading memory of Welsh conquests? How long before we are nothing more than an English county with an English heart and an English soul?"

Many in the crowd nodded their assent.

His voice rose to a clarion ring. "I say that a man without a voice of his own is a slave!"

A murmur of agreement rumbled through the crowd.

"I say that when the English take away the red dragon's fiery tongue, they take away his power!" He paused, his expression dark and earnest. "Will you let that happen, my countrymen?"

"Nay!" the crowd cried as one.

"Will you let them trample our identity into the dust?"

"Nay!" they shouted, shaking their fists.

He smiled, his face flushing with the glow of his success. He had his audience in the palm of his hand, and he knew it. Even Juliana sat in rapt attention, waiting for his next words.

When they came, they were quiet and more powerful than any ranting. "Then we must follow the example of our companions in America."

Several gasps pierced the air. Many in Wales sympathized with the colonists, but many were also opposed to the war, and talking about the war in glowing terms was considered seditious. Juliana had heard her father argue many times that the war would only end in a loss of men and wealth for everyone.

Mr. Vaughan held up a pamphlet and shook it. "Some of you have heard of our countryman, Richard Price, who writes on the American war. In his *Observations on Civil Liberty and the Justice and Policy of the War with America*, he says the natural rights of men should prevail over English law." He paused. "I believe that, too. And I believe it's time to found a Wales governed by all the people and not just a few squires."

His mention of the squires was met by stunned silence.

He went on feverishly. "The American Declaration of Independence states, 'We hold these truths to be self-evident, that all men are created equal.' Yet here in England, Welshmen are far less than equal to their English lords."

"Aye!" cried some voices from the crowd.

"We too want equality!" he shouted.

"Equality!" they shouted in return.

Suddenly, Juliana felt Lettice rise to her feet. Juliana flashed her maid a shocked glance, but Lettice ignored her.

"And at what price?" Lettice called out. "My grandfather fought the English, and he died for it. Thanks to him, my family lost everything. Is that what you and your friends want of us? Do you wish your wives and sisters and children to starve for the cause of equality while you and your brave friends fight a futile battle?"

As everyone in the room fell into a stunned silence, Juliana held her breath, waiting for Mr. Vaughan to mock Lettice's womanly concerns. Father and Darcy would surely have done so. But Mr. Vaughan settled his disquieting gaze on Lettice and smiled. "I believe, Miss Johnes, that though it may cost some lives, this is not a futile battle. I think we *can* succeed."

Mr. Pennant, who'd tensed up when Lettice rose, now settled back in his chair, obviously content with Mr. Vaughan's attempt to appease her.

But Lettice wasn't appeased. "Every man thinks he

can succeed, but many do not. Then we women are left holding the country together without our men!"

Before Mr. Vaughan could answer, a voice piped up in back. "If ye need a man, Lettice, I'll be glad to satisfy ye. Come by the shop anytime! Any time at all!"

When the other men laughed and Lettice colored, Juliana clenched her fists in her lap.

"Mr. Lloyd, you wouldn't know what to do with me if you had me!" Lettice snapped.

"Never know until you try!" called another raucous male voice. Mr. Pennant cast the man a vicious glance and half rose in his seat.

"That's enough!" Mr. Vaughan shouted and pounded the podium, his scowl of disapproval including Mr. Pennant.

Mr. Pennant sank into his seat as the crowd quieted.

"Miss Johnes has asked a legitimate question," Mr. Vaughan said. He addressed Lettice as she sat down. "All I can say is this cause will eventually bring better things for *all* of Wales, women and children included. And isn't that worth the cost?" Turning his attention from her, he smiled and held up one of the pamphlets. "Our Welsh friend, Mr. Price, thinks that it is. But don't take my word for it. You must read his essay yourself."

How smoothly Mr. Vaughan had led the conversation out of dangerous waters, Juliana thought. A pity he hadn't further addressed Lettice's statements. They'd raised intriguing thoughts in Juliana's head. Why weren't women's wishes considered whenever men went to fight for their "just causes"?

That thought was thrust from her mind when Mr. Vaughan drew several pamphlets from a box behind the podium. He waved them before the crowd. "Hitherto, Price's essay has been available only in English, but I have translated it into Welsh. Here are printed copies, along with a work by Price's friend, Thomas Paine." He paused. "I could talk on this subject all night, but I believe 'tis better for you to read *their* words. So I've brought pamphlets for all."

A murmur of approval rose from the crowd. Political writings were rarely made available in Welsh, and certainly not writings on such controversial topics.

As if on cue, Mr. Pennant moved to the front where

Mr. Vaughan was already handing out pamphlets to those nearest him. "Take as many as you like," Mr. Vaughan urged. "Read them. Think about them. Then think about your country. 'Tis time the Welsh understand why the colonists are fighting English oppression. And why we should do so as well."

Mr. Pennant joined Mr. Vaughan in distributing the pamphlets, both of them taking different sides of the room. Mr. Vaughan, Juliana suddenly realized, had taken her side of the room. He moved into the crowd, passing out pamphlets as he strode down the aisle. People grabbed at them, pushing and shoving to get copies. "There's more in the front," he declared.

The disorderly crowd completely disintegrated then as some people rushed forward to stuff their pockets with the pamphlets, while others gathered to whisper, cautious of approaching the seditious materials.

"I wonder how he managed this," Lettice whispered to Juliana, eyes narrowing. "The English generally suppress such publications. No local printer with any sense at all would have risked printing it."

"Perhaps Mr. Pennant?" Juliana asked.

Lettice scowled. "Well, he'd certainly qualify. He's local and he has no sense. He's also Mr. Vaughan's friend, but I swear I'll have his head if he did something so dangerous." Lettice set her shoulders. "Look here, I think the meeting is over, and I want one of those pamphlets. You stay here, all right? I'll be back in a moment and then we'll leave."

Juliana nodded as Lettice slid into the aisle without waiting for an answer. Shrinking into her corner, Juliana watched people surge from their seats.

Unfortunately, Mr. Vaughan hadn't altered his direction and was still moving through the crowd toward her, shaking a hand here and speaking a word there. His frequent glances in her direction warned her of his intention to waylay her. She searched for Lettice, but the maid had been accosted by Mr. Pennant, and the two were arguing at the far end of the room.

Oh no, Juliana thought. She'd best leave if she wanted to avoid Mr. Vaughan. But as she reached the end of the aisle, so did Mr. Vaughan. He stepped in front of her, blocking her exit.

Clearing his throat, he thrust a pamphlet at her. "Would you like one?"

She sucked in her breath, waiting for him to notice the quality of her clothing and denounce her. But when he merely pressed the pamphlet more insistently upon her, she relaxed and took it from him.

As she did so, his fingers brushed hers. The brief contact made her feel suddenly warm in the damp cold of the basement. With a jerk of her hand, she stuffed the pamphlet under her arm and dropped her gaze from his unsettling one. "Th-thank you," she said in Welsh, praying that her Welsh would pass muster.

Apparently it did, for he flashed her a smile. "Would you tell Miss Johnes I'm sorry for the other men's insulting remarks? They were uncalled for."

"I'll tell her." Hoping her words were sufficient conversation, she tried to slide past him, but he caught her arm.

"I hope *you* didn't take offense," he said in that low-thrumming voice.

She shook her head. "Of course not. And now . . . you must let me go, sir. I have to go home."

He released her arm, but followed her down the aisle. "Why so soon? Miss Johnes seems to be staying. Can't you?"

By that time, she'd reached the door. She passed into a dimly lit hall and headed toward the stairs, shaking her head.

Once more he caught her arm. "Here now, I think you've been lying to me."

She went very still, lifting her face to his with fearful trepidation. He didn't appear angry, but she couldn't be sure in the faint light. "Wh-what do you mean?"

"I think you did take offense at what the men said, or else you wouldn't run off so soon."

Relief flooded her. She forced a smile to her face. "I promise their words gave me no offense. Now please excuse me—"

She turned and took a step up the stairs, but he moved once more to block her way, halting a couple of steps above her. "Then perhaps 'tis my speeches driving you off."

"Oh, no! You were wonderful!" Then she groaned. This was not the way to escape him.

A sudden, blazing grin transformed his serious features. "Thank you." He took her hand and rubbed his thumb over the knuckles, making her feel inexplicably short of breath. He stared down at her hand, seemingly at a loss for words. But when she tried to extricate her hand, he said, "You know, 'twas you who helped me speak so well. Everyone else seemed determined to dislike me."

He lifted his gaze to her. "Except you. Every time you smiled at me, I felt welcomed. How could I not? You have a sympathetic face. 'Twould make any man feel welcome."

She blushed, unused to such extravagant praise. Father always chastised her for being too familiar with people. But she couldn't help it. Some people drew her. Of course, she had other reasons for feeling sympathy for Mr. Vaughan, reasons she certainly couldn't tell him about.

"If you don't mind my asking," he went on, "what is your name?"

"M-my name?"

Her distress seemed to amuse him. "Yes, your name."

Dear heaven, what had she gotten herself into? She turned her head, frantically searching for Lettice, but the hall in which they stood was empty. Everyone else was still inside.

"Is it so difficult a question to answer?" He clasped her other hand.

She stared down at his hands. Except for the merest sprinkling of dark hair on the backs of them, they were smooth-skinned, with the long, tapered fingers of a musician ... or a poet. Those fingers held fast to hers like the ropes mooring ships at the docks of the Towy, and she wasn't the slightest bit certain how to set herself adrift of him. "I—I must go, sir."

That wasn't the way to do it, she realized when a mock frown creased his forehead and he quoted, " 'Let her who was asked and refused him, beware!' "

Her eyes widened, her caution momentarily forgotten. "Why, that's Huw Morus's 'Praise of a Girl'!"

"You know of Morus?"

"Of course!" Her enthusiasm spilled over into her voice. "He's one of my favorite Welsh poets, and I do so love that poem. I have every line memorized. Let me think ... what is the rest of it?"

When she bit her lip in concentration, he answered for her, his voice dropping into an enticing rhythm, " 'Give a kiss and good grace/And pardon to trace,/And purity too, in your faultless face.' "

"Oh ... yes." Too late, she remembered the words ... and their inappropriateness. The color rose in her face.

His thumbs traced circles on the backs of her hands. "I think he wrote the words just for you."

"Oh, I doubt that." She tried for a light tone. "Morus died before I was born, didn't he?"

He lifted one eyebrow. "For a servant, you're quite a scholar."

A servant. Bother, she'd forgotten all about her role. And if she stood here like a goose much longer, letting him say such adorable things, she'd give everything away. "That shows how little you know about servants."

"I know you have the most beautiful eyes of any servant I've ever seen—like rare emeralds winking in the sun. Poets write paeans to eyes like yours."

"Oh," she said inanely. Her heart's pace quickened. Why must he be as silvery-tongued as all those poets? "You shouldn't say such things to me."

Now his fingers were stroking her palms, sending strange shivers up and down her arms. "Why not?" he murmured. "Have you a husband?"

"Nay, but—"

"A sweetheart?"

She shook her head. Then seizing upon the only thing she could think of, she said, "I'm not worthy of your attentions. Please, I must go now."

But rather than giving him pause, her words seemed only to hearten him. "Nonsense." He descended to her step, putting him so close she could feel his warm breath on her forehead. "I don't care if you're a servant."

She wanted to cry from sheer frustration. And his nearness was making her resolve crumble like a scone in a fist.

"Since I have no estate," he continued, "it scarcely matters that I'm not a squire. So you see, perhaps I'm not worthy of *you*. At least you do honest labor, while I am still finding my place in the world."

His self-doubt tugged at her heart. "But you *have* found your place in the world, don't you see? You show people the truth. That's important, isn't it?"

A quick flash of satisfaction glimmered in his eyes. With a smile, he cupped her cheek in his smooth palm. "Do *you* find it important, my nameless friend?"

His palm warmed her skin and the warmth seemed to radiate throughout her body, driving all thoughts from her mind. "Yes."

He trailed his fingers along the curve of her cheekbone to her jaw. "You *are* my friend, aren't you?"

"Yes." This time her voice was more earnest.

"Good, I can use a friend these days." His eyes searching hers, he smoothed his voice into a silken murmur as he quoted, " 'Give a heart that's alight/With kindly delight,/Gentleness, faithfulness, and we'll do right.' "

Before she could even register that he'd spoken the next verse of Morus's poem, he was lowering his head. Then he pressed his mouth to hers.

At first she was too shocked to move. His smooth lips against hers held an intimacy she'd never experienced. No one had ever touched her like this. No one had ever been *permitted* to touch her like this. It was the utmost affront to her dignity. And the utmost excitement of her life.

Instinctively, she closed her eyes, relishing the soft pressure, wondering if Arthur had kissed Guinevere in this manner. Yet as Mr. Vaughan rubbed his lips over hers in a tantalizing rhythm, even those thoughts disintegrated.

When she made a sound deep in her throat, he caught her about the waist, forcing her to clutch his shoulders to keep from falling. The movement brought her flush against him, her skirt crushed between them, and she felt sure he could hear her heart pound madly in her chest.

If he did, he merely took advantage of it to keep kissing her, scattering thrills through her body like a ploughman sowing seeds. His mouth was soft and coaxing at first, a mere breath against hers. But as he prolonged the kiss, he shaped her mouth to his with more insistence until she went utterly limp.

"My lady!" came a sharp voice in English. "Juliana! Stop that at once!"

Hearing Lettice's voice boom in the midst of all that stimulating excitement was like hearing the voice of God descend from the heavens. With a gasp, Juliana jerked back from Mr. Vaughan, her fingers going at once to her burning lips.

She turned a guilty, flushed face to Lettice, who had pushed through the crowd and out into the hall, followed by Mr. Pennant.

Mr. Vaughan ignored both of them. He smiled, the seductive lips curving upward to entice her further. "Juliana. At last I know your name."

Then Lettice was beside them. "Come," she said, pulling Juliana away from Mr. Vaughan and casting a meaningful glance back at Mr. Pennant. "We must go home."

"No, stay!" Mr. Vaughan demanded as Lettice pushed past him, Juliana in tow.

As Lettice dragged her up the steps, Juliana looked back at him, her heart catching in her throat. "I'm sorry, Mr. Vaughan. I'm so sorry. I told you I had to go."

Lettice stopped short on the top step and looked down at Mr. Vaughan's upturned face. His eyes were filled with fire as he took a step upward.

She jerked Juliana behind her. "She's not for you, do you hear? You're a fine man, Mr. Vaughan, and I wish you luck. But Juliana is not for you!"

"Why not?"

Mr. Pennant stepped forward. "Come on, Rhys, let the women go if they wish it."

Juliana scarcely heard Mr. Pennant's words, for she and Lettice had already reached the street, and Lettice thrust her into it none too gently.

"I knew something dreadful would happen if I let you stay," Lettice muttered as she broke into a quick stride, still clasping Juliana's arm. "You must not have told him who you were, or he wouldn't have been putting his hands on you like that."

Embarrassment made Juliana hang her head. "I tried to get away from him, truly I did. But he was so . . . so . . ." *Wonderful*, she thought, a brief smile crossing her lips.

"He quoted Huw Morus to me, Lettice. He quoted 'Praise of a Girl.' "

A grim expression crossed Lettice's face. "Aye, I'll bet he did. He's smooth, that one, smooth as a fine brandy. But brandy has a bite, too, and so does he. 'Tisn't at all what you need, that squire's son."

"It was merely a kiss," Juliana whispered, trying to sound nonchalant. It was merely the only kiss she'd ever had from a man, and it had stripped her youth from her in one clean swipe.

Lettice took one look at her face and snorted. "Merely a kiss, eh?"

"Juliana!" came a shout from behind them. Mr. Vaughan had apparently broken free of Mr. Pennant.

Instinctively, Juliana turned, but Lettice yanked her forward. "Don't look back. You'll only encourage him."

Juliana choked down a cry of protest, but she knew Lettice was right. Rhys Vaughan might speak like an angel and kiss like someone straight out of a Welsh myth, but the minute he found out who she was, he'd spurn her. It was better to get the pain over with now, before she let herself hope too much.

So when he called her name the second time, she ignored the hint of betrayal in his voice. She kept walking and didn't look back.

Chapter Two

"Such my woes, sorrow's harvest,
She, day-bright, won't let me rest.
Spellbinder, lovely goddess,
Speaks to my ears magic, no less."
—Dafydd ap Gwilym,
"His Affliction"

"Tell me who she is," Rhys demanded as he stared hungrily after the woman named Juliana. "I know her Christian name, but that's not enough."

Morgan wore a noncommittal expression. "Forget about the girl, all right?"

With an effort, Rhys tamped down his temper. "Why?"

"As Lettice said, she's not for you."

Coming from Morgan, that stung his pride. Besides, Morgan was wrong. Rhys could still feel her lips softening under his, could see her brilliant green eyes grow dreamy at his words. She *was* for him, no matter what Morgan said.

But why would his friend claim otherwise? Rhys surveyed the now empty street. Hadn't Miss Johnes called Juliana "my lady" at first? Surely not.

He shifted his gaze to Morgan. *My lady.* That would explain why she was "not for him." "My lady" was not what one called a servant. Nor did servants speak such cultured, almost archaic Welsh, or know poetry or even have lavender-scented, soft skin. She should have smelled of lye and had callused hands. "She's not a servant, is she?"

Morgan groaned and glanced away. "Nay."

"I'll make a nuisance of myself trying to find out who she is if you don't tell me, Morgan."

"Trust me, you don't want to know."

"Why not?"

"For one thing, she's English."

Rhys's jaw dropped. English? It couldn't be. "But she spoke Welsh . . . beautiful Welsh."

"She's fluent in it. From what Lettice says, she's a bit of a bluestocking, likes to read Welsh tales and such."

The blood rushed to Rhys's head as he tried to remember if she'd spoken with an accent. God, as if he could tell. English was his own native language, for his father had always had them speak it at home. He'd learned Welsh from the servants.

Then something else Morgan had said made his throat grow dry. "A bluestocking? How did a bluestocking come to be a friend of Lettice's?"

With a sigh, Morgan turned back toward the shop.

Rhys followed. "Well?"

"She's Lettice's mistress."

"Mistress?" A slow dread burned through him. "And her name?"

Morgan glanced at him, a trace of pity in his eyes. "Lady Juliana St. Albans. Her father is the Earl of Northcliffe."

Rhys stared blindly at Morgan's face, a thousand awful thoughts whirling through his head.

St. Albans . . . the Earl of Northcliffe . . . "I lost Llyn-wydd, son, lost it in a bet with Northcliffe" . . . " 'Twas the earl what killed your father, sure as if he pushed him into the river himself" . . .

"No," Rhys said numbly, thinking of how sweetly she'd encouraged him during the lecture. "I don't believe it!"

"Nonetheless, 'tis true. She followed Lettice here this eve, and Lettice didn't send her home."

A murderous rage consumed Rhys. He stared wildly in the direction the two women had gone. "That liar! That little, conniving—"

"Here now, don't talk that way about the lady. I understand why you're upset, but—"

"Lady?" Rhys whirled on him. "What was the 'lady' doing at a gathering like this?"

"Just curious, I suppose. Lettice didn't say why her

mistress wanted to come. But Lady Juliana does like Welsh things."

"By thunder, why didn't someone warn me who she was?" He felt like breaking something, like tearing into someone, anyone. Why did she have to be Northcliffe's spawn?

Morgan seemed unperturbed by his anger. "No one knew who she was but me, I suspect."

"Then why didn't *you* warn me?"

Morgan shrugged. "Why? So you could badger her for her father's crimes? Lettice would have cut my tongue out if I'd caused trouble for her mistress."

"Caused trouble for her mistress? Her mistress could cause trouble for us! She could name our members to her father, and we'd all find ourselves hounded by the burgesses. Or worse yet, sought by the press gangs. You know how fond the press gangs are of carrying off radicals to serve in His Majesty's Navy."

"She wouldn't turn us over to them," Morgan protested, though Rhys heard the note of uncertainty in his voice.

"Wouldn't she? Damn it all, Morgan, she might do it for her father!"

Morgan shook his head. "I don't think so. Besides, she's only a girl."

"Nay," Rhys said, thinking of her soft body pressed to his. "Lady Juliana is not 'only a girl.' "

"Maybe not, but you're accusing her of being a spy!"

"Aye, I'm accusing her of deceit."

Morgan laid a hand on his shoulder. "You're thinking with your cock now. She's a pretty thing that you can't touch, so you're taking that out on her."

Rhys recoiled from the truth in Morgan's words. "Don't talk to me as if I'm some green lad! I know all about her family's damnable tricks! Leave me be, and I'll take care of this!"

Morgan's eyes narrowed. "What do you mean, you'll 'take care of this'?"

"That's none of your concern." Rhys stalked off, wanting only to be clear of Morgan and his too sound logic.

"Don't do anything foolish now, lad!" Morgan called

out after him, but Rhys shook his head and kept walking, heading for the river.

"Damn!" he muttered under his breath. "Not only English, but the earl's own daughter!"

He could still hear her saying she wasn't worthy of him. What stupid answer had he given? Ah, yes, that he might not be worthy of *her* since she did honest labor. Honest labor, hah! Her honest labor was sneaking about at night, spying on her father's enemies, seducing them with her smiles.

He pounded his fist into his palm and tried to blot out her image, the intent expression she'd worn as he'd talked, the satiny texture of her cheek, her yielding lips—

Damn her for doing this to him! How could a woman look so innocent and be so deceitful?

And she'd certainly looked innocent, hadn't she? Her face had been not so much beautiful as arresting. The wide eyes and full mouth had seemed to signal a generosity of spirit as well as an unconscious sensuality. She hadn't flirted, hadn't smiled coyly, and she'd kissed with an untutored wonder.

His eyes narrowed. Obviously, he was more easily fooled by appearances than he'd thought.

By now he'd reached the bridge. He strode along it, then stopped at the railing, staring into the swirling waters of the Towy. In the dead of night, his father had leapt to his death here, knowing he couldn't swim.

"May God have mercy on his soul," Rhys muttered as the anguish hit him all over again. If only he'd been here a month ago instead of racing back from Paris, summoned by an urgent letter from his father that read, "I lost Llynwydd, son."

A keening moan escaped his lips as he bent over the rail. Why hadn't he followed his instincts the first time Father suggested sending him away? He should have refused to leave Llynwydd. But he'd been too young to stand up to Father and refuse the "education befitting a gentleman" that Father had wanted for him—Eton and Oxford and then the Grand Tour.

A gentleman's education was all very well and good for a boy who didn't have to shore up the family estate at every turn, who didn't spend his holidays poring over

Llynwydd's books. But he should have known better than to leave Father alone. Left to his own devices, Father had never been able to settle his mind to work, and he'd always relied too heavily on a land agent who overlooked his outrageous expenditures.

So while Rhys had played the dutiful son in Paris, making stupid notes on French architecture and history and art by day and meeting with *philosophes* at night, the damned Earl of Northcliffe had deceived his father into gambling away Rhys's inheritance. While Rhys had been traveling across the Channel, numb with shock from his father's letter, which had taken some time to reach him, his father had been throwing himself into the Towy, having decided he couldn't face his son. Rhys had arrived in time to watch them pull the body from the river after someone found it snagged on a tree limb two miles downstream.

"Well, Father," he said, looking down into the unforgiving waters, "I'm a squire now, with that 'education befitting a gentleman.' And what good is it to either of us?"

The wind whistling around his ears was his only answer. He gripped the rail, a tightness constricting his chest. He and his father had never agreed on matters of political importance, nor on how to run the estate, but they'd been close in other ways. Rhys could remember his early childhood, when he'd risen early on crisp fall mornings to accompany his father on his monthly rounds of the tenant farms. He'd watched with awe as his father had put even the most timid farmers at ease with his robust voice and good humor.

Yes, that good humor had proven in later years to mask a nature that was frivolous and bent only on pleasure. Yes, Father had been much too fond of drink and cards, of hunting parties and balls. Mother had been a sobering influence on him, reminding him of his duties, but once she was dead, he'd reverted to what had probably always been his nature. The estate had fallen into disrepair, despite Rhys's best efforts, and his sojourn abroad certainly hadn't helped. Now it would take a great deal of money to set things right again.

With a jolt, he remembered that it wouldn't be him

setting things right. The estate belonged to a damned greedy Englishman who would no doubt bleed it dry.

He groaned and buried his face in his hands. "As usual, you left me a muddle, Father." Then he lifted his head to stare out into the unfeeling night. "But I'm going to make it right. You'll see. I *will* make it right."

He'd already been to a solicitor about the possibility of regaining Llynwydd. The man had claimed Rhys had a chance of winning a dispute over the title, since his father had not been in his right mind when he'd signed it over to the earl and since there were rumors that the earl had cheated. The solicitor and his agents had been gathering all the facts for the case, having already given notice to the earl that Rhys was disputing the transfer of ownership.

But apparently Lord Northcliffe intended to use his own methods in putting a stop to Rhys's actions—like sending his daughter to the Sons of Wales meeting, where she could take notice of every radical in the place. Such knowledge would be useful to an earl known for his intimidation tactics.

Well, it was time Rhys talked directly to his lordship and put a stop to it. Aye, he'd go to Northcliffe Hall and set the damned earl straight before this spying business went any further. And if Lady Juliana was there, so be it. He'd set her straight, too.

Juliana sat in the breakfast room the next morning, swirling her spoon in her hot chocolate. She'd been the last to rise, thanks to her sojourn to the Sons of Wales meeting . . . and the sleepless night following it.

Overton had teased her about being a sleepyhead. He was back from Cambridge for good, and with him and Darcy roaming the house, it was hard for her to keep much secret. But this one thing they must never know about. If her brothers ever learned that a Welshman had kissed her . . .

She touched her finger to her lips. Had oafish Overton ever kissed a woman so? Had Darcy ever spoken poetry to a woman?

Not likely. Neither of them had such finesse, such nobility of mind as Mr. Vaughan. They bussed a woman. They didn't kiss her with gentle feeling.

Sighing, she laid down her spoon and rested her chin in her hands. What a wonderful man Mr. Vaughan was, so fiery, so learned.

Of course, Lettice hadn't shared her opinions at all. She'd spouted nonsense about how a man would say anything to get a woman in his clutches. Juliana sniffed. Mr. Vaughan wasn't like that. He was merely impassioned. Like her, he couldn't contain his feelings.

Ten minutes later, she was still staring dreamily into space when the sound of the entrance door opening, following by loud voices in the entrance hall, jerked her from her reverie.

She rose and left the room, wondering who would call at such an hour. Father was already up and in his study, but it was still too early for visitors.

"I don't care what time it is," came a voice from down the hall. "I want to see his lordship immediately!"

Her eyes widened, and she froze beside the staircase, her view of the entrance hall still blocked. But she didn't need to see. She'd heard those ringing tones last night. From a podium.

The door to her father's study opened across from her, and oblivious to her lurking in the shadows, he stormed into the hall from the other side of the staircase. She crept forward, her heart in her throat as she peered around the edge of the staircase to see her father come face-to-face with Mr. Vaughan.

Two footmen were attempting to reason with Mr. Vaughan, but he was standing firm, his eyes following her father's entrance. He looked exactly as she'd remembered him—all lean muscle animated with a vibrant energy that put the spark in his eyes and the glow on his face. Why on earth was he here?

Her father voiced the question for her, although less gently. "What is the meaning of this, sir? You cannot force your way into a man's house without—"

"I am the son of the man you ruined," Mr. Vaughan announced. "My name is Rhys Vaughan, and William Vaughan was my father."

As Juliana sucked in her breath, her father's expression shifted to one of shrewd calculation. He gestured to the footmen, who stopped buzzing around Mr. Vaughan and returned to their posts.

Then he turned his hard-eyed gaze on Mr. Vaughan. "I heard you'd returned to town."

"I'm sure. If none of your other spies told you, then I suppose you heard it from your daughter."

Juliana's knees buckled. So he'd found out who she was. From Mr. Pennant, she supposed. But why tell Father that he knew her? Didn't he know what trouble he'd get her into?

Her father's jowls filled with air like a bagpipe. "What do you mean, my daughter?"

"Don't pretend you didn't send her to spy on me and my friends last night."

"Last night?" her father bellowed.

For Juliana, the effect of Mr. Vaughan's words was more profound. A spy? He thought she was a spy? What happened to all his sweet words? And his gentle kiss? She choked back the sob rising in her throat. Had Lettice been right after all? Had he not meant a word of what he'd said?

Mr. Vaughan's eyes narrowed. "I should have expected this of you. You couldn't allow the wheels of justice to take their slow turn in this matter. No, you had to skulk behind your daughter's skirts, sending her out to spy for you."

Slowly, Juliana's hurt changed to good, solid fury. How dare he accuse her of such a . . . a vile thing! She'd obviously been quite wrong about his nobility of mind. He was beastly, simply beastly! If she were a man, she'd walk right out and thrash him!

But she could only watch helplessly as her father drew himself up, a vein bulging in his forehead. "You, sir, are insane if you think my daughter would involve herself with your band of ruffians!"

You tell him, Father! she thought, warmed by her father's support until she realized that she had indeed involved herself with Mr. Vaughan's "band of ruffians." She chewed on her lower lip. Perhaps Father would refuse to believe Mr. Vaughan's words. Perhaps he'd dismiss them as mere troublemaking nonsense.

But Mr. Vaughan dashed those hopes. "Your daughter's name is Juliana, is it not?" Then he proceeded to describe her with an accuracy that was as astonishing as it was damning.

Juliana buried her face in her hands as her father sputtered, then shouted, "Juliana! Juliana, girl, you come down here at once!"

She hesitated in the shadows. How could she face Father's temper, especially in front of Mr. Vaughan, that betraying wretch? Yet she must defend herself. Not that Father would listen to her defense.

She could cheerfully throttle Mr. Vaughan at the moment, kiss or no kiss. The wicked creature obviously didn't care that he was ruining her life.

"Don't take it out on the poor girl," Mr. Vaughan said, and for a moment, Juliana thought him repentant. Until he added acidly, " 'Tisn't her fault that she isn't as practiced at deceit as her father." The urge to throttle him surged in her again.

"Juliana!" Her father's tone brooked no argument as he started toward the stairs. And he'd keep at it until the entire household had come to watch.

With a sigh, she emerged from behind the staircase. "Here I am, Father."

Her father took her arm and dragged her in front of Mr. Vaughan. "Now tell me truthfully, girl, do you know this man?"

She stared woodenly at the floor. Briefly, she considered lying. But that might force Mr. Vaughan to elaborate on her adventure. "Aye, Father, I know him."

Her father's hand tightened painfully on her arm. "Is he telling the truth? Were you at this gathering of his friends last night?"

She cast a glance at Mr. Vaughan, but his face was stony and remote as he stared at her without a whit of concern for what happened to her. Any guilt she'd felt for misleading him last night rapidly dissipated.

"Were you?" her father repeated, shaking her.

Lifting her chin in defiance of them both, she said, "Aye."

Her father shoved her away from him. "Go wait for me in the study. I'll be there presently to administer your punishment."

A tremor of fear skittered along her spine. Father would cane her for this. She knew he would. He'd caned her twice before for offenses far less heinous than this one.

Perhaps if she reasoned with him. . . . "Please, Father, let me explain—"

"Go to my study!" He shook his thick finger in that direction. "Now, or I'll cane you thrice as hard!"

With a shudder, she backed away. She'd seen Father angry before, but not like this. Still, she mustn't let him reduce her to a quivering puddle, or it would go worse for her. With all the dignity she could muster, she flashed both men a regal stare. Then she stalked off to the study.

Rhys watched her go, a vague uneasiness settling in his gut. What in the devil was this? An elaborate show for his benefit? Surely the earl wouldn't cane his daughter for this, would he? She'd done only what he'd put her up to.

But she'd been caught in the process. Perhaps her punishment was for that. A surge of unwarranted pity made Rhys tighten his fists. "You shouldn't punish Juliana for merely carrying out your orders."

The earl remained silent, grim-mouthed, until the study door opened and closed. Then he fixed Rhys with a cold gaze. "I assure you, sir, I wouldn't send my daughter within ten miles of you and your scoundrel friends. If I needed spies, I'd use one of my two sons or a servant. I'd not send an innocent girl into a nest of vipers, even to crush the likes of you!"

The logic behind the man's words struck Rhys hard. If the earl spoke the truth—and somewhere in the fog of Rhys's anger, it seemed plausible—then Juliana was about to receive a caning.

And it was all his fault.

At that thought, he snapped, "If she didn't go at your request, then why in God's name was she there?"

Lord Northcliffe's eyes narrowed. "I have no idea. The girl has strange notions about the Welsh, to be sure, but I'd never thought to see her sneaking about at night."

A chill shook Rhys. Morgan had said she liked to dabble in Welsh things. Nor had Morgan seemed overly concerned about her presence at the meeting. By thunder, had Morgan been right? Had Rhys jumped to conclusions?

The earl ran his gaze contemptuously over Rhys's less than formal attire. "As for your 'wheels of justice' and that solicitor you've hired . . . don't think they worry me. I acquired Llynwydd fairly, and I'll hold what is mine, no matter what some upstart Welshman's son thinks to do about it!"

As Lord Northcliffe's words registered, Rhys momentarily forgot his concern about Juliana. "You didn't 'acquire' that estate, my lord. You *stole* it. And I intend to prove it!"

They stared at each other for a long moment, hatred boiling up between them. Then Lord Northcliffe nodded. "We shall see, my boy. We shall see."

Abruptly, he turned to summon his footmen. "Charles! James!" They were at his side in an instant. He motioned to Rhys. "Escort Mr. Vaughan to the gate. And I never want to see his scurrilous face in this house again!"

Rhys smiled grimly. "I can see myself out. And don't worry, Lord Northcliffe. I shan't set foot here again until you resign your claim to Llynwydd." He fixed the old earl with a fierce glare. "And rest assured, you will one day resign your claim."

Then turning on his heel, he strode for the door, ignoring the earl's snort of derision and the footmen who flanked him.

Rage choking him, he passed through the entrance and down the steps with the footmen trailing after him. They did exactly as their lord had commanded and accompanied him to the gate. But after Rhys heard the wrought-iron gates clank shut, his anger receded and his earlier worries resurfaced. He stared back through the bars at the gloomy, brooding mansion.

Juliana was in there somewhere, awaiting a caning. Would Lord Northcliffe really do it? Would he really cane his own daughter, the bastard?

His own father could never have done it. Not that there'd been a daughter to cane, for Rhys's mother had died giving birth to the only sister he'd had, and his sister had followed his mother in death only a week later. But even for Rhys, discipline had been given in other, more effective ways.

Rhys saw again the earl's murderous expression, the way he'd thrust Juliana aside when she'd given him an unsatisfactory answer. If she truly had attended the meeting for her own perverse reasons, then she was suffering on Rhys's account.

"Damn it all!" he muttered under his breath. He ought to be on his way to his solicitor's right now to prod the man forward in his work. Instead, he found himself moving along the stone walls, searching for a way to get back in.

It wasn't as if he could do anything. He couldn't leap into the earl's study and whisk Juliana away, even if she'd allow it, which was unlikely now. But he also couldn't let her be caned.

Maybe he could create a distraction and get her father away from her. Or maybe he could find her afterward and soothe her hurts. Beg her forgiveness.

He shook his head. Had he gone completely soft? Beg her forgiveness indeed! He still didn't know if she'd intended to betray him to her father.

Then an image flashed through his mind, of the sheer fright suffusing her face when her father had promised to cane her. And there was her flawless command of Welsh. Was it possible she *had* gone to the meeting out of sympathy for all things Welsh? She obviously hadn't lied about her love of Welsh poetry, and Morgan had called her a bluestocking who liked Welsh tales.

Today, she'd worn an expensive gown of blue satin, yet even through his fury he'd noticed that the undersides of her cuffs were dingy, much as his were from having well-inked paper rub up against them as he pored over books. He'd remarked last night that she was a scholar. And scholars were rarely spies.

Riddled by guilt, he followed the wall around, now even more determined to find a way in. When he came to a tree branch that extended several feet over the wall, he heaved a sigh. He could probably reach it if he stretched. Then he could walk his way up the wall and throw a leg over....

A rustling on the other side gave him pause. The sound seemed to move up the tree. Puzzled, he edged in closer, staring up at the top of the wall. Was someone climbing the tree, or was he merely hearing an animal?

A sudden, low grumble wafted over the fence. *Definitely a person*, he thought, wondering if he should call out. As he peered up into the tree branches, he caught a glimpse of blue satin, and a smile split his face, followed by an instant surge of relief. He should have known Lady Juliana wouldn't stay to be beaten. Running away seemed to be her specialty, thank God.

More satin spilled over the top of the wall as she crept backward along the branch. Her unruly blue skirts, tangled with the white of her petticoats, dripped over either side of the branch. He saw a flash of shapely calf before her silk hose caught on the bark. She grabbed at it, but her hair, a rich coppery red that had been hidden from his sight last night, masked her face and blinded her.

He moved under the branch, and none too soon, because in disengaging her hose, she lost her balance and fell off, only managing to keep from hurtling to the ground by catching the branch at the last minute. She groaned as her arms strained with her weight, but before she could even look down to gauge how far she must drop, he caught her under the knees with one arm and tugged her loose from the branch into his arms with the other.

It took her a second to shove her hair from her face, but as soon as she saw him staring down at her, she went stiff all over.

"You! What are you doing here?"

"Catching you," he said as he shifted her weight so she lay more comfortably in his arms.

"Why? So you could make sure I got my caning, after all? Are you planning to march me back in to Father?"

He winced. If he hadn't already been convinced that she was innocent of everything, her wounded tone and attempt at escape would have done it. "Nay. I thought I'd rescue you instead."

"Oh, indeed," she said bitterly.

When she tried to struggle free of his arms, he set her down on the grass. She brushed leaves and twigs from her gown, which now had a number of small tears in it. "I am doing fine rescuing myself, thank you very much."

"What are you planning to do, hide?"

"Not that it's any of your concern, but yes. For a while. Until Mother can talk Father out of his punishment. Or at least get it reduced."

"That works?" he asked in surprise.

"Sometimes." She gave him a stiff look that sent guilt

spiraling through him. "I don't relish being caned, you know. I had to do something."

"Thanks to me and my blundering." He dragged a twig from her hair. When he couldn't resist letting his fingers linger over the silken strands, she swatted his hand away.

"How dare you! You say unconscionable things to Father about me ... you get me in trouble, and then you act as if it never happened!"

Unshed tears glittered in her eyes. They lacerated his already beaten conscience. "What I did this morning *was* unconscionable, and I *am* sorry. I can say nothing in my defense."

"Quite true." The passionate, low-pitched timbre of her voice made him ache to touch her again. But he knew better than to try that. Not until he explained. "You must understand—your father and his candidate for Member of Parliament are persecutors of radicals. When I found out you were his daughter—"

"You jumped to conclusions. Oh, I understand quite well, you ... you scoundrel, you *diawl*!"

Her easy use of the Welsh word took him off guard even more than her calling him a devil. He stared in surprise as she flounced away from him toward the woods that skirted the estate walls. Then he hastened after her.

"You ignored my obvious sympathy for your cause and ... and for you," she said, "and instead believed horrid things about me. I know Father committed a great wrong against your family. But I had nothing to do with it!"

She stomped through the grass, heedless of how it ruined her skirts. "Of course, because I was a St. Albans, you decided I was in it up to my neck!" She halted to fix him with a piercing stare. "Correct?"

"Something like that," he muttered, irritated that she had so succinctly described his mad thoughts over the last night.

"So you came to Father with your suspicions instead of coming to me." She broke off, her voice catching. "Even though last night you praised my eyes and quoted Huw Morus to me."

"I'm sorry."

But she went on shakily. "Y-you told me I had a 'sympathetic' face. You told me ... Oh, it doesn't matter what you told me. All of it was lies anyway."

"Not so!"

"Aye. Lettice explained it all to me last night."

He didn't know if he liked the way she was eyeing him as if he were an insect she wanted to squash. "And what did she say?"

"That a man will say anything to tear down a woman's defenses, so he can get at her person." She lifted her chin, her sweet mouth trembling, and he felt like a bastard all over again. "She said a man lies to get what he wants. And obviously 'tis precisely what you did. You said all those lovely things to get me to kiss you, yet it meant nothing to you."

Every word dug into his conscience like an untipped rapier point. "That's not true! I meant what I said last night!" He reached for her, but she backed away.

"Don't touch me! If you lay a hand on me, I'll call the footmen!"

"And let them carry you back to your father for that caning?" When she blanched, he stepped forward and caught her hand. "Please, Juliana, you must believe me. This morning was a temporary madness, that's all. Last night when I met you, I realized I'd met my ideal woman. Then I discovered that you were out of my reach. It infuriated me to have you snatched from my hands before I'd had a chance to know you. That's why I struck out today."

"Against me," she said, glancing away.

"Nay. Against everything that took you from me. Unfortunately, that included you."

"You're speaking in riddles and trying to confuse me."

"I don't mean to." She tried to snatch her hand from his, but he only gripped it harder, filled with a desperate urge to make her believe him. "I know this sounds insane, but from the moment I saw you smile at me, I wanted to know everything about you. And after we spoke, I wanted to know you even more."

She looked as if she might waver, then pressed her lips together. "Pretty words, but they won't work this time. I know your game now."

Instantly, his heart lurched. Damn it all, why did he want so badly to convince her that he wasn't an ogre? He ought to be running as fast as he could away from this place. Lettice and Morgan were right—she wasn't for him.

Yet something in him railed at that. Without even thinking, he clasped her hand to his chest, holding it against his heart. "What can I do to change your mind, *anwylyd*?"

"D-don't call me that! I'm not your 'darling'," she whispered, but he could tell she'd begun to waver.

"Please, tell me how to make up for my poor behavior. I can't take your caning for you, but I could tell your father I was mistaken, that I saw some other woman at the meeting."

That brought a wisp of a smile to her face. "Too late for that, I'm afraid."

He clasped her about the waist and drew her close, the blood thundering in his ears. "Doesn't it mean something to you that I came back to rescue you, even knowing who your father is? Doesn't my attempt to apologize mean anything? That's why I was under that tree, you know. I was going to pull myself up on that branch and go after you."

She sucked in her breath.

"You do believe me, don't you?" He must make her believe him. He didn't know why, but he must. This one English girl had enticed him beyond bearing. He wanted to taste her again, to crush her mouth under his, to revel in its warmth.

Her lavender scent filled his nostrils, wafted to him by a soft breeze, and it only drove him more insane. In a half-trance, he bent his head to her hair, burying his nose in the smell of her, then pressing a kiss into the silky mass. "Say you believe me."

"No ... yes ..." She looked at him with those flawless, luminous eyes. "Please, you mustn't—"

"Mustn't what? Touch you? Kiss you? I can't help it, *anwylyd*. I truly can't help myself when I'm with you."

She glanced back frantically at the estate walls, and he saw her stiffen.

"What is it?" he muttered.

"My brothers. Father has sent my brothers looking for me!"

He swung his head around in time to see two burly young men round the corner of the wall. One of them he recognized, for he'd seen Viscount Blackwood before. Swiftly Rhys pulled her into the forest, praying that the men hadn't seen either of them.

But when he tried to drag her deeper, she halted. "Please, I must go back. They won't rest until they find me, and if they find you with me, 'twill be very bad for me."

"I can't let you go." He cast a furtive glance at the two men who stalked along the wall with grim purpose. "I want to protect you. You shouldn't suffer for my error—"

She silenced him with a finger to his lips. "It doesn't matter. I can endure the caning now that I know ..." She broke off, coloring.

"Yes?" He caught her finger and kissed it, then pressed a kiss into her palm. "Now that you know what?"

She ducked her head shyly. "That you no longer believe those awful things you said. That you didn't lie last night."

"I don't. I didn't." He stroked her hair. "And do you forgive me for mistreating you today?"

When she said nothing, but merely glanced up at him, forgiveness shining in her eyes, he caught his breath. He didn't deserve her kindness, her trust. No matter what her father was, she was an innocent. She trusted him, and he shouldn't let her. He shouldn't desire her or let her desire him. Yet he did. And he would, despite everything that lay between them.

He held her close, afraid to release her. "Don't go back right now. Stay awhile." He managed a smile. "Give your mother time to plead on your behalf."

She cupped his cheek, looking as if she might do as he asked. But just then one of her brothers called out, "Darcy, I see something. Over there ... in the woods!"

She pushed him away hard. "Go!" When he hesitated, her voice turned pleading. "If you care for me at all, run and don't come back, because if they find me with you, I'll be caned within an inch of my life!"

Only that gave him the strength to leave, to flee into the woods. But he stopped not far away, hiding behind a tree and watching as her brothers caught up with her.

"Juliana, you little fool, you're in big trouble now," said the viscount. "Father will have your hide for running off!"

"You could tell him you couldn't find me," Juliana said hopefully.

Although the younger brother appeared to waver, the viscount shook his head. "This isn't like when you were a girl and I hid you from Father. If you don't come now, 'twill be worse for you later. You know that."

She nodded with obvious resignation.

"Come on then. 'Tis better to get it over with."

Despite the viscount's sympathetic tone, Rhys had to fight the urge to jump out and snatch her from her brothers. But he did as she'd asked and stayed put. Thrashing her brothers would only get her in more trouble.

By thunder, this was such a damned mess. He shouldn't have come at all, shouldn't have gotten her into trouble. And he certainly shouldn't have held her again, allowing her to steal once more into his heart.

Look at me, he thought wryly, *lurking behind trees, longing after an Englishwoman, and one beyond my station at that. She ought to hate me. I ought to hate her.*

Yet he didn't. More was the pity. And given the chance, he would see her again.

That was what worried him the most.

Chapter Three

"Where there's love it's all in vain
to draw the bolt or fix the chain;
and locks of steel, where there's desire,
and doors of oak won't hold that fire."
—Anonymous,
"Stanzas for the Harp."

The sun sank behind Northcliffe Hall, and the temperature dropped, making Darcy draw his surtout more closely about his bulky frame. He peered from behind the tree at Lettice who was pacing back and forth, heedless of the two men watching her. "Lettice looks a mite nervous to me," he told Overton.

Overton grunted and shifted from foot to foot. "Who cares? I can't believe we're out in the cold forest, watching a bloody maid when we could be inside having a nice nip before dinner."

"Watch your tongue. You're speaking of the woman I love."

"Love, is it?" Overton shook his head. "You're a greedy man, brother. Already you've a beautiful fiancée, and now you want to bed a maid, too. I'm surprised you haven't cornered her in one of the rooms and taken her by force."

"You know Father forbids that." Darcy watched as Lettice suddenly turned and listened. He lowered his voice. "Besides, I don't want to rape her. I want her willing. I want her for my mistress."

"What?" Overton said, a little too loudly, and Darcy clapped a hand over his mouth.

"Aye," Darcy whispered in his brother's ear, "my mistress. Elizabeth may be my betrothed, but she's cold as a fish, and you know it. Lettice, on the other hand, is a blazing good woman, just the type to warm a man's bed. You know Welshwomen. They choose their own men. I'd have her choose me."

When his brother eyed him skeptically, he added, "Besides, she's not entirely averse to me. I've stolen kisses from her a time or two. 'Tis only lately that she puts me off. But she won't do that after tonight."

He drew his hand from Overton's mouth and straightened his shoulders. "A few more minutes and 'twill be completely dark. Then I'll go to her. All I need from you is to watch and alert me if anyone comes. If I can have a moment alone—" He broke off when he saw a form melt out of the shadows. "What the deuce? Who's that?"

They both leaned forward, glancing through the brace of trees at the man who'd emerged into the clearing, a tall, handsome figure wearing tradesmen's clothing.

Overton's eyes narrowed. "I know that fellow. It's Morgan Pennant, the printer."

"Printer?"

"Aye. He has a shop on Lammas Street."

Darcy watched as the Welshman drew Lettice into his arms and kissed her. Jealousy boiled up inside him. "I'm moving closer." Then without waiting for an answer, he sidled near enough to overhear their words.

After returning the Welshman's kiss feverishly, Lettice jerked back. "I swear, Morgan, sometimes you try my patience!"

Darcy was thankful Lettice was more comfortable with English than Welsh. Otherwise, he wouldn't have understood a word of their conversation.

"I see I'm a trial to you," Morgan said with a laugh.

"I told you not to come here anymore." Lettice glanced around nervously, and Darcy flattened himself against the tree trunk. She lowered her voice. "You deliberately ignored me, sending me that note that said to meet you here. I told you last night, find someone else and leave me alone."

Morgan pulled her against him, ignoring her faint resistance. "You don't mean that. I swear, you're such a coward sometimes." He tried to kiss her again, but she turned her head.

"Yes, I'm a coward. I don't want to lose my position.

I won't ever be forced to scrabble for a living like my parents."

He nuzzled her hair. "What makes you think I want that for you?"

"You may not want it, but that's what I'll get if I keep on with you." Darcy could hear the pain in her voice. She pushed Morgan away. "I know you printed those seditious pamphlets for Mr. Vaughan. One day you'll be found out, and I don't want to be linked with you when you are!"

Darcy's eyes narrowed. Was she speaking of the same Mr. Vaughan who was his father's enemy? The one who'd landed Juliana in trouble this morning? And what was all this about sedition?

Morgan laughed. "I told you last night. I had nothing to do with that."

With a loud groan, Lettice turned her back to him. "Aye, and I know otherwise. I'm not a fool, you know. You're the only printer among the sons of Wales."

Darcy clenched his fists. The Sons of Wales, a deuced group of bastards. Radicals, all of them. Father and the burgesses had been attempting to stamp them out for some time. Lettice was right to be concerned. Being mixed up with that lot would definitely get her turned off from her position.

Morgan shrugged. "Those pamphlets could have been printed anywhere in Wales ... or in England, for that matter. Why accuse me?"

"Because I know you. I know how dedicated you are. And Rhys is your friend. If he asked it of you, you'd do it. Besides, he's been working with you at the shop, hasn't he, ever since he came to town?"

Morgan didn't deny her words this time. He came up behind her and clasped her about the waist. "Why must my private business change what lies between us?"

"I can't risk losing my position for you," she choked out. "I shouldn't even have gone last night. 'Twas very foolish."

When Morgan began nibbling her ear, she groaned and leaned her head back against his chest. "Oh, Morgan, why must you do this? Can't you ... can't you forget about the radicals?"

Morgan turned Lettice to face him. "Nay, *fy anwylaf,*

I cannot. And you don't truly want me to. If I were one of those puling cowards who paid lip service to English laws, then grumbled about it in the taverns, you wouldn't love me."

"I—I don't love you. I don't!"

Morgan frowned and dragged her against his body. He framed her face in his hands, then kissed her with a passion that made Darcy burn just to watch it. The scoundrel! 'Twasn't right that he should have Lettice!

When Morgan stopped kissing her, Lettice drew him back for another kiss. He chuckled. "Say again that you don't love me, and I'll show you again that you're lying."

She clung to his shoulders in near desperation. "You devil, how could I care for a foolish Welshman who doesn't have the good sense to see the danger he puts himself—and his friends—in?"

Morgan embraced her, and Darcy felt something twist in his gut. Gritting his teeth, he strained to hear the words Morgan half whispered to Lettice. "You've nothing to worry about, *anwylaf*. If I'm found out, you and I will start anew in London or maybe even America. You can be sure I'll never leave you to the tender mercies of your master." He stroked her cheek. "But no one will find out unless you tell them. No one but Rhys knows I printed the pamphlets, not even my fellow radicals. So unless you tell someone, I'll be perfectly safe."

"I swear I'll never tell!" She threw her arms about his neck. "Oh, but you will be careful, won't you?"

"Only if you promise to keep meeting me." His voice grew serious. "I couldn't bear it if you truly broke with me."

She turned her face up to his. "I must be ten kinds of a fool. . . ." She paused. "But God help me, I do love you, Morgan."

His laugh was his answer, full of confidence and self-assurance as he held her close and kissed her so passionately, Darcy had to dig his fingernails into his palms to keep from leaping out and tearing into the too handsome printer.

But he knew better than that. If he jumped in now, Lettice would side with her lover and Darcy would never have her. Nay, there were other ways to get what he wanted.

First he'd see what he could find out about Morgan's and Rhys Vaughan's activities. Then he'd make sure Morgan was no longer around to tempt Lettice.

Juliana lay on her belly in bed, listening to the sounds that rose up from the dining room, of clinking cutlery and her brother's loud laughter. The scent of roast duckling, mingled with the sugary smell of cinnamon apples, wafted up to her. With mouth watering, she thrust her head under her pillow.

No doubt Father had thought up this unique torture, since Mother had prevailed upon him not to cane her. The punishment he'd hit upon instead—confinement to her room for the next two weeks—was appalling enough, although she did have her secret stash of books to keep her company. But being sent to bed without supper when her favorite meal was being served—that was truly cruel.

She threw her pillow aside restlessly. Father had certainly been furious. Had last night's adventure been worth his rage? Had it been worth being humiliated in front of him and then forced to suffer confinement?

With a sigh, she rested her chin on her folded arms. Aye, it had. One kiss from Rhys Vaughan had made it all worth it.

She ought to be cursing that quick-tongued Welshman right now. Aside from the fact that he'd gotten her punished, he'd put her in the abominable position of lying for him. Father had badgered her for information about the meeting she'd attended and who'd taken her there. She'd kept silent, of course, which was why she was being tormented now. But she couldn't betray Lettice and the others. She just couldn't, no matter how much Father stamped his foot and swore and asked about Mr. Vaughan.

Like as not, she'd never see the Welshman again. How could she? She wished she could get a note to him, to explain. . . .

She punched the pillow. Oh, what was there to explain? That she wished she were a Welsh girl, who could kiss whomever she wanted? It was true. At the moment, she'd rather be a scullery maid than Lady Juliana St. Albans, daughter of an English earl.

She glanced around her spacious bedchamber. The candlelight cast a flattering glow on every polished surface. It drew the eye away from the fraying edges of the draperies and the yellowing color of the bed linens. Even her towering canopy bed of expensive mahogany with its drapings of Indian embroidery attested that Father had once been wealthy enough to spare no expense on a young girl's bedchamber.

That wealth might be sadly depleted now, but her father still had a position to uphold and very firm ideas about the kind of man she could kiss. And a penniless Welsh radical would certainly not qualify.

The door swung open suddenly, making her jerk her head around. Her mother slipped into the room and came to sit on the bed beside her. "I wanted to make sure you were all right. You do understand why your father punished you, don't you?"

Juliana swallowed back her resentful words, knowing that speaking them would do her no good.

"He merely wants what's best for you, dear. If you're to make a good marriage, you must learn to control these wild urges of yours. You cannot simply go off on your own. There are men who would—" Her mother broke off, lips tightening.

"Would what?"

Drawing a hank of sheet between her fingers, her mother dropped her voice as if speaking of a deadly secret. "Assault your person."

Juliana's eyes widened. Lettice hadn't told her that. "You mean they would hit me?" Juliana didn't count Father's canings as hitting. That was merely punishment for transgressions, although she was glad she'd escaped it.

"Not exactly." A pained smile tipped up Mother's lips. She pleated the sheet between her fingers. "Men can assault a woman in other ways. They can touch a woman...." Her mother trailed off, obviously embarrassed.

"You mean, like kissing them?" Julian added helpfully.

Her mother glanced up, startled. "What do you know of kissing?"

Juliana dropped her gaze. "I—I've watched Lettice."

Her mother's sigh of relief sounded loud in the room. "That maid of yours is entirely too forward with men for an unmarried woman. But then, she's Welsh."

What did that have to do with it? Juliana wondered. "Do only Welshwomen let men kiss them like that?"

With a rigid expression, her mother nodded. "An unmarried Englishwoman would never allow a man to kiss her, unless he were her betrothed, of course, and then only on certain supervised occasions. Only married people may kiss ... and ... well, touch each other." Her voice grew brittle. "The trouble is, men ignore those rules. Men have trouble curbing their strong ... ah ... feelings. So women must keep them from letting their feelings get the best of them."

Juliana thought of how Mr. Vaughan's kiss had made her feel inside, all tingly and pleasant. She'd wanted to stand there kissing him forever. "Don't women have strong feelings, too?"

"Certainly not!" Her mother covered her mouth in horror. "Not proper Englishwomen and well-bred ladies. The Irish and the Welsh and the Scottish ... well, they're different, because they don't have our pure blood. But English ladies are a higher breed, you know. Strong feelings aren't in their constitutions. There are some exceptions, of course—unmarried women with impure blood who are willing to be the paramours of any man—but certainly no one who travels in *our* circles...." Her mother trailed off, obviously content to let it go at that.

But Juliana needed to know more. She'd heard the word "paramour" and knew it had something to do with living in the same house with a man who wasn't related to you either by blood or marriage, but that was all she knew. "Paramour" had always sounded so foreign that she'd dismissed it as a Continental peculiarity. But if she understood Mother correctly ... "These women of impure blood ... they're English?"

Her mother sat up straight on the bed. "In name only, I should think. Their behavior demonstrates that they're not—" She broke off. "I shouldn't have mentioned it. In any case, you mustn't think about such women. Suffice it to say, you aren't of that kind, not with your breeding."

"So you're saying that if a woman, even an Englishwoman, lets a man kiss her and likes it, she has impure blood."

"Of course." Her mother's eyes narrowed. "You're awfully curious about this, Juliana."

She managed a smile. "Well, my window is over the garden, you know, so I see the servant girls with their sweethearts all the time. I—I never could understand why they kiss so much."

Her mother gave a tight-lipped smile. "Now you understand. And in future, you must tell me when you witness such behavior. The servants know they're to behave properly on these premises. I must have another talk with them about this."

Juliana felt a twinge of guilt at having garnered the poor maids another lecture from her mother, but she couldn't regret having asked. Impure blood? That explained everything—why she'd always felt so different from her family, why they always told her to control her emotions when she only wanted to let them out. She was one of those women with impure blood. She wasn't sure how she got that way—some accident of birth, no doubt—but she was clearly more like a Welshwoman than an Englishwoman.

Juliana pursued her lips. That must be why she loved Welsh things and had strong feelings when Mr. Vaughan kissed her.

She dragged in a bracing breath. Knowing she was so flawed should upset her, but it didn't. If anything, it relieved her. Now when her family talked about the Welsh as if they were odd creatures, she would know why she felt out of place. Now she understood why she found Welsh stories about heroic conquests so much more exciting than the dry English lady's manuals Mother made her read. She had impure blood.

"I'd best return downstairs," her mother said, interrupting her thoughts. "Your father would be disturbed if he knew I'd broken your isolation."

Juliana bit back a wry smile. "Disturbed" was Mother's polite term for furious. And indeed Father would be furious if he learned Mother had sneaked into her room. Perhaps that was one more way Juliana's impure blood betrayed her. After all, she'd always been angered by Mother's meek acceptance of Father's commands.

And last night when Lettice had asked about men going off to war without a thought for the women, Juliana had been intrigued rather than appalled. It was her impure blood again. It made her want to fight like Lettice instead of bowing her head and taking her medicine as Mother always said a lady should.

Her mother stroked Juliana's cheek, then reached in her pocket and pulled out a handful of dried fruit and a hunk of bread. "Here. You needn't completely starve."

When Juliana stared at her mother, shocked by this show of bravado, her mother merely shrugged and said, "I can't have you wasting away or we'll never find you a husband." Then she rose and slipped out the door.

As soon as the door closed behind her mother, Juliana fell upon the bread and fruit. Her breakfast had been cut short and she'd missed lunch, too. She was ravenous.

Unfortunately, the bread and fruit only dulled the keen edge of her hunger. Long after she'd devoured them, she found herself imagining slices of roast duckling with crisp skin, meat pies stuffed with savory pork and onions, creamy Caerphilly cheese....

A strange bumping noise summoned her from her thoughts. She sat up, suddenly alert, and stared at the door to her room, but when the noise came again, it came not from the door, but from the window.

She turned to see an uplifted arm plastered against the glass. She opened her mouth to scream, but didn't, for just then the candles lit the face that went with the arm, and she recognized Rhys Vaughan.

Mr. Vaughan? What in heaven's name—

She left the bed to stare at him in astonishment. He was apparently balanced on the thin ledge outside her window, holding onto God knows what. When she hesitated, uncertain what to do, he bumped his elbow against the glass, imploring her with his eyes to undo the latch. How on earth had he—

No, she knew how he'd done it. The madman had climbed the tree outside her window and had somehow crept far enough along the branch to maneuver himself onto the ledge. But that ledge was so narrow....

Hurrying to the windows, she flipped the latch and opened the window next to him, reaching through to clasp his arm and make sure he didn't fall. "You fool!"

she whispered as he slid over, then climbed across the sill. "You could have fallen! Or my brothers might have found you up here ... you might have been killed!"

He dusted off his breeches and flexed his arms as if to work out a cramp. Then he turned his eyes on her, the candlelight giving them a devilish gleam. "Are you so worried for me, then?"

The combined light of candle and fire cast intriguing shadows upon the angular planes of his face and shone off the raven-dark hair he wore pulled back in a queue. Quickly, he strode across the room and fastened the lock to her door.

Suddenly, it dawned on her what she'd done. She'd let a man into her bedchamber. Dear heaven, and he'd locked the door. She reddened. This wouldn't do, not at all.

"You shouldn't be here," she accused, but the words came out weakly and she cursed herself for it. Impure blood definitely ran through her veins. Most definitely, for despite her feeble protest, his presence was already affecting her.

He stepped nearer, a rueful smile on his face. "I told myself the same thing. I told myself I should stay clear of you and your family."

"Y-you should."

He shook his head. "I can't. I had to see you, to find out if you survived your caning. So I scaled the outer wall, then watched downstairs until I saw all of your family comfortably ensconced in the drawing room, your father and brothers with their liquor and your mother with her needlework." He kept his gaze trained on her face. "But in truth, I expected you to be with them. I thought I'd have to wait until everyone was in bed." Taking off his coat, he tossed it across a chair.

Obviously, he planned to stay awhile. She should discourage him. Instead, she confessed, "I'm confined to my room for two weeks. I'm not to have any visitors except Lettice, who brings my meals." When her stomach groaned, as if lamenting the scarcity of those meals just now, she added, "And no dinner at all tonight."

An anguished expression crossed his face. "Because of me?"

She bit her lip and nodded, warmed by the remorse clouding his brow.

"And the caning? Was it very awful?"

With a bright smile, she said, "Oh, Father changed his mind about the caning, as I'd hoped. Mother assuaged his anger, and he abandoned the idea, thank heavens."

"Yes, thank heavens." An odd look passed over his face. "Your mother must have a great deal of power in your household."

"Not really. Besides, being confined is nearly as bad as being caned. To be shut up in this room is dreadfully dull, you know. I suppose Father knew that."

His eyes darkened. "I'm sorry for getting you into trouble."

She shrugged. "Well, it's done now, and there's no use crying over it."

"Perhaps you're right. But at least I can help enliven your confinement."

A wary expression crossed her face. "Oh?"

He hesitated, then reached into his waistcoat to draw out a wrapped parcel. "I brought you a gift. I thought it might ... um ... make matters all right between us and take your mind off your punishment."

Her eyes grew round. He'd brought her a gift? Truly?

He mistook her expression for disapproval. Thrusting the parcel toward her, he murmured, "I suppose I should have brought a loaf of bread instead, but I didn't know— In any case, no gift could make up for the trouble I got you in."

"No ... I mean ... it's all right." She took it from him with trembling hands. "It's so kind of you."

His lips tightened. "I'm nothing if not kind."

She paid no heed to his sarcasm, too intent upon unknotting the string that encased the leather-wrapped present. "I can't believe you brought me a present." The string came undone and the leather fell away to reveal a book, very new by the look of it.

Casting him a quizzical glance, she opened the flyleaf to find the title—*Gorchestion Beirdd Cymru*, which meant *The Masterpieces of Welsh Poets* in English. Her breath caught in her throat as she pored over the list of contents.

"There's no Huw Morus," Mr. Vaughan murmured, "but it has poems by Taliesin and Dafydd ap Gwilym—"

"It's delightful!" She lifted her face to his, all smiles. " 'Tis the most wonderful present anyone has ever given me!"

He let out his breath in one great sigh. "You like it."

"I love it!" She caressed the leather-bound volume. "I have many books of Welsh history, but my Welsh poetry is only bits and pieces transcribed for me by the servants or their friends from their own small collections. I've never had a whole book of poetry to myself."

He smiled. "That's probably because there aren't many collections in existence. The Morrises in London did that one."

She opened the book and thumbed through the pages, careful not to bend the paper or crease the spine too much. "However did you get a copy in such a short time?"

" 'Tis my own copy."

Her pulse quickened. She flipped to the front cover and saw his name written in ink on the flyleaf.

"I have a small library of Welsh books that I carry about with me," he added. "That's one of them."

She held the book out to him. "Oh, but you mustn't give me your only copy—"

Covering her hands with his, he murmured, "I want to. I knew you of all people would appreciate it." He skimmed his fingers over her skin as if it were silk.

Her breath grew unsteady. "How can I ever thank you, Mr. Vaughan?"

He squeezed her hands. "You could start by calling me by my Christian name. Rhys."

"Rhys," she whispered. When his lake blue eyes locked with hers, dark and searching, she added, "I'll cherish your gift always, Rhys."

The words had the ring of a vow, she realized when he stared at her as if caught up in the web of some magic spell. Indeed, it must be a spell that kept her from protesting his intimate touch or drawing her hands from his or looking away. For a long moment, they stared at each other, both transfixed by the same mysterious enchantment.

Then he took the book from her and laid it on a

nearby table, and before she could even move away, he drew her close. She could hear the slight quickening of his breath, could see the pulse beat in his neck.

"You honor me by cherishing my gift," he whispered.

She didn't speak a word, afraid it would shatter the spell. He was going to kiss her, and she wanted him to. She'd never wanted anything so much.

True to the promise of his gaze, he bent his head to hers. At first his kiss was the merest of breaths, his lips hardly touching hers, but as she slid timid arms about his waist, he sighed, then covered her mouth with his.

The warm pressure drew an instant response from her. Hunger had already made her light-headed, but the soft texture of his mouth and the musky scent of him sent her floating in a sea awash with vivid colors in glorious hues.

"Juliana," he whispered almost worshipfully against her mouth. "Sweet, sweet Juliana."

"Rhys," she said on a breath, her eyes sliding shut.

As soon as his name left her mouth, he altered the tenor of their kiss, pressing harder and skimming his tongue along the seam of her lips. She shivered all over, assailed by totally foreign sensations that seemed to originate in her lower belly.

"Open to me, *cariad*."

Dear heaven, he'd called her his "love."

She opened her mouth to answer him and instead felt his tongue plunge between her teeth. Shock held her motionless for a moment as his tongue swept the sensitive inner skin of her mouth. But as it sparked a wanton heat inside her, she relaxed and gave herself up to what he was doing.

Instantly, he deepened the kiss, thrusting into her mouth with bold strokes and toying with her tongue. How strange that it should feel so good to have his tongue toy with hers, first playful, then rough. It was quite intriguing.

And it made her want to feel him pressed more closely to her. But when she tightened her arms about his waist, he moaned.

She drew back. Had she hurt him? But he stared at her wild-eyed before dragging her back for a kiss so intense, he scarcely gave her the chance to breathe.

She hadn't recovered from that delightful assault when

he began scattering kisses over her cheeks, her hair, her neck. Each touch of his heated mouth bedeviled her with strange urges until something wild and molten and insistent spread through her body like hot honey. She raked her fingers through his unruly hair, freeing it of its ribbon tie so she could stroke the springy black curls.

Suddenly, she heard footsteps in the hall. She twisted away from him, and he swore under his breath. The light footsteps hesitated outside her door, but after a long, terrifying moment, continued down the hall.

As soon as they both heard a door open and close, he let out an indrawn breath. "Who was it?"

"Probably Mother going to her room." She stared up at him. "Lettice will come soon to help me undress for bed. You mustn't be here when she does."

A faint smile quirked up the edges of his finely drawn lips. "I suppose not, although I wouldn't mind watching."

She reddened under his burning gaze. "You shouldn't talk that way."

"You're right. Why waste time talking?" He reached for her once more, but she slipped out of his grasp.

"I'm serious, Rhys. You must leave. If you're not concerned about Lettice finding you here, then think of this—Father will soon follow Mother to bed. Although I don't think he'll stop to speak to me, there's no telling."

Rhys speared his fingers through his loosened hair in sheer frustration. "I see. And we wouldn't want your father to find me with you. He's liable to make good on that caning."

He turned toward the chair where he'd flung his coat. She sighed. "He's really not as bad as he seems. . . ."

Halting, he glared at her. "Don't speak to me of your father's good points, Juliana. I'm quite aware of what kind of man he is." Angry now, he snatched up his coat.

"I told you, the punishment he gave me isn't so bad—"

"I'm not speaking of that. And I don't think we'll agree on the matter of my estate, which your father stole from my family."

"That's not true!"

The firelight flickered over the unyielding lines of his

face as he met her gaze. "What's not true—that your father stole Llynwydd?"

"Nay. That we're not likely to agree about it." At his uncomprehending expression, she added, "I don't know whether Father came by your estate fairly, but I do know he shouldn't have taken it. I only wish I could do something."

His expression softened. "I don't expect you to do anything. As you said before, you're not to blame for it."

His generous dismissal of her guilt in the matter only increased it. She *was* partly to blame. If Father hadn't wanted a fine dowry for her, Rhys might even now be sitting comfortably in his own drawing room.

What would he say if she told him that his former home was now legally her property? He'd be angry. He'd accuse her as he had that morning, and she couldn't bear that. Besides, it wasn't as if she could do anything about Llynwydd's being hers.

"I'd better go," he said as he donned his coat. "I've done what I came to do." His gaze flicked to her lips. "And more than I should have."

"Won't you come again?" she blurted out. Oh, bother, what a foolish thing to say. This was hardly a social call, where it was proper to invite guests to return. Yet she wouldn't take back the words.

He sucked in a ragged breath. "You mean, come here? To your room?"

She shrugged. "Only if you want to—"

"I want to." He tipped up her chin, so she stared into his face, startled by the blazing desire that shone there. "I'll return as often as you wish. Next week I must go to London, but until then, I can come every night if you want."

"I'd like that. But come after everyone is asleep and Lettice has left, so we won't be found out."

He traced a line along her jaw, his eyes glittering. "I don't think you know what you're asking."

She turned her face into his palm and kissed it. "Perhaps I don't. But I want you to return all the same."

"By thunder, I must be insane to let you put me through this *uffern-dân*."

"I wouldn't want you to suffer the 'fires of hell' for

me, but if this is your insanity, I like you when you're insane."

With a choked cry, he dragged her to him and gave her a long, plundering kiss that stunned her. His tongue stabbed deeply as if staking a claim, and his hands roamed her body, taking liberties they hadn't before.

Then he released her and strode for the window. She followed him, her head reeling from the enormity of what she'd just said.

He sat on the sill and threw his leg over it. Then he glanced at her and saw the hesitation in her face.

His eyes narrowed. "Are you sure about this?"

She met his gaze. Here was her chance to change her mind, to refuse to meet him. Yet wouldn't it be lovely to see him again, to have more time to talk of poetry and the Sons of Wales and . . . oh, just everything? He'd understand what her family never could. He'd explain to her what it meant to have impure blood. And he wouldn't laugh at her for her enthusiasm, either.

"I'm sure," she whispered, coming up to the window.

He threw his other leg over. "Then I'll be here tomorrow." And without warning, he stood on the ledge and jumped for the branch.

She sucked in her breath, startled and terrified by his daring. But he caught the branch easily, hanging from it a moment before he dropped to the ground. He looked up at her. "Tomorrow," he mouthed the word.

"Tomorrow," she whispered back, lingering at the window until there was no more sign of him.

Pray heaven that tomorrow came soon.

Chapter Four

"Much love will you see,
   And my heart and its key,
My dear, if you say you will come with me;
   But if you draw back
   'Tis a perilous lack—
My life is so wounded, there's no return track."
                              —Huw Morus,
                                 "Praise of a Girl"

Nearly a week later, Rhys reached for the branch over-
hanging the walls and pulled himself up, pausing a moment at the top before jumping to the ground.

Juliana won't expect me so early, he thought as he
passed through the gardens toward the dining room.
He'd been coming to her long after the St. Albans
household was asleep. Sometimes even she was asleep
and he had to wake her.

Every night began the same, with him determined to
keep his hands off her while she seemed completely unaware of his raging desire. Every night they talked about
the poetry of Huw Morus and Dafydd ap Gwilym, about
the Gwyneddigion Society, and even about the war in
the colonies. To his surprise, Juliana had shown an un-
common thirst for knowledge. The sheer outrageousness
of his presence in her bedchamber seemed to free her
to ask any question that popped into her head.

If they'd only talked, it would have been fine. But
they'd done more. Every night began the same ... and
every night ended the same, with his arms around her,
his mouth on hers, his body pressed against her thinly
clad one.

It was getting no better either. Two nights ago, he'd
unbuttoned the top of her nightdress—the sheath of

muslin that only hinted at the pleasurable curves and dark cleft it veiled, tormenting him every night as much by what it concealed as what it revealed. Two nights ago, he'd slid his hand inside to cup the soft, heavy warmth of her breast.

Ah, yes, two nights ago. Just thinking of it made his loins harden. After her initial shock, she'd allowed him to stroke and then pluck at her nipples, teasing them to hard little points. She'd even let him suck at them with all the greed that had built in him since the first time he'd seen her. Her skin had been smooth and firm, like ripe fruit and just as luscious to taste. He'd wanted to go on tasting and touching her forever.

Then last night . . .

Damn it all, last night, he'd pressed his advantage too far. They'd been disagreeing about whether Huw Morus's ballads were on a par with Goronwy Owen's poetry when he'd pulled her onto his lap to shut her up with a kiss. That kiss had led to other things, to hotter and sweeter caresses. Before long, he'd inched his hand up under her nightdress and between her legs to stroke the triangle of curls that hid her pleasure places.

Though she'd pushed his hand away at first, her face alive with her blushing pleasure, it hadn't taken him long to buy her acquiescence with kisses. Then he had slid his hand once more between her thighs until he'd found her sensitive nub, already wet for him, and stroked it until she moaned.

It had been a week of such delights.

And a week of sheer hell.

He swore under his breath as the familiar heaviness in his loins grew almost painful. Tonight he'd put an end to this limbo one way or the other. He couldn't go on craving her body every waking and sleeping moment.

After each night of touching her, never touching her quite enough, he awakened with an ache in his loins that wouldn't be quenched. He didn't want to awaken like that anymore. He wanted to wake up with her at his side, after going to sleep in her arms. He wanted to rescue her from her bastard father.

Right now, however, he couldn't even rescue her from himself. That was why he'd arrived early. Knowing that Lettice might show up any minute would keep him from going too far. If Juliana rejected his proposal, he wouldn't stay and torment himself further. And if she accepted it, he could wait a few days to enjoy her delights.

He hid behind the tree that grew outside Juliana's bedchamber. Peering around the trunk, he was pleased to see the family already engaged in eating dessert. In a few minutes, he thought as he scanned the table, he could climb up.

Then he caught sight of Juliana sitting there, and his eyes narrowed. Why wasn't she in her bedroom? Wasn't she supposed to have been confined to her room for two weeks?

An uncomfortable tightness clutched his chest. Had she lied about that? Was this like the caning that had never materialized? After all, he'd been here late every night, at a time she'd specified. He wouldn't have known that her punishment had been rescinded unless she'd told him. Perhaps she hadn't been confined to her room for two weeks, after all. Perhaps she'd only been sent to bed without her supper that first night.

He dug his fingers into the coarse tree bark as all his doubts about her surged to the fore. She *had* sneaked into the Sons of Wales meeting and pretended to be Welsh. Her father *had* stolen Rhys's estate. And she was English, no matter her interest in Welsh poetry. So why would an English earl's daughter take an interest in him, a Welsh commoner?

Her father said something to her, which effectively banished her from the table. She nodded and left. A few moments later, lights appeared in her window above him, signaling that she'd been sent to her room.

He relaxed. Perhaps he'd misunderstood the nature of her punishment. Perhaps she could partake of meals outside her room, but that was all.

Or perhaps he was excusing her actions because his lust blinded him to her true character. He muttered a curse as he waited impatiently for the rest of the family to leave the dining room, so he could climb up to her room.

Lust blinded him, that was true. And he didn't have to take drastic steps in assuaging that lust. He could always take advantage of her obvious willingness to be seduced. He could make her his and say to hell with the consequences. Indeed, if she'd been another woman, not a virgin, they'd have ended up in bed long ago. He'd have already laid that adorable body down and planted himself between her smooth, white thighs.

The trouble was, he felt more than lust for her. More and more he longed to talk to her during the day, saving up things to tell her at night. At odd moments, her favorite phrases would pop into his head. She occupied his every thought.

A movement in the dining room caught his eye. Everyone was leaving. Seconds later, he was shinnying up the tree. Yet even after he'd gained his balance on the branch, he hesitated, watching her through the glass. She was sitting at her dressing table, combing her hair. He sucked in his breath. The mass shimmered with each stroke like a cascading flame.

He shifted uncomfortably. Maybe it was only lust that drew him to her. Maybe he was being a fool to care for her.

Thrusting that disturbing thought from his mind, he reached into his pocket and pulled out some pebbles. The first night he'd forced the issue by stepping onto that narrow ledge and hoping she'd open the window. No need for such tactics tonight.

It took only a few pebbles to catch her attention. She hurried to the window and threw it open, her cheeks flushing as soon as she saw him.

"You're early," she whispered. "Why—"

"I'm coming in." Bringing himself to a stand on the branch, he stepped forward onto the ledge and grasped the upper sill to pull himself inside.

As soon as he'd cleared the window, she said, "Lettice will be here in a little while. We won't have much time."

"I know." Her anxiousness made him say the accusing words he'd told himself he wouldn't say. "You told me you were confined to your room for two weeks, but I just saw you eating dinner downstairs."

When her lips tightened, he immediately regretted his hasty words. "You were spying on me?" she asked in hurt tones.

"Nay, I'd come early because—" He broke off as she turned her face from him. What a bastard he was to her, when anyone could see that she was an innocent darling. "Oh, *cariad*, I'm sorry. I don't know why you put up with me. I'm a suspicious Welshman who doesn't deserve to be in the same room with you, let alone touch you."

Her eyes remained lowered and her face still showed her distress. "I ate dinner with the family tonight because Father is leaving on a trip tomorrow, and he wanted me at the dinner table before he left." Her lower lip trembled now. "He sent me back to my room right after dinner was finished, b-but you probably saw that."

"Aye, and ignored the evidence of my eyes like the foolish man I am." He *had* seen her father send her away, yet he'd let his ridiculous doubts eat at him.

He could think of only one way to erase the tears glittering in her eyes. "Listen to me, *anwylyd*. I didn't come to spy on you or hurt you. I came to bring you a gift." He reached into his waistcoat pocket and drew out an oblong object wrapped in cloth.

When she merely stared at him, a trace of wariness in her gaze, he thrust the package at her.

To his relief she took it and unwrapped it. She studied it a moment, her eyes widening. "Why, 'tis a spoon."

"A *llwy-garu*. A love-spoon."

A pink flush touched her cheeks as she glanced at him. "I see. A love-spoon."

"Do you know what it means?"

She chewed on her lower lip. " 'Tis a gift Welshmen give to their sweethearts."

"Aye. I carved this one myself—for you—during the hours I wasn't working with Morgan at the shop. Morgan showed me how. It took me most of this week to complete it."

Almost reverently, she ran her finger over the carved wood, the handle with intricate Celtic crosses ending in two entwined hearts next to the spoon's bowl. "It's lovely. I—I've seen one before, but this is the first anyone has ever given to me."

"The first," he echoed. "And the last, I hope."

"Wh-what do you mean?"

He took a deep breath, then plunged right in. "You know I leave for London day after tomorrow."

Trying to mask her disappointment, she nodded.

He took courage from her obvious misery. "I want you to go with me."

Her face registered shock. "Go with you?"

"Aye."

Cradling the love-spoon in her hands, she walked in a daze to the bed. She sat down, her brow knitting in confusion. "I—I don't understand. Are you asking me to be your paramour?"

He swore under his breath. "No, no. *Uffern-dân*, I'm doing this badly." He strode to the bed and sat next to her, taking her hand. "I thought you understood about the love-spoon. 'Tisn't just a gift from a man to his sweetheart. 'Tis a gift from a suitor to the one he wishes to marry."

She lifted her face to his. "Marry?"

"Aye." He held her hand to his lips, then kissed each finger. "I'm asking you to run away with me, Juliana. I want you to go to London as *fy mhriod* . . . as my wife."

She was silent a long time. He forced himself to wait for her answer, not to press her while she was still absorbing his words. Yet not until she pried her hand loose from his did he realize he'd been squeezing it so hard.

Rising from the bed, she went to her dressing table where the book he'd given her a week ago lay. She stroked it, her expression neutral. "Why do you wish to marry me, Rhys?"

That wasn't the answer he'd expected. He stood up, feeling a sudden painful tightening in his chest. "What do you mean?"

"I mean, is it because of all this mess with Father? Is it because your estate is my—" She broke off with a sigh, then faced him. "Do you hope that marrying me will force Father into acknowledging your claim on Llynwydd?"

All his uncertainty about her surged to the forefront once more. Was that the only way she thought of him, as some damned Welsh bastard out to get his estate back at any cost? "Your Father and his paltry claim on Llynwydd have nothing to do with this. And if you can think so after this past week, then I see I made a mistake coming here."

Anger choked him as he pivoted toward the window, but she hastened to his side, clasping his arm to halt him. "Please, Rhys, don't go. I—I just want to understand." When he refused to look at her, she added, "I'm sorry if I offended you, but I have to know why you want to marry me."

She sucked in her breath. "We've ... shared things I've never shared with any other man. But you haven't once said ... that is ..." She trailed off, then dropped her hand from his. "Men marry women for many reasons. I—I think I have a right to know yours."

Warily, he turned to stare at her. Her porcelain face looked even more delicate than usual, hesitant, even afraid in its virginal innocence. Abruptly, all his anger faded. He thought he'd shown his feelings for her in many ways. Still, women liked words, and he'd never said the words.

Lifting his hand to stroke her cheek, he murmured, "I could say I want to marry you because I want to make love to you, and that would be true."

She colored prettily, though she didn't turn away.

He went on. "And I could say I want to marry you because you and I both love poetry and Wales. That would be true, too."

He took her face in his hands, staring into her uncertain eyes. "But the main reason I want to marry you, Juliana St. Albans, is because I love you. With all my heart."

Astonishment lit her face, replaced a few seconds later by the most brilliant smile he'd ever seen. She covered his hands with hers. "I love you, too, Rhys Vaughan."

Her words shattered a tight knot of fear inside him. He wondered if he'd ever feel the same about anything after tonight. "You'll marry me then?"

"Yes."

"You'll run away with me?"

Her face clouded. "Must we elope? Can't we simply ask Father for permission to marry?"

He gave a bitter laugh. "Do you think he'd allow it? If I asked your father for your hand, do you think he'd say, 'Certainly. I'd be honored to have my enemy, a penniless dog of a Welshman for a son-in-law'?"

Dropping her head, she sighed. "No, I suppose not."

His throat constricted. "By thunder, I *am* a dog for asking this of you. I have some money, but until now my main hope for the future was in regaining my estate from your father. Now I'm not so certain how wise that is. My fighting your father would put you in an untenable position."

"Perhaps not." She gave a secret smile. "You see, I—"

"Nay." He pressed a finger to her lips. "I don't want to talk about that. I won't have you thinking I'm marrying you to get your aid in regaining Llynwydd. I'm marrying you because I love you and you love me. Once we're married, we'll sort the rest out. Even without the estate, I have prospects. I can teach. Or I can continue to work for Morgan if I have to."

She smiled. "So it *was* Morgan who printed those pamphlets."

He gripped her arms. "Who told you that?" When she flinched from his harsh tone, he softened it. "I'm sorry. What makes you think that?"

Looking guilty, she ducked her head. "Lettice thought perhaps ... well, she said—"

"Lettice shouldn't be saying anything about that, damn it all! Morgan would be in great danger if anyone knew."

"Oh, but I shan't tell a soul that I know. I swear it."

He relaxed. Trust still came hard for him, but he must learn to trust her if they were to marry.

"Besides," she continued, "if you're to work for him and thus support us both, that would be cutting off my nose to spite my face, wouldn't it?"

He stared at her aristocratic features, and his throat tightened. "What kind of bastard am I to deny you the wealth you deserve? Your father no doubt plans to marry you to some duke with vast estates."

"I don't want a duke with vast estates." She trailed her finger over his cheek. "I only want you."

With a low moan, he kissed her, his pulse racing at the thought that he'd soon be able to kiss her whenever he wanted, to linger in her arms forever.

Only with great reluctance did he draw back from her enticing mouth. "Listen, *cariad*, Lettice will be here any minute, and I've much to tell you."

"Yes?"

"Tomorrow night I'll come as soon as Lettice is gone.

We'll go out the window." When she glanced uncertainly in that direction, he added, "Don't worry, I'll bring a ladder. I've searched the ground these past few nights and found one behind the stables." He took a deep breath. "We'll go straight to the bishop's house. He'll have a special license awaiting us."

"The bishop will help us?"

Rhys grinned. "He's my godfather, and a true Welshman none too fond of your father."

"You're a devious one, aren't you?" she said with a laugh.

"Aye. 'Tis why you love me." He smoothed back a lock of hair from her forehead. "After we leave the bishop's, we'll take the coach that stops at Carmarthen in the wee hours of the morning on its way east to London." He paused. "No one here suspects that we've been meeting, do they?"

She shook her head.

"Good, then it'll take them a few days to discover where you've gone. And even if they guess that you've run off with a man, they're sure to go to Gretna Green, which would send them on a merry chase north. By the time they discover we're not there and start asking questions here, we'll be safe in London and too well-known as a married couple for your family to do anything but accept the marriage."

Juliana worried her bottom lip with her teeth. "But I—I can't leave without saying anything. They'll be anxious. Couldn't I leave a note in explanation? By the time they find it, we'll be gone and—"

Rhys clasped her by the shoulders. "No note." When her face clouded, he said more gently, "I know you don't want them to worry, *anwylyd*, but leaving a note is too risky."

She dropped her gaze from him. "You're right, of course."

He tipped up her chin, forcing her to stare into his eyes. "Promise me you'll do as I ask."

After staring at him earnestly, she smiled. "I promise."

Suddenly he heard a hesitant tapping at the door. Both of them froze.

"It's me," came Lettice's voice.

Rhys drew back from her. "I'd better go."

They heard Lettice try the door. Rhys swore under his breath and strode for the window. Juliana ran after him as he thrust his leg over the sill.

He threw his other leg over as he said in a low voice, "I'll be here tomorrow night. If you change your mind, leave the window closed, and I'll know not to bother you."

"I'll not change my mind, you can be sure of that."

Lettice rattled the door and called out, "Juliana? Are you in there?"

Rhys glanced at the door, then at her.

"Go," she urged. "Before she makes a fuss."

His eyes glittered. "I love you. Remember that."

Leaning forward, she pressed a kiss to his cheek. "I love you, too."

"I'll be here tomorrow night."

Juliana watched as he stood on the ledge and jumped forward for the branch. It no longer gave her the fright it used to, but she still held her breath every time. As usual, however, he caught the branch and swung to the ground with leonine grace. Then he blew her a kiss.

Lettice hissed through the door, "I don't know what you're up to in there, Juliana, but I'm going to fetch your mother!"

Juliana raced to the door and unlocked it, opening it just in time to see Lettice striding down the hall. "Lettice!" she called to the maid in a low voice.

Lettice stopped and came back, eyes glowing with suspicion. She hastened into the room and swept it with a searching glance as Juliana held her breath. Then she caught sight of the open window. Striding to it, she looked out.

Juliana thought her heart would drop into her stomach as she waited for Lettice to call out, or worse yet, call the footmen to stop the thief on the grounds.

But Rhys had apparently made his escape without being seen. With a frown, Lettice shut the window and faced Juliana. "You shouldn't let in all this unhealthy night air. You'll make yourself sick."

Juliana's gaze fell on the love-spoon that she'd laid beside the book on her dressing table. As Lettice strode for the wardrobe, Juliana snatched up both the book and the love-spoon and hid them under the chair cushion.

"I—I was looking at the stars," she stammered. " 'Tis a beautiful night."

"Aye, a beautiful night. So beautiful you were wool-gathering and didn't hear me knock?"

"I dozed off. And you know how soundly I sleep." Juliana gave her a look of challenge, doing her best to exert her authority as mistress for once.

Eyes narrowing, Lettice stared at her, but said nothing else. Then she sniffed and opened the wardrobe, and without further comment, helped Juliana undress.

Somehow Juliana managed to keep silent as Lettice sulked. Somehow she kept from blurting out her news. Once Lettice was gone, however, she sank onto her bed with a sigh of relief.

How wonderful it all was! She and Rhys were to be married! She smiled. The foolish boy thought he was damning her to a poor future. He'd be shocked to find that in marrying her he'd regained his estate.

Shocked, she thought soberly, and perhaps angry and suspicious. Any mention of Father infuriated him, and he seemed not quite to trust her either. Would he be suspicious of her when he found out that Father had taken Llynwydd for her? Oh, but how could he be, when it meant he'd gotten it back?

Still, men's pride was a strange thing. He might worry that people would claim he'd married her for Llynwydd. He might even refuse to marry her if he knew what she brought to the marriage.

Perhaps she shouldn't tell him anything until they were married and on their way to London. Then it would be too late for anger or suspicion. Besides, he'd asked her not to speak of Llynwydd, so she'd only be doing as he asked.

And once they were joined forever ... Dear heaven, what would it be like to live every day of her life with Rhys? Was it a dream, or had he truly asked her to elope with him?

No dream, she thought as she remembered the love-spoon and went to remove it from its hiding place. She fingered the whorls and curlicues etched into the wood and the shallow bowl which wasn't meant to be used for

eating. He'd made it himself. For her. With a smile, she
held it to her heart. Wouldn't Lettice eat her contemptuous words about Rhys if she saw this?

Too bad Juliana couldn't show it to her. Or tell her
about the impending elopement. Lettice might be loyal,
but she wouldn't approve. After all, well-bred ladies
didn't elope.

Juliana threw out her arms and began to dance about
the room. Aye, well-bred ladies stayed at home and listened to their frowning fathers. Well-bred ladies read
*Instructions for a Young Lady in Every Sphere and Pe-
riod of Life* and worried about their portions.

But not Juliana. She was a wicked woman of impure
blood. And she would marry Rhys.

She sighed, thinking of the scandalous way Rhys had
touched her most private places and made her burn last
night. A well-bred lady would have felt shame. But she'd
felt wild exhilaration. And tomorrow night Rhys would
do that again to her!

Nor would he feel compelled to stop as he'd done last
night. Nay, tomorrow night she would finally know the
full enjoyment of having impure blood. Tomorrow night,
Rhys would initiate her into all the pleasures of love.

And she couldn't wait.

Darcy sat in The Bull and Onion and stared over his
ale at a burly Englishman named Shuter. The seaman
had a face like a crumbling Roman bust, with a smashed-
in nose, cauliflower ears, and cruel eyes. On the whole
quite appropriate.

"So that's clear then," Darcy said in low tones. "Tomorrow night you'll make sure the press-gang takes
Morgan Pennant as he enters his house."

"Why not tonight?" said Overton, who sat beside
Darcy.

Darcy flashed his younger brother a scathing look.
"Because the ship doesn't leave until day after tomorrow, fool. We mustn't give anyone the chance to find
out he's been taken."

"Oh, right."

" 'Twill be done exactly as y're lordship wishes."
Shuter gave a gravelly laugh. "People say they 'ate the

press, but without it, 'ow would 'onest gentlemen get rid of troublemakers?''

Overton laughed along with the seaman, then shut up when Darcy gave him a quelling glance. "This man Morgan may show papers that would exempt him from the press."

The seaman's expression altered. "Well, now, that'll cost ye more. The officer in charge of the gang will need a bit of persuadin'. Ignorin' a man's papers can be dangerous."

Lifting his ale, Darcy drank deeply from it, then fixed Shuter with a penetrating gaze. "All right. But the man has no family who'll dispute the impressment, so it shouldn't cause you too much trouble. Will this do?" Darcy set a small purse on the table between them.

The seaman's eyes widened as he hefted the purse, then peered inside. He gave a gap-toothed grin. "Aye. It will."

In a low voice, Darcy explained where to find Morgan Pennant, then snatched up the bag of coins. As Shuter's eyes narrowed, Darcy said, "You'll get this tomorrow night after I see that you've got him. Is that clear?"

The man grumbled, but nodded his head.

"Good. Then I'll meet you here at the appointed time. The tavern owner has agreed to stash him here until dawn."

Standing, the seaman cast a covetous look at the bag of gold, then smiled. "A pleasure doing business with ye, milord."

Darcy said nothing, merely watching as Shuter weaved his way through the tavern crowd, then sauntered out the door, his chest puffed out like a peacock's.

"Does Father know what you're up to?" Overton asked in hushed tones, glancing around at the rough-looking drunks and sailors who frequented The Bull and Onion.

Sliding the bag of coins into his pocket, Darcy shook his head. "And since Father is going to visit his friend in Pembroke tomorrow, he won't be implicated in the least."

Overton frowned.

"Don't worry. I'm sure he'd approve. After all, Pennant printed those pamphlets that have everyone in an uproar."

"Is that why you're doing this? Or is it because you fancy Pennant's sweetheart?"

Darcy gritted his teeth and shot Overton the look that always made the younger man squirm. "I can't believe you'd think that of me. I merely wish to do my civic duty. Nothing more."

"Then why not bring Pennant before the court and charge him with sedition?"

"That doesn't always work. Some courts have found such defendants not guilty, if you can believe that. 'Tis better this way. We're merely doing what the burgesses have done countless times before with Dissenters. So if he disappears in the night, no one will be surprised, will they?"

A heavy sigh escaped Overton's lips. "I suppose not. It just seems . . . I don't know . . . ungentlemanly."

Darcy chuckled. "I see you've been listening to your fellows at Cambridge." He slid a companionable arm about his brother's shoulders. "Listen to me for a change. Being a gentleman is for the ballroom and the club. But you don't get anywhere by being a gentleman in business. That's why Father has brought our finances down to the deplorable level they're in right now. He doesn't go for the throat when he should. Except for acquiring Llynwydd, he's been unimpressive in his endeavors to restore our family to its former glory."

He flashed his brother an earnest glance. "But I shall change that, Overton. After I marry my heiress and make Lettice my mistress, I'll turn our family into a force to be reckoned with in this poor excuse for a shire." He smiled. "You'll see. One day we'll have it all—power, money . . . everything. I'll not be a nearly impoverished earl like Father. When I inherit, the earldom will be something to behold indeed."

Chapter Five

"Like honey musk is
Your unconcealed kiss,
The kernel of your lips I cannot dismiss."
—Huw Morus,
"Praise of a Girl"

Juliana and Rhys left the church on his horse long after
midnight. Rhys's chest pressed hard and unyielding
against her back, and she shuddered. What was wrong
with her? He was her husband now. And he loved her,
truly he did.

It was still such a shock to her that he loved her. Her
love for him seemed as natural as spring waters bubbling
up from the earth. But his love for her . . . was a marvel.
He should hate her, after all Father had done. Instead,
he'd married her.

She was glad he'd married her. Yet the furtiveness of
it bothered her. She told herself that the near solitude
of their wedding, witnessed only by the bishop and his
wife, made it no less real than if a huge assemblage had
been there, but it still felt unreal to her. What kind of
world forced lovers to marry in secret, to make their
vows in the dead of night at a deserted cathedral? And
could she and Rhys have a secure future when their
marriage had begun so inauspiciously?

His arm tightened about her. But he kept quiet and
that worried her, too. Did he doubt the wisdom of the
marriage now that they were bound forever?

The longer they rode in silence along the rutted road,
the more she worried. The moon cast an eerie light
through the vaporous mists, and the trees swayed their
branches toward her, ghastly arms trying to snatch her
from Rhys. She shivered and snuggled against him.

He grunted as if she'd given him pain, so she tried to hold herself upright. But the rustling wind whispered dire predictions, and the damp autumn air slid beneath her cloak like probing fingers. Before long, she was sinking back against him, wanting to hide inside his arms. Then an owl flew across their path in a panic of hooting, and she jolted straight with a cry.

Rhys lowered his head to hers. "Don't worry, 'tis nothing. In any case, I've promised to protect you from harm, haven't I?" When she merely nodded, he added, "You're having no regrets, are you, my love?"

Had she been so obvious in her fears? She turned her face to his, venturing a smile. "N-No, of course not."

He gave her a searching glance, then nuzzled her hair. "I wouldn't blame you if you did. Not until we made our vows did I realize how much I asked of you—to leave your family and abide with me 'in sickness and in health, for richer or poorer.' I might be poor for some time, depriving you of all the luxuries you are accustomed to."

The watery moonlight glimmered over his face, kissing the high brow and well-defined cheeks as if the moon, too, had chosen him to love. He looked so uncertain that she felt her heart grow tight with love for him.

The poor darling. He was as anxious as she. "I don't care about all of that. You're all that matters to me."

A faint smile crossed his face, and then he planted a kiss in her hair. "You shan't regret marrying me, *cariad*. I promise I'll make you happy."

She settled herself against his hard body and sighed in contentment. "And I'll do the same."

Rhys said nothing else as the horse clopped along, but instead spoke with soft kisses and caresses, his long fingers stroking the underside of her breast as he nibbled on her ear. By the time they reached the inn on the outskirts of Carmarthen, she'd forgotten every misgiving.

But as they neared the inn yard, Rhys's low curse jarred her.

She straightened in the saddle. "What's wrong?"

He was looking over her head into the inn yard. "The coach isn't here. We were to board it as soon as possible to prevent anyone from finding us. They told me it generally arrived before 2 A.M." He pulled out his pocket watch and squinted at it in the moonlight. "It's nearly that now. Where is the damned thing?"

He rode the horse into the inn yard and quickly dismounted as a groom ran to take it. "Where's the coach to London?" Rhys asked as he helped Juliana dismount.

"Ain't arrived yet, sir. They sent a boy on ahead to say they'd be late by an hour or two."

Rhys groaned. In sharp tones, he arranged with the groom to have his horse cared for while they were in London and the bags put on the coach when it arrived.

Then he told Juliana in a low voice, "We can't stand out here waiting for the coach, and we can't sit around inside either where anyone can see us. 'An hour or two' may turn into five or ten, so we'd best take a room."

Oh, no, five or ten hours! She thought of the note she'd left on her bed. In the end, she hadn't followed Rhys's stricture, unable to let her parents worry. So if she and Rhys didn't leave soon, her family would be up and have come across it. It said nothing of where they'd gone, but still . . .

She didn't realize she was standing there with a worried expression on her face until Rhys took her arm.

"Something wrong?" he murmured.

She ducked her head. She didn't dare tell him that she'd disobeyed his instructions. "N-No, everything's fine."

Casting her another concerned glance, he shook his head, then led her into the inn. As soon as they entered, Rhys sought out the innkeeper. Juliana waited for him, feeling lost and anxious. She hadn't expected they'd have to wait for the coach.

Rhys returned with the innkeeper, a gaunt and hawkish-looking man whose dark eyes flitted about the room as if searching for malcontents. He looked oddly familiar to Juliana, but she couldn't think why.

"This is my wife," Rhys said. "As I told you, we only need a room for a few hours while we're waiting for the London coach."

The innkeeper eyed Rhys suspiciously, then turned his gaze on Juliana. As he stared down his pointy nose, she felt sure she'd seen him before. But where could she have met him?

"Begging y'r pardon, sir," the innkeeper asked, "but

can ye prove y're married to this woman? She seems young for a wife."

She held her breath, cursing her short height.

"Of course," Rhys snapped. He drew out the marriage certificate and waved it before the man's face, careful to keep her name covered with his hand. "We're newly married, and are going to London so I can introduce my wife to my family there."

The innkeeper glanced at the certificate. "I see, Mr. Vaughan. Well then, I believe I've one or two rooms available. If you'll come with me ..."

He strode to the stairs and they followed, but they'd moved only a step when Rhys stopped short. "Wait, I've forgotten something in our bags." He smiled mysteriously, then turned to the innkeeper. "Take my wife up. I'll be there shortly."

She and the innkeeper began to climb the stairs. Juliana felt the innkeeper's intent gaze on her. What in heaven's name was wrong with the man?

At the top of the stairs, he stopped before a closed door and unlocked it, then opened it and gestured for her to enter. When she walked inside, the first thing she noticed was the bed. One large bed, and only one.

Instantly, all her curiosity about the innkeeper fled. Were she and Rhys to sleep in that bed together? That seemed terribly improper, even for a woman of her impure blood. But then, he was her husband, so perhaps that was all right.

Still, Father and Mother didn't share a bed. Or was this simply because Rhys was short of funds? Oh, of course, that must be it. And she mustn't make him feel bad about it.

The innkeeper walked around, showing her where the chamber pot was kept and extolling the virtues of the room, but she paid attention to none of it. All she could think of was Rhys and her, lying together in that bed. Why did the mere thought of it warm her all over? And frighten her, too.

Just then, Rhys entered, a book tucked under his arm. He asked the innkeeper to notify him when the coach arrived, then paid for the room. Within moments, they were alone.

Nervousness suddenly assailed her. Remembering her

determination not to make Rhys feel bad about his lack of funds, she took a deep breath and faced him. " 'Tis a lovely room."

He lifted one eyebrow. "That's a bit generous, don't you think? But 'tis the best I could do under the circumstances."

"Truly, it's fine."

"I'm glad you approve."

An awkward silence ensued between them. Then he brightened and held out the book he'd gone to fetch. "This is my wedding gift to you."

She took the slender volume from him with a smile. "Another volume of poetry?"

"Yes." His own smile was almost embarrassed. "I—I suppose it's vain of me, but . . . you see . . . these are *my* poems. Ones I wrote myself."

"Truly?" She opened the cover to find an exquisitely illustrated frontispiece. She turned the pages slowly, skimming the Welsh poems copied out in a bold, male handwriting.

"The last few were written for you," he said.

She flipped to the back and read aloud, " 'Mine is a dank and cheerless song/Hung with heavy tears as long/As Juliana sits above/And is not mine to love.' "

"Not quite Huw Morus," he said, reddening. "But it captures the way I felt when I feared you'd reject me."

She clasped the book to her chest. "How could I reject you when you bring me such wonderful gifts?" she said, teasing him.

He came toward her. "So it's my gifts you married me for, eh, *fy mhriod*? What a greedy little thing you are."

"Aye." She giggled as he snatched her to him, then took the book from her and set it on the table. "I *did* marry you because I'm greedy, you know. Greedy for your presence, for your smiles, for—"

"For this?" He pressed his mouth against hers in a swift kiss.

She sighed deep in her throat. "Oh, yes."

"So you like my wedding present," he said huskily as he reached up to bury his hands in her unbound hair, crushing the strands between his fingers.

"Aye. 'Tis the best gift you could have given me." Her eyes widened as she remembered the rolled-up piece of parchment in her own bag. "Oh, but Rhys, I have a gift for you, too. It's in my bag! You must let me fetch it!"

"Later." He buried his face in her neck, then began to nibble her skin in a way that made her shiver all over with excitement. "We've all the time in the world for that."

She started to pull away and insist, but when he drew her back to him, kissing a path along her throat to her ear, she let him do as he would. Aye, later she'd show him the deed to Llynwydd. Later she'd reveal that she, too, could give presents. But now . . .

He sucked her earlobe, and she moaned. Who'd have thought one's ears could be so . . . so sensitive?

When she made some contented sound, he drew back from her. Shrugging off his coat, he tossed it on a chair, then moved his hands to the front of her gown, fumbling for the ties of her stomacher. "Juliana?"

"Yes?"

"Are you very tired? Would you like to sleep?"

She glanced at him, wondering why he was eyeing her like that. What did he mean, sleep? Surely he didn't think they could remain here for several hours.

She thought in horror of the note sitting on her bed. "N-No, we really don't have enough time for that anyway, do we?"

"Not for sleeping," he said in a low rumble. "But for other things."

"Other things?"

He swallowed, and she wanted to touch his throat and make him do it again to feel how the muscles worked. She wanted to know everything about him—how he ate, how he slept, how he bathed. . . . Oh, but that was a truly scandalous thought!

Suddenly, she realized he was removing her stomacher. She put her hand over his. "What are you doing?"

A half-smile crossed his face. "Has your mother or Lettice ever explained to you about what a man and his wife do in the bedroom after they're married?"

"What do you mean?"

"I mean, about lovemaking?"

She blushed. "Like kissing and . . . and touching?"

He chuckled. "Yes, like kissing and touching."

Juliana screwed her face up, trying to remember exactly what Mother had told her. "Mother said kissing and touching were only permitted between married people."

"Yes, and we're married now," he reminded her.

"That's true." The intent way he was watching her frightened her a little.

"Did she tell you what kind of touching takes place?"

"Not exactly." Thinking of the night he'd touched her between the legs, she turned a bright red. "But I imagined it would be like . . . what we did before."

"It will be. But we shall do much more." He made the promise in a thrilling deep voice as he clasped her waist.

She remembered the hours they had spent kissing. Then she thought of her note lying on the bed. What if they missed the coach? What if they were discovered? "We don't have time to do 'much more,'" she said, unable to hide the panic in her voice.

Cupping her chin, he searched her face. "We have time." He paused. "Is that what's bothering you? Or are you simply scared of what we're going to do?"

She hesitated, disturbed by his dark, intent expression. He looked as if he might eat her alive, and for a fleeting moment, she remembered how little time they'd known each other. "I—I don't know."

Her confession didn't seem to disturb him. "Tell me this then. Do you like it when I kiss you?"

She started to blurt out a yes, then thought of what her mother had told her. Only women of impure blood liked kissing. If she said yes, would he think her an awful woman?

At her silence, he pulled her close and kissed her long and deep, then drew back. "Now tell me. Do you like it when I kiss you?"

"Oh, I—I do," she couldn't help admitting, afraid to meet his gaze. "I know it means I'm not well-bred, but I can't help it and—"

"Wait, wait." He lifted his chin. "What do you mean?"

She swallowed. "Well . . . Mother explained to me that men have strong feelings that well-bred women don't have. She said only women of impure blood like Lettice have such feelings, and since I *do* have strong feelings when you ... you touch me and ... and kiss me, I realized I must be one of those women with impure blood."

He looked stunned.

She turned her face from his. Perhaps she shouldn't have told him about her impure blood. "You don't mind that I have impure blood, do you? Mother says all the Welsh and Scottish and Irish have it and even a few Englishwomen, although well-bred women like me aren't supposed to."

Something flickered in his eyes as he tightened his hands on her waist. "Your mother was wrong, *cariad*. Plenty of Englishwomen, even well-bred ones, have the feelings you speak of, although they pretend otherwise."

She eyed him with suspicion. "Why would they pretend?"

"Because people like your mother hold them to such an impossible standard that they don't dare admit the truth." He bent to press a kiss to her forehead. "Believe me, you have the purest blood of any woman around, and your enjoyment of what we shall do in this room together in no way reflects upon that."

Should she believe him? The way he made her feel had to be scandalous. Still, if he didn't mind her having scandalous feelings, why should she? "You said we'd do more than kiss and touch. What did you mean?"

She felt his dark smile to the tips of her toes. He grasped one end of the neckerchief tucked into her bodice and drew the piece of silk toward him, so it whispered over her skin like butterfly kisses until it came loose. Then he skimmed his knuckles over the swells of her partially exposed breasts, making her breath catch in her throat.

His voice sounded almost strangled when he answered. "I think 'tis something better understood in the doing. All I ask is that you trust me."

That had an ominous ring to it, she thought. "Why?"

He chuckled. "Because I'm your husband, and I intend to give you pleasure."

Then he allowed her no more time to think about it, but began to undress her, accompanying the removal of every piece of clothing with hot, fervent kisses that made her blood race.

Only when her corset fell away, leaving her in just her

shift, did she draw back in sudden embarrassment. It had been different before, when he'd seen her in her high-necked nightdress. In her shift, she felt almost naked. Still, she scarcely noticed the cold air chilling her body, for the look he gave her had such fire she had to drop her eyes.

He didn't chide her for her shyness or even try to pull her back into his arms. Instead, he distracted her by pulling off his neckcloth and unbuttoning his waistcoat.

Her eyes went wide when he tossed the clothing aside and began loosening the ties of his shirt. Dear heaven, he was undressing, too! She hadn't anticipated that. After the night he'd caressed her bare skin beneath her nightdress while he'd remained fully clothed, she'd assumed lovemaking was one-sided—he did things to her and she let him.

But when he bared his chest and she lifted her fingers in fascination to stroke the curly black hair that covered it, he pressed her hand to his chest. "Yes, touch me, *anwylyd*," he rasped. Then he released her hand and stood motionless, waiting with crystalline eyes for her to do as he asked.

Wetting her lips, she touched the springy hair first, then flattened her hand against the muscles. Unlike her brothers, who were all bulk and weight like battle-axes, he was lean and sleek as a rapier and nearly as frightening, for she could feel the strength he held in check.

Wearing a half-smile, he let her explore his body a few moments. He shrugged out of his shirt so she could run her hands over the muscles swathing his shoulders and arms, the skin taut and smooth over hard sinew, like silk over steel. The longer she stroked his skin, the more quickly his chest rose and fell as if he couldn't quite catch his breath. Oddly enough, neither could she.

Suddenly, he captured her hand and moved it to the buttons of his breeches, his eyes darkening to a rich cobalt. She jerked her hand back in shock.

With a strained expression, he said, "I don't suppose you're ready for that, are you? Never mind. I can do it."

As she watched, worrying her lower lip with her teeth, he unbuttoned his breeches, and slipped them off, although mercifully he left his drawers on.

This time when he took her in his arms, she felt something she hadn't noticed before, a hard bulge between his thighs that dug into her skin.

"Juliana," he whispered against her ear, then tugged at the earlobe with his teeth. "I want to touch you all over, as a husband touches his wife. Will you let me?"

All over. It sounded wonderful. And scary, too. "Yes." Had she said the word aloud or merely thought it? Whichever, he heard it and wasted no time in slipping his hand inside her shift to cup her breast.

She sighed happily, pressing herself against his hand. This was familiar. He'd done it before, and she'd liked it. A lot. His fingers were warm against her chilled skin as he rubbed circles around the nipple until she ached to feel his touch there at the tip.

With a groan, he obliged her, brushing his thumbs over her nipples until they tingled, then filling both hands with her breasts. When she clutched his waist, he plundered her mouth, delving deep with his wicked tongue that found all her sensitive spots and tormented them deliciously. She scarcely noticed when he pushed her away from him long enough to slide her shift off her shoulders so it whispered to the floor around her ankles.

But she couldn't help noticing when he unhooked his drawers and slid them off, leaving them both naked. As he took her in his arms once more, the feel of hard flesh pressing into her belly distracted her for a moment, but when he returned to caressing her breasts, thumbing the nipples with an increasing roughness that burst pleasure through her like cannon fire, she forgot everything.

"Oh, Rhys," she whispered, twining her arms about his neck.

"There's more, my love. So much more."

He drew back and gave her a scorching look as his hand left her breast to slide down sensuously over her belly to the secret, throbbing place between her legs. When his fingers parted the damp curls and he smiled like a devil scenting sin, she gasped and closed her eyes, unaccountably embarrassed. Although he'd touched her there the other night, he hadn't made her so aware of it. That time had been more furtive. This time he was bold about what he wanted. Nor was he content with merely cupping her and rubbing the cleft. This time he stroked further until she felt his finger plunge deep inside her.

What in heaven's name was he doing? She tried to pull away, but he wouldn't let her, capturing her mouth with a possessive kiss. This time his tongue stabbed restless and deep as his finger probed inside her. Soon her faint urge to protest faded. What he was doing was so delicious she wanted more. Much more. His fingers gathered her strange ache and stretched it, then soothed it all at once. Blindly, she grabbed his shoulders, wanting him to . . . to . . .

She didn't know what. Something truly wonderful, no doubt. When she arched into his hand, rubbing against the palm, he gasped.

"You like that, don't you?" he whispered.

She could only whimper and clutch him tighter.

"Ah, you're so warm, so wet. . . ." He fell on her neck in a frenzy of kisses that he worked into the skin as he moved further down until he'd caught her breast in his mouth and was devouring it as he had the rest of her.

She clamped his head to her in a kind of half-mad joy that made no sense to her at all. It was like the quick pierce of fear and anticipation whenever she raced her horse into unfamiliar territory. His mouth drew on her breast, hot and ravening, making her resonate and hum with excitement, especially in that place between her legs where his fingers ravished her.

Then he lifted his head and walked her backward to the bed, his mouth scorching kisses over every place it touched. He tumbled her down, then lay half over her, one knee parting her legs. She wanted his fingers inside her again, but she didn't know how to ask for such an embarrassing thing. When his knee brushed between her thighs, she gripped his waist and arched upward in an unconscious bid for more.

With a sound that was half-laugh, half-groan, he caught her face in his hands, his dark head hovering over hers. "Listen to me, my dear, wanton wife. I'm going to put myself inside you. 'Twill hurt at first, but I'll make it as easy for you as I can."

But you've already put yourself inside me and it didn't hurt, she wanted to say, thinking of his fingers. He gave her no chance, for he slanted his mouth over hers and drugged her with kisses, long, hungry ones that intensified the sweet ache in her lower belly.

Then his legs were between hers, spreading her thighs apart, opening her to his questing fingers. Suddenly, his fingers were replaced by something else, something long and hard and wholly unfamiliar, sliding up inside her.

She tore her mouth from his in a panic. "Rhys, what—"

"Trust me," he choked out. "I promise I'll be gentle."

As that mysterious part of him pushed deeper, stretching her inside, she wiggled beneath him. "Oh, but you're not! It feels ... too tight. There's something wrong. There must be something wrong!"

"Nay, 'tis always this way the first time for a woman," he whispered against her ear, dropping his head to kiss her neck, then sliding his tongue along the ridge of her jaw.

"How do you know? You're not a woman," she snapped, but then he stopped inching further inside her, and she relaxed slightly.

"That's it, my love. Let me in. Relax."

He worked his hand down between their bodies, then caressed the hidden nub that seemed to be the source of all her enjoyment. She gasped and arched unconsciously upward, planting him further inside her.

But that wasn't enough for him. After a moment, he began to move once more. "Hold on, love, and 'twill be all right in the end." Then he thrust deep, making her cry out in pain as something tore inside her.

"Rhys," she whimpered helplessly. "Please ..."

His mouth cut off her protest, all warmth and sweetness. Then he began to move, drawing out, then in, then out in a motion that at first gave her discomfort.

"Never forget that I love you," Rhys whispered against her mouth. "It gets better, I promise. But you must relax."

In truth, when she tried to do as he bade, she felt the intrusive pressure lessen. And as he slid into her with slow, long strokes, his movements even began to warm her.

"Ah, *cariad*," he murmured, "you feel so good, so tight." He covered his mouth to feed on hers, making her forget the invasion in her nether regions.

The more he caressed her mouth while driving that hard part of him into her, the less discomfort she seemed to feel. Her breath started to quicken and her heart to pound in anticipation of she knew not what.

Soon conscious thought forsook her. Her body seemed taken over by a strange and wonderful bundle of urges that made her cry out without meaning to, arch up without her mind giving the command, and strain toward a greater closeness with him.

Apparently he felt it, too, for he abandoned all attempts to be gentle. His arms bracketed her body, the muscles straining as he fell into a thrusting motion that put him deeper inside with every thrust. To her shock, she reveled in the lusty way he plunged into her, his mouth covering hers, keeping her breathless and feeling half-insane. He was consuming her ... no, he was annihilating her and yet in the annihilation was such ... such untold freedom. To give one's body up like this ...

"Juliana ... my love ... *fy annwyl mhriod* ..." he chanted, but she was so beyond thought she scarcely heard him calling her his "darling wife."

He drove himself into her, filling her until they merged like two streams that joined into a torrent rushing toward the sea. The current swept them both up, plunging them faster and faster toward the edge of a cliff by the dark, wild ocean, their limbs tangled together.

She strained against him, feeling the mad rush, the roar of pleasure in her ears. She didn't know when she began chanting his name, nor did she care. Mindlessly, she writhed beneath him, with him.

"Juliana!" he cried hoarsely. Then only a little more softly, "My God, Juliana!"

"Yes ... oh, yes ..." she cried out in answer, feeling weightless and free.

Suddenly, he gave a mighty thrust, and it was as if they both hurtled over the waterfall and into the thunder of vast, crashing waves. With a choked cry, he poured his seed into her and she reveled in the feel of it, clutching him to her until she was swamped by a fluid enjoyment she'd never dreamed of.

For a moment, she feared she'd drown in it ... never come up for air again, but die like this in his arms. Her body shook, and only when she realized that Rhys's body did the same did she lose her fear of it.

Some time passed before the wildness in them subsided. Rhys buried his head in her neck with a sigh, his whiskers tickling her skin. He stayed silent for so long, she feared he might be dead. Then again, she felt near to death herself—depleted and yet utterly satisfied.

Nothing she'd ever experienced compared to this. If this heaven was allowed only to impure women, then she pitied all those Englishwomen with pure blood.

"Rhys?" she whispered as his weight began to crush her. "Could you,... I mean ..."

With a groan, he shifted off her, lying on his side and propping his head up with one hand. He bent his head to kiss her shoulder. "Sorry, my love. You make a pleasant bed."

Now that he no longer lay atop her, she felt an odd stickiness between her thighs. She looked down to see blood smearing her skin.

She sat up in alarm. "Rhys! I'm bleeding!" She stared at her thighs. Although she felt only a vague soreness between her legs, he must have wrought terrible damage inside her.

"It's all right." He laughed, pulling her back into his arms. "A virgin usually bleeds the first time a man takes her."

She eyed him uncertainly. "Are you sure?"

Amusement glittered in his bright blue eyes. "Quite sure, dear wife of mine." He kissed her on the lips. "Of course, the second time is much less messy. . . ." Trailing off with a meaningful smile, he slid his hand over her breast.

She could feel his arousal growing against her thigh, but his certainty about the blood worried her. "How do you *know* so much about what happens when a man ... when he ..."

"Makes love to a virgin?" He smiled. "Well, other men warn a man of these things, of course. 'Tis a pity women aren't as forthcoming about such matters to each other."

"True," she said absently, but her mind was working further on the subject of Rhys's previous experience. He'd undressed her so easily. He'd seemed to know ex-

actly how a woman's clothes were fastened together . . .
and how they came undone.

She frowned. "Am I the only woman you've ever . . .
done these things with?"

His smile faded and he swallowed. "You're the only
virgin I've ever made love to."

A quick jealousy surged through her, startling her with
its intensity. She tried to sound nonchalant. "So you've
made love to another woman."

His face grew solemn. "No one that mattered, I assure you."

"Who then?"

He groaned. "Juliana, none of them are even worth
talking about—"

All pretense at nonchalance ended right there. "Of
them? There was more than one?" She thought of him
touching other women's bodies, kissing them with those
warm lips, sliding his sensuous fingers deep inside them.
Mother had told her that people only did these things
with the ones they married. Was that all a lie, too?

Without speaking, he slipped from the bed and went
to the basin. He wetted the towel lying there and began
to wash her blood off himself, then returned to the bed
with another wet towel for her. He sat down and began
to cleanse her.

"You're not going to tell me, are you?" she
whispered.

A muscle worked in his jaw. He finished what he was
doing, then tossed the rag aside and looked at her with
exasperation in his face. "Do you really want to hear a
recitation of the women I've bedded?"

When she stared at him, uncertain what to say, he
said, "All right then, there was Mrs. Abernathy, the
young wife of one of my tutors who invited me to tea
when her husband wasn't home, and the dairymaid at
Llynwydd—"

"Enough." She realized she didn't want to know any
of it.

"Listen, *cariad*." He leaned over her. "There were
only a few. They were experienced women who took it
in their heads to have a tumble with a young, randy
buck of tolerable looks. It meant as little to them as to
me." He kissed her, his eyes solemn. "And not a one of

them was good enough to touch your boots, do you hear? Not a one."

The fervent look in his eyes warmed her, but she was still confused. "Some of these women were . . . married?"

He sighed. "Some of them."

"But Rhys, I thought married women weren't supposed to . . . well, do these things with men who weren't their husbands."

A cynical smile played over his lips briefly, then was gone. "You thought right. But as you've seen, lovemaking is quite pleasurable. People sometimes do it for its own sake, and not because of any deep feelings for the person they join with. If their husbands—or wives—won't oblige them or don't give them pleasure, they may not choose to abide by society's rules."

She sucked in her breath sharply. "D-did I give you pleasure?" she asked, afraid to hear the answer.

He gave her a blazing smile. "Oh, yes. A great deal of pleasure."

Relief coursed through her. "So then you *will* abide by society's rules, won't you?" She didn't think she could bear it if he made love to other women after making love to her.

He looked stricken. "Of course, *anwylyd*. What I did before . . . 'tis what most young men do in their salad days. Even your brothers have probably done the same." He stroked her hair, his expression earnest. "But people who love each other . . . they don't need anyone else. And I love you very much. It shall take me till the end of our lives and beyond to express how much."

Ah, but can't he turn mere words into poetry? she thought. How could she stay angry with him when he said such sweet things and looked at her with such adoration? Indeed, she could forgive him those other women as long as he was hers now.

When he saw her smile, he let out a long breath. "All right?"

She nodded. "All right." Then she thought to add, "And I shall abide by society's rules, too. I promise."

He quirked one eyebrow up. "You'd better. Some men beat their wives for such behavior, you know."

"Oh?" Her eyes went round. "You would never beat me for anything, would you?"

Lowering himself to cover her, he murmured in a husky voice, "Never. I plan to cherish you all my life." He nudged her knees apart as he bent his head to suck her breast, starting an ache deep inside her. "Beginning now, *cariad*."

Then he demonstrated exactly how he intended to cherish her.

Chapter Six

"A tryste with Morfudd true I made,
'Twas not the first, in greenwood glade,
In hope to make her flee with me;
But useless all, as you will see."

—Anonymous,
"The Mist"

Darcy paced the floor in his private sitting room. Despite the late hour, he was fully dressed. So was Overton, who dozed on the settee. Darcy glanced at the clock. It was nigh on to 3 A.M. What was taking so damned long? The press-gang should have had Morgan by now, yet they'd not sent word as agreed.

A discreet knock came at his door. He growled, "Come in," and his man entered the room, looking perturbed. "Well, have you a message for me?" Darcy barked.

"Not exactly, my lord. But there's a boy downstairs who says he must see you."

"A boy?"

"He says naught of who sent him and insists he'll speak only to you."

Darcy frowned. It must be the press gang at the tavern where Morgan was being held until the ship left. Perhaps they were more discreet than he'd given them credit for. Darcy gestured to the door. "Show him up."

When the servant returned with the boy, Darcy scrutinized him, wondering why the lad was dressed so respectably. The Bull and Onion was run-down, a seaman's haunt. Why would its owner give his servants such fine clothing?

He waved his servant out. As soon as the door closed, he fixed the boy with a sharp gaze. "You have a message for me?"

"My master at The White Oak sent me to tell you that your sister is at our inn with a man whom she says is her husband."

Darcy glared at the lad. The White Oak? Juliana? "What in the deuce are you talking about?"

The boy squirmed under Darcy's intent gaze. "A—a man and a woman arrived at the inn an hour ago ... said they were going to London and only wanted a room until the coach left. My master recognized the woman as your sister."

By this time, Overton had roused from his place on the settee and stood staring at his brother with his wig all askew. "Here now, what's this about Juliana?"

Darcy shrugged. "I don't know if this is some scoundrel's idea of a joke or if some poor man is seeing things, but this lad claims Juliana and some man have taken a room at The White Oak."

Overton chortled. "Juliana? With a man at an inn? What a lark! And who in the bloody hell would she run off with?"

"A Welshman, sir," the boy answered helpfully.

"Come, boy, this jest is getting out of hand," Darcy growled. "My sister doesn't know any Welshmen. Besides, she's been confined to her room for the past week, and I'm sure she's there at this very moment. So what's the meaning of this trick?"

The lad's brow clouded with uncertainty. " 'Tis no trick, sir. My master is sure 'tis your sister in our inn."

"And how would he know?" Darcy snapped.

"My master came here often last year, courting your sister's maid, Lettice. He says he saw your sister once when he was here. He said to tell you the woman at our inn has red hair."

At Overton's muttered curse, Darcy gritted his teeth. Plenty of women had red hair. Still ...

"And why is he so eager to turn her over to us?"

The boy shrugged. "I don't know. Perhaps because your sister's maid spurned him, and he thought to strike back at the maid through the mistress."

Darcy shivered. A spiteful innkeeper might give information, but he might make up stories, too. Then again, what advantage would there be in that?

"What about this Welshman?" Darcy said with heavy sarcasm. "Did your master recognize him, too?"

"Nay, but my master thinks the man's name is Vaughan. That name was on their certificate of marriage, although Mr. Vaughan wouldn't let him see the woman's name."

Vaughan. Darcy went very still, his pulse quickening.

Overton bounded from the settee. "Vaughan? Surely not that blackguard Rhys Vaughan." His face darkened. "But he did come here about Juliana last week. And about Llynwydd." He hit his head with his palm. "God save us all! Llynwydd! If Vaughan marries Juliana, he gets Llynwydd back! That must be his plan!"

"Shut up, and let me think!" Darcy commanded. Vaughan had indeed confronted the earl a week ago, implying that he'd met Juliana, but from what Father had said of the conversation, Vaughan had been furious at her. Hadn't he?

In any case, there was no harm in checking the boy's story. Juliana was most likely asleep in her room, but if she wasn't—

"Stay here," he told the boy. "If you're speaking the truth, I'll have a nice reward for you. But if you're lying—"

He didn't have to finish the threat, for the boy was already shrinking back from him. Overton followed as Darcy stalked down the hall. No need to awaken the household just yet, Darcy thought. Besides, Father was gone, so 'twould be better to keep Mother in the dark until it became absolutely necessary to give her an explanation.

By the time he'd reached Juliana's room, he'd half convinced himself it wouldn't be necessary at all. The boy and his master must be mistaken. Juliana couldn't possibly run off with a blackguard like Vaughan. For all her odd ways, she wasn't a fool, and surely she'd realize that Vaughan was only interested in her for the property Father had foolishly deeded to her.

Then he tried Juliana's door and found it locked. Cold dread trickled through him. Juliana never locked her door, and certainly not when she'd gone to bed. Besides, why would Juliana lock her door if she had nothing to hide?

He knocked and waited. No answer. He knocked more loudly and shouted Juliana's name. Again, no answer.

The door to his mother's room opened and she emerged, drawing her nightdress tightly about her. "What's going on?"

Darcy made his tone as unalarming as possible. "There's a boy in my sitting room who claims Juliana has eloped with Mr. Vaughan and is even now preparing to take the coach for London." He nodded at the door. "Juliana isn't answering. Someone will have to go for the keys."

His mother paled. "I have a key. Wait a moment." She was back in a trice, holding the key out to Darcy with trembling hands. "Please ... I—I can't manage it."

Darcy took it from her and unlocked the door. When he walked into the room with Overton and their mother hot on his heels, he could see at a glance that the room was empty.

His mother gave a horrified cry, pressing her fist to her mouth as she scanned the room. "Look there," she whispered, pointing to the bed. A note was propped against the pillow. She snatched it up and read it.

Then she began to wail. "Mercy on my life! My baby, my poor baby! I should have known last week when she asked me all those questions— Oh, why isn't Horace here! Why did he go see his wretched friend just when we need him?"

As she alternated between berating their father and lamenting the loss of her "poor baby," Darcy took the note from her and read aloud:

Dear Father and Mother,
    Do not be alarmed. Rhys Vaughan and I have decided to marry, and since we knew you wouldn't allow it, we've run off together. Please try to be happy for us. Rhys and I are very much in love, and hope you will come to accept this marriage in time.
                                    With great affection,
                                    Juliana

Darcy crushed the note in his fist. "When I get my hands on that scoundrel, I'll kill him!"

Overton glanced at Darcy. "The boy said they were already married, so they must have left awhile ago."

"Already married?" his mother cried. "Already married?!"

Darcy ignored his mother and spoke to Overton. "Could Vaughan have gotten a special license, do you think?"

"I don't know. The bishop might have given him one. The man's Welsh and not too fond of Father."

Their mother let out a choked sob. "Why are you just standing there? You must go after them! You must rescue her from that beast!"

Darcy faced his mother grimly. "Aye, if we can't stop the wedding, we can at least stop the consummation and get an annulment." He turned to his brother. "Come on, Overton." They both went out the door and descended the stairs quickly.

Darcy's man met him at the bottom. "Sir, there's still no message from The Bull and Onion."

Darcy waved him away. At the moment, Morgan's fate was the furthest thing from his mind. Instead, he barked out several commands, ordering that the boy in his sitting room be held until their return and that horses be saddled and his sword brought.

In a matter of moments, he and Overton were racing to the inn. As they rode, Darcy pondered a thousand ways of dealing with Vaughan. Much as killing the bastard would give him immense satisfaction, it wouldn't be wise. Too many people knew of the battle between Rhys Vaughan and Father. If Vaughan were found dead, the entire family would be under suspicion, and that would hurt Darcy's own political plans.

But having a deuced radical for a brother-in-law wouldn't help either. Besides, it infuriated him that Vaughan was using this deceitful way to get his hands on Llynwydd. Juliana would soon discover that Vaughan hadn't married her for love. Somehow he'd seduced her into believing otherwise, but Darcy knew better. He knew what men who'd lost their livelihoods were like, and he had no doubt that Vaughan wanted only one thing from Juliana.

But if she'd been so blind as to run off with the man, she'd not listen to reason when they found her. How was he to get her out of this? What if she wouldn't see sense once he wrenched her from Rhys? What if the marriage had been consummated?

Somehow he had to manage this so Juliana wasn't ruined forever, either by having her reputation sullied or her heart broken.

When they reached the inn yard, the innkeeper ran out to greet them, apparently realizing that these must be the brothers he'd summoned. "My lord, I hope I wasn't mistaken about your sister, but I felt sure—"

"You weren't mistaken," Darcy interjected. He only wished the man were. He glanced up at the darkened windows of the inn. "How long have they been here?"

"More than an hour, I'm afraid." The innkeeper dropped his gaze to the ground. "And I believe they've been ... ah ... using that time to ... well ..."

"I understand." Darcy clenched his fists on the reins. The deuced bastard. So much for putting a stop to the consummation. "Where are they?"

"Their room is at the top of the stairs, but Mr. Vaughan came down a few moments ago to ask about the coach and get food. One of the servants is making a cold supper for them while he waits in the kitchen."

Darcy dismounted, handing his reins to the groom who'd run out. Then he started for the door as Overton also dismounted. Suddenly, he stopped. Vaughan was in the kitchen without Juliana, eh? Perhaps there was another way to deal with this problem—one that would allow Darcy to keep Juliana out of it. He paused to think through everything, to consider every avenue.

Then for the first time that evening, he smiled. He turned to the innkeeper. "Listen, my good man. Here's what I wish you to do. Go in and find some excuse for luring that scoundrel out here ... but without telling my sister, do you understand? Bring him out that door there, and my brother and I will deal with him."

The innkeeper looked confused. "What will you do, my lord?"

"Don't worry, I shan't murder him. I'll merely make certain he takes himself off elsewhere and puts an end to this marriage. Quietly." He handed the innkeeper what he knew was an ungodly amount of money and watched the man's eyes widen. "That is yours as long as you keep silent about whatever you see this night, and that includes not saying a word to my sister. Agreed?"

The man hesitated, looking down at the gold. Darcy could see the indecision in his face. But at last his greed overtook whatever conscience he had. He nodded.

As he headed back into the inn, Overton growled, "I don't know what you're waiting for. We should go in there and slit the bastard's throat, and the more public the better. Let them see what happens to the man who defiles our sister!"

"Aye, and let them hang us afterward. Father's influence couldn't get us out of that one, I assure you." Darcy searched the ground until he found a rock the size of two fists. He hefted it and smiled.

"What the bloody hell are you going to do with that?"

"Knock Vaughan unconscious." Darcy's mouth tightened. "But after that, I've got plans for our Mr. Vaughan. When I'm through with him, we'll never have to worry about him again."

Rhys walked from the kitchen into the hallway of The White Oak. The innkeeper had told him the coach had arrived and the coachman wanted to speak to him outside. Rhys hadn't heard much noise coming from the inn yard, but then he was having trouble concentrating on anything tonight.

That came from bedding his lovely wife, no doubt.

His wife. He smiled. Juliana was his wife in every way now. No more torturous nights lusting after her while he lay alone in his bed. No more torturous days wanting to speak to her and knowing he couldn't.

Their life ahead might be difficult, but he could do anything with her at his side. His lack of an estate made no difference, and tonight he could even tolerate her family. Ah, the poets were right to say that love would make a man mad. It surely had made him so.

But madness was pleasant indeed when shared with Juliana.

He thought of her complete innocence, of her lack of restraint once he'd initiated her to love's delights. She'd been edgy at first, but once he'd made love to her, that had faded. They'd joined together twice, and the second time had been even more glorious.

But he'd known it would be that way. Of course, it had gotten tricky when she'd asked about other women he'd bedded. Still, he'd navigated that crisis fairly well. And he would make her forget he'd ever bedded others, for in truth, he hadn't lied when he'd said he wanted only her for the rest of his life.

Rhys reached the side door leading into the inn yard and walked out. For a moment, he stood there blankly. There was no coach here. Had the innkeeper lost his mind?

Then something hit his head and everything went black.

Rhys awakened to the sound of a voice swearing close by. Gradually he realized he was lying on a cold earth floor in what seemed to be a cellar. Other voices argued from beyond an open door, but he had a devil of a headache and couldn't yet take in the words. He sucked in a deep breath only to get a mouthful of rank-smelling air, and when he tried to move, to stretch his cramped limbs, he discovered his arms and legs were bound.

"Uffern-dân!" How long had he been lying here?

The arguing voices didn't seem to hear him, but the voice that apparently belonged to someone beside him said, "Rhys? Is that you? Devil take them, they got you, too?"

He recognized the voice instantly. "Morgan? What in thunder is going on?"

" 'Tis the press. While they were dragging me in here just now, I heard them say they're taking us aboard ship in a few hours to serve in His Majesty's Navy. The damned wretches."

Rhys's blood ran cold. The press. It couldn't be. Only a while ago he'd been making love to his new wife at The White Oak. Of course, he had no idea how long he'd been lying in this stinking, dank hole. "Where are we?"

"I don't know. They put a sack over my head when they took me, but I suppose it's some tavern near the docks. They got me when I came home after meeting Lettice."

Rhys's heart pounded. "It can't be the press. Press-gangs don't take people like us—craftsmen ... squire's sons. They take vagabonds and criminals."

"And radicals."

With a shiver, Rhys fought to take in Morgan's words. "Aye, but what good could we be to them? We're landsmen. I don't know about you, Morgan, but I don't know a sail from a bed sheet, and I'll tell them, I will!"

"Don't waste your breath," Morgan muttered.

But Rhys had already pushed himself into a sitting position and was calling out in English, "You there, outside! I want to talk to you!"

There was silence. Suddenly, the door was filled by a bulky man who had to stoop to clear the low door. He straightened once he entered the room, a lantern in his hand. When he held it up, Rhys saw his face. Shock went through him. It was Darcy St. Albans, Viscount Blackwood, heir to the Northcliffe title and Juliana's brother.

Had the viscount found out about him and Juliana? But how? And what in thunder had the bastard done with Juliana?

Rhys cursed the fact that he was trussed up and lying helpless at the man's feet. It made it hard to adequately convey his contempt. But he made his voice as imperious as he could manage. Viscount or no, the man wouldn't get away with this. "What's this all about, Blackwood?"

The viscount fixed him with eyes the same green as Juliana's, but cooler, like icy sea water. "You thought you'd done it, didn't you? You thought you'd finally pulled it off—gotten Llynwydd in your clutches. Well, thank heavens you didn't succeed, Vaughan, that's all I've got to say."

Rhys shook his head to clear it. Perhaps this wasn't related to Juliana, after all. Was the man referring to Rhys's attempts to have the acquisition of Llynwydd investigated by the authorities? "I don't know what you're talking about."

Blackwood's face tightened. He looked as if he were struggling very hard to contain his temper. "I'm talking about marrying my sister to get at the estate my father deeded over to her."

Rhys stared at him in disbelief. "What estate? What do you mean?"

"Don't pretend you didn't know that Juliana owns Llynwydd. When my father won it from your father, it was to make it her dowry. And to protect it from any false claims—such as yours—he deeded it over to her."

"Wha— You're lying! She'd have told me!"

"She didn't tell you?" Blackwood looked confused for a moment. Then his eyes narrowed. "Well, 'tis true all the same. Llynwydd belongs to her. And I'm sure those solicitors of yours told you that before you approached her."

Llynwydd belonged to Juliana? It couldn't be, could it? Then again, why should Blackwood lie about it? But if Blackwood wasn't lying, why hadn't Juliana mentioned it? Rhys cast the man a glance of withering scorn. "I knew nothing of it. I married your sister because I love her."

Blackwood's expression hardened. "Did you indeed? Well, I know better." He shrugged. "In any case, none of it matters. You won't have Llynwydd after *this* night, to be sure."

Rhys tasted fear in his mouth, cold and bitter. If Blackwood spoke the truth and Llynwydd was indeed Juliana's, then there was only one way the bastard could hope to take it from Rhys now. "You plan to kill me."

"Nay." Blackwood set the lantern on a nearby shelf. " 'Tis what I ought to do, but Juliana begged me not to go so far. My sister has a bit of a soft heart even if she did want you out of her life."

Rhys stared blankly. "Juliana?"

"Aye. Once she found herself married, she got cold feet, and of course, called on me to clean up the mess."

He gritted his teeth. "What in God's name are you talking about, you bastard?"

"I'm talking about Juliana and her tendency to get herself into trouble, then leave it to her family to extricate her. Only this time, she's gone too far."

Rhys knew he should ignore the man's words, but he couldn't. Juliana *did* tend to run away when she found herself in a sticky situation. But surely he didn't mean that she— "What do you mean, she got cold feet?"

"*Sais yw ef Syn*," Morgan ground out.

With a glance, Rhys acknowledged the ancient Welsh warning, *He is a Saxon, beware*. And yet . . .

"I want to hear what he has to say," Rhys told Morgan. Then he shot Blackwood a malevolent glare. "Out with it."

Blackwood sat on a nearby barrel and drew a snuff box out of his pocket. " 'Tis simple ... or as simple as it ever is with women. By the time you two reached The White Oak, she realized she'd made a big mistake. It finally dawned on her that marrying you meant giving up any chance at having a husband of title and great wealth. I mean, even with Llynwydd back in your hands, you'd have had to struggle to put it to rights."

Putting a pinch of snuff beneath his nose, he cast Rhys an assessing glance. "For some peculiar reason, she'd been blinded by your Welsh charm. Perhaps she'd even enjoyed your advances. But faced with the reality of marriage, she saw how foolish she'd been to marry a penniless Welshman who was probably only interested in her for her property anyway. Juliana acts on impulse at times, but she generally comes to her senses afterward."

A hundred thoughts swam through his head ... Juliana had been so skittish after the wedding ... once at the inn she'd been alone with the innkeeper while he'd gone back to get her gift ... and she'd even wanted to go out to get a gift she'd said she had for him. Worst of all, he remembered the night of his proposal, when she'd asked if he were marrying her to get Llynwydd. Had she mentioned then that it was hers? Surely he'd remember that.

Then another image intruded ... of the sweet way she'd given herself to him. No, he'd stake his life on the fact that she'd been willing, quite willing to marry him and to consummate their marriage. "You're lying, Blackwood. Juliana wanted our marriage. She'd never have backed out of it like a coward, and she would certainly never have sent you out to kidnap me!"

"Believe what you want," the viscount said with a shrug, "but ask yourself how my brother and I knew where to find you tonight." He paused to let that sink in, then flashed Rhys a contemptuous glance. "She had the innkeeper summon me as soon as you reached The White Oak. She probably thought to have us rescue her before you could—" He clenched his fists, a muscle working in his jaw. "In any case, the message didn't reach us in time, and we were too late for that. But not too late to deal with her mistake."

"Don't listen to him," Morgan said. "He's spouting nonsense. You know Lady Juliana would never be so fickle."

"Morgan's right," Rhys declared. "And she'll let you have no rest when she finds out what you've done!"

"Think whatever you want," the viscount said. "I don't care. The fact remains, once you're aboard that ship, you're as good as dead, for you'll not escape His Majesty's Navy. And Juliana will be free of you."

He smiled. " 'Twas Juliana's idea to have you impressed, you know. After I threatened to murder you right there, she suggested impressment instead." Dipping more snuff, he added, "I don't think she understood what impressment entails except that it would allow her to be free of you in the least scandal-provoking way possible."

Rhys's mouth gaped open. There was no way in thunder that Juliana would have had him impressed. The very idea was absurd. Obviously, her brother had thought this whole thing up himself.

"They won't let you do this," Rhys gritted out. "Even the British Navy doesn't allow men to be impressed solely at the whim of an English lord!"

"Oh, but Juliana gave me the perfect reason." Blackwood chuckled cruelly. "She was hysterical after we knocked you out, said she must have been mad to marry you. She wanted you away, but she didn't want you dead either, so she suggested impressment. When I pointed out that one can't have men impressed willy-nilly, she said she'd heard that radicals were sometimes sent off to sea, and that you were a radical. Then she told me about what you two have been up to, printing sedition and passing it out in the streets. She said Lettice had told her."

Rhys heard Morgan curse and clamped down on the doubts Blackwood's words were rousing in him. It would have been easy for the bastard to find out that Rhys had distributed the pamphlets. But there were other printers in Carmarthen and many in Wales. In fact, Blackwood had no reason to believe that Rhys hadn't had the pamphlets printed in London. So how could he have found out that Morgan had printed the pamphlets? Unless Juliana *had* told him.

"I don't know what you're talking about," Rhys said as calmly as he could.

The viscount scrutinized his fingernails with a bored look. "Of course you do, Vaughan. Juliana was eager to tell me about your illegal activities if it meant she could get you out of her hair. She told me about the meeting that you spoke at, and she recounted all you said about the Welsh language. And she told me about the pamphlets you two printed up."

Stunned into silence, Rhys wondered if someone else might have betrayed them. If so, who?

"In any case," Blackwood went on, "I was happy to oblige her by having you impressed. With you gone, no one need know about your outrageous marriage at all. We can arrange a proper marriage for her. After all, Llynwydd will be a plum for some other, more worthy gentleman."

Casting a withering glance at Blackwood, Rhys retorted, "The bishop who performed our ceremony will have something to say about that!"

Blackwood's eyes narrowed. "Will he risk tangling with my father so publicly? I doubt it. He may be Welsh, but he still answers to the Church of England, and they might frown on a man giving a special license to a known radical and a young woman of eighteen. No, I don't think your bishop is quite that brave. If he is, we'll insist on an annulment. 'Tisn't what we'd want, of course, but—"

Rhys let out a roar that made Blackwood jump back a step. "*Cer i'r diawl!* Aye, to the devil with you! This marriage has been consummated!"

"Juliana will say otherwise, I'm sure. And if she claims your marriage wasn't consummated and you're not there to refute her, then everything is done, over, complete. She's free to marry another, with a fine property to attract him."

Rhys gritted his teeth, wishing he could wipe the smug smile from the viscount's face, wishing the man's words weren't so convincing. He made himself remember Juliana's face as she'd sworn to love, honor, and obey him for a lifetime. She'd meant her words. He could swear she did.

But someone *had* summoned her brothers to the inn this night. It wasn't likely they'd figured it out on their own, for they hadn't even known he was seeing Juliana, and she'd promised not to leave a note telling them about the elopement. He'd certainly told no one where they were going, not even the bishop. And she'd been alone with the innkeeper while Rhys had gone back to the horses to get the book. . . .

He beat back the doubts devouring him. Who would he believe—a black-hearted Englishman like the viscount?—or his sweet Juliana?

His sweet Juliana . . . who'd always run off at the first sign of trouble . . . at the meeting . . . after her father's threat to cane her. . . . He'd heard Darcy tell her that day in the forest that he wouldn't hide her anymore. And she'd relied on her mother to get her out of her caning.

Yes, his sweet Juliana did have a penchant for acting impulsively, then doing whatever it took to avoid the consequences. And if she'd thought that he'd somehow learned Llynwydd belonged to her, would she have balked at the marriage?

Worse yet, she *had* known that Morgan had printed the pamphlets. And she was, after all, a pampered young English noblewoman.

That thought made him curse himself. He knew Juliana. Pampered she might have been, English she certainly was, but she wouldn't run from their marriage. Would she?

He fixed Blackwood with a threatening gaze. "I won't listen to your lies about my wife. My *wife.* She'll be my wife until the day I return. And I *will* return, you son of a bitch, you can be sure of that!"

"If you do, it'll be your death." The viscount scowled and gestured to Rhys's neck. "They hang deserters, you know. And while I might not kill you now, if you ever come back, I'll make sure they hang you. You and Pennant both!"

"If you won't release me, then at least release Morgan," Rhys gritted out. "No matter what you think, he had nothing to do with those pamphlets. I had them printed in London. And if Juliana says otherwise, she's lying."

A dark smile creased Blackwood's face. "Is Lettice lying, too, then?"

"You whoreson Englishman!" Morgan exploded at Rhys's side. "If you think to malign my woman as well—"

Blackwood's harsh laugh seemed to cast a chill on the already cold room. "You two are such fools. Women are cowards at heart. All I had to do after I brought Vaughan here tonight was confront Lettice with what Juliana had told me. She confirmed it all as soon as she realized what hot water she was in." He gave Morgan a hard stare. "Once I knew for certain you'd been involved, of course, I had to take you, too. We can't have you radicals stirring up the Welsh—not with an election nigh at hand. Lettice understood that."

"Nay, not Lettice," Morgan choked out. "She would never betray me. She couldn't—"

"Couldn't she? Do you think she'd lose her position over you?" Blackwood shoved the snuff box back into his pocket with sudden, vicious energy. "When it came to choosing between her post and a deuced Welsh radical, she certainly didn't throw herself into poverty."

"I don't believe it," Morgan whispered.

But his anguished tone said he might. Rhys himself couldn't say, for he knew little about Lettice, except that she hadn't wanted him involved with Juliana.

The viscount drew himself up, surveying both men with a cold gaze. "Well, that's that. I've tarried here with you long enough. Now that you know why you're being impressed, I hope you'll not trouble the men with questions. They've been well paid to ignore them."

Rhys could no longer answer. He felt as if a boxer had been pummeling him for hours. In truth, Blackwood's words had been like blows, primed to hit each man's most vulnerable spot.

The viscount rose from his seat on the barrel. "I'll leave you two gentlemen to your happy thoughts. After all, once you're aboard ship, you won't have much time for thinking, will you?" He moved to the arched doorway, then paused and turned. "And remember what I said. Return to Wales and you're both dead men. I'll see to it myself."

With that, he was gone, shutting the door behind him and leaving them in total darkness.

"You know he's lying," Rhys said aloud in Welsh, hoping that speaking the words would make him believe them.

"Did Lettice tell Juliana who printed those pamphlets?"

"Yes."

"So she did know." Morgan cursed until his breath. "I told Lettice not to tell her. She swore she'd not say a word to anyone."

An acrid taste filled Rhys's mouth. "You know women. They can't keep secrets at all."

Morgan's breathing grew heavy. Rhys could hear him shift his position on the floor. "Yes, but to tell Blackwood? If he didn't find out from either of them as he said, then from whom?"

"A spy in our midst, perhaps? One of our compatriots?"

"Our compatriots didn't know who printed them. As I recall, you even told them once it was a printer in London."

"Maybe one of them overheard us discussing it." Rhys stared blankly into the darkness, praying that was the answer.

Then again, even if Blackwood had found out about the pamphlets through spies, that didn't explain how he'd known where to find Rhys tonight.

Rhys could explain how Blackwood knew about the Sons of Wales and even why Juliana hadn't told him about Llynwydd. Perhaps she hadn't known it belonged to her. Perhaps Blackwood was simply lying about that.

But Rhys couldn't explain how Blackwood had known where to find him. That was the one piece of damning evidence that ate at him. And he couldn't forget how nervous she'd been when they reached the inn, how skittish.

"At the moment, it hardly matters whether the women betrayed us or not," came Morgan's voice, dragging Rhys from his painful thoughts. "We're still bound as tightly as two dead sheep being hauled to market, and

I don't think we're like to get out of this. I don't know about you, but I have no weapon. No knife, nothing." His tone hardened. "After all, one doesn't take a weapon when one is out courting."

Nor does one take a weapon to a wedding, Rhys thought bitterly.

"So what do we do now?" Morgan asked.

Rhys thought of all he'd heard about the navy. Impressed men were given the worst tasks. And in truth, the only reason the navy resorted to impressment in the first place was conditions were so bad on a British man-of-war that men died or deserted at alarming rates. Rhys had heard of the wretched food that bred disease, of the floggings ordered by tyrannical captains. There were prisoners who, when given the choice of the navy or death, chose death.

Uncontrollable shudders racked his body. Juliana wouldn't have wished such a nightmare on him, would she? Of course, Blackwood claimed she was too naive to know what impressment entailed. And he could believe that easily.

"Rhys? What do we do?" Morgan repeated.

Rhys could tell that Morgan's thoughts mirrored his. He clenched his fists, feeling the stone floor scrape his knuckles. "We survive. We survive, and one day we return. Because no matter what that son of a bitch Blackwood says, we will avenge this. And none of his paltry threats will prevent it."

Chapter Seven

"I gaze across the distant hills,
  Thy coming to espy;
Beloved, haste, the day grows late,
The sun sinks down the sky."
—William Williams Pantycelyn,
    "I gaze across the distant hills"

Overton rode beside his brother back to the inn where they'd left Juliana. He'd wanted to go there as soon as they'd given Vaughan to the press-gang, but Darcy had insisted on waiting at the tavern until the ship pulled out of port. Now the sun had risen well above the horizon.

Glancing at his brother's rigid expression, Overton swallowed. "I hope you know what you're doing. Shuter didn't like taking a squire, even after you gave him all that money and told him Vaughan was a radical."

Darcy's grimace drew his heavy brows together. "I don't care. That blackguard Vaughan carried off our sister for his own devious purposes. Don't you understand? They *consummated* the marriage. That deuced bastard would have been our brother-in-law if we hadn't done something. And when Juliana realized he desired her only for her property, she'd have been miserable. Is that what you wanted?"

No, he thought. But this whole business didn't seem right, especially with Vaughan being an Oxford man and a gentleman. "Perhaps he truly cares for her."

Darcy snorted. "For the daughter of the man who stole his estate? I doubt it." They rode into the inn yard for the second time that day. "Besides, Juliana deserves better than some Welsh radical. We've saved her from an awful fate. Trust me, if we'd let it go on, a week from now she *would* have been regretting the marriage and crying to us for help."

Overton remained silent as they dismounted. Darcy had always set the rules for everything they did. Overton never questioned him. But this was making him bloody uneasy.

As they approached the entrance to the inn, Overton caught Darcy's arm. "I heard all those things you told Vaughan, you know. I stood outside the cellar listening. It was cruel to lie to him. The poor chap will suffer in the navy anyway, so why kick him when he's down?"

"Because if he believes Juliana loves him, he'll return to take advantage of her." Darcy's tone was patient, like that of a physician explaining a painful treatment to a child. "Vaughan must be forced to realize he'll gain nothing by coming back."

Overton shivered as he remembered Vaughan's threats to wreak vengeance on them. "Do you think he *could* return?"

"Return? After the navy gets through with him, he won't want to come near England." He patted Overton on the shoulder. "Don't worry, brother. I won't let him come after you."

When Overton squirmed at his brother's touch, Darcy added, "Come now, you're not worried about that puny Welsh squire, are you? You saw the man. Either of us make two of him. He'll probably struggle through the navy, then slink off into some remote corner of the world with his tail between his legs, thanking his good fortune that he needn't deal with us ever again."

Overton chafed under his brother's condescending tone. Rhys Vaughan hadn't seemed either puny or a coward to him. Nor had that printer fellow. "Well then, what about Morgan Pennant?"

Darcy shrugged. "What about him?"

"What if *he* comes back? He looked rough."

"Rough? A printer?" Darcy chuckled. "You certainly are spooked by shadows, aren't you?"

"No, but I don't understand why you said all that rot to him about his sweetheart and got him riled up. You told me you only wanted to rid the town of radicals." He crossed his arms defiantly. "Now I wonder if you did this to get him out of the way, so you could have Lettice."

Darcy stared at him, eyes glittering. "I hope you don't

voice that theory to anyone but me, dear brother. You'd best keep this night's events a total secret. Remember, when Father dies I'll hold the purse strings. And I never forget a slight."

Overton blanched. He and Darcy had always had an easy relationship. Darcy had never threatened him, but then, he'd never needed to. Overton had always deferred to Darcy's superior intellect in any decision, and in return, Darcy had always made certain Overton received sufficient funds for hunting and gaming. Overton had never seen his brother so determined to get his way. Lettice must have affected him as no other woman had before.

"Do you understand me, Overton?" Darcy added. "I have to be sure you'll support me, no matter what."

Overton thought about making another token protest, but decided against it. If Darcy wanted this so badly that he'd make threats to get it, Overton wouldn't cross him. Rocking boats wasn't one of his favorite pastimes, to be sure. "I'll support you," he muttered.

"Come on then." Darcy entered the inn.

It took them only moments to find the innkeeper and determine that Juliana hadn't left her room.

"I think she might have fallen asleep," said the innkeeper. " 'Tis awful quiet up there."

"Good." Darcy gave the innkeeper more money and admonished him once again in the story he was to tell anyone who asked. Then he added, "Be sure all those in your employ say the same."

They all climbed the stairs. But Darcy paused outside the door the innkeeper indicated. "Remember, this is our first visit to the inn. We know nothing about Vaughan's disappearance."

When Overton nodded, Darcy gestured to the innkeeper to unlock the door. Then Darcy threw the door open.

The innkeeper had been right. Juliana was asleep. But as soon as Darcy boomed out "Where is he?" she jolted awake.

Overton averted his face as she sat up, exposing her nakedness. And though she scrambled to cover herself with the sheet, rage surged through him to see her obviously deflowered.

"Where is he?" Darcy repeated. He too wore a tortured look as he strode inside and scanned the room. "Where's that scoundrel Vaughan?"

Darcy was so convincing in his search that Overton had to remind himself it was merely an act. Despite her obvious confusion, Juliana also looked convinced. She clutched the sheet to her chest and watched Darcy prowl the room as an expression of horror grew on her face.

Darcy pounded a fist against the wall and fixed her with a fierce gaze. "Where's Rhys Vaughan, Juliana?"

Her gaze flitted around the room. She looked so pitifully bewildered that Overton had to look away. "I—I don't know," she whispered. "I fell asleep and then . . ."

She trailed off as she shook her head to clear it. As her sleepiness began to wear off, her gaze shot to Darcy. "What are you doing here? H-how did you know where to find us . . . I mean, me?"

"Mother found your note this morning, and we've been searching inns ever since. When we got here, the innkeeper said there was indeed a young couple staying here." He surveyed her sheet-wrapped body with contempt, and poor Juliana cringed. "I see we came too late to rescue you from that fortune hunter, but not too late to make him face the consequences of his act, I promise you. So tell us where he is!"

Juliana shook her head helplessly. "What time is it?" She glanced toward the closed curtains. "What time?"

"Milord," said the innkeeper, in keeping with the instructions Darcy had given him. "The maid told me Mr. Vaughan came downstairs a few hours ago. He said he had to get something from his horse, and he went out. The maid didn't stay around to see him come in, and I had just assumed he was up here—"

"Where did he go, Juliana?" Darcy demanded. "Tell us!"

Tears welled in her eyes. "I don't know!"

Overton's heart twisted at the confusion in her voice.

Darcy searched the floor until he found her clothes and then threw them at her. "Then you're coming home with us."

"No. I want to wait here for my husband."

"So you really did marry that fool Welshman, did you?"

Juliana's lips tightened as she tilted her head back regally. "Yes. And there's nothing you can do about it."

Darcy's tone was deceptively casual. "Prove you're married. Show me your marriage certificate."

Overton held his breath. If they could get their hands on the certificate, they could make the marriage disappear, provided the bishop cooperated.

Juliana, however, dashed those hopes. "I can't. I'm not sure where it is. Rhys might have it with him."

Overton and Darcy exchanged glances. Neither of them had thought to search for such papers on Vaughan's person. And the ship had already sailed. Overton shifted from foot to foot. If Vaughan ever returned with that paper ... He swallowed. Darcy was so sure the man wouldn't return. Overton could only hope his brother was right in this as in so many other things.

"The marriage certificate is gone ... your husband is gone," Darcy said coldly as he paced the room. "It appears, madam, that your 'husband' has abandoned you."

"He hasn't!" Despite her words, Overton could hear the faint doubt in her tone. "He ... he wouldn't have. Why would he marry me, then abandon me?"

"Why?" Darcy cast a scathing glance over her. "So he could bed you. And take your lands. But he's nowhere in sight at the moment so you might as well come home with us."

"I—I can't." She turned an imploring gaze on Overton. "I must wait for him."

Overton bit his tongue to keep from telling her everything. But he dared not. Even if he wanted to go against Darcy's wishes, doing so now would be futile. Telling poor Juliana that her husband had just begun a lengthy stint in the navy wouldn't exactly comfort her.

Still, not to tell her anything ... He forced himself not to think about it. "Listen, love," he heard himself saying. "There's no point to waiting here by yourself, and Mother is sick with worry. Come back to the house, and I'm sure this good innkeeper will send your"—he nearly choked over the word—"husband on to Northcliffe if ... when he returns."

Darcy shot him a cynical look, which he ignored. "We'll leave so you can dress. But then you must come with us, if only to put Mother at ease. I'll bring you back here later if you want."

When Juliana cast him a grateful smile, he swallowed his guilt. In truth, she was lovely, and it would be a bloody shame to waste her on a chap like Vaughan, who might indeed have married her for her property.

Yes, he and Darcy were doing what was best for her. She deserved a better husband, he told himself.

It was the only way he could silence the clamoring of his conscience.

Tense and fearful, Juliana descended the stairs to the ground floor, where she'd been told Father was awaiting her in the study. It had been hours since she'd left the inn, and she was now frantic with worry over what might have happened to Rhys. She'd checked with the groom and found their bags, including the deed to Llynwydd, intact, which only increased her worries.

She gave a sob and pressed her fist to her mouth. Something awful had happened to him. She just knew it. But what?

As she reached the door to her father's study, Lettice emerged from the shadows, her normally vibrant eyes dull and red.

"What is it?" Juliana asked in alarm.

"Have they not told you? Darcy said he'd heard about it in the streets. They've been out looking for your husband and—" She broke off with a little cry. "Oh, my lady, the press-gangs were out in the wee hours this morning. And someone reported seeing them take two men aboard a boat." Lettice's voice wavered. "My Morgan . . . and your Rhys."

Juliana flattened her hand over her heart. "Oh, no . . . not Rhys . . . not my husband . . ."

"It's true, my lady." She wiped away fresh tears. "I asked around myself. No one's sure which ship they were meant for. There are several that set sail from Carmarthen Bay this morning, and the boat likely headed for one of them. The other Sons of Wales think the burgesses learned who was responsible for those pamphlets and told the press-gang to take them."

" 'Tis all a mistake! I know it! Who would have known where to find Rhys?"

"Anyone might have sent word to the press-gangs."

She thought of Rhys aboard an English man-of-war and shuddered. He wasn't a seaman but a scholar. How would he survive?

Suddenly, the door to her father's study opened and her mother stepped into the hall. She flashed Lettice a reproachful look before turning to Juliana. "Come in, they're waiting for you."

With a nod, Juliana squeezed Lettice's hand, then followed her mother into the study. As soon as they entered, Juliana's heart sank, for standing behind her father's desk was not only her father, but Darcy, both scowling at her. Only Overton looked the least bit friendly, and even he wore a worried expression.

Juliana stood mute while her father shouted his disappointment at her, his outrage over her foolish actions, his disbelief that she had done something so scandalous. Yet none of it seemed to touch her, for she was still reeling from what Lettice had told her. Dear heaven, what Rhys and Morgan must be suffering! To be taken by the press-gangs! The very thought of it made an acid tide of fear spurt through her.

If only she'd gone downstairs with Rhys. If only ...

Suddenly, she realized her father was asking her a question. She looked at him blankly.

"Are you listening to me, girl?" Rage made his eyes look like two bulging marbles.

"Yes, Father." How calm her voice sounded. And how odd that her fear of Father seemed to have vanished. It was as if the marriage ceremony had transformed her into a different person. She was no longer Lady Juliana St. Albans, but Rhys's wife, Lady Juliana Vaughan. She had a husband now, so she didn't need her family's approval.

Her father's ramrod posture didn't alter. "We will have the marriage annulled today. You'll tell the bishop that it wasn't consummated, and—"

"But it *was* consummated!"

Her father looked at her as if a doll had suddenly opened its porcelain mouth to speak to him. In truth, in the past she'd been like a doll in her father's presence, always doing what he wanted and only daring to be different in the privacy of her own room.

But no more. She was a married woman now, and she wouldn't stand for him treating her like a little girl. They were trying to make this marriage go away, for heaven's sake. Well, she wouldn't let them.

"It doesn't matter if it was consummated," Darcy interjected. "You'll tell the bishop what Father says you'll tell him."

She planted her hands on her hips. "I certainly won't! And I won't let you have my marriage annulled!"

"I'll lock you in your room forever, girl!" her father roared. "I'll keep you from eating and—"

"You can't bully me anymore. None of you can. I'm married now, and only my husband can tell me what to do. If you bring me to the bishop, I'll tell him the truth, so don't even think of it."

"Come now, Juliana," Overton cajoled, "this is the best way. We've heard that the man's been impressed."

A tight fist closed on her heart. "So it's true?"

Overton nodded.

"A piece of good fortune for us," Darcy said. "Now you don't have to live out a miserable existence bound legally to a man who didn't want you."

"He *did* want me!" Darcy's assured words lacerated her. "He still wants me."

Darcy's eyes narrowed. "Well, it doesn't matter even if he does. He'll be at sea for years, whether you like it or not."

She wrung her hands. "Perhaps he can escape."

"He'd be a fool to try it. The punishment for desertion is hanging or if he's lucky, whipping through the fleet."

"Whipping through the fleet?" Juliana whispered.

"Aye," Darcy said. "The master-at-arms takes the unlucky deserter in a boat from ship to ship, and at each stop the deserter receives lashes from that ship's boatswain. I heard tell of a man who was dead by the time they reached the last ship. They flogged him anyway. When they buried him, the flesh was completely flayed from the bones of his back."

That was all it took to give Juliana a complete picture of hardships at sea. "Oh, no . . ." Bile rose in her throat. "My poor Rhys!"

"And even if he doesn't escape, he'll be lucky to survive at all," Darcy went on relentlessly. "They treat sailors abominably on those warships—flogging them for any infraction, feeding them maggoty biscuits—"

"That's enough, Darcy!" Overton bit out.

But Juliana was already numb. How would her dear, sweet husband bear it all?

"In any case," Darcy said, "he'll not be back for a long time. So this whole thing can be fixed if you'll just—"

"Nay!" Juliana felt a painful pressure in her chest. "Nay. I love him. I don't care what has happened. He'll come back some day, and when he does, I'll be waiting. I know he'll communicate with me as soon as he can."

"No doubt," Darcy snapped. "He'll communicate with you so he can get his greedy hands on Llynwydd. 'Tis why he married you, isn't it?"

"Of course not! He didn't know Llynwydd belonged to me. He married me for love."

Darcy snorted. "Indeed! And it would have simply been a happy coincidence that once you were married, he'd have regained his estate. I'm sure he didn't intend that at all."

"He didn't!"

"None of this matters!" her father roared. "There's been a scandal, and we must keep it quiet, do you hear? We must! You'll get this marriage annulled, girl, if I must force you into it!"

"Now, Horace," her mother said, "stop shouting at the girl. It does no good to be like that."

Juliana's newfound courage wavered a fraction. Could her father force an annulment? He couldn't force her to agree to one, but if he pressured the bishop, could he bring it to pass without her? If so, she couldn't let that happen.

She sucked in a deep breath, considering her choices. Desperate to say something, anything, that would keep them from acting to end her marriage, she lied. "If you try to annul my marriage without my permission, I'll make sure every man, woman, and child in this town sees my marriage certificate and knows the truth of what happened."

Darcy scowled. "You said you didn't know where the certificate is. You said you thought Vaughan had taken it."

She forced herself to sound calm. "I lied. And I have it now, in a safe place where none of you will find it. So either you let me have my way in this, or I shame the family by revealing what I've done."

Her father paled, and for a moment, he actually looked vulnerable. "You wouldn't do that to me, would you, love?"

Something twisted inside her heart. He never called her "love" unless he wanted something from her. "I don't want a scandal any more than you do, Father. I wouldn't want to bring shame on the family or on Rhys. But I *am* his wife."

Darcy came around from behind the desk, his expression calculating. "Listen, Juliana. What if Vaughan doesn't return? And if we never hear from him again? What if, God forbid, he dies at sea? You'd likely never know it. You'd live your whole life in some half state between widow and wife, never having a family or a husband."

She wanted to ignore the harsh truth behind his words, but she couldn't.

Darcy shot their father a glance. "I have a proposal that might settle this to everyone's satisfaction."

Crossing her arms over her chest, she said, "Oh?"

"If you don't wish an annulment, you don't have to get one. We can speak to the bishop and ask him to keep silent about the marriage under the circumstances. He'll agree. As for anyone else who knows about the marriage—like the innkeeper—I've already ensured that they'll keep quiet."

She eyed him warily.

"For the time being," he continued, "why don't you also keep quiet? Take time to consider what you wish to do. There's no hurry. You may decide you're unwilling to sacrifice your future for the memory of one Welshman."

She hesitated, surveying the expectant faces of her family. In truth, she wasn't up to facing people right now, to telling them about her marriage when she had only sorrow in her heart.

"What if I find—" She broke off and swallowed hard. "What if I find I'm with child?"

"Oh, mercy," her mother squeaked and dropped into a chair. Her father looked almost ill.

But although Darcy's expression grew more stony, he held her gaze. "If that should happen, we'll announce the marriage, of course. Still, it's unlikely. You only spent one night together, didn't you?"

Turning crimson, she nodded.

"So what do you think?" Darcy prodded. "Why don't we give it a little time and keep it quiet until you make up your mind?"

As Juliana stared at him, a great weariness stole over her. It had been a long day and night. Darcy's words held too much logic for her to ignore. Yet wouldn't she be betraying Rhys if she did as Darcy asked?

She sighed. Yes. But he'd left her few other choices. And Darcy's proposal did have merit. It would also give her time to explore possibilities, to determine if she could buy out Rhys's service or something. As soon as Rhys wrote to say which ship he was on, she could take care of it.

But if she stayed here with the family, they'd work on her to change her mind and get an annulment. She thought a moment, thought of all the plans she'd made with Rhys. Then her brow cleared. "All right, I'll consider it." The group breathed a collective sigh until she added, "but only under one condition."

"Condition?" her father said, the color returning to his face. "What condition?"

"That I be allowed to live at Llynwydd in the meantime."

"Llynwydd?" her mother protested. "Alone?"

"Yes." Juliana cast them all a defiant glance. "It belongs to me, after all."

"I should *never* have given it to you," her father grumbled. "Maybe if I hadn't, none of this would have happened."

"Yes, but you did give it to me. I won't let you take it back. It belongs to me and Rhys now. And until he returns, I want to live there and make certain it's cared for properly."

"Oh, of all the stupid ideas—" her father began.

"If you don't allow it, Father, I swear I'll trumpet my

marriage to the rooftops. I'll tell everyone I know, and devil take the scandal."

Darcy and Overton exchanged glances, but she stared at her father with a resolute expression. He scowled, but the fight seemed to have gone out of him. For the first time in her life, she realized he was looking terribly old—and worn down.

She softened her voice. "Please, Father?"

Anger flickered briefly in his eyes, but he quelled it. "Very well, girl, as you wish." He stiffened. "But I tell you this, if I ever get my hands on that scoundrel Welshman, I'll wring his bloody neck, I will."

"Yes, Father," she said absently, too relieved by his acquiescence to protest.

She had a home of her own now, even if she had no husband to share it with. No husband. Her heart wrenched in her chest. Rhys was gone, and it might be years before he returned.

Nonetheless, having Llynwydd to care for was something at least. And if she could gain that, then perhaps fortune would smile on her and bring Rhys back to her soon.

All she could do was hope.

PART II

Carmarthen, Wales
June 1783

"Hard blow, why care where's my home,
You broke faith, and it grieves me."
—Llywelyn Goch ap Meurig Hen,
"Lament for Lleucu Llwyd"

Chapter Eight

"O, when you eye all Christendom's
Loveliest cheek—this girl will bring
Annihilation upon me ..."
—Dafydd ap Gwilym,
"The Seagull"

The harsh smell of vinegar brought Juliana half conscious. But it took the sound of arguing voices to drag her from her faint. She caught snatches of words—"liar," "crazy Welshman," and "my wife"—and shook her head wildly. She hadn't dreamed it? She hadn't dreamed that Rhys had returned from the dead after six years of total silence?

She forced her eyes open. Her mother bent over her, holding a ghastly bottle to her nose. Juliana brushed it away and attempted to sit up, but Overton appeared next to her mother and said, "Don't rush it, love."

Overton looked so pitying that it was to him she turned and not her mother, who was near hysterics. "I—is he truly here?" she whispered through dry lips. She wet them and repeated, "Is Rhys here?"

With a nod, Overton moved to let her see across the room. Stephen stood silent and angry at the window, the very picture of the haughty lord, and beside him stood Darcy, his face red with fury. The object of both men's fury was a man she still could hardly recognize. Rhys Vaughan.

Ignoring Overton's restraining hand, she sat up. Somewhere in the back of her mind, she realized they were no longer in the ballroom, no longer surrounded by guests. Her family had gotten her away from prying eyes into the drawing room, for which she was grateful, although they'd done it only to minimize the scandal. But none of that concerned her as much as Rhys's miraculous appearance.

The three men on the other end of the room hadn't yet realized she'd awakened. They were busy bandying forth phrases about "rights" and "betrayal" and "honor," which gave her a chance to study the man she hadn't seen in six years.

Such a very long time. Had Rhys really been so tall? Or so handsome? To be sure, his clothing made him look more imposing and sophisticated than before, but there was something else, too. Six years ago he'd emanated an enticing blend of flame and raw energy. But now ... she could tell just from the deliberate way he parried every one of her brother's verbal thrusts that the flame and energy had been banked into a furnace that burned even hotter under such control. In truth, his obvious control frightened her as his unstudied fervor never had.

And he was here, determined to pick up their lives as if nothing had happened in the interim. Her temper flared at the thought, especially when she looked at Stephen, whose stony expression barely masked the hurt in his eyes.

How dare Rhys do this! Six years without a single letter, no message of any kind to tell her he'd survived the navy. The investigator Darcy had helped her hire had turned up nothing on him until a year ago when he'd found a mention of Rhys's death in a ship's log.

Yet Rhys had obviously not died. In fact, while she'd struggled to bring Llynwydd into its glory, waiting for him, fearing for him, and finally mourning him, he'd been off somewhere prospering. His fine clothing told her that. So why in heaven's name hadn't he returned sooner?

She'd thought he'd been blown up in a battle or drowned at sea. Well, he certainly hadn't. And he was obviously here to stay. What had he said? *I've come to reclaim my lands ... my inheritance ... you. I've come to take you home.*

He was alive and here before her, ready to continue as if his six years of silence were nothing. He wanted to take ownership of the estate that *she* had nurtured, to benefit from the work *she* had performed, when he'd apparently not cared enough about her even to let her know he was alive.

She sat up stiffly on the settee, gathering her strength. Before God, he could go to hell if he thought she'd simply acquiesce to his plans.

He'd been silent for six years, and six years was a long time, blast him.

Six years was an eternity, Rhys thought as his attention was caught by a movement on the other end of the room. He turned to see Juliana rise from the settee, her wan face set stubbornly.

"I'd like to participate in this discussion," she said, her feminine voice edged with steel.

Lord Devon and the new earl, who'd gained the Northcliffe title at his father's death, pivoted at the sound of her voice, breaking off their argument. With everyone's attention on her, she settled her skirts and came forward.

Inexplicably, a harsh pressure built in Rhys's chest. It had been building ever since he'd first seen Juliana this evening, dressed in a golden satin gown that showed her assets to their best advantage. When she'd come down the stairs to that bastard English lord, her face alight, the pressure had grown worse. He didn't know if anger or frustration or perhaps even jealousy had caused the tightness, but it had been wholly unexpected.

It had only increased when he'd stood before them all and made his announcement. He'd expected to feel nothing but elation, and indeed that had passed through him at the sight of Juliana's guilty, alarmed expression. But there'd been something else—the tight clutch of memory in his chest.

No matter what he told himself about her character, he couldn't forget that she was his wife, that those soft, red lips had once parted beneath his kisses.

At eighteen, she'd been pretty, her green eyes bright with the promise of youth and her full figure a lusty young man's dream. But now . . . now she was beautiful. Damn it all, she was beautiful, with a lush form and lovely face. In the years he'd spent wishing he could make her feel a tenth of his tortures, he'd forgotten about the pleasures of her, the way her hair flashed copper in the candlelight, the quick turn of her hand when she spoke.

Tonight he'd had ample time to watch her. And remember.

Cursing himself for falling once more under her spell, he rubbed his wrist with its scars where the spun yarn had cut into his flesh during his many floggings aboard the H.M.S. *Nightmark,* or Nightmare, as the tars had privately called it.

It reminded him of his purpose. "I see my wife has finally chosen to join us."

"You keep referring to her as your 'wife,'" Northcliffe cut in. "You have no proof of any wedding."

Under other circumstances, Rhys would have been amused by Northcliffe's petty attempt to put a good face on things in front of Lord Devon. But he was not amused now. "I suppose a marriage certificate won't suffice?"

Everyone gave a collective gasp. Everyone except Juliana.

Northcliffe turned on her. "A marriage certificate? Does he have a marriage certificate?"

With a stiff nod, she gave Rhys a scathing glance.

Rhys drew it from his pocket and handed it to her. "That should serve to jog your memory about our marriage—the one you conveniently forgot."

She waved the certificate away. "If I'd wanted to forget our marriage, I'd have had it annulled!"

"Not having the marriage certificate might have made that difficult," Rhys said as he slid the certificate back into his pocket, "and I'm sure my godfather the bishop wouldn't have agreed to perform an annulment in any case. Then after he and his wife died, there were no more witnesses and no need for an annulment, was there? No need for a public scandal."

Her silence confirmed that he'd hit upon the truth.

"But there will be an annulment now," Northcliffe put in.

"Now that you're acknowledging the marriage?" Rhys quipped, with a knowing glance in Lord Devon's direction. The poor man had grown pale.

"Yes," Northcliffe bit out.

"No." Rhys said the word savagely. "There will be no annulment."

"Why not?" Juliana asked.

Rhys leveled a withering glance on her. To her credit, although she colored, she didn't flinch from his gaze.

"Have you forgotten," he said in a silky voice, "that our marriage was consummated? Or will you pretend it wasn't?"

"Consummated?" Lord Devon said, his voice quiet but bitter. "Is he telling the truth, Juliana?"

Rhys watched with pleasure as her sweet, lying mouth trembled and all her confidence faltered. His puny taunts scarcely repaid her for the loss of his illusions, but they did give him a certain hollow satisfaction.

"You don't have to answer," Northcliffe warned.

"But if you don't," Rhys told her calmly, "I'll be forced to give your fiancé a detailed account of our joyous wedding night ... how you cried out my name as I—"

"That's enough, Rhys." Juliana's face was a deathly pale color, emphasizing the fragility of her slender throat. Her beautiful, slender throat. He cursed inwardly. Why did he notice such things even now, knowing what she was?

Lowering her gaze, she turned to her fiancé. "I'm so sorry, Stephen. I never thought this would happen. I thought—"

"Is he telling the truth?" Lord Devon's eyes filled with pain.

She bit her lip. "Our marriage ..." She faltered a moment. Then she lifted her head, though not her gaze. "It was consummated."

"Oh, dear, now you've gone and done it!" exclaimed her mother as she collapsed onto the settee.

Lord Devon looked shattered, the very picture of a cuckolded husband.

Poor sot, Rhys thought. *A cuckold and not even married yet.* Still, Rhys reminded himself, a few weeks more and the blameless marquess would have been full owner of Llynwydd. Rhys's tone hardened as he faced his wife. "Now that we all agree it was consummated, there will be no more talk of an annulment."

"If you'll both claim that the consummation didn't

take place, we can still have the marriage annulled,"
Northcliffe persisted. He shot an imploring glance at
Lord Devon. "Then Juliana could marry his lordship
as planned."

Lord Devon's face turned even more ashen. "Surely
you understand that I can't ... I mean ..." He turned
to Juliana, a trace of pity in his eyes. "I'm sorry, my
dear, but I must ... I have to reconsider my offer. I
have family obligations to think about. And my reputation. You understand, don't you?"

Juliana nodded, but Rhys could tell she didn't understand at all. A welter of emotions assailed him—anger
at Lord Devon for his callousness ... anger at her for
caring about the damned marquess ... and anger at himself for noticing her reactions at all. This was what he'd
wanted, to separate her from her wealthy nobleman, to
make her face the consequences of her unthinking act of
six years ago. He should be delighted that she was hurt!

But when Lord Devon took her hand and she stared
up at him with regret, Rhys felt his insides twist.

"If you'd only told me of the truth in the first place,"
Lord Devon said, "if you hadn't lied to me—"

"Lying to you was a necessary part of getting you to
marry her, you fool." Rhys couldn't stand to keep silent
in the face of their obvious feelings for each other.

"Stay out of this, Rhys," Juliana whispered in an aching voice. " 'Tis none of your concern."

"I see," he snapped. "I hadn't realized the fiancé takes
precedence over the husband."

She flinched, but ignored him otherwise, taking both
of Lord Devon's hands in hers. "I *am* sorry I didn't tell
you, Stephen. I believed him dead, or I'd never have
allowed you to propose."

Rhys gritted his teeth. She would never have allowed
it if she hadn't believed him dead. What rot! She'd
wanted Rhys out of her life precisely so she could gain
a better husband. The little liar.

"I do understand why you feel you must ... reconsider your offer," she continued as she gazed up into the
marquess's face with the look that had once entranced
Rhys.

It entranced the marquess still, for he said fervently,
"Let me know if there's an annulment, and I'll speak to

my solicitor. Perhaps . . ." He trailed off with a sigh. "I hope you'll understand if I go now. I can't bear—" He shot Rhys a hard look. "You must work things out with your husband, and I think 'twould be better if I weren't here to watch."

Then he released her hands and strode to the door.

As he disappeared through it, Juliana's mother, who'd been watching in horrified disbelief, gave a shriek, her hands fluttering like a captured bird's wings. "The scandal! The dishonor! Oh, mercy on my life, what shall become of us?"

"Call Elizabeth to get Mother out of here," Northcliffe urged his brother as the door closed behind Lord Devon. "Mother can't handle discussions of this nature."

St. Albans went to the door and called for Northcliffe's wife, who was attempting to get rid of the guests in as subtle a manner as possible.

She hurried in, casting her husband a quizzical look, but he merely asked, "Have the guests all gone, Elizabeth?"

"Only the local ones. I couldn't very well throw out our houseguests. You'll have to take care of that."

Northcliffe shot Rhys an angry glance. "I will. Later. For now, take Mother upstairs and stay with her."

Lady Northcliffe did as her husband bid her, helping the dowager countess from the room.

As soon as they were gone, however, Northcliffe whirled on Rhys. "You must agree to an annulment. You can't do this to Juliana."

Rhys raised one eyebrow. "After what she's done to me, I'm letting her off easy, don't you think?"

Juliana had been staring at the door Lord Devon had left through, her face marked with pain, but now she whirled to face him. "And what have I done to you that's so dreadful that you purposely reappear on the eve of my engagement to torment me? To snatch my fiancé from me?"

He flinched at the surprise in her voice. Damn her for seeming so innocent! "How dare you act as if you don't know! How dare you pretend you didn't collude with your brothers to have me impressed?"

She stared at him aghast.

That only inflamed his anger further. "I wouldn't have

blamed you for having had second thoughts about our marriage. 'Twas an ill-fated union from the beginning." His throat tightened. "But then to behave like a coward, instead of telling me ... to summon your brothers behind my back and bid them to rid you of me—I can't forgive that. You may have thought you were doing me a favor by saving me from death and letting me be impressed instead, but I nearly died from it anyway."

Her face had grown bloodless, but he went on relentlessly. "Unfortunately for you, I didn't. My ship was captured by the Americans after I'd served three miserable years, and they gave me the choice of imprisonment or fighting for freedom with them. I chose to fight. And they rewarded me well. Very well."

"Which means you were either a privateer or a spy," Northcliffe interjected coldly, "for 'tis the only way a man gains wealth during a war."

Rhys's dark chuckle seemed to disconcert his enemy. "Listen, Northcliffe, if you think to use any of that against me, think again. Nor can you carry out your threat of having me hanged for a deserter. Being taken captive by the Americans doesn't constitute desertion. What's more, the war with the Americans is over, and I had a part in negotiating the peace. As a consequence, I've made some powerful friends—the Duke of Grafton and the Duke of Rockingham, for example. They've assured me that my debt to the nation has been paid."

He reveled in the way Northcliffe paled. Grafton and Rockingham were not only the current leaders in Parliament, they were also firmly supportive of the colonists. Of course, they wouldn't have countenanced Rhys's privateering, but Northcliffe needn't know that. And in truth, they'd listened to Benjamin Franklin when he'd presented Rhys as a model representative of both British and American concerns.

He smiled. The irony of that statement appealed immensely to him.

"I—I don't understand," Juliana broke in. Confusion and horror warred in her expression as she glanced from her brother to Rhys. "Why on earth would you think that I had summoned my brothers to the inn? How could you believe that I had you impressed?" Her eyes widened as she searched his face and backed away from him. "Did your years in the navy give you these delusions? Did it make you mad?"

How dare she act so innocent! Rhys stepped forward, ruthlessly pursuing her as she tried to put some distance between them. "No, the madness was in trusting you. God, I was so enamored of you that it took several floggings for me to accept what you'd done." He caught her arm, and she flinched from his touch. Good, he thought. Let her fear him. She seemed to understand fear better than love.

"But after I sent letter after letter and all remained unanswered," he continued in a deadpan voice, "I had to accept it was true."

"What letters? What are you talking about?" she whispered, her eyes wide with fright.

He ignored her. "I considered never coming back—abandoning any dream of Wales and making a life in America. But once the Duke of Grafton made it possible for me to return without fearing repercussions, I realized I had to come back ... to make you face the marriage you ran away from, to make you face what you'd done to me by having me impressed."

"Why do you speak these lies about me! You've lost your mind!"

"Lies? Then why are you here preparing to marry another as if our wedding never existed? And not just any man but a wealthy English marquess, exactly the kind of man your brother said you would find." His voice dropped menacingly. "So don't pretend you had no part in any impressment. The innkeeper at The White Oak confirms what your brother told me six years ago—that you had him send me aboard that ship because you wanted to end our marriage!"

His voice had risen to a shout in his tirade, but he didn't care. He'd waited six long years to confront her with her act, to watch her tremble as she realized he'd returned to exact his vengeance.

True to his expectations, she did tremble. But when she opened her mouth, he realized it wasn't fear that made her tremble. It was anger.

"My brother?" She wrenched her arm from his. "My *brother* told you those things?" She turned to her brothers, fury transforming her into a red-haired devil of a woman. "Which of you told him these lies? Which?"

"Darcy," St. Albans responded, stepping away as if to give his sister fighting room.

In truth, she looked as if she were spoiling for a fight as she turned on the earl. "Why would you lie to him like that, Darcy?" Her voice seemed to catch, and a look of betrayal spread over her face. "Why?"

Northcliffe shot a glance at his brother. "Now, Juliana, you know you wanted him gone. And when I brought him to the ship, I told him the truth—that you had cold feet about the marriage. I'd have killed him if you hadn't suggested the impressment, so you have nothing to be ashamed of."

"You!" she hissed. "You had him impressed? And then you acted as if ... oh, God, how could you have done that to me?"

"Come, love," he said in a gentle voice. "This pretense is foolish. I know you didn't want me to tell him the truth, but I couldn't resist it. I was so angry about his marrying you for your dowry that I said more than I should have."

"The 'truth'? That I'd sent my own husband off to a terrible fate? That's the 'truth' you told him? How could you speak such lies?"

Northcliffe spoke as an adult would speak to a foolish child. "There's no point in pretending to innocence now, Juliana. He knows everything, so we'd best deal with the bastard and see if we can't negotiate some arrangement mutually acceptable to all of us."

For a moment, she remained totally speechless. Then a look of understanding dawned on her face. "What about the letters he speaks of, Darcy? Letters did come here for me, didn't they? You never sent them to me. And ... and that man who told me Rhys was dead ... It was all your doing, wasn't it?"

Northcliffe shrugged. "If that's the way you want it." He turned to Rhys and said blandly, "I lied. It was all my doing."

She seemed to realize that Northcliffe's words only reaffirmed her guilt. Her entire body trembled, and Rhys tensed against the instant sympathy that spiraled in his gut. *She's an emotional woman,* he reminded himself. *She's merely angry that her brother has told her secrets.*

With a wild look in her eyes, she approached her

brother and grasped his coat. "Tell Rhys the truth." She shook him in near desperation. "Darcy ... don't ... How could you lie about me that way? Why don't you tell him the truth?"

Northcliffe looked extremely uncomfortable as he pushed her away from him, no doubt disgusted to watch his sister pretend to innocence. St. Albans, too, hid his face from her.

Her pretense was beginning to eat at Rhys, too, no matter how much he told himself it was an act. "Stop accusing him of lying, Juliana. Yes, Northcliffe handed me over to the press-gang, but you were the only one who could have summoned him to the inn that night. No one else knew of our presence there. And you and Lettice were the only ones who knew that Morgan and I printed those seditious pamphlets, which gave North-cliffe the excuse to have me impressed. Are you going to explain that away, too, in this foolish attempt to save yourself from me?"

She rounded on him, her eyes confused. "I—I don't know how they found us. Maybe from the note—"

"What note?" he said, pouncing on her slip.

Guilt suffused her face. "I left a note that said we'd eloped. But that's all it said, I swear it! I didn't tell them where we'd gone!"

"As I recall, we'd agreed not to leave any note."

"I know, but I couldn't let them worry."

"So you're saying that your 'note' is how they knew to come to the inn only an hour after we got there?"

"Only an hour? What are you talking about? They came the next morning, and told me—" She broke off in horror, whirling on her brothers. "You must have come earlier, while I was asleep. Is that when you caught him? Is that when you told him all those terrible things about me?"

"Stop it!" Rhys hissed. "Do you think I'll believe this invented tale? You might as well give up all hope of that, for the innkeeper says you sent him to get your brothers while you were alone with him."

"Then he lies!" Absolute desperation was in her voice now.

"Does he? The innkeeper lies. Your own brother lies. Even your fiancé has abandoned you now that he has seen your true character. Tell me then, why is everyone lying about you if you're so pure and innocent?"

"I—I don't know," she whispered, casting a beseeching glance at her brother. She lowered her voice to a pained whisper. "But no matter what they say, I loved you then. I *wanted* to be your wife. I would never have summoned my brothers."

He fought the feelings her words called up, especially since she'd used "love" in the past tense. Even knowing her to be a fickle, foolish woman, she could affect him, and that was dangerous. "Someone brought them there at four in the morning, long before anyone could have found your supposed note. And what about the pamphlets? No one knew who was responsible for printing them but you. And Lettice."

She jerked her head around. "You and your friend Morgan pranced about town with a devil-may-care lack of concern for what happened, and you blame me for that? I'm sure it wasn't the secret you make it out to be. We all knew of your part in it, for you announced it at the meeting—"

"The meeting you boldly sneaked into, then fled from when you realized you'd acted impulsively. Just as you married me, then fled the marriage after you changed your mind." He smiled, knowing he had her trapped.

She recoiled. "Is that who you think I am? Some . . . some irresponsible fool who'd marry you, then change my mind on a whim?"

"Not only on a whim . . . because you *thought* I'd married you for your property. The night I proposed, you accused me of wanting to marry you to get Llynwydd. I denied it, but you persisted in your fears, didn't you? And once we were married, you let those fears eat at you until you decided you'd made a big mistake."

"And that's when I'm supposed to have summoned my brothers and told them to pack you off to the navy?" She shook her head in disbelief. "Nothing I say will convince you that I couldn't have done such a thing, will it? You've tried and sentenced me, and I'm to have no word in my defense."

"I'm relying on the evidence, wife, and the evidence says you betrayed me. Perhaps you did it not knowing what impressment would mean for me, but you did it all the same."

With helplessness in her face, she turned to St. Albans. "And you, Overton? Shall you let Rhys believe all these awful lies about me that Darcy has concocted? Will you say nothing in my defense?"

St. Albans glanced at his brother, then said unsteadily, "I know you for what you are, Juliana."

"A foolish nitwit who'd send her husband off to certain torment to avoid her marriage?" she choked out. "Is that what you know me for, Overton?"

Lord Northcliffe stamped his foot. "That's enough, Juliana. We know you were young, and none of us blames you for behaving as you did." He turned to Rhys. "No one but your husband. And in light, sir, of your dislike of your wife's behavior, I would think you'd welcome an annulment."

"No annulment," Rhys repeated calmly.

Lord Northcliffe paled. "But surely, now that you know all of it—"

Juliana shot her brothers glances of betrayal. "You see what your plotting has wrought you? Now I'm married to a man who believes horrendous things of me, yet refuses to release me from my vows." She faced Rhys. "You want to ruin us all? Fine. Divorce me."

"Divorce?" her brother exploded. "Certainly not!"

"This is none of your concern, Darcy. You've already meddled quite enough, thank you."

Rhys's gaze met Juliana's. A divorce would make it nearly impossible for her ever to marry again. How strange that she'd risk it. But perhaps she thought her obvious attractions would ensure that matters turned out her way. And they probably would.

"No divorce," he said evenly. "You had the chance to be rid of me legally, Juliana, and you didn't take it." His eyes narrowed to slits. "You know, if you'd asked for an annulment that night, I would have given it to you. I loved you that much." His tone hardened. "But you didn't ask. You took a more treacherous road, and now you're mine, Juliana. And you'll be mine for as long as I want you."

"You mean, for as long as you wish to torment me." Her chin came up and her eyes glowed with bitterness.

"That's what this is all about, isn't it? You want to keep me in your power so you can punish me for a slew of imaginary crimes, not first of which is being English."

He stiffened. "Being English is certainly a deficit in your character, *fy mhriod,* but I could have tolerated it if you hadn't frivolously thrown me into the lion's den."

"I never did that, but of course you don't believe me. You always were a suspicious man, Rhys Vaughan. I should have known you'd never trust me. It was all a sham, wasn't it? All the soft words and kindnesses. Inside, you merely waited for me to make some mistake so you could show me to be the unworthy Englishwoman you already believed I was."

She said it with such conviction that he had to grit his teeth against the emotions she roused in him. "Stop twisting the past! I didn't make you unworthy—you proved yourself to be unworthy! You took a man's life and played with it, never caring what destruction you wrought!" He thrust his hand at her, then jerked back his cuff to show the scars on his wrists. "This is only one illustration of what your actions brought me!"

At the sight of the thick scars, she backed away with a gasp. But then, to his surprise, she tentatively touched them, before lifting a tortured gaze to him. " 'Tis a terrible thing you've endured. A terrible thing." She clasped his hand. "But I swear it was not of my making. I could never have—" She broke off with a choked sob.

It was the first time she'd touched him in six years, and it seared him more thoroughly than any flogging ever had. He snatched his hand from her, damning her for her pity. By thunder, she still had the power to move him. After all these years, she could make him believe her to be innocent even when everyone said otherwise.

"We've wasted enough time discussing this," Rhys managed to say. "You're my wife now, Juliana, and nothing will change that." He turned to address her brothers. "There will be no annulment or divorce." His eyes narrowed. "Nor, I hope, will you attempt to repeat the activities of six years ago. I assure you that this time I'll bring all of you down if you so much as try to destroy me."

"You're going to do that anyway, aren't you?" Northcliffe gritted out.

Rhys regarded the new earl steadily. Northcliffe had

grown leaner in his absence, as if the privileges of power and money had been gained at the cost of his physical self. In truth, the young man looked far older than his years, especially with that gray powdered peruke on his head. Rhys had heard of Northcliffe's successes—how he'd taken the reins after his father's death and climbed upward until he associated with some of the greatest men in London.

Northcliffe might sputter and complain about Rhys's plans, but he wouldn't thwart him. Not, at least, until he'd considered the consequences. "I shall not take my revenge that way," Rhys said, relishing the power he held over his enemy. "Not if you give me what I want— my wife and my estate. Much as I prospered during my years in America, 'tis Wales I love and 'tis in Wales I'll stay." He turned and caught Juliana's arm, forcing her to stand beside him. "I merely wish to make sure that my wife lies in the bed she's made, as I had to lie in the bed she made for me."

For one brief moment, Northcliffe's eyes glittered with terror. He glanced at his sister, then back at Rhys. "And what does that mean exactly?"

"From this night on, Juliana is my wife in every way. In a few moments, we'll leave here to spend the night at my town house. Tomorrow we'll go to Llynwydd. You, my lord, are not to interfere, unless you wish to relinquish your tidy position in England's political hierarchy. If you cross me, I swear I'll do whatever it takes to ruin you politically and socially."

Northcliffe stiffened. "You want us to stand by and watch while you torment our sister?"

Rhys shrugged. "I won't beat her, if that's what you think." He leveled a threatening gaze on the two men. "But I will deal with my wife as I see fit, and I won't tolerate any interference."

Casting his brother a long, meaningful glance, Northcliffe hesitated. Then he sighed. "All right."

Juliana glared first at her brothers and then at Rhys. "And what if I refuse to go? What if I tell you to go to hell?"

He nearly smiled. She certainly had changed since he'd first met her. Six years ago, she would never have uttered the word "hell" in his presence, or anyone else's, for that matter. But she'd soon learn that strong words had no effect on him.

He forced her to face him. "I don't think you fully appreciate the precariousness of your position, wife of mine. It's not too late to put a good face on this, to tell the world that it was all a misunderstanding. We eloped and then you thought me dead, so you hid the elopement from the world. Eventually, society will forgive you for that, especially if we live publicly as husband and wife."

She stared at him stony-faced, her eyes livid.

"But if you resist me," he continued, "I'll reveal what really happened. I'll show off that lovely marriage certificate and bemoan the fact that you went to terrible extremes to get out of our marriage."

"No one will believe you."

"They'll believe me over a woman who nearly committed bigamy. Oh, yes, they will. And you'll never be able to hold your head up in society again, I assure you."

"If you hate me that much," she whispered, "why do you want me as your wife? I—I don't understand it."

He lifted a hand to her cheek, trailing his fingers over it with a cold smile. She flinched from him, and he felt a mixture of delight and dismay. The delight he understood—to have her at his mercy had been his goal all along. But the dismay—that made no sense.

Angry at himself for being so affected by her reactions, he released her and stepped back. "There are reasons I might give, of course. I need you to maintain my hold on Llynwydd." He added viciously, "And I want an heir."

He waited until his last remark registered and the fear rose in her eyes. Then he went on. "But the truth is more basic than that. You see, I simply refuse to give you the pleasure of being free of me."

She surprised him by meeting his gaze. "That works two ways, dear husband. I may not be free, but neither are you. And if you persist in tormenting me because of Darcy's foolish lies, I swear I'll make your life hell."

He stared into her flashing eyes, wondering if she'd always been this stubborn. Or this achingly beautiful.

That thought made him lower his voice to a menacing whisper. "Then it's hell we'll be headed for, Juliana. Because this time you won't escape our marriage."

Chapter Nine

"Too great desire is evil,
Every step unlucky still!"
—Dafydd ap Gwilym,
"Trouble at a Tavern"

When the doors closed behind Juliana and Rhys Vaughan, Darcy slammed his fist against a wall. "That deuced bastard!"

"Aye," Overton retorted. "And you just gave him carte blanche with our sister. Have you gone mad? Don't you see what you've done?"

Darcy crossed to the sideboard and jerked out a decanter of whisky and a glass. "What the hell did you want me to do?" He poured himself two fingers of whisky and downed it all at once.

"To tell the truth! I should have told it myself, but—"

"But you knew what I'd do to you if you did." Darcy threw the glass at the wall, feeling only the faintest satisfaction at the sound of breaking glass.

Overton's face looked pasty as he dropped into a nearby chair. "I can't believe that you did that to her. There's no telling what dastardly torments Vaughan will invent for her now that he believes she betrayed him."

"Damn it, don't you think I realize that?" He roamed the room like a desperate prisoner, halting beside the fire.

"Then why did you lie? Why?"

Darcy stared blindly into the flames. "At first I hoped he'd agree to an annulment if I held to my story and painted a foul picture of Juliana."

"And when he refused to get an annulment? Why didn't you tell him the truth so they could at least have an amiable marriage?"

"He won't hurt her. Juliana can fend for herself. She always has." Darcy knew he was trying to convince himself of something he didn't quite believe, but he kept on. "Besides, he still cares for her or he wouldn't want her so badly."

"You're a bloody fool if you believe that. He just promised her a marriage in hell! You'd stand by and let her live it when a word from you would end it?"

"Which am I supposed to choose—a marriage in hell for Juliana?—or complete destruction for the family?"

Overton gave a gesture of exasperation. "What are you talking about?"

Darcy swung his gaze to his brother. "Didn't you hear him? He said he'd do nothing to us as long as we let him have Juliana and Llynwydd. But if we tell him the truth, all those assurances are gone. You know that. As long as he believes we acted at Juliana's request, he'll leave us alone. But if he learns she's an innocent ..."

"What? What would he do?"

"He'll destroy us. Grafton and Rockingham are his friends, for God's sake! Do you know what would happen to me if they ever turned against me? I'd lose everything I've accomplished!"

Overton frowned. "It would be worth it to have Juliana happy."

"I'm in a deuced marriage from hell myself! Why shouldn't *she* be? He said he wouldn't beat her!" He stared blindly at the door Vaughan and Juliana had left through, remembering how the bastard had spoken of being flogged. Deuce take it, what would a man who'd suffered so do to the woman he thought had caused it?

And to the men who really did cause it? He stiffened. "After a few weeks with her, sweet as she is, he'll come around." But his assurances sounded hollow even to him.

"No matter how you excuse it, you've still made her the scapegoat for your own crimes, poor innocent Juliana, who never spoke ill of anyone in her life."

Every word sliced through Darcy. Overton spoke nothing but the truth. He sank into a chair and buried his face in his hands. "How was I to know he'd return? How was I to know he'd make something of himself?"

"It was a stupid business, all of it. She loved him, and we hurt her. But we can fix it now."

Darcy lifted his head. "And what about Mother and Elizabeth? What about everything we've gained? Juliana wouldn't want us to risk everything for her."

"Everything *you've* gained, you mean. Besides, you don't know that you'd lose it all."

"Vaughan's the vindictive sort, Overton. Surely you can see that."

Overton jumped to his feet. "Aye, I *can* see that. And he'll be vindictive toward Juliana if we don't tell him the truth."

"I don't know if he'd believe the truth now even if we admitted it. He's already spoken to the innkeeper. He's sure to find suspect anything we say."

"Yes, and what about that innkeeper? Did you tell him to lie, too? Did you anticipate Vaughan's return?"

Darcy rose stiffly from his chair, unwilling to face his brother's penetrating gaze. "Vaughan's last letter here made me worry, so I ... I told the innkeeper what to say if Vaughan ever sought the truth. But honestly, I thought Vaughan would write him, and after receiving confirmation of Juliana's behavior, would decide against returning."

"And that man who brought proof of Vaughan's death? Did you pay him to lie as well?"

When Darcy remained silent, Overton exploded. "You bastard!" A look of complete disgust filled his face. "What a treacherous web you wove! You lied to Juliana, you lied to her husband—"

"I thought I was doing the right thing. For all of us."

Raking his brother with a contemptuous gaze, Overton said, " 'Twasn't the only reason for the plotting, I daresay."

Darcy whirled to face his brother. "What do you mean?"

"Your mistress, Lettice."

"Sh," Darcy whispered, glancing toward the door. "Elizabeth will hear you."

"Elizabeth knows, you dolt. Everyone knows. You're not the least bit discreet about her." His eyes narrowed. "Lettice doesn't know you were behind the impressment of her sweetheart, does she?"

Darcy's stomach twisted into knots. A pity that Overton wasn't always dense and unobservant. Sometimes his brother could be astute indeed.

How to answer him? To win Overton to his side, he'd have to play on his sympathies, and that meant telling the truth. "No, she doesn't know. And I don't want her to know . . . ever."

"Well, she's sure to find out now. Vaughan will tell her out of sheer spite."

Darcy swallowed back the agony of that thought. "Aye. And Pennant might have returned with Vaughan. The two men left together . . . they could have come back together." And if they did? he thought. Were the tales he'd told Pennant about Lettice betraying him strong enough to keep the man from her?

He shot his brother a pleading glance. "Now you know why I tried to make sure that neither Vaughan nor Pennant returned. I love Lettice, Overton. I love her completely. She's the only thing that keeps me sane around Elizabeth." His voice dropped to a pained whisper, and it wasn't in the least pretended. "If Lettice leaves me, I'll die. She has borne me my only son, and I can't live without either of them."

The thought of her taking little Edgar away nearly killed him. He choked back the doubts he'd nurtured through the years, doubts about Edgar's paternity. It didn't matter that the birth had taken place eight months after Pennant's impressment. Edgar was *his* son, *his!* Pounding one fist into the other, he hissed, "A pox on Vaughan! Why did he have to return? Why?"

Overton shook his head. "What will you do about Lettice and Edgar?"

"I'll hope she never learns the truth. And if perchance she does, I'll pray that six years of taking care of her will compensate for my sins. Perhaps when she sees how far I went to secure her love, she'll not hold them against me."

"For a man of intelligence," Overton remarked dryly, "you're surprisingly stupid when it comes to women."

He hated to admit it, but Overton was right. "Do me this one thing, Overton."

Overton eyed him with suspicion. "What?"

"Don't tell anyone the truth until I see what Vaughan

does about Lettice. There's a chance he won't bother with speaking to her, since he assumes that she, like Juliana, betrayed her lover." He swallowed. "But if Vaughan learns the truth, his first strike to hurt me will be to drive Lettice from me."

"How long do you think you can keep the truth from her? Juliana is sure to tell her. And Lettice isn't the sort of woman you can easily fool. Then there's the boy—"

Darcy clenched his fists. "Just give me some time to think of a way out of this mess ... to gather my friends behind me and counteract whatever plan Vaughan might use against us if he learns the truth. Time to tell Lettice myself." He stiffened, finding it hard to swallow his pride. "Please, Overton. Bear with me awhile longer."

With a sigh, Overton nodded. Then he jutted out his chin. "Not much time, however. If you haven't come up with anything in a few weeks—"

"I'll tell Vaughan everything. I swear it."

As Rhys led Juliana out of the mansion into the dark night, she roused from her numb state to look around at the lanterns lighting the walks for her engagement party. Bitterness choked her. This hadn't been quite the celebration she'd anticipated. If not for Rhys, she'd be dancing in Stephen's arms at this very moment. Stephen would be treating her with his usual kindness and consideration, and later he'd kiss her while she closed her eyes and ...

And thought of Rhys, she admitted. A curse welled up in her throat. Oh, but she'd been so stupid! To have wasted all those years pining for Rhys, comparing every man she'd met to him!

As Rhys led her toward the entrance gates, she stole a glance at the man she'd once worshipped. He was certainly as handsome as he'd ever been, if not more so. And earlier when he'd spoken, he'd demonstrated that he still had that orator's voice.

But in every other way he'd changed. There were angry lines etched into his forehead and his jaw seemed permanently clenched, locked into a rage she couldn't fathom. As she stared at his cold profile, outrage swelled in her chest.

Had she really been so foolish as to marry this man,

who now spoke to her with a callousness she'd never known even from Father? Had she truly once thought him kind? She jerked her gaze from him. She had indeed. But the Rhys she'd fallen in love with hadn't been quick to believe lies.

Then she remembered the first time he'd come to Northcliffe Hall, when he'd accused her of spying on him. Even after all these years, the memory started an ache in her heart. The Rhys she'd fallen in love with six years ago had been just as quick to believe the worst of her.

But back then he'd recognized his tendency to jump to conclusions. And back then he hadn't been able to act on his assumptions in such a sweeping manner, for his fury had merely resulted in a confinement for her.

Now he had a power over her that was frightening, a power she'd given him. A power that her wretched brothers sanctioned, blast them!

She gritted her teeth. Oh, when she got her hands on Darcy again, she'd strangle him! She should have strangled him the minute he started lying to Rhys in front of her. But then she'd been too stunned to believe what he was saying. The lies! The abominable lies! What madness had possessed him to lie about her like that?

And Overton, too! Tears started in her eyes, and she wiped them away viciously, hoping Rhys hadn't noticed. Her brothers were traitors, both of them, and didn't deserve her tears! In faith, they deserved to be hanged, that's what they deserved!

In her fury, she made some choked sound, and it was that which attracted Rhys's attention at last. "Don't worry, I shan't make you walk all the way to my town house," Rhys said. They were the first words he'd spoken since they'd left the drawing room. "My carriage is just outside the walls. I didn't want to rouse questions earlier by having it bring me to the doorstep, so I came in the way I used to."

The blatant reminder of how he used to slip onto the grounds, how he used to love her, roused her temper and she snapped, "Oh, yes, you were very good at sneaking into places."

"As I recall, I was invited."

Another reminder, this one of how eagerly she'd accepted his advances. She remembered how quick she'd been to welcome him into her bedchamber. He'd probably thought her the worst of wantons.

Was this to be her punishment? A constant litany of her past faults? If so, she had a surprise for him. She could do nothing about his misreading of the past and of her character, but she *could* refuse him the satisfaction of rousing her anger every time he sought to wound her.

Tense and silent, they reached the gates, which the gatekeeper opened as he saw her approach. No doubt the news had traveled through the household like wildfire, she thought. It was all she could do to hold up her head and face down the gatekeeper, who stared at her with barely disguised curiosity.

The carriage that awaited them surprised her by being fashionable and expensive. A liveried coachman sat on the perch and the horses were blooded. Apparently, Rhys hadn't lied about his improved circumstances.

Outrage swelled in her again. While he'd been amassing a fortune, nursing his unfounded distrust of her, she'd been mourning him!

Full of righteous indignation, she refused his help when he reached to hand her up, even though it meant clambering into the carriage in a most unladylike manner.

As she settled herself on the plush seat, he sat opposite her, one half of his face lit by moonlight, the other in shadow. "If you think to annoy me with your petty shows of resistance, Juliana, you might as well give it up. No annoyance you invent can compare with the many 'annoyances' the captain of the H.M.S. *Nightmark* invented for impressed landsmen."

True to her determination not to react to him, she merely stared out the window, her face expressionless as the carriage jolted to a start and rumbled away from Northcliffe.

"And ignoring me won't work either," he added in a tone that sounded almost amused.

Her gaze shot to him. Indeed the kind of smile a man wears when he thinks he's had the last laugh. Only with a supreme effort did she keep from retorting, from attempting to wipe that gloating smile from his face.

But her fury must have shown in her eyes, for his smile widened, though it grew somehow colder. "Tell me, *cariad,* did you ever look at your fiancé that way?"

He spoke the Welsh endearment with an absolute contempt meant to wound. She stiffened all over, fighting the urge to scratch his eyes out, and said with as much cool nonchalance as she could muster, "Unlike you, Stephen never deserved my fury. He was always a dear to me. I never even had to raise my voice to him, for he at least was a gentleman."

"A rich, powerful gentleman. A pity he never saw your true self until today. He might have saved himself some grief. But with all that money and position hanging in the balance, you had to hide your true self."

Madly, she searched her brain for some retort that would stop him dead. "Just as you did when you courted me, speaking lies and giving me gifts. With your estate hanging in the balance, you had to hide *your* true self."

A dark satisfaction skittered through her when his smile faded completely. He leaned forward to glower at her. "You know I was unaware that Llynwydd belonged to you. That had nothing to do with why I married you, no matter what you thought."

"That's not what Darcy said, and of course, he always speaks the truth." Hah! she thought. Wriggle out of that one!

"And you believed every word he said."

She leveled on him a solemn gaze. "No. Because I knew in my heart what you were. 'Tis why I waited so long for you."

"So long?" He laughed harshly. "Yes, you waited at least until a marquess came sniffing after you!" His eyes shimmered with anger in the dark coach. "How long did you wait before you let him court you, before you went hunting for a husband?"

She hid the hurt his words gave her. He had a right to ask it, but she hated the way he was doing so. "Surely you heard what Darcy said. Stephen came to court me only a year ago. He came to the house to see Darcy before that, of course, but I didn't encourage his ... overtures until Darcy's investigator told me you were dead."

"Which was a lie."

"Yes, but I believed it or I wouldn't have let Stephen court me at all."

"Of course. And the little matter of your previous marriage didn't come up, I suppose. I wonder ... how did you plan to deal with your Stephen on your wedding night?"

She couldn't prevent the guilty flush that spread over her face and prayed the darkness hid it from his intent gaze.

"Were you going to wait until he spread your pretty legs to tell him you'd already given the prize to another? Or did you plan to sprinkle pig's blood on the sheets while he wasn't looking?"

Recoiling from his crude, though astute observations, she crossed her arms over her chest and sank into herself, wishing she could leap from the coach and escape his accusing words.

"Or perhaps that wasn't even an issue." His voice grew more cutting as he spoke. "Perhaps he'd already sampled your delights and knew he was getting damaged goods. I daresay any man who'd had you wouldn't have cared about your lack of innocence, not once he'd discovered what a wanton you are in bed."

She shot up in her seat. "How dare you! Stephen would never have—"

"Did you tell him about that convenient tree outside your window, so he could enter your bedroom at night and take you at his whim?" He leaned forward, a wild expression on his face. "Did you cry out every time he thrust deep into you as you did with me? Did you—"

"Stop it!" She covered her ears as sobs welled up in her throat. "Stop it! Stop saying such awful things! You're the only man who's ever touched me that way, and you know it!"

He fell back against his seat, panting hard, like a savage beast that had just run its poor prey to ground.

She fixed him with an accusing gaze. "I *meant* it six years ago when I promised to be faithful to you."

"Obviously your definition of faithfulness differs vastly from mine."

"What did you expect? That I'd languish away forever? You never sent any word. If I'd known you still lived, no power on earth would have kept me from awaiting your return! But I didn't know, don't you see? I thought you were dead!"

"So you say," he bit out.

She gasped for breath, forcing herself to be strong, to fight him with his own weapons. "And you, Rhys? Were you faithful to me, as you promised on your wedding night?" She felt a lump stick in her throat. "Were there . . . were there other women over in America?"

He stared at her with mouth agape, then snapped his mouth shut. "Are you asking if I bedded other women?"

She nodded, unable to speak the words. She shouldn't have brought it up. She'd already spent six years at Llynwydd remembering their wedding night when he said he'd bedded one of the dairymaids. Many a time she'd tortured herself, wondering which of the buxom women was the one who'd known him intimately.

He hesitated as if uncertain whether to tell her. Then his jaw tightened. "What do *you* think? In America there were plenty of willing wenches who wanted to bed a war hero and who didn't mind being loose with their reputations. Do you think I threw them out of my bedchamber? Do you?"

Each word was designed to cut deeply. And he certainly succeeded in drawing blood. She felt as if he'd gone after her with a butcher knife.

But somehow she fixed him with a steady gaze as the coach shuddered to a halt outside a town house. "What do I think? I think you're a two-faced bastard who has one set of standards for himself and another for his wife."

For a long moment, he simply glared at her, face livid with rage. Then he thrust the coach door open and pointed to the town house door. "Get inside! Now!"

With all the dignity she could muster, she stepped down from the coach, grateful that the coachman had appeared from out of nowhere to assist her, for she knew she couldn't bear Rhys's hands on her.

She walked primly to the entrance steps, scarcely noticing the expensive Palladian house with its marble columns and sashed windows. All she could think of was how to get out of this mad marriage with Rhys. She couldn't continue in it, not when he sought to destroy her at every turn.

She heard him behind her and hastened her steps to avoid his touch. She needn't have worried. He kept a marked distance from her as the doors opened before them, manned by servants who'd been watching for them from the windows.

A portly man stepped forward and bowed to Rhys. "All the rooms are in readiness as you instructed, sir."

"The master bedroom is finished?"

"Yes, sir. Being as you only bought the place last week, we had a time getting it ready, but it's done."

"Good," Rhys said, staring absently about him.

Juliana followed his gaze. In truth, everything looked newly furbished, as if some genie had swept through the house and changed out all the old fittings with new ones.

A genie that had started work at least a week ago. She frowned. Too late she remembered hearing gossip among the tradesmen about the eccentric American who'd bought the old Webberley town house. Dear heaven, if she'd only realized . . .

Then the implications of that sank in. Instead of coming to speak rationally to her like an honest man the minute he'd arrived in town, Rhys had sneaked into her engagement party like a thief, then aired his grievances before all of society. It was one more insult she'd add to his account. And someday she'd make him pay for every one.

"Will that be all?" the servant asked.

Rhys nodded. "Yes. We leave for Llynwydd in the morning. In future I'll notify you in plenty of time whenever we plan to be in residence here." He cast her an enigmatic glance, then swung his gaze back to the servant. "For tonight, you're dismissed. You and all the servants. We don't wish to be disturbed."

Her gaze flew to his. There was an ominous meaning behind his words. "I shall require a maid to help me undress—"

"We do not wish to be disturbed," he repeated.

Although the servant looked curiously at them both, he wisely said nothing and disappeared through one of the many doors off the downstairs hall.

"Come, my dear wife," Rhys said, "let me show you the master bedchamber."

She shook her head. She didn't want to go anywhere

with him, and certainly not the master bedchamber, especially when she had no idea what torment he planned for her.

But he clasped her arm, making it clear he wouldn't tolerate any resistance. And what good would physical resistance do anyway? He was stronger than her by far, and in his present angry state, liable to harm her if she tried to escape him.

He'd said he wouldn't beat her, which left only one other way she could think of that he might punish her. But surely he wouldn't attempt *that* ... not after the obvious contempt he'd shown for her. Still, why bring her to the master bedroom?

"Rhys, I'd rather just go to my own bedchamber," she said in a low voice as he forced her up the stairs. "And I'm sure I can find it myself."

"Oh, no," he said in clipped tones. "I fully intend to accompany you to your room. And to bed. I wouldn't miss that for the world."

Perhaps he didn't mean that the way it sounded, she thought, clutching at straws. Perhaps he merely meant that he would see her safely taken care of for the night.

Then why hadn't he allowed her a maid?

They'd reached the top of the stairs already, and to her horror, the master bedroom proved to be the first door on the hallway. Frantically, she sought for some other delaying tactic, but before she could think of anything, he'd opened the door. Then with his hand on her back, he urged her inside.

Her mouth dry, she entered and glanced around. The room shouted its masculinity. The dark woods, the rich blue velvet curtains and bed drapings made her feel like a trespasser. She caught sight of a pair of man's boots, newly polished and sitting at the foot of the bed, then sucked in a breath as the full implications of where she was hit her.

She whirled to face him. He'd entered behind her and now made a point of locking the door with a key on a thin chain, dropping the chain around his neck.

He'd locked them in together. Her heart sank. Either he indeed planned to beat her, despite what he'd said, or he intended this to be a marriage in every respect. Somehow she didn't think beating was his intention, not judging from the way he now stared at her as a hungry man stares at a succulent hen.

She shuddered when he loosened his neckcloth and removed it, tossing it over a chair, then sat down and removed his boots. In faith, he planned to bed her. Now. Tonight.

Was this to be her punishment for all her taunts in the carriage? Or had he intended it all along? Did he truly think she'd let him bed her as if six years hadn't passed between them?

Backing into a corner, she glanced wildly around. There was no other exit, no escape. But he wouldn't take an unwilling woman, would he? He couldn't have changed that much.

As if to draw out her torment, he stood up and strode to a table against a window where a crystal decanter of bloodred liquid sat. With slow, deliberate movements, he poured two glasses. "Wine?" he asked, turning toward her.

She shook her head. At the moment, she couldn't hold a glass steady, and she didn't want him to know how much he frightened her. If his plan was to reduce her to begging him to spare her, she wouldn't let him. Nor let him seduce her either. She was no longer the untried, foolish girl he'd enticed with poems and gifts. She knew her own mind now, and what a mistake she'd made in marrying him.

Her only salvation lay in remaining unaffected by his tactics and hoping he'd give up when she didn't succumb to his seduction.

Don't look at the bed, she told herself. *Don't let him see you frightened.*

That proved difficult to do, for while he sipped his wine, his gaze raked her body with the insolence of a horse trader picking a prize mare.

"Can you believe," he said after a moment, his voice brittle, "that I'd forgotten how beautiful you are?"

When she said nothing to that, only backing farther into her corner, he set the wine aside and rounded the bed toward her. She forced herself to remain still and outwardly calm as he approached. He stopped inches away, reaching up to draw one of her jeweled pins from her hair.

A cursed trembling began in her body as he removed the pins one by one until her hair tumbled down about her shoulders. He was so close she could touch him, could brush her fingers over the clean-shaven chin and the thin blade of a nose if she wanted. His wine-scented breath feathered over her face, summoning up long-buried memories—of the way his mouth once covered hers, teasing, possessing.

She stiffened, fighting the memories. This wasn't the Rhys who'd taken her with care on their wedding night. This was the Rhys who believed her a schemer and a liar. And she would *not* let him seduce her.

He lifted her hair, letting it fall over his hands, then rubbing the strands between his fingers. His eyes glittered as he stared at it glimmering in the candlelight. "I'd also forgotten how soft your hair is." As she held her breath, her emotions rioting, he stroked her hair back over her shoulder.

Suddenly he stiffened and jerked his hand back, pivoting away. He crossed to the other side of the room, his expression grim as he picked up his wine again, not looking at her.

"Take off your clothes," he said tersely and took a gulp of wine, then set the glass down hard on the table.

She stood there in stunned amazement. "Wh—what?"

He faced her, eyes wild. "I said, remove your clothes."

"No! N-not until you leave."

To her chagrin, he laughed, a mocking, hard laugh. "Perhaps I didn't make myself clear earlier, *fy mhriod.* You're my wife now, and I'm not leaving. Not ever again." He trailed his insolent gaze over her body. "When I said I intended to take you and my estate back, I meant in every way. And if you were wise, you'd try to appease my anger, instead of playing the innocent and fighting me thus."

"I'm not playing at being i-innocent."

"One day you'll admit the truth." He rubbed his chin. "I'll see to it. But in the meantime, I expect you to obey my commands as you promised to do when you spoke your vows so frivolously. So take off your clothes. Now!"

She tilted up her chin, fighting to keep from showing her cowardice. "I don't want to."

"I don't care." His merciless expression showed he

meant it. "Do as I say, or I'll tear the clothes off you myself. And I'd hate to ruin such a lovely and expensive gown."

As if she could ever wear it again without feeling nauseated. In desperation, she glanced at the door, but he caught her subtle movement and gave her a taunting smile, waving the key on the chain around his neck to remind her that she was trapped.

While she watched in horror, he removed his cutaway and threw it across a chair, then unbuttoned his gray waistcoat. "The servants have been instructed to ignore any sound that comes from this room tonight, so don't think you'll enlist their aid."

The implications of that terrified her. It was clear he meant to have her, willing or no. She couldn't bear to feel the force of his violence. Yet she couldn't make her hands do what he asked.

When she still stood motionless, he stepped toward her, fists clenched. "Take ... your ... damned ... clothes ... off! I wish to see what I paid in blood for!"

In a state of numb fear, she did as he commanded, unfastening her stomacher with shaky fingers, then her bodice, skirt, hoop, and petticoats. As she bared her arms, then shrugged out of her armor, his gaze darkened and his face grew taut with undisguised hunger.

"The stockings," he said hoarsely. "Take off your stockings."

Heart pounding, she stepped out of her slippers, then lifted her shift only enough so she could untie the garters and draw down her white silk stockings. She felt his eyes following the slide of her hose down her legs.

"Now the corset." His voice sounded more unsteady now.

She hesitated. "I—I can't undo it by myself."

Her words seemed to jerk him from some dark prison. With a curt nod, he came to stand behind her. She sucked in a quick breath when she felt his fingers unknotting her laces, brushing her skin as he drew the corset apart. She suddenly remembered how adept he'd been at undressing her that first time, too, and an irrational pang of jealousy clutched at her.

When the corset had dropped to the floor, he stepped in front of her once more and rasped, "Now the shift."

That was when her control broke. She couldn't remove everything and stand there completely naked in front of him when he was staring at her without an ounce of caring in his expression. She simply couldn't!

"Please, Rhys, don't do this," she begged, all her pride gone. "You can't be as uncaring as you seem."

"Oh, but I can be," he ground out, the intensity in his eyes hot enough to burn her to ash.

"I don't believe it. What could possibly have happened to turn you into ... into—"

"A heartless beast?" he finished for her. He stared at her a long, cruel moment, his jaw tightly clenched. Then he tore off his shirt. "Have you ever seen a man flogged, Juliana? Have you any idea what happens to a man after several floggings with a cat-o-nine tails?"

He pivoted to show her his back, and she gasped. She'd expected scars of some kind. But the reality was far worse, for there were no scars on the upper back at all. It was simply an expanse of mottled skin that looked like healed pulp. There *were* marks lower down in the small of his back, however, where the cat apparently hadn't reached as well, leaving on the skin a dense mesh of white scars.

She'd heard of the horrors men suffered in the navy, but she'd never dreamed anyone could be so cruel to another human being. Still, she couldn't deny the evidence before her, especially when she remembered how beautiful his back had been before, how proud and finely shaped.

Now it was so covered with healed welts that she could only stare in horror. What pain had he endured to have a back like that? And what other pains had he not yet told her of?

He left nothing to her imagination. "They clean the cat after every stroke, you know, to make sure it doesn't become so clotted with blood and flesh that it's ineffective. And when they're done, they wash the back with brine, so it will heal. Men generally pass out from the shock of salt water against torn flesh—if they haven't already passed out. But the skin does heal. Until the next flogging, of course."

Bile rose in her throat. How many such floggings had he suffered? And how had he endured them at all?

He whirled around to face her. "The law supposedly allows no more than six strokes at each flogging, but a tyrannical captain may order up to three hundred with impunity."

He scowled when he saw the horror in her face. "And I had a tyrannical captain ... a cruel man who hated Welsh landsmen, especially known radicals." He stared past her at the wall as if remembering. "He had me flogged for the least infraction, and for some I didn't commit."

Pity welled up in her. Despite everything he'd said or done to her in the last few hours, he'd never deserved such treatment. "Oh, Rhys, I'm sorry you suffered so."

His gaze snapped to hers. "I didn't tell you so you could pity me. I told you so you'd understand a fraction of what you did to me when you decided marriage didn't suit you after all."

"I didn't—"

"Enough!" he thundered. "I don't want protestations of innocence from you, nor pity either. I want only one thing from you tonight. So take off your damned shift!"

He looked so frightening, so fierce, she did what he said without further protest.

As her shift slipped to the floor, he dragged in his breath. She numbed herself to the shame of standing so exposed before him. And when he scoured her with his gaze, pausing at her breasts, her belly, the juncture of her thighs, she tightened her fingers into fists, determined to endure it, determined to let him have this one thing of her, even though he demanded it for false reasons.

If he could endure countless floggings, she told herself, she could endure this. So when his eyes moved slowly back up her body, burning like blue flames as he assessed her every attraction, she made herself stand proud.

By the time he brought his gaze back to her face, his expression had altered, softening a fraction. "Do you know how many times I survived a flogging simply by remembering you ... the curve of your hips ... the full weight of your breasts ... the silkiness of your skin...."

He walked up to her, then lifted his hand to run a finger

down her throat, over the swell of one breast and then over her belly.

It was such a sensual gesture, almost sweet, that for a moment she forgot how much he'd changed. For a moment, she half believed that the old Rhys stood before her, coming to her as she'd dreamed of him doing every night for the past six years. She waited, breath held, for him to kiss her.

Instead he shook his head, as if suddenly coming to his senses. He yanked his hand back and stepped away. "Lie down," he commanded, unbuttoning his breeches. "On the bed."

She stared at him, shocked to the core by the sudden change in him. Once again, he was perfunctory, cruel. Was this what he planned for her—to take her like an animal, to reduce their former lovemaking to a bestial act in repayment for the many bestial acts committed against him?

She wouldn't let him. If he meant to rape her, he'd not have her help in it.

"Lie down, I said!"

She said nothing, but merely waited until he stepped closer. Then reaching up, she snatched the key, breaking it free of the chain. But even as she turned toward the door, he lifted her and threw her across the bed, covering her body in a flash. He pried her fingers open and took the key, throwing it at the door. Then he pinned her wrists with his hands.

She writhed against him, panic-stricken as she felt his weight upon her naked body. Lowering his face to within inches of hers, he growled, "There's no escaping me, Juliana. I don't need or even want your cooperation in this. Fight me if you will, but I'll have what I want of you this night."

She twisted her head from side to side as he brought his head down, attempting to kiss her. A few seconds ago she might even have met his mouth with her own ravenous one, reveling in the pressure of his muscular body against hers, but now all she wanted was escape.

"What, don't you desire your husband anymore?" he muttered in her ear as she continued to avoid his mouth. Forcing his knee between her legs, he settled his body there, allowing her to feel the arousal growing beneath his drawers and pressing into her soft flesh.

"Don't do this, Rhys!"

His tone grew mocking. "What happened to wild, wanton Juliana, moaning and begging for more even while she awaited her brothers' arrival to 'save' her from her Welsh husband?"

His cruel words helped her fight off her panic. "I won't let you do this!" She bucked against him in a fruitless effort to throw him off.

He chuckled. "You're only making it worse." Crudely, he ground his hips into her to demonstrate that she was indeed only arousing him further.

"Stop it," she begged.

But he ignored her, bending his head to suck at her neck. Planting hard kisses as he went, he moved down the slender column to the rounded slope of her shoulder and then lower until his mouth reached the very edges of her breast.

Not even conscious of it, she went completely still. So did he. He glanced up at her, his face stark with raw desire, and for a second, their gazes met, both of them assessing each other. Then, without shifting his gaze from her, he ran the tip of his tongue around the outer circumference of her breast.

At first it was a taunt, his way of showing he could do anything he pleased to her and she couldn't stop him. But as his tongue moved in smaller and smaller circles around her nipple, stroking the skin wetly so the cool air made it tingle after he passed over it, his expression shifted to one of intense awareness, of a great, dark pleasure.

To her horror, she realized his actions were affecting her. Now he no longer stroked with his tongue, but pressed kisses with his mouth, and every one of them felt like flame against her skin. It had been six years since anyone had touched her like this, six long years of craving him.

Suddenly his hands released her wrists, allowing him to knead her other breast, then caress it with deft, enticing strokes. She drew an unsteady breath. This couldn't be the same man who'd coldly told her a few minutes ago to undress, who'd threatened to take her with violence. This man was a lover. Or was pretending to be a lover.

With a shudder, she fought the flood of warmth that centered in her loins. It was a trick, all a trick. She must get away from him. Her hands were free now. Why didn't she simply push him away?

Because she couldn't. She just couldn't.

She closed her eyes, trying to concentrate on how much she despised him now, but that only made it easier to forget what he'd become and remember what he'd been. When his mouth closed over her nipple, hot and sweet, drawing and tugging on it, she went soft all over.

"Please don't ..." she whispered, hating him for reminding her of how easily he'd once seduced her.

She felt his hand slip down between their bodies, cupping her, fondling her intimate places. Wherever he rubbed, she burned, and when he continued the magic, she opened her eyes, amazed and horrified that he could still rouse her body so thoroughly.

He had closed his own eyes and was now sucking her breast as if he'd craved it for an eternity. Suddenly, his finger slid inside her, delving deep. She couldn't help it. She moaned, arching up against his hand and bringing her arms around him.

But at the touch of her hands on his back, he went stiff all over and his eyes shot open. With chilling abruptness, he lifted his head away. He glanced at her, his breath unsteady, his face a mask of anger.

She watched him in total confusion. What had she done?

"Damn it all, Juliana!" Cursing foully in Welsh, he pushed himself off her and left the bed. He still wore his unbuttoned breeches, and he buttoned them up now with furious movements.

Quickly she sat up and dragged the velvet coverlet over her naked body. But he no longer seemed to see her as he paced beside the bed, his arousal still clearly visible beneath his glove-tight breeches.

She stared at him. "Why are you so angry? This was what you wanted, wasn't it?" Her voice grew bitter. "To make me want you despite myself? To ... to have me fall into your bed willingly again?"

"It took very little to get *that* from you, didn't it?" he

snapped. "It took very little to have you moaning and writhing with pleasure!"

At first embarrassment made her blush, but as she realized that he seemed to be angry *because* she'd had pleasure, she grew cold inside. "If you didn't want me to have pleasure, then . . . then what did you intend? To use me cruelly? To hurt me?"

He stopped to scowl at her, not saying a word.

"That's it, isn't it?" The truth started a hollow ache in her stomach. "You wanted to force me, to make me suffer as you suffered, to punish me!"

" 'Tis what you deserve!" he burst out.

She shook her head. "It isn't. And somewhere in that toughened heart of yours, you know it. And you know you don't truly want to hurt me. 'Tis why you gave me pleasure, 'tis why you touched me with gentleness!"

"That's a lie!" He stalked toward the bed as if to renew his assault. He even jerked the cover from her, his hot gaze settling over her naked body once more as he set one knee on the bed. But when she lifted her face to him in challenge, her eyes unafraid, he threw the cover back at her.

"Damn you!" he hissed, his mouth forming a grim line. *"Cer i'r diawl!"*

He turned and strode to the door. He paused only to scoop up the key on the floor. Then he unlocked the door and stormed out.

She held her breath, waiting for him to return, for him to make a liar of her and attack her in earnest. But when he merely locked the door from the outside and strode away cursing, she collapsed onto the bed, finally allowing her tears to flow.

She didn't care what he claimed. For a few minutes, he'd forgotten all the lies he believed about her. For a brief time, he'd been the Rhys of six years ago.

That glimpse heartened her, despite his anger, despite his curses. She'd won the first battle. Somehow she'd won it.

Still, how many more battles like this could she endure?

Chapter Ten

"O how I long to travel back,
  And tread again that ancient track!
  That I might once more reach that plain
  Where first I left my glorious train . . ."
                                    —Henry Vaughan,
                                      "The Retreat"

Lettice opened the door to her son's room, careful not to awaken him. It was a nighttime ritual with her, checking on Edgar before she went to bed herself.

Tonight the full moon cast its kindly light over his sweet face, kissing his soft cheeks with moonbeams. His childish features were so painfully familiar to her. She had tried not to notice over the past few years how much he looked like Morgan with every passing day, but it was impossible not to.

Darcy, however, saw none of it. It sometimes amazed her that Darcy had never questioned why his "son" didn't resemble him in the least.

She closed the door, her throat tightening. If Darcy ever did realize how she'd tricked him . . . what would he do? What would *she* do?

As she walked down the hall to her own bedchamber, memories flooded her, memories of that fateful morning when all her dreams were shattered in one fell swoop. First she'd learned of Morgan's impressment. Then Darcy's father had dismissed her, because he'd heard of her involvement with Morgan. He'd been furious that she'd been out with some radical while Juliana had been eloping with Rhys.

The dismissal hadn't been unexpected, for Lettice had known the old earl would dismiss her when he learned of her pregnancy. But having it come sooner rather than later had been terrifying.

Then Darcy had rescued her. He'd told her he was appalled by his father's actions. He'd offered to care completely for her. And all he'd asked in return was that she be his mistress.

His offer had stunned her. Even then she'd known how he felt about her, but she'd thought it was merely the kind of infatuation many young men felt for pretty maidservants. Once or twice he'd even snatched kisses from her, and she'd taken them to be casual, meaningless.

But when he'd begged her to be his mistress, she'd realized how deep his feelings ran. And she'd been torn. She couldn't give him her heart ... her heart was still with Morgan. Yet she was in a terrifying quandary. Pregnant and without a position or family, she had no way to care for her child—Morgan's child.

Darcy had offered her the perfect solution, but only if she lied. Only if she gave him her body as soon as possible and told him the child was his. She'd thought about it a great deal, but in the end she'd lied. It had been her only choice.

Her thoughts snapped back to the present as she entered the neat, modestly furnished bedroom she shared with Darcy whenever he visited. Glancing around it, she sighed. In truth, Darcy hadn't been a bad choice. He treated her like a queen. He came to her often and brought her endearing gifts. She had her own cottage away from prying eyes, and plenty of time to care for it.

Of course, the townspeople looked down on her, not only for being a mistress, but the mistress of a married English nobleman whom they all despised. Still, she tried not to let it bother her. At least she had a home for herself and her son. Besides, Darcy treated Edgar well, since his wife had given him no children. Although he couldn't acknowledge Edgar as his son except to her, he gave Edgar a generous allowance and promised to educate him as a gentleman. And Edgar thought the world of "Uncle Darcy."

So why wasn't she content? she thought as she disrobed, then drew on her nightdress. Why was it whenever she looked into Edgar's sparkling black eyes, she thought of the one man who'd made her melt with just a touch? Darcy couldn't do that. Their lovemaking was pleasant and adequate . . . but with Morgan it had been a glorious feast day, a celebration of joy.

A knock at the door downstairs disturbed her thoughts. She opened the door of her bedchamber. Had she merely heard the wind hitting a branch against the side of the cottage? Another knock came and she scurried into the hall.

Could it be Darcy? she wondered as she flew down the stairs. He'd said the engagement party would go late and that he wouldn't see her for a day or so. Had he changed his mind? Sometimes he did that when he and his wife were on particularly bad terms.

She reached the door and threw the latch, opening the door without a second thought. "I didn't expect—"

Her words caught in her throat. Standing before her was a ghost, a flesh-and-blood ghost she'd never hoped to see again.

Her face lit up as six years melted away. "Morgan! Is it really you?"

His only answer was a hard stare.

She wanted to throw herself into his arms and cry for joy, but the chill in his expression halted her. What was wrong? Why did he look at her so sternly?

Then she remembered. She was another man's mistress now. And he couldn't have found her without learning that.

Her heart sank as she stared at him. He'd changed, not so much that she wouldn't have recognized him, but a great deal nonetheless. His clothing was richer than it had been before, and he wore it with the arrogance of a man of position. A jagged scar creased one of his cheeks, and his hair was quite long.

But his black eyes were what truly showed the years, for they were no longer merry. They were solemn and unsmiling. And they remained fixed on her with an unnerving intensity.

"May I come in?" he rasped.

"Yes, of course." She stood aside to let him pass. She shut the door and slumped against it, needing something to hold her up. The shock to her heart was so great, she didn't know if she could absorb it all. Morgan was here, alive and standing before her. But he was obviously not happy to be here.

Somehow she contained her tumultuous emotions, so that the words that sprang to her lips showed none of her feelings. "Would you like some tea?"

He turned from surveying her cottage to fix her with that same icy gaze. "You see your 'true love' after six years and all you can do is offer him tea?"

The sarcasm he put into the words "true love" wounded her. He'd been gone for six years without sending word, and now he expected everything to be exactly as it had been before? She swallowed her hurt, smoothing her expression into one of nonchalance. "To be honest, after six years with no word from my 'true love,' I'd assumed I didn't have one anymore."

Her coldness seemed to rouse him from his own aloofness. He came toward her, fists clenched. "I sent a letter to Northcliffe Hall. It was returned with the words 'No longer at this address' written across it. I didn't know where else to look."

"Obviously you found me tonight," she answered, wondering how long she could maintain this cool exterior.

His eyes glittered. "Yes. I went to Northcliffe Hall, and they told me of your whereabouts. And of the nice cottage that your lover, the new Lord Northcliffe, bought for you."

As the force of his contempt washed over her, righteous anger surged in her. How dare he accuse her! Thanks to *his* dangerous politics, he'd left her pregnant with no way of supporting herself, no possible future. Yet he'd expected her to wait for him? Forever?

Dragging in a bracing breath, she met his gaze. "It took you a very long time to come searching for me. I know you must have served in the navy for a while." She trailed her gaze over his rich attire. "But obviously you went on to greener pastures. I suppose making a fortune in some far-off country kept you too busy to return." She straightened her shoulders and walked toward the fireplace.

But he caught her arm. "What kept me busy was finding a way to return without being hanged for desertion!"

All the stored-up resentment of six years exploded in her. "Hanged for desertion? If you hadn't gotten yourself involved with those damned Sons of Wales, you wouldn't have had to worry about it! If you hadn't printed those wretched pamphlets—"

"And if you hadn't told Northcliffe about them!"

She looked at him in stunned amazement. "What in heaven are you talking about?"

He thrust her away from him, disgust contorting his face. "I didn't believe Northcliffe when he said you'd betrayed me." His sweeping gesture encompassed the cottage interior. "But I talked to the servants and discovered that you've been here for six years. Six *years*! Ever since I left, you've lived here as his mistress. . . ." He shook his head. "You were obviously willing to go to any extent to stay out of poverty, weren't you?"

She stared at him in disbelief. "What are you talking about? What did Darcy tell you? Did you see him tonight?"

"No. If I had, he'd be dead for what he did to me six years ago." He drew in a ragged breath. "For what he and you did together."

Her heart's pace slowed to a crawl as her voice took on a note of sheer desperation. "A pox upon't, *what* did he do? What is it you think I did?"

His eyes narrowed. "You know he had me impressed."

She staggered back from him, her legs suddenly too weak to hold her up. Somehow she found a chair and dropped into it. She shook her head mindlessly. "Darcy? He was the one who had you impressed? Are you sure?"

Morgan clenched his fists at his sides. "I'm very sure. I'll never forget his face as he stood in that tavern cellar and gloated about now you'd confirmed that I was the one who'd printed those pamphlets, how you'd done it to keep from losing your damned position."

She jerked up straight in her seat. "I *never* told him that! I wouldn't have! How could you even believe it?"

"It's hard not to when you're sitting here as his mistress, obviously snug as a cockle in your secure cottage!" His voice rose to a shout. "How stupid do you think I am? You expect me to believe you had no part in it?"

"Yes, I expect you to believe I had no part in it!" Jumping from her chair, she prepared to give him a thorough set-down, but a childish voice coming from the stairs stopped her. She turned to find Edgar standing on the bottom step, rubbing his eyes.

"Mother, why are you shouting?" He eyed Morgan with curiosity. But when Morgan gave him a hard stare, he fidgeted. "Good evening," he said bravely, then destroyed the effect of his manly speech by sticking his thumb in his mouth.

Lettice scowled at Morgan. Edgar only sucked his thumb when he was frightened. "Go back to bed, Edgar. Everything's all right, and we'll try to be more quiet."

"Wait," Morgan said. He glanced from Edgar to her and then back to Edgar. When Edgar stared at him with the faintest trace of fear, Morgan softened his expression and went down on one knee. "Good evening to you, my boy."

With mixed emotions, she watched Morgan examine Edgar's features. She wasn't sure she wanted Morgan to know he had a son, not after what he'd accused her of. Even if he was telling the truth and Darcy had spoken such lies about her, how could Morgan have believed them?

"Your name is Edgar?" Morgan asked.

"Yes, my lord." Edgar's eyes were round as saucers as he stared at the big stranger.

The faintest smile touched Morgan's lips. "You need not call me 'my lord.' "

Taking his thumb out of his mouth, Edgar cocked his head to one side. "But I call Uncle Darcy 'my lord.' "

Morgan's smile faded. "That's because . . . Darcy *is* a lord. I'm not."

"What should I call you then?"

" 'Sir' would do nicely, I suppose."

"Yes, sir."

Morgan paused a moment, staring at the boy, then said, "I've seen your mother and now I've met you, but where is your father?"

Lettice sucked in a harsh breath. Must he torment poor Edgar like this? She stepped forward to intercede, but Morgan gave her a hard glance that froze her in place.

Edgar shifted from foot to foot and stared down at the steps. "I haven't a father, sir." He screwed up his face into a frown. "Other children do, I know. Is it odd that I have no father? I mean, Mother says Uncle Darcy is as good as a father."

Morgan visibly tensed. "And do you like Uncle Darcy?"

Edgar's face brightened. "Oh, yes, very much. He brings me lovely presents. And he likes to play quoits. Do you like to play quoits?"

"Yes, of course."

Lettice could stand it no more. "Edgar, it's time for you to go back to bed. It's very late."

Morgan stayed the child with one hand. "Only one more question, Edgar, and then you must do as your mother says." His voice sounded shaky. "How old are you?"

Lettice closed her eyes and sighed.

"I'm five. My birthday was this past May Day, you know. We always have a jolly time on my birthday. I'll be six years old next May Day, and a very big boy."

Morgan remained silent an endless moment. She could almost see him figuring the dates.

After scrutinizing Morgan carefully, Edgar blurted out, "Would you like to come to my birthday party?"

Morgan stood up and patted Edgar on the head, but the pat turned into a caress before he drew his hand back. "It sounds like fun. I should love to come."

Lettice bit her lip to keep from crying. "Go to bed, Edgar," she choked out, and this time the boy obeyed.

As soon as they heard the upstairs door shut, Morgan whirled on her, eyes alight with fury. "Does Northcliffe know that Edgar is my son?"

She turned from him, trying to hide the emotions she knew must be blazing in her face. "Who said that Edgar is your son?"

"Don't lie to me, Lettice! I can look in his face and tell he's my child!"

Her only answer was a barely stifled sob.

Coming up behind her, he grabbed her arm and made her face him. "Does Northcliffe know?"

"No!" She wrenched her arm from his. "Why in God's name do you think I'm here? Why do you think I've been with him for six years?"

He stared at her uncomprehending.

"When the press-gang took you," she whispered, "I had just realized I was pregnant. And on that same day, the old earl dismissed me without a reference for 'consorting with radicals' and not properly watching out for Lady Juliana." Her voice rose. "I was with child and without a position or family, and you were nowhere to be found!"

She planted her hands on her hips. "So when Darcy asked me to be his mistress, what do you think I said? 'No, my lord, I'd rather take my chances that some fool would hire a pregnant woman'? 'No, my lord, I prefer to wait endlessly for my lover while my child and I starve'?"

Her rage made her voice shake. "What would you have had me do, Morgan? What grand plan had you made for me in case you were punished for your illegal activities?"

He was staring at her, a stunned expression on his face. "The old earl dismissed you? But Darcy said you betrayed me in order to keep your position!"

"I never betrayed you! I wouldn't have. But my position *was* precarious, and my association with you was all it took to have me lose it!"

He raked his hand through his hair, the color draining from his face. "Good Christ, I never dreamed ... You didn't tell me you were pregnant. . . . I didn't know. . . ."

"I had only just found out myself. And in any case, if I'd told you, would you have stopped what you were doing?"

Pacing the room, he muttered, "I don't know ... perhaps. . . ."

"And another thing," she bit out. "Why in God's name would I have betrayed you to Darcy when I was carrying your child? I'd have been a fool to endanger my child's father!"

Morgan flinched, then turned to stare at her, the truth dawning on him. "So Northcliffe lied. You had nothing to do with the impressment."

"I told you, I knew nothing of it!"

Remorse shone in Morgan's eyes. "Devil take it, I'm sorry. I'm so sorry, love. I ... I didn't believe him at first, you understand. I truly didn't." He paused. "But you don't know what hell Rhys and I went through. We had a cruel captain who flogged his men at the slightest provocation. Rhys suffered through many floggings. Fortunately, I had only a flogging or two once the captain discovered I was a good cook. That was my salvation. Still—" He broke off, his voice shaking.

She stared at him wide-eyed. He *had* suffered. She could see it in his eyes. "I—I've heard life on a man-of-war is horrible."

"Aye," he clipped out. "And after a while you start to hate anyone and anything that put you there."

Her anger had dimmed to a low flame now, but the hurt burned even brighter. "E-even your true love?"

He closed his eyes against the accusation in her voice. "Especially your true love, if you think she betrayed you. Forgive me, Lettice, for doubting you. Now I see how wrong it was." Then his eyes shot open, and his jaw tightened. "But Northcliffe is also responsible for keeping us apart. He told me you betrayed me."

She clutched at her stomach, thinking of the Darcy she knew, the one who could be infinitely kind. "I—I don't understand it. He has always treated me with gentleness. He—"

"Don't you see?" Morgan stepped forward. "He'd probably been making plans to steal you from me for a long time. That's why he took such pains to be rid of me."

She shook her head, but couldn't deny the logic of his words. Darcy had never hidden his desire for her. And he'd been right there, ready to make her his mistress after the earl had dismissed her. What she'd construed as an act of kindness had been plotted out from the beginning.

"He was obviously in love with you," Morgan said tersely, "so much in love he'd have done anything to get you."

A tear slipped between her lashes and fell onto her cheek. "He has always said he loves me to desperation. It . . . It frightens me sometimes how much."

Morgan clasped her shoulders. "The question is, are you in love with him?"

She averted her face. "That hardly matters. He's been so kind to me—"

"Taking away your sweetheart, the father of your son? Is that kind?"

She lifted her tear-stained face to his. "I still have trouble thinking of him that way. I mean, I'm beginning to believe he did this terrible thing. But I've never seen that side of him.''

He obviously didn't like that answer, but instead of continuing to badger her, he asked, "If you won't tell me what you feel for him, can you tell me what you feel for me after all these years?"

The question shouldn't have taken her by surprise, but it did. And even more surprising was her inability to form a coherent answer. "I—I don't know."

His hands tightened on her shoulders. "I think you do. I think you're merely afraid to answer. Darcy has made a comfortable place for you here, and your misguided sense of loyalty makes you think you owe him for that. But I'm not talking about loyalty or kindness. I'm talking about love."

She wanted to turn her face from his, to hide her raw emotions, but he caught her chin and made her look at him.

"When you opened that door tonight," he persisted, "in that first second when you saw me, there was joy in your face. Was it born of love, Lettice? That's all I want to know."

She closed her eyes, hoping to avoid the question until she could be alone to ponder what her answer should be. Did she dare tell him the truth? And if she did, what would that mean . . . for her . . . for Edgar . . . for Darcy?

He gave her no time to think, however. Before she could free herself from his hold, she felt his lips on hers, gentle . . . soft . . . and every bit as sweet as she remembered.

It was as if six years had never been. He still smelled of bay rum, and his mouth still covered hers with blatant possessiveness. She started to draw back, but he clutched her head, holding her immobile as he moved his lips over hers, coaxing them apart until she opened to him, letting him plunge his tongue into her mouth.

His kiss was utterly sensual and as exciting as a kiss ought to be. It seemed to go on forever. When he finally drew back, her breath was coming hard and fast, and she was even more confused than before. How could he still make her blood sing, even after all these years, even after all the time she'd spent with Darcy?

He stared at her, triumph in his eyes. "You do still

love me. No matter what you say, I know it. I feel it in my bones."

She hid her face in his shirt, feeling both shame and joy at his words.

"Come with me, Lettice," he whispered against her hair. "Come with me tonight. Let me make you my wife. Let me care for you . . . and for my son."

It took every ounce of her will to resist the plea in his voice, the tempting comfort of his arms. But she did. She couldn't simply wrench Edgar away from his home without giving it careful thought. Nor could she pay Darcy back with such treachery after he'd cared for her. She owed Darcy a chance to explain, to defend his actions.

"Please, Morgan." She shifted away from him when he tried to draw her back into his arms. "I—I need some time to take care of this. I need to speak to Darcy—"

"And listen to more of his lies?"

"At least he took care of me—"

"If he hadn't had me impressed," Morgan gritted out, "*I* would have been the one to take care of you!"

"I know." What a coil this was. How could she untangle it without hurting someone? "Still, I owe him a great deal."

Morgan's scowl was etched with pain. "And what of me? Am I to lose you again, because he was here when I couldn't be?"

"Nay!" When his scowl faded, replaced by a hopeful look, she added, "Come again tomorrow. By then, I'll have spoken to Darcy. And I'll have made my decision."

He looked as if he'd argue, then clamped his mouth shut and strode for the door. But when he reached it, he faced her, his eyes flashing with determination. "Listen well, Lettice. I'm not going to disappear for six years this time. So no matter what decision you make about Northcliffe, I shan't give you up easily. Nor my son. I want you both, and I'll fight for you. Because I know you want me, too. And until that changes, I'll brave any obstacle Northcliffe throws up at me to have you."

With that, he went out into the night, leaving her feeling breathless and unwillingly excited.

Pray God he meant what he said. Because despite her

indebtedness to Darcy, despite her son's feelings, she knew she wanted Morgan, too.

Very much.

From where he sat beside a writing table in the library, Rhys heard the clock in the hall strike two, but he ignored the pealing and poured himself another glass of brandy. His head ached, his eyes throbbed, yet he welcomed the liquor as it seared his throat.

He should go to bed. Tomorrow he and Juliana would travel to Llynwydd, and he'd need a clear head for that. And for his next bout with his wife.

Groaning, he stared into the flames. His wife. A curse on the witch and her delectable body! What spell had she put on him?

He'd meant to frighten her, to punish her, to make her know she could never again ignore him. Instead, she'd turned his punishment into a seduction, tempting him to make love to her, to give her pleasure and seek his own pleasure with her.

By thunder, what had happened to him? Had he forgotten so easily all he'd suffered, thanks to her?

An image flickered into his mind, of Juliana standing tall and proud, even in her nakedness, even as he'd ordered her to lie on the bed. Her soft moan of pleasure echoed in his mind over and over. Despite her avowed hatred of him, he'd aroused her, and remembering it made his loins grow heavy and hard once more.

How could that be? How could he desire her so fiercely after all she'd done? For the past year, he'd dreamed of this night, of how he would humiliate her and make her beg. Instead he'd been the one humiliated. He'd been the one to flee in terror. Once he'd touched her, he'd been lost, eternally lost.

It was her wanton nature, he told himself. It made him lose all control when he was with her. He'd forgotten she wasn't like other women. Even now, he could almost hear her proclaiming to him on their wedding night that she had impure blood because she found pleasure in his caresses.

The memory brought a fleeting smile to his lips before he caught himself. Damn it all, that had been part of the trouble tonight, all those sweet memories of the first time, when she'd willingly given him her body.

He gulped some brandy, needing the fiery liquor to purge such thoughts from his head. By now, he should have lost his pleasant memories. Yet he could still remember their wedding night, and how it had felt to be inside that enveloping warmth—

The door opened. He turned, thinking perversely that he'd conjured her up with his thoughts, but instead Morgan walked in.

"Ah, Morgan." He returned his gaze to the leaping flames and wished for some ice water to cool his hot urges. "I wondered where you'd gone off to."

"I went to see Lettice."

Rhys glanced at him. "And how was *your* faithless lover?"

Morgan's jaw tightened as he took the chair on the other side of the table. "I found her to be not what I thought."

"Oh?"

"As it turns out, she wasn't faithless after all."

Rhys snorted and set the brandy decanter down a few inches from Morgan, then offered him an empty glass. "Indeed? I suppose being another man's mistress is not a sign of faithlessness? Or didn't you tell me that was what you discovered this week?"

"Yes, she's Northcliffe's mistress." Without another word, Morgan poured himself a glass of brandy, sipped it, and stared into the fire.

Rhys stiffened. "And?"

"She's also the mother of a child nearly six, who was born eight months after we left. His name is Edgar."

It suddenly occurred to Rhys that he'd never asked Juliana about children. But surely she'd have told him if their one union had produced a child. Still, he must question her on it tomorrow.

He spoke more unsteadily now. "I suppose Lettice claims that this Edgar is yours."

Morgan glared at him. "I *know* Edgar is mine."

Rhys shook his head and pulled the brandy decanter back to his side of the table. "Perhaps you shouldn't have any more of this. Your mind is more befuddled than I'd thought."

"He's mine," Morgan said through gritted teeth. "If you'd seen him, you'd know he was mine. He's the very image of me, and he's the right age, besides."

"Looks can be deceiving—"

"She told me herself that he was mine."

"She might have lied—"

"Why, Rhys?" Morgan twisted in his chair to fix Rhys with a dark scowl. "Why lie about it? 'Tis to her advantage to claim the child is *not* mine."

"Why is that?" Rhys bit out.

"She has let Northcliffe think the child is his all these years, which is why the bastard provides for her. In telling me the opposite, she's risking everything with him. Surely she realizes I could tell him the truth at any time, so why would she give me reason to do so?"

In truth, he didn't know. Rhys settled back against the chair, trying to make his half-sotted brain understand the implications of it.

"She didn't have to admit it, you know," Morgan continued. "She was fixed nicely, with a nobleman to provide for her all her life if that was what she was after. But she risked throwing that all away to tell me about my son. So I believe her. I believe Edgar is mine."

"I see. You're going soft on me, ready to forgive her all because she's given you a son. Have you forgotten everything that happened to us? Will you let her insinuate herself into your good graces now that she has tired of Northcliffe?"

Setting his brandy glass down, Morgan jerked his gaze from Rhys. "You're a cynical son of a bitch, you know that?"

"Aye, 'tis what kept me alive."

" 'Tis also what made you so blind with vengeance, you can't see the truth."

He sneered at Morgan. "Oh, and what damned truth is that?"

Morgan shot to his feet and began to pace the room. "Lettice is innocent of any involvement in our impressment. And perhaps Juliana is, too. Perhaps Northcliffe concocted the scheme to separate me from the woman he coveted and his sister from an unworthy Welshman."

Rhys set down his glass. "I see it took little to erase your memory of the night we were impressed! *Someone* betrayed us—at least one of the women and probably both." He snorted. "I may be a cynic, but at least I'm not a besotted fool. I didn't fall for Juliana's tearful protestations of innocence tonight."

Morgan stopped his pacing, his jaw twitching. "I'd rather believe Lettice's protestations than the lies of that twisted sot Northcliffe. And you should believe Juliana over him as well."

"It's hard not to believe him when he repeats the accusations to her face."

Astonishment crossed Morgan's face. "What do you mean?"

Rhys felt the bitterness surge in him again. "Tonight he was quite adamant about Juliana's participation, even when she called him a liar. So even if—and I do mean *if*—your Lettice is innocent, Juliana is not."

Morgan looked troubled. "He still claims she got cold feet and had us impressed to get her out of the marriage?"

"Aye, he claims it staunchly." He clenched his fist around the decanter. "So does his brother. And the innkeeper."

Morgan looked thoughtful. "Well, his brother would support anything he says, but the innkeeper— What did she say to the innkeeper's accusation?"

Rhys scowled. "Nothing. She 'didn't know' why the innkeeper would lie. Just as she 'didn't know' who summoned her brothers to The White Oak in the middle of the night when no one knew where we were." He slid the decanter aside. "And she certainly 'didn't know' I was alive, which is why she was marrying her precious marquess."

"What? She denied that you'd sent her letters?"

"She claims Northcliffe never gave them to her."

Morgan was silent a moment. "It's possible, isn't it, if his is a household where the mail is brought to him first?"

"Aye, it's possible her brother invented everything!" Rhys exploded, jumping up from his chair. "But he couldn't have invented the time discrepancy, could he? She claims her brothers came to the inn mid-morning, but you know I was taken only an hour after we'd entered the inn. So if she's blameless, how do you explain their presence there at that hour? She claimed they'd learned of the elopement from the note she'd left behind. But she also said that the note didn't mention where we'd gone. It couldn't have anyway, for I didn't tell her where I was planning to take her. Of course, we'd agreed she wouldn't leave a note for them in the first place, so obviously that was an invention. Someone brought them there in the middle of the night, and you and I both know it could only have been her!"

Rubbing his eyes, Morgan sank into an armchair. "Devil take it, Rhys, this is a muddle. All I know is that Lettice is innocent." When Rhys scowled, he added, "But maybe Juliana *isn't*. I didn't know her well six years ago, but she did seem to have a penchant for getting into trouble, then taking the easy way out."

"Aye."

"Still . . ." Morgan shook his head. "The young are often like that. And she always seemed so sweet, so innocent—"

"Exactly. Sweet, innocent, and irresponsible as hell. She ran away from canings and sneaked into meetings without a thought to the consequences." He paced the room. "And she never trusted me. The night I proposed, she accused me of wanting to marry her to get Llynwydd."

"You can see how she might have thought that."

Rhys breathed unsteadily. "Thinking it is one thing, but going behind my back to act on it is quite another. I don't blame her for her vacillations nor even her fickle character. I blame her for letting me go through hell because she was too cowardly to get out of the marriage through some honorable way."

"That's not all you blame her for, is it? I daresay your anger would be much reduced if you'd returned to find her unwed and ready to accept the marriage."

Rhys shot Morgan a furious glance. "Are you implying that I'm jealous?"

"Aren't you?"

Swearing under his breath, Rhys slammed the brandy decanter down on the table. "Not jealous. Angry. Angry that she planned to use my estate to buy that English noble as husband. By thunder, how can you even consider she might be innocent when she was about to marry another man, to commit bigamy? If she'd been innocent, she wouldn't have taken up with that damned marquess! She wouldn't have kept our marriage secret!"

"You have a point." Morgan leaned forward. "Did you ask her why she did that if she's as innocent as she claims?"

"She claims that some hired man of Northcliffe's found out I was dead. But since that's impossible, I know that's a lie. As for why she kept our marriage secret in the first place ... she didn't say why, but she probably has a tale for that one, too. It doesn't matter. Eventually I'll make her admit the truth."

"What if she has a valid explanation for everything? I wouldn't have believed Lettice was innocent either until she explained how she had to choose between starvation for herself and Edgar or an alliance with Northcliffe. I can't blame her for that."

Rhys stared into the fire. "Juliana's situation is different. She's given me no reason to believe her innocent."

"Still, she claims she is."

"She lies. I have the word of three people on it! *Ufferndân*, Morgan, two of them are her damned brothers! Tell me, why in God's name would her own brothers lie about it, and take such a chance with her future?"

"I don't know," Morgan admitted.

"I could punish her any way I wanted. Surely they wouldn't wish that on her if they could prevent it!"

Morgan clenched the arms of his chair. "And how *do* you intend to punish her? All you said before was that you would take back Llynwydd and your wife. But what will you do with her now that you've got her? What kind of marriage can you have when you trust her so little?"

"What I do with Juliana is my business," he retorted hotly.

Morgan hesitated. "That's true. But let me give you some unsolicited advice, my friend. If after maligning her character, you should discover she's indeed innocent, you won't be able to erase all that time of distrust. And you may find that after showing her so little faith, she has lost complete faith in you. What will you do then?"

"That is indeed 'unsolicited advice,' " Rhys growled. "So let me give you some. Do as you wish with Lettice and your supposed son. Pretend we were never torn from our country and made to suffer aboard the H.M.S.

Nightmare. If it pleases you, pretend the last six years never happened." He turned on Morgan fiercely. "But leave me and Juliana alone, do you hear? I will do with her as I see fit, and nothing you say will change that!"

Morgan gave him a hard stare. "Yes, I can see that. I only hope you're not making an irreparable mistake." He turned and left the room, closing the door softly behind him.

Rhys cursed at the closed door. "I'm not making a mistake," he insisted to the silent four walls. "I'm not."

So why did he wonder if Morgan might be right?

Chapter Eleven

"Despite what good comes from holding land,
World's a treacherous dwelling ...."
   —Peryf ap Cedifor,
   "The Killing of Hywel"

A persistent clicking sound resonated through Juliana's dream, then dragged her slowly from the heaviness of deep sleep. Trying to return to the soft soundless world she'd been floating in, she punched up her pillow, snuggling into it with a sigh as her mind grasped at the wisps of whatever pleasant dream was already fading.

But it was too late. Wakefulness intruded, forcing her to hear morning's arrival—the rumble of carts in the street, the hushed steps of servants in the corridor. She wouldn't be able to go back to sleep now.

With a groan, she opened her eyes and stared at the wall opposite her. And found herself completely disoriented.

Where was she? This wasn't Northcliffe or even Llynwydd.

Nay, she thought with an awful lurch in her stomach as she remembered the previous night's events. This was Rhys's town house. She dragged the pillow into her arms and derived a fleeting comfort from squashing it. Everything that had happened came flooding back to her, every disturbing moment, including the hours she'd spent shifting and tossing in the bed, trying to think of how to go on.

Once she realized how determined Rhys was to keep her as his wife, she'd decided there was only one way to continue. Somehow she had to turn this mad battle of wills into a civil marriage. "Civil" was the best she could hope for, what with him hating her so. And much as she dreaded the thought of living with him as if they were two strangers, even that seemed preferable to the gut-wrenching fight he seemed to want.

She was tired of battles. For six years she'd battled her fears, then her grief over what had happened to Rhys. For six years she'd fought her family to keep her place at Llynwydd and she'd fought the creditors to get Llynwydd on its feet. When she'd decided to marry Stephen, she'd thought the battles would finally be over. She could get on with her life and have a haven at last.

Her mouth twisted into a bitter smile. Of course, that had proven too good to be true. Thanks to her blasted brothers and their sudden betrayal—well, not so sudden, since they had apparently been the ones to have Rhys impressed—she was now in the midst of the worst battle of all.

Closing her eyes, she willed back the hurt that crawled inside her belly like an insidious worm. Why had Darcy told Rhys those dreadful things last night? She could understand why he'd lied to Rhys the first time—to keep Rhys away from her. She could even understand why he'd lied to her about Rhys's death, since he'd been eager to see her marry Stephen. But after Rhys's return, why had Darcy lied to Rhys again about her? Why?

None of what had happened the night of Rhys's impressment made any sense. She'd had no inkling that her brothers were involved. After all, they'd come to the inn long after the press had taken Rhys.

She shook her head. Obviously, that wasn't true either. Rhys said they'd taken him in the middle of the night, so Darcy and Overton had clearly come to the inn earlier. But how had they known where to find her? They'd had no time to search for her. Some memory of that night struggled to surface, but no matter how she concentrated, she couldn't bring it to mind. Six years was a long time.

So Darcy had come to the inn, then lied both to her and Rhys about how he'd found her, telling them different tales. And the blasted innkeeper was supporting Darcy's story. No doubt Darcy had paid him off.

That still didn't explain how her brothers had found her that night. Or why Darcy had lied tonight. Was there some way she could sneak out and return to Northcliffe

Hall to ask him all her questions? Otherwise, it would drive her insane not knowing how and why he'd done it.

Darcy had always been ambitious, arrogant, and strict, but he'd also had his moments of kindness. A fleeting smile crossed her face. She remembered when she was six years old and he'd hidden her from Father for a whole day. She'd drawn flowers all over Father's legal papers with his best ink pen. While Father had ranted and swore, Darcy had claimed not to have seen her even while he hid her in his closet. Darcy had always looked after her, and perhaps he'd even thought he was looking after her when he'd sent Rhys off.

But last night ... Her eyes welled with tears. Last night, he hadn't been looking after her. Not at all.

She must find out why. Feeling better now that she'd hit upon a course of action, she pushed herself into a sitting position on the bed. And that's when she saw Rhys.

She'd been lying with her back to the door, which was why she hadn't spotted him before. He was standing just inside, his gaze trained on her. Barefoot and wearing only an open-throated shirt and tight breeches, he looked more like a pirate than a squire, especially when he watched her with a dangerously hooded gaze.

Her breath caught in her throat. How long had he been standing there? He undoubtedly hadn't realized she was awake. But when had he entered?

As the silence stretched between them, he stated, "I came to see if you were up. Your mother sent your clothes this morning. I'll have them brought to you. We'll be leaving soon, and you'll probably want breakfast." His words were crisp as his gaze drifted down to fasten on a spot well below her throat.

Too late she realized she was wearing only her shift, and she didn't need to look to realize that it hung quite low over her bosom.

Hot color rose up her neck to burn in her cheeks as she dragged the sheet up to her chest. "H-how long have you been standing there?"

His gaze snapped back up to her face. "Not long."

Suddenly, she remembered the clicking sounds that had awakened her from her dreamy sleep—the sounds of a key being turned in a lock and a door being opened and shut. In faith, he'd been watching her all that time.

"Why didn't you knock?" she blurted out.

" 'Tis *my* bedchamber, if you'll recall. Why would I knock at my own bedchamber?"

"To be polite perhaps?" she snapped. "You do remember courtesy, don't you?"

Her boldness seemed to startle him. Then a dark smile crossed his lips. "I remember lots of things. One of them is how enticing you used to look, all curled up in your bed at Northcliffe. I wanted to see if my memory served me correctly."

His soft words took her completely off guard. The thought of Rhys watching her sleep made her feel trembly and warm inside. "And . . . and did it?"

"No." He stepped forward, eyes hungry and his full lips slightly parted. "You're much more enticing than I remembered."

His gaze on her was alarming. She didn't want a repeat of last night. She searched for something to say to carry them from the dangerous subject of his desire for her. "I—I heard voices in the hallway late last night. Did you have a visitor?"

His expression grew shuttered. "Yes. Morgan came to tell me about his visit to Lettice."

Juliana's face lit up. "He returned with you? Why, that's wonderful! Lettice must be thrilled!" Then she remembered that Lettice was now her brother's mistress and had a child. She colored. "I—I mean, she must be pleased that he survived the navy. Though I suppose everything's different between them now."

"Morgan doesn't think so." Rhys snorted. "He means to continue where they left off . . . if she'll have him. That damned child of hers instantly grabbed his sympathies."

What could she say to that? Obviously, Rhys didn't approve of Morgan's desire to take up with Lettice again. He probably thought that like him, Morgan should torment his former love for getting involved with another man.

She shifted her gaze from Rhys to the curtained window. The muted light peeking around the edges of the curtains reminded her there was a world outside his house, outside his presence. 'Twas the only thing that kept her emotions even.

When she continued to gaze blindly at the diffused light, her lifeline to sanity, he drew a deep breath and said, "I have a question for you."

"Yes?" She couldn't look at him.

"Did you ... was there ..." He paused, seeming to struggle for words. "Did *we* have a child, too?"

The question shocked her, and she wasn't quite sure why. Was it because he hadn't asked before? Or simply because his voice was threaded with a quiet yearning completely at war with his behavior last night?

Either way, speaking about those first horrible days after he'd left was more than she could bear. She shook her head no.

With a sharp intake of breath, he stepped closer. "I want the truth about this, Juliana. This is one thing you mustn't lie about. If we had a child, I want to know."

The pain settled sickeningly in her belly like sour milk. "I haven't lied to you about anything, but I certainly wouldn't lie about that. Did anyone mention children last night when you were wresting me away from my family? Don't you think they would have?"

"Actually, I thought you might have sent the child to be raised elsewhere." When she swung her gaze to his, anger boiling up in her with fierce swiftness, he added, "If you did, I won't hold it against you now. I just need to know the truth so I can regain my child. That's all I want."

"The truth? You don't want truth! You only want more crimes to lay against me!" Her voice dropped to a ragged whisper. "Have you no good memories of our time together? Did the sea wash them so completely from your mind that you could think I'd send away my own child to be raised by strangers?"

With a bitter shrug, he murmured, "You kept our marriage a secret, didn't you? I didn't expect that. And to keep it a secret, you'd have *had* to hide any child of our union."

She thrust the sheet aside and leapt from the bed, no longer caring that she wore only her shift. "If I'd had a child, I wouldn't have kept our marriage a secret! I'd have shouted it from the rooftops, you fool!"

"You didn't need a child for that!" He balled his hands into fists at his sides. "You should have done that anyway, instead of pretending it never happened!"

"If I'd wanted to pretend it never happened, I would have had it annulled, wouldn't I?" Her breath came in sharp gasps as she met his furious gaze.

His eyes narrowed. "You couldn't have. You didn't have the marriage certificate, and my godfather, the bishop, wouldn't have let you, not while he was alive."

She rolled her eyes. "Neither of those things would have stopped my father from having it annulled, I assure you. Father had the power to make your godfather do whatever he wanted, certificate or no certificate! And Father wanted to annul the marriage. Immediately." Rage building in her, she jabbed a finger at her chest. " 'Twas *I* who kept him from it! I told them I'd spread the story of my elopement throughout the land if they attempted an annulment!"

"You should have done that anyway!" His eyes were alight with outrage. "You were my wife, but you told not a soul! You hid it in your bosom like some dirty secret that shamed you!"

"Aye, 'tis true. I did hide it." How different things would be now if she hadn't. "But Rhys, remember my youth. I was eighteen. I'd been wedded and bedded for only one night, then told my husband was lost to me for a long time, if not forever. They said you'd been impressed." Her voice caught, remembering that nightmarish time. "And despite what you believe, what they told you, I knew exactly what impressment entailed. What I didn't know, they were sure to tell me. They all said you could easily die at sea."

She turned toward the window, unable to face him, fearing the condemnation she'd find in his expression. Slowly, she approached the window and pulled aside the curtains, looking out at the bustling market streets below. "It was hard enough for me to stand up to them, to say I wouldn't allow an annulment. You weren't there to give me strength and protect me from my family's anger. So when Darcy suggested . . ."

She trailed off as that day came back to her. Half in a daze, she dropped the curtain. She'd forgotten how much Darcy had shaped her behavior in those early days. He'd orchestrated it all so well, and in her grief and uncertainty, she'd fallen in with his plans easily. He'd wanted her to hide the marriage so there'd never be a question of her going back to it. Blast the wretch! Had Darcy really thought Rhys would stay away forever?

He must have. And when she'd stubbornly held on to her hopes, Darcy had cut them off by paying that investigator to say Rhys was dead. Darcy had cold-bloodedly betrayed her, and she hadn't even known it. A tightness built in her chest as she stared blindly at the heavy green brocade in front of her.

"What *did* your damned brother suggest?" Rhys prodded, his words laced with anger.

She swallowed back a sob and faced him. "He said there was no point to proclaiming my marriage when you might never return." As memory flooded her, her tone grew more and more biting. "He pointed out that I might never know if you survived the navy. If you died, who would tell me? Why should I ruin my life, he said, when 'twould be better merely to wait and see what happened?"

"You mean, to wait and hope that I never returned." Rhys's face wore a look of betrayal so deep she wondered if anything she said could ever erase it.

Still, she had to say it all. "Perhaps Darcy hoped for that. I never did. But I feared terribly that you wouldn't return, especially when the investigator Darcy hired for me found no trace of you. Then when he said you were dead—"

"A convenient addition to your story," he muttered. "Except for one thing. There was no evidence of any death for your supposed investigator to find."

"I realize that. Darcy obviously paid the man to tell me you were dead."

"Can you show me this investigator?"

A sob welled in her throat. "What do *you* think? Darcy hired him. And now that Darcy is ... persisting in his lies, he's certainly not going to have someone come along and refute them in my defense."

"How convenient for you."

She flinched. "Why won't you believe me?"

"Because you never told your precious fiancé about

your marriage, even when you supposedly believed yourself a widow. And why didn't you? Because you'd been hiding the marriage from the very beginning, and there was no need to tell him of what you'd pretended didn't exist. You did exactly as Darcy predicted—you hid your marriage so you could make a more advantageous one later."

"No! I mean, I didn't hide it for that reason!"

"Any reason was a betrayal of what we'd shared."

Guilt overwhelmed her. He was right. In a sense, she had betrayed him by listening to Darcy. "I suppose you could see it that way. But I only hid my marriage out of fear and confusion. I couldn't bear to face the scandal of an elopement when I had no husband to show for it. And Darcy played on that. He pointed out that I was neither widow nor wife, that I'd be in that limbo forever unless I kept the marriage secret."

Rhys glanced away, but his jaw began to twitch.

"I was weak, Rhys," she continued, "not as weak as you've believed me to be, but weak nonetheless." She drew a ragged breath, weighing her next words, knowing they would make her even more vulnerable to him. Yet she had to make him see her side. "In truth, I prayed that I'd find myself pregnant with your child, for then I'd have part of you with me. Then they'd have been forced to let me announce the marriage."

As if drawn by a witch's spell, he turned his face to her. A glimmer of sympathy shone in his eyes as she stared at him, caught by his yearning gaze. "I wanted your child so badly. When my courses came, I wept for two days."

She paused. The silence drew them in together, into a mourning for what might have been, what never was.

He let out a long-drawn breath. "So there was no child."

Wordlessly, she shook her head, clamping down on the tears that waited to engulf her control. The sorrow in his face tore at her, made her want to touch him, to comfort him.

Instead, she went on. "That's when I began keeping the secret they counseled me to keep. I made them promise to let me await you at Llynwydd, and I moved there under the pretext of caring for my estate. But it was really to avoid their pressure on me to annul the marriage."

He was staring at her in astonishment. "You awaited me at Llynwydd? For how long?"

Her pulse quickened as her face mirrored her surprise. "I thought you knew. You seemed to know so much else, I thought you realized that I've been living at Llynwydd all this time."

Raking his fingers through his hair, he turned away from her. "I haven't been there since I reached Wales two weeks ago. I didn't want to go until everything was settled, so I could arrive as owner. I also didn't want anyone recognizing me and warning the family of my arrival. When I asked around, I was told it was closed up."

She nodded. "I closed it up a month ago when I came to town to plan my engagement party. Until then, I'd been living there."

He whirled on her. "As what? Obviously not as my wife."

"Nay, as the owner. 'Tis my property, you know."

His eyes blazed at her. "So you were happy to live in my estate, yet not to acknowledge our marriage."

It sounded so callous when he said it that a defensive note crept into her voice. "I would have been happy to acknowledge our marriage if I'd had any word saying you were alive or if the investigator hadn't proclaimed you dead."

"The letters." His face paled. "They went to Northcliffe Hall. Not to Llynwydd. And you were at Llynwydd."

Her heart began to pound. He understood. He did. "Aye, I was at Llynwydd. And Darcy obviously never sent the letters."

He seemed to ponder that a moment. Then his face hardened. "Even if that's true, it doesn't change anything. You set out to keep this marriage a secret from the moment I was impressed, long before you would have expected to hear anything from me, and all because you hoped to marry someone else later."

"Nay! I told you, I didn't keep it a secret for that reason!" A tear escaped her eye, and she rubbed it away fiercely. "Can't you understand what it was like for me?

You said yesterday that you could forgive me for having second thoughts. Why can't you forgive me for being weak when I believed you were gone forever? I couldn't do anything but wait . . . without word, without hope for the future."

She choked the words out through a throat raw from the effort of holding back tears. "I wasn't strong enough for that, Rhys. I just wasn't. So when the investigator told me you were dead, I felt free to let Stephen court me. And to accept his offer."

At the mention of Stephen, his face went stony. "Yes, and while you were gleaning the fruits of my estate and preparing to turn them over to another man, I was serving the damned English navy, letting them drain my very life's blood from me!"

"I know. But you escaped that, didn't you? And look at you now. You're obviously successful and wealthy." A faint bitterness swelled in her. "You spent three years in America. If you'd come back then instead of waiting—"

"I couldn't come back then," he snapped. "I had no money and no desire to feel the hangman's noose about my neck. I assure you, those three years in America weren't blissful and carefree." Smoothing his face into nonchalance, he spoke in a near monotone. "I repaid the Americans for saving me by risking my life daily. I did it because I wanted to return to Wales, because I needed the money to do so and the most money was paid for the riskiest tasks."

His eyes locked with hers, and the bleak abyss that yawned deep in them made her ache once more to comfort him. But how did one comfort a wounded beast who bit anyone who ventured near?

Then his gaze hardened once more. "I won't say what I did," he ground out. "You might tell your brothers, and get me hanged despite my newly gained influence. But I can tell you this—there are wounds and scars on my body that your countrymen inflicted long after I left the navy."

He yanked back a handful of hair to reveal a long, jagged scar just above his right temple where no hair grew. "This was done by an English saber. I nearly died from it—I was completely unconscious for two weeks, and then very ill for weeks after that. But I survived. I survived the same way I survived everything else, by telling myself I had to live to regain what I'd lost—my wife, my home, my birthright. I had to live to repay you for your thoughtless act." Stepping close to her, he lowered his voice to a threatening hiss. "You think to purge me of my anger with all your false tales, but 'twas my anger that kept me alive, and I will honor its cry for vengeance!"

It took all her strength not to back away, to look into the harsh face that showed the ravages he spoke of. But she managed it by remembering how that face had once smiled at her, the corners of his eyes crinkling in amusement.

Reaching up, she smoothed her fingers over the scar he'd shown her. " 'Twasn't anger that kept you alive, don't you see? Nor even your thirst for vengeance. 'Twas love. Love for your home. And yes, love for me. 'Tis the love you can't purge, and you hate that."

He seemed frozen, unable to turn away from her as she trailed her fingers down his bristly cheek, remembering a time when he'd welcomed her caresses. He reached to pull her hand away, but covered it instead. For a moment, they remained locked that way, his rough hand engulfing her small one.

Then he drew her hand from his face. "You think all your soft words—and your touch—will save you from me, don't you?" His breath came hard and fast, but he still clasped her hand. "You think it'll make me forget that I found you betrothed to another upon my return, that you hid our marriage from the world, that you toyed with my life without one thought for the consequences?"

Twisting her hand behind her back, he jerked her against his body, then lowered his face until it was inches from hers. "It won't, I assure you. No matter what you say, I know you for what you are. And one day you'll beg my forgiveness for what you did to me!" Releasing her hand, he smoothed his fingers over her buttocks. "One dark night I'll *make* you beg my forgiveness."

She swallowed at the threat in his voice, but this time she wasn't so cowed as before. She knew now what he would do. And what he wouldn't. "I've told you why I behaved as I did, and you've seen for yourself how callous Darcy has become. If you still choose to think ill of me, I can't change that."

She drew a deep breath as she stared him down. "But regardless of what you think I did to you, I am your wife. Thanks to your stubbornness, I'll be your wife forever. So don't you think 'twould be better to put the past behind us and find a way to live amicably together? Will gaining your vengeance erase your wounds? Will tormenting me ease your pain?"

His eyes met hers, stormy with anger ... and with something else she couldn't mistake—desire. Despite everything, he still felt that for her. And that was something, wasn't it?

She waited breathlessly, holding his gaze, wondering what he would do and how she would fight him if he tried to force her once more.

Suddenly, he thrust her away from him with a low curse. "You expect me to take up where we left off, don't you? To act as if you hadn't betrayed me. To forget."

"Nay. But I think you're a practical man. You've seen war now, and you know peace is preferable." She sought for words that would bridge the chasm between them, that would spark the good memories inside him.

Suddenly, they came to her, words she'd read only a few weeks before. She spoke in Welsh, "You know how to 'fashion peace, which is richer than gold.' You know that 'Mercy will never die or grow old.' 'Tis time to fashion peace, don't you think? 'Tis time to find mercy in your heart."

He stared at her, stunned silent for a moment by her quotation from *The Black Book of Carmarthen*. She could tell that in his quest for vengeance, he'd thrust from his memory all the pleasant hours they'd spent speaking of poetry and books. He'd spent so long focusing on her past mistakes—real and imagined—that he'd forgotten all the sweetness between them.

So this was what she must do. Remind him of the sweetness. She must uncover the old Rhys buried inside the new one.

Drawing a shaky breath, he shook his head, his face mirroring his torn emotions. "You're wrong," he murmured in Welsh. "I don't know how to 'fashion peace' anymore. I don't even know what peace is."

Her heart clamored in her chest as she stepped toward him and held out her hand. "Then let me teach it to you. Let us learn peace together."

For a moment, he wavered, his gaze fastening inexorably on her outstretched hand. But he closed his eyes and turned from her toward the door. "Get dressed," he commanded. "We leave in an hour."

Then he was gone.

She dropped her hand and stared through the open door. It was true he'd spoken aloofly, but now she knew what a thin facade was that aloofness. Inside, he ached for love, no matter what he said.

Perhaps there was a spark of hope for them both after all, she thought. If there were, she'd feed that spark with the tinder of her own precious memories. And maybe one day soon, the flame would melt the ice in Rhys's heart.

Wiping the sweat from his grimy brow, Rhys shifted in the saddle and looked back as the coach lumbered into view, spewing clouds of dust behind it. Juliana was in that coach, riding alone because he'd chosen to accompany the vehicle on horseback.

He twisted the reins about his hand until the leather bit into his gloves. Two hours of riding on horseback had taken its toll on a head that throbbed from the lingering effects of last night's brandy and a stomach that churned as badly as when he'd eaten maggot-ridden hardtack.

Still, he couldn't make himself join her in the coach for the last half hour of the ride, even though it was only there he could lay his head back on soft cushions and close his eyes. Nay, joining her also meant enduring her quiet, long-suffering presence, and that he couldn't do.

But this solitude wasn't much better, he thought as he waited on a rise for the coach to catch up with him. No matter how hard he rode, he couldn't push her words from his mind.

You know how to fashion peace. He'd expected her to fight as she had yesterday, to snap and growl at him, to accuse him of tearing her from her damned fiancé. When she fought him, it was easy to think of her as a light-headed, spoiled flirt, who'd ruined his life on a whim. It was easy to remind himself of all she'd cost him through her unthinking act.

But when she met him with Welsh poetry, so perfectly spoken that it might have been a bard of old intoning the words about "peace" and "mercy," all his convictions about her grew shaky.

Then memories assailed him. Like the memory of one night long ago when she'd sat on his lap and recited the whole of "Praise of a Girl," each Welsh word flowing from her mouth like rich music. Her face had glowed from the pleasures of poetry spoken aloud, and she'd taken a childish delight in the kisses he'd given her after each stanza. There'd been no hesitation in her that night, no sign of dislike for his penniless state or his Welshness.

The memory was so intense and immediate, Rhys had to clutch the reins to remind himself of where he was. That she could still quote Welsh poetry to him made him question all his assumptions.

Snatches of what she'd told him a few hours ago came to him now. At the time, he'd been too angry to listen, but over the long ride, her words had simmered in his brain. Her family's pressure on her not to have the marriage annulled ... Darcy's urging her to keep the marriage a secret ... her reasons for her betrothal ... All of it rang too much of truth.

Rhys rubbed his aching neck. He no longer knew what to believe. Morgan had doubts about her guilt, but no answers to explain what had happened that night—how the St. Albans brothers could possibly have found him without her help or could have known about his role in distributing the pamphlets. And every time Rhys thought of Juliana defending that handsome marquess, turning to him for support, it made his blood boil.

But when she'd spoken of not having his child ... By thunder, the yearning shining through the tears in those brilliant green eyes couldn't have been false. Even now, it sparked a yearning inside him, a clawing desire for something he'd never wanted before.

His child. Their child. Would their children be pale as cream like their mother or dark like their father? Would their hair capture the sun like Juliana's or reflect the black night like his own?

Thoughts of children led him to thoughts of how children were made. With a low curse, he tightened his legs on the horse's sides, spurring him to run on once more, but the motion didn't help to ease the throbbing in his loins. Too easily, he remembered Juliana standing before him in that thin shift that hadn't completely veiled the dusky rose of her nipples or the triangle of dark auburn hair between her legs. Then there was her heady lavender scent ... after all these years, it still made him want to bury his face in her hair ... in her neck ... between her legs.

"Cer i'r diawl!" he swore aloud. She was making him as insane as she'd made him all those years ago. It was merely lust, but powerful nonetheless. And he was woefully tired of fighting it.

He drove the horse until it flew over the pockmarked road. Keeping well to the edges where the ruts smoothed out into level, packed dirt, he thundered toward Llynwydd, trying, but failing, to keep his lustful thoughts in check.

Perhaps he shouldn't fight it anymore, he thought as he bent low over the horse's well-lathered neck. Perhaps that was where he'd made his mistake last night, trying to punish her with his desire. It had been as much a punishment for him as for her, not to be able to caress every inch of her body or watch her face flush when he kissed her slow and deep.

Damn it all, last night he hadn't even kissed her. And suddenly he wanted quite badly to kiss her, to see if he'd only imagined the intense connection they'd once had. In truth, he didn't want her to lie there like a whore and let him spend himself inside her. He wanted her moaning beneath him, lifting her mouth to his of her own accord to find her pleasure.

Aye, he told himself as the ache in him started to ease a bit. Aye, that was it. He wanted her willing. He remembered too well how sweet it had been when she was willing.

And he wouldn't be giving up anything to have her willing. It was what he wanted, and what she wanted, too, no matter what she claimed.

Her words came back to him. "Fashion peace," eh? Let them fashion peace in the marriage bed. She *was* right. They did have a lifetime to live together. And as long as he made it clear who controlled their lives, who would be master in their house, they could have that one pleasure together.

Of course, he wouldn't let pleasures shared in bed negate her duty to make amends for her unthinking act of six years ago. He wouldn't trust her, but he could bed her as often as he wished, and if she drew pleasure from it, that was even better.

Last night, she had said she feared being seduced against her will. That would be a kind of vengeance, wouldn't it? he told himself as he mounted the last rise before Llynwydd. Ah, to make her desire him, to tempt her with her own weakness! The thought nearly swept the breath from his body. Why should he resist her? She was his wife. He had a right to enjoy her body.

Just then he topped the hill that looked down on Llynwydd, and his breath caught in his throat. Home. His home. After six years, he'd come home.

The old passion for the land glowed in him again as the wind swept his hair from his brow. He'd forgotten how it was to crest the hill and come all of a sudden upon Llynwydd, nestled like a jewel within the hanging beech woods.

Now he was glad he hadn't come here until he could enter the estate as owner, for it made the pleasure all the more intense. Llynwydd was his. Every garden, every field, every tenant farm. No one could deny that any longer.

With a deep sigh, he savored the sight of it—the long drive leading to the massive wrought-iron gates that had awed him as a child, and beyond those gates, the expanse of outbuildings and the thriving orchards of plum and peach. A lump grew in his throat. How tall were the trees along the Irish yew walk his father had planted when Rhys was barely eight! Twenty years later, they'd lost their stripling look and their lush dark green foliage brightened the garden.

Then there was the squire hall itself—a central block of aged brick flanked by the newer wings his grandfather had put in. Sunlight glinted off the white painted rails of the entrance steps, as if off the pearly gates themselves, and the oak door looked as solid as he remembered it. For the first time in nearly seven years, he could ride up to that very door and walk into the halls of his childhood home with impunity.

He smiled. Finally, he had his birthright back, and not even the treacherous St. Albans brothers could wrest it away from him.

But Juliana already had. Unbidden, their conversation came back to him. She'd been living here for six years. He hadn't expected that. He hadn't expected her to take over his estate. His heart lurched painfully. After living here all this time, she must have changed things to suit her whims. Some changes were evident from where he stood—a new tile roof on the coach house, expanded stables, and the new vine house that showed she'd revived the practice of growing cucumbers and melons at Llynwydd. What else had she altered?

Shifting in the saddle, he stared at his childhood home. It didn't matter what she'd done. Llynwydd was his now, and he would make it his own once more. If her changes were good, he'd certainly let them stand. But *he'd* make that decision, not her.

She'd soon learn he was master here. When she accepted the role of dutiful wife she'd once refused—and when she came willingly to his bed—he'd accept the peace she offered.

But not until then.

Chapter Twelve

> "I'd go back to my father's country,
> Live respected, not lavish nor meagrely,
> In sunlit Mon, a land most lovely, with
> Cheerful men in it, full of ability."
> —Goronwy Owen,
> "The Wish"

When Rhys opened the carriage door, he was smiling, and that disturbed Juliana a great deal. Had he considered her words and found them to be sensible? Judging from the glint of calculation in his eyes, she didn't think so. Yet something had changed in him during the journey. She just couldn't figure out what.

Behind him, the servants were scurrying out of the entrance door to line up along the rails of the stairway, obviously drawn by their arrival. There weren't as many as usual—when she'd closed the house, she'd let some of them go—but their well-scrubbed faces and impeccably clean attire made her proud. At least Rhys couldn't accuse her of hiring a slovenly staff.

No sooner had Juliana alighted from the carriage than the housekeeper, Mrs. Roberts, came rushing up to her. "Milady, we weren't expecting you or we'd have readied the house. I'm afraid everything is still under covers and all in a muddle." She cast Rhys a quizzical glance. "But it won't take us long to get all in readiness if you're wanting to stay."

"Thank you," Juliana said. "We will be ... that is ... Mr. Vaughan and I—"

"What my wife is trying to say is, we'll be in residence at Llynwydd from now on, aside from occasional trips to Carmarthen or London."

Mrs. Roberts's jaw dropped. "In residence?" Then as

everything Rhys had said registered, she stammered, "Y-your wife?" She looked to Juliana for confirmation. "Milady?"

Rhys did the same, his smile widening as he lifted his hand to the small of her back in a blatant gesture of possession. Obviously, he planned to enjoy watching her announce her six-year-old marriage to her staff.

Juliana sighed and wished she hadn't kept her marriage quite so secret. No telling what Mrs. Roberts, with her vivid imagination and penchant for gossip, was thinking. Lifting her chin, Juliana fought to retain some semblance of pride as she said in a voice meant to carry only to Mrs. Roberts, "This is Squire William Vaughan's only son, Rhys. As you've probably heard from other members of the staff, his family were the previous owners of Llynwydd." She swallowed hard. "Mr. Vaughan is also my husband."

As Mrs. Roberts continued to stare at her with the wide eyes of a startled rabbit, Rhys leaned close to whisper in her ear, "Very good, *mhriod.* Finally you're beginning to learn some compliance."

She shot him a scathing glance, but he'd already turned to the astonished Mrs. Roberts. "You are the housekeeper?" he asked in Welsh.

It was the first time Juliana had heard him speak entirely in Welsh since his return, and she could tell he probably hadn't used it much while he was abroad, for he had an accent. After all, other than Morgan, to whom would he have spoken Welsh?

But the housekeeper seemed surprised to hear him use Welsh at all. It wasn't usual for a squire. "Aye, sir," she said quickly. "I've been with Lady Juliana for six years."

He assessed Mrs. Roberts with a quick look. "You weren't the housekeeper here when Squire Vaughan was in residence."

"Nay—" she began.

"Mrs. Roberts and many of the other servants were hired by my father," Juliana put in as she stared blindly ahead at the open door. If only this could all be over and she could simply disappear inside. "When Father acquired the estate, he dismissed your father's servants and hired his own. After I moved in, I tried to hire as many of them back as I could, but most had already found other positions by then, including your father's housekeeper."

She waited for him to rail about that, but he merely surveyed the line of servants ranged stiffly down the stairs in front of the house. He paused here and there to peruse a face as he made a thorough appraisal of the staff.

Juliana could only continue to gaze through the open door, unable to meet the inquisitive glances of her servants. She knew what they were wondering, for they'd all seen her fiancé on several occasions, and must know that Rhys was not he. The few servants who'd worked for Squire Vaughan might recognize him, but he'd changed so much in six years that she doubted it.

Flashing Mrs. Roberts a smile, Rhys drew Juliana out of earshot of the servants. " 'Tis best that we get this over with now, so here's what I want you to do. Announce to them, as you did to Mrs. Roberts, that I am your husband and that we've been married for six years. Explain that you thought me lost at sea, which is why you never said anything. They're going to hear rumors anyway—"

"Because you insisted on making this whole thing public."

His eyebrows drew together in a dark frown. "Aye. If I'd confronted you and your brothers privately, I might not have lived to tell anyone else about it."

She opened her mouth to refute that horrible accusation, but he went on ruthlessly. "Do as I say, Juliana. Tell them I'm your long-lost husband returned to life. It must be done sooner or later, and sooner is best."

He clasped her arm and pulled her close. To anyone else, it probably looked like an intimate gesture, but she could feel his fingers digging into her arm. "And for God's sake," he murmured, "wipe that expression from your face. You look like a virgin facing the sacrificial knife. Try to appear as if you're actually glad to have your husband back."

"If you're so concerned about how this is done, why don't *you* tell them?" she snapped. "Embarrassing public announcements are *your* forte, not mine."

The edges of his mouth tipped up, and she could see

amusement glittering in his eyes before he masked it. "At present their loyalty is to you. They're liable not to believe me—or to accept me—if I thrust myself forward in your place."

"And why should I help you gain their acceptance?" She twisted her arm out of his hand, careful to block the motion with her body.

"You said you wanted peace, didn't you? Show me that you mean it. Because if you refuse to support me in this, you won't have a moment's peace, I assure you."

Glancing at the servants, whose faces reflected their curiosity even though they avoided her eyes, she weighed her choices. But she had none to weigh. A battle before the staff was unthinkable. Aside from being mortifying, it would only gain her Rhys's enmity, and she had that already. Nor would it help matters at Llynwydd to have the servants confused by who was in charge. This wasn't a matter for the servants. This was between him and her, and she wouldn't give him the satisfaction of seeing her lose her dignity before the staff.

Besides, her people would be loyal to her no matter what Squire Arrogance told her to say, so it wouldn't hurt to acquiesce to his wishes.

With a quick nod, she faced the staff. He settled his hand once again on the back of her waist, and the slight pressure of his fingers against her rigid spine made her more aware than ever of the reality of their marriage. If only he were touching her with the tenderness of a husband who cared for his wife.

But his touch was only to control, to aim her in the direction he wanted. And for now, his direction was the only one to take. So with a ragged sigh, she did as he'd asked and announced to the servants her marriage, putting as much sincerity into her tale as she could muster while she fought to ignore the warm hand fitted familiarly into the small of her back.

As soon as she finished, he spoke. "None of you need fear for your positions as long as I find you're doing your jobs well. However, there may be changes in the way the household is managed, depending on what I discover when I tour the grounds and meet with the housekeeper and agent. As a minimum, there will be additions to the staff. In the meantime, if you have a question about the running of the household, you are to come to me, not to my wife. Is that understood?''

When the servants nodded, cowed by his commanding stance and firm voice, Juliana groaned. Must he imply that she might have been mismanaging the estate? And must he humiliate her so in front of her own servants?

Aye, she realized, it was all part of his infernal quest for vengeance—to make her powerless in her own house. Well, she did want peace, as she'd said, but she wouldn't let him tear down everything that was good in Llynwydd out of peevishness. And if that appeared to be his plan, she'd fight him tooth and nail to prevent it.

"That's all for now," Rhys told the servants. He pointed to two footmen. "You and you, unload the coach. And Mrs. Roberts, I need a word with you. The rest of you are dismissed.''

Their faces mirroring their questions, the servants nonetheless obeyed Rhys and returned to their duties, except Mrs. Roberts who stood watching her mistress expectantly.

Rhys frowned when he noticed the direction of the older woman's gaze, but merely told her, "I wish to see you and the agent in the study in an hour. Bring with you all the books and whatever other papers you think might need my perusal.''

With a curt nod, Mrs. Roberts too was gone, and Juliana was left alone with Rhys.

"Shall we go in now, *fy mhriod*?" Rhys asked.

His triumphant smirk made her want to slap him, but she resisted the urge as she hurried up the entrance stairs. She had to get away from this public place before she lost her temper. She managed to keep her temper long enough to enter the house she'd called home for so long, the home now usurped by the devilish Welshman at her side.

But as soon as they passed into the drawing room, she pivoted away from him, eyes glittering. "I think you should know something before you start changing everything to suit your fancy. Ever since I've been managing this estate, it has gained steadily in profits, and that was no small feat. Your father left this place sorely run-down and destitute. If it hadn't been for me—''

"I know." Turning to a nearby table covered with a yellow stuff cloth, he whisked off the cover, then drew his leather gloves off one finger at a time and dropped them on the marble-topped surface. "I know Father ran this estate into the ground. He gambled too much, and he drank too much. After his death, I had planned to restore it to its former glory once I took it back from your father." His smile faded and his tone grew acid. "Of course, my impressment altered that plan, for a while anyway."

He pivoted, folding his hands behind his back as he scanned the room. Although the furniture was still covered with white and yellow cloths, she knew he must notice the new Chinese-patterned wallpaper and the fireplace, whose chipped sandstone facade had been replaced with black marble.

"Yes, I can see you've done much to restore the place. And for that, I'm in your debt." His gaze snapped back to her. "But 'tis my estate now, and *I* will see to its care. Which may require some changes."

"Fine," she clipped out. Let him think he was running the estate, the blasted fool. Once his back was turned, each of her servants would find some way to ask her in private what to do. And she'd have no qualms at all about telling them.

Aye, Squire Arrogance, we'll see how far you get trying to run this estate without me.

At her continued silence, a small frown creased his forehead. "You act as if this surprises you. But surely you'd anticipated what would happen upon my return." He cast her a mocking smile. "After all, you told me that you waited for me those first few years. Hadn't you realized I would take charge of my estate upon my return?" His smile faded. "Or were you so sure I'd never come back that you didn't consider that?"

She flushed at his nasty words, but caught herself before she could react in anger. Anger did her no good, she reminded herself, thinking of her resolution that morning.

Truth seemed to work better. She tilted her chin up at him and forced her voice to soften. "Whenever I thought of your return, I imagined your knocking at the door and my opening it. I imagined your taking me in your arms and kissing me until I ached from it, then recounting all your hardships so I could soothe them away." When he looked taken aback by her words, she added, "I confess that my dream never passed much beyond that."

His gaze locked with hers, and it took all her strength to meet its intimidating force. He stepped closer until he stood only inches from her, a myriad of emotions flitting over his face—disbelief, confusion . . . desire.

The last seemed to fill his face. "Your dream never passed beyond kissing?" Lifting his hand, he stroked her cheek with the backs of his hair-roughened fingers.

The unexpected caress gave a turn to her words that she hadn't entirely intended. Shivers coursed down her spine, then radiated outward into a cursed trembling. Oh, bother, there it was again, that same longing he'd always made her feel. Why hadn't six years crushed it to bits? Why did he alone hold the key to her desire?

A distinctive urge toward self-preservation hit her, and she backed away, but he caught her around the waist, drawing her to him until he'd fitted her snugly against his lean, hard body. "I *have* been lax, haven't I?" he whispered, nuzzling her temple. "Already I've been with you several hours, and I haven't yet kissed you."

Before she could protest that she didn't *want* him to kiss her, he bent his head to touch his lips to hers. After last night's near assault, she expected a brutal kiss. But this was the sheerest caress, a whisper of his lips against hers.

Confused by the change in him, she stood completely motionless, her eyes wide. He took advantage of her astonishment to brush his mouth over hers, meeting her lips then sliding away, enticing her with his gentle playing, but never quite settling in one place. His hot breath mingled with hers until she lowered her defenses, her body going limp and her eyelids sinking shut.

As soon as her eyes closed, he settled his mouth upon hers, covering it with a warmth almost too intense to bear. Her pulse raced, her breath caught in her chest, and she realized she was sinking fast, falling into the quicksand of seduction he'd always been so good at creating. But when she tried to draw away, to resist him, he captured her head between his two hands, holding her still.

Then the kiss began in earnest, for he brought his thumbs down to caress her throat as his mouth fed on hers, coaxing her to soften. In a sensuous invitation to deepen the kiss, he ran the tip of his tongue along the seam of her closed lips.

I must stop this. I can't let him do this, she thought dimly. But it was all too much like the dream she'd spoken of. With a silent sigh, she parted her lips, then heard him groan as he buried his tongue in the waiting warmth of her mouth.

Her own groan she quickly stifled. But she couldn't stifle the wealth of memories he conjured up in her as he drove his tongue into her mouth over and over, marking his possession of her as surely as he'd marked his possession of Llynwydd only moments ago.

As his hand slid down to clasp her shoulders and hold her tight against him, six years melted away—six long, lonely years. Once again they were in her bedchamber at Northcliffe Hall. Once again he was kissing her for endless hot hours and touching her with brazen caresses that had made her young, virginal body sing.

Now, however, his caresses were far bolder. Clutching her waist with one hand, he used the other to cover her breast, kneading it, rolling it beneath his palm. Despite the layers of clothing that separated her from his intimate touch, she could feel her nipple harden.

This time, she couldn't restrain her groan. And her groan brought an answering one from him. His hand stroked down to cup her bottom and thrust her against him so she could feel his arousal. "Ah, *cariad,*" he murmured against her mouth. "You see what you do to me?"

The spoken endearment shot her own arousal to new heights. He *did* care, no matter what he said. He *was* still hers. She threw her hands about his neck and gave herself up to him, to the poetry of his mouth plundering hers in an ancient rhythm more compelling than that of the bards, to the sweet slide of his hands relearning every contour of her body.

Before she knew it, he was drawing aside the robings of her dimity Levite gown and inching down the lace-trimmed edge of her shift to bare her breast to his fingers. Then his mouth left hers to trail kisses down her throat as he flicked his thumb over her nipple until she whimpered, arching her head back to give him better access.

She was waiting breathlessly for the first touch of his mouth on her breast when a knock at the open door behind her brought her to her senses.

Dear heaven, they'd been kissing here in front of God and everybody! she thought in a panic as a violent blush stained her cheeks. Ducking her head, she pushed away from him, and he released her reluctantly.

Then he fixed whoever stood in the open doorway with a fierce gaze. "What is it?"

Fumbling to pull her bodice up over her breasts, she half turned to peek at who stood there. It was one of the younger footmen, David, who appeared to be blushing almost as furiously as she. David had a tendency to knock first, and look later. He would undoubtedly be cured of that after this, she thought wryly.

"I—I'm sorry, sir," the hapless footman stammered, "but I—I wasn't sure where to put the trunks."

"You haven't forgotten where the State Bedroom is, have you?" Rhys bit out.

The young man looked crestfallen by the reproof. His head bobbed furiously. "Of course not, sir. But I didn't know if . . . well, I mean, milady has been sleeping there and—"

"Put *all* the trunks in the State Bedroom. From now on, Lady Juliana will be sleeping there with me."

David's head bobbed again and he fled.

As soon as the doorway was clear, Juliana blurted out, "Did you have to be . . . to imply . . . oh, heavens, they'll think that—"

"That I plan to share a bed with my wife?" Rhys raised one eyebrow in amusement. "I should hope they'd realize that."

"But what kind of woman will they think I am, to . . . to share a bed with you the night after I'd pledged to marry Stephen?"

When his amused expression abruptly faded, she cursed herself. What a stupid thing to say.

Pivoting away from her, he moved to the door and

shut it. When he faced her once more, the expression on his face could have frozen fire. "They'll think you're my *wife,* and not the fiancée of some *uffernol* marquéss, I assure you. They'll think I plan to *bed* my wife. Because that's precisely what I intend to do. Thoroughly and often. Beginning tonight."

Thoroughly and often. She ruthlessly suppressed the thrill his words gave her. "I won't share a bed with you, Rhys. If you wish to have the State Bedroom, you may, but I won't share a bed with you. There are plenty of other rooms I can sleep in."

He settled an enigmatic gaze on her. "I don't condone the new fashion of husbands and wives sleeping and dressing apart. My parents slept in that bed together, and so shall we." Reaching out to skim the tip of his finger over the upper swells of her breasts, he lowered his voice to a silky murmur. "Besides, you know you want to share a bed with me. Don't deny you were willing just now. I daresay if I'd laid you down on that settee, you'd have been willing enough."

The crudeness and complete self-assurance of his words shattered her hopes for peace between them. He saw her only as a receptacle for his urges, and not as a wife. "Perhaps I would have. But we'll never know, will we? Because next time I won't be so foolish." She ignored the hurt that snaked its way through her insides. She'd deal with that later.

"If you're wise, you'll use that beautiful body of yours to make amends, to soften my heart." He dragged his finger up her throat along the pulse, which quickened immediately. "I'm very interested in seeing if our last joining was everything I remembered."

"Why?" She lowered her eyes, unable to meet his probing gaze. "I don't understand you. Last night you couldn't bear to kiss me and today . . ."

"I want you, Juliana." He tilted her chin up, forcing her to look at him. "I couldn't take you by force, so I'll take you willing. But one way or the other, I'll have you in my bed."

Blast him! To him, bedding her meant conquering her. But she wanted it to mean so much more. "You would make love to me even though you think I'm foolish and fickle? Though you think I betrayed you?"

His mouth went taut. "One thing has nothing to do with the other. Fickle you may be, but you're also beautiful and enticing. And you know how to appreciate pleasure. Why shouldn't we appreciate it together? I'm willing. And no matter what you claim, you're willing."

Rubbing his thumb along her lower lip, he watched her with a secretive smile.

And despite herself, her breath quickened. Oh, yes. She certainly was willing. One touch, and like tinder held to a spark, she erupted into flame. He knew it, too. But that didn't change anything.

"What if I say I'm not?" she whispered. "What if I resist you? Will you then resort to force again?"

His eyes glittered blue as the icy waters of the Towy. "Nay, I've no need for that. You won't resist me forever, I assure you. You're not a skittish eighteen-year-old anymore, and I'm not a hesitant young man. You burn as much as I do. And as you said this morning, we have many years ahead of us. Even you can't hold out for an eternity. One day you'll say yes."

"I won't," she protested.

"You will." Confident in his position, he released her chin, stepping away from her toward the door. Then he paused to look back at her, his face determined. "And I'm betting you'll do it soon. Very soon."

When he passed through the door, she released the breath she'd been holding and sank into the nearest covered chair, her heart pounding.

Pray heaven he was wrong. Because if he came to her as he had the night of their wedding and made love to her like that, it wouldn't matter to her what awful things he believed about her. She'd be lost forever.

Chapter Thirteen

"Maybe so sharp is exile,
  Not to love were more worth while."
          —Goronwy Owen,
            "The Invitation"

Looking up from the ledger, Rhys rubbed his tired eyes, wondering if he should close the windows and call for someone to light a fire in the grate. The room was growing chill and dim as nightfall approached. Soon it would be time for dinner. And after dinner, then bed. . . .

"*Uffern-dân,*" he muttered as he clenched his thighs.

He slammed the ledger shut. For two hours he'd pored over the records, studying the management practices of his lovely wife. And in that time, he'd learned two disturbing things.

One, despite her youth and inexperience, Juliana had run the estate as efficiently as she'd claimed.

Two, he could think of nothing else but bedding her.

The last disturbed him more than the first, for judging from their last encounter, he wouldn't be bedding her anytime soon.

He hadn't meant to be so abrupt with her, so obvious about what he wanted. Women didn't like being told they were wanted only for their physical attributes. He'd planned to be smoother than that, to seduce her with compliments, even use poetry as he had years ago when he'd been a starry-eyed fool in love.

But when she'd mentioned her beloved Stephen and reacted in such horror to the idea of sharing a bedchamber . . . Damn it all, he'd hastened to remind her that she was *his* wife and not Lord Devon's fiancée.

With a low curse, he rose to pace the room like a miner trapped in the shaft he'd hollowed himself. Why couldn't he do as he wanted with her? He couldn't force her, and his attempt at seduction had ended with her even more determined to fight him. She wanted him. He knew it. And God knows he wanted her.

Why did he desire her so? She'd asked him that. And she had a good point. Why did he want her even though she'd taken six years of his life from him?

Because the damned woman intrigued him. She had defied all of his expectations. He'd expected her to be either frightened of him or penitent. He'd expected her to throw herself on his mercy. Many an hour he'd spent envisioning the penance he'd require of her before he allowed her a wife's privileges, and each scenario had included his bedding her in various enjoyable ways.

In none of his dreams had she stood firm in declaring her innocence. In none of his dreams had she refused to share his bed. It drove him mad.

She was an absolute enigma, even more so than when he'd first known her. For one thing, she'd obviously put her life and soul into caring for Llynwydd. He'd not expected to find her living at his former estate, and certainly not improving it. True, it belonged to her, but few women controlled the properties that belonged to them. Why had she chosen to do so? Merely to be sure it would garner her a titled husband?

Or for some other reason.

Slowly, he turned to survey the study. Little had changed in it from all those times when he'd spent his holiday leave trying to put to rights what his father had neglected. The desk of mahogany inlaid with brass was as sturdy as ever, and the Indian rug, though faded, still had many serviceable years left. The brass fender and irons were polished to a fine sheen, and the walnut wainscotting had been swept clean of dust and cobwebs.

There were some additions to the room—a cast-iron fireback, some walnut chairs ... and a small stepladder that sat at the end of one of the mahogany bookcases, a concession to Juliana's short height, no doubt. He scanned the shelves at that spot, noting that they didn't contain the same volumes on estate management that graced the other shelves. There were novels by Fielding and Richardson as well as several volumes of poetry by an assortment of poets, Welsh and English—Donne, Pope, Dafydd Jones. . . .

Suddenly, he caught sight of a gilded cover farther down the shelf, and his eyes narrowed. Curious, he moved closer to examine the spine. He removed that book and several others, opening their covers to find his name printed on the flyleaves.

My books, he thought. *But how?*

These books had not been at Llynwydd when he'd left. They'd been from his own private collection at Morgan's house, where he'd lived briefly before his impressment. Had Juliana brought them here? And why?

Of course, she appreciated fine books as much as he did, and his collection was fine enough to meet anyone's standards. Still, the image of her going to Morgan's house and packing away his belongings gave him pause. If she'd believed him out of her life forever, why had she bothered with something like that?

Juliana's words came back to him—*No matter what they say, I loved you then. I wanted to be your wife.*

Rhys sucked in his breath. Yet she'd hidden her marriage from the beginning. She'd come here as mistress and never told anyone, not even the staff, that she had a husband. She'd tried to marry again, for God's sake!

But everything she'd told him that morning pressed into his mind, and he found himself seeking allowances for her behavior, reminding himself of her youth, of how easily her brothers might have manipulated her into doing the wrong thing.

A sobering thought struck him. Perhaps the truth lay somewhere between her version and Northcliffe's. Perhaps she'd balked at the marriage and summoned her brothers, but then had been pressured by them into letting him be impressed. He could understand why she wouldn't want to admit to that.

It didn't matter anyway. No matter how much complicity she'd had in setting him aboard that ship, she'd still been the one to instigate it all. And then she'd blithely proceeded with her life as if he'd never existed. She'd betrothed herself to a wealthy English nobleman.

And yet . . . Like a curse, her words played in his head once more, and he replaced the books on the shelf, wishing he knew how to find his way through this morass of lies and half-truths.

The sound of laughter wafted up through the open window. Curious, he went to the window and planted his hand on the sill, leaning forward to look out at the pleasure garden below, only to find the very object of all his torments just beneath his window.

Still wearing her fetching dimity gown, Juliana was kneeling in the grass to clip roses and place them in a basket.

And the basket was held by a child.

Rhys caught his breath painfully until he realized that the boy with her had to be at least eleven. No child of his, that was sure. Or of hers either.

Then the child spoke in the lilting Welsh of a commoner, and Rhys strained closer, just able to make out the words.

"So you've come back to Llynwydd for good?" the boy asked.

She smiled at him, the kind of smile Rhys suddenly realized he wanted her to give *him*. "Are you pleased, Evan?"

Her exquisite Welsh once more took Rhys by surprise. It didn't fit with his image of a pampered English lady who balked at marrying a penniless Welsh radical.

The boy named Evan ducked his head, digging at the dirt with his bare toe. "I suppose. Are you?"

His voice sounded so hopeful that she leaned over and kissed his cheek with a laugh. "Of course I am. I love Llynwydd. And I missed having you help me in the garden."

Stabbing his toe deeper into the dirt, Evan reddened. "Mama said I shouldn't come and bother you just now, but I thought . . . well, you might need me about . . . you know, to carry things and kill bugs."

An amused expression passed over Juliana's face. "And I bet you were curious to know why I'd come back."

"We *were* surprised, my lady. I mean, you said you weren't coming back for a while. Then this afternoon, Mrs. Roberts came and told Mama you were here with a husband, but not that man you went off to marry."

Juliana's lips tightened as she stared blindly at the wall. "Mrs. Roberts is certainly quick, isn't she?"

He looked at her quizzically. "Do you think so? I don't. She's too old to be quick."

Rhys stifled a laugh. He'd judge Mrs. Roberts to be in her mid-thirties, and no doubt proud of her limber legs. But to an eleven-year-old, of course, thirty was ancient.

When Juliana merely smiled, Evan grew fidgety. "So. Did you bring a different husband back or not?"

With a sigh, Juliana rose from her kneeling position. "Yes, I brought back a different husband."

"Is he another stuffy Englishman like that Lord Devon?"

"Not hardly." A strange, uncertain expression passed over her face. Then she began to stroll down the walk toward the garden door as Evan followed behind her. "Do you remember the man I told you about? The one who went to sea?"

Rhys leaned half out of the window, straining to hear their words.

"Mr. Vaughan?" Evan asked.

"Aye."

" 'Tis he who is my husband."

Evan said something in response, but by then they were too far for Rhys to make out what they were saying. With a frown, he drew back from the window.

She'd told the boy about him? Why? Why had she kept her knowledge of him secret from an entire staff, yet revealed it to a stripling of a lad? And how much had she told the boy?

Suddenly, he heard footsteps approaching the study and realized from the voices that Juliana and Evan were coming his way. The door opened, and he slid into the shadows as a perverse urge to continue his eaves-dropping assailed him.

"I have the paper here somewhere," Juliana was saying as they entered. " 'Tis a shame it was spoiled by water like that. Are you sure you won't have some un-spoiled paper?" She went to the desk and opened a drawer, rummaging about in it.

"Nay, the spoilt paper will be jolly fine, thanks." A wistful expression on his face, Evan sighed the heavy sigh of the young. "If Father saw me with good paper, he'd take a brush to me. Long as I tell him I got paper from the rubbish heap, he lets me keep it, 'cause he thinks 'tis spoilt for anything but playing with. But good paper would make him suspicious. He'd ask what I was doing with it and make me tell him the truth."

"The truth?" Juliana drew the paper out, her face tight with anger. "That you're studying and writing? That you're bettering yourself? Why shouldn't he know that?"

Evan lifted solemn eyes to her. "Father says there's no use in me taking lessons. He says I'll have to help my brother run the farm one day, and I shouldn't waste my time with foolishness like lessons." He folded the paper reverently and slid it into his grimy pocket.

"You know better, don't you?"

He ducked his head, but nodded.

She put her arm on his thin shoulder. "You ought to be in school, you know. You've got a superior mind that would benefit from schooling."

The boy shrugged. "Father won't let me go. He needs me at the farm. He only lets me come here 'cause he thinks I'm helping you with the garden." A worried look passed over his face. "And he told me to be back before dark, so I best go."

"Perhaps if I spoke to your father—"

"No!" The word was almost frantic as he turned a pleading gaze on her. "Please don't, my lady. 'Twill only get me into trouble."

When Juliana sighed, he pulled away from her, headed toward the door. But he stopped there and looked back, outright adoration shining in his eyes. "I thank you for the paper. 'Tis kind of you to do such things for the likes of me."

"I don't do it for kindness, Evan." She smiled. "I do it because you're my friend. And you know if you ever need anything, you can come to me. All right?"

He grinned. "Aye, my lady. I'll do that."

Then he was out the door.

Rhys watched as she stared after the boy with longing, and his throat felt suddenly tight and dry. The desire for a child was blatant on her face. Would she be a good mother? he wondered.

A foolish question. After seeing her with the Welsh boy, he knew she would be.

Watching her, seeing her so soft and gentle with a child when she bore nothing but distaste for Rhys, made him briefly wish he'd gone about everything differently and hadn't made her his enemy from the outset.

He curled his fingers into his palm. He'd merely behaved as anyone would have who'd been betrayed by his wife. Damn it all, he hadn't beaten her. He hadn't divorced her. She ought to be glad of that.

But she didn't look glad. She looked ... lost. There was no other word for it. With a sigh so heavy it wrenched at him, she turned to the desk, standing beside it as she ran her hand along the ledger, then studied the papers he'd laid out there. Her face grew tighter as she saw what he'd been working on.

He shifted his feet and made some little noise in the process. She lifted her gaze.

And saw him standing in the shadows.

"Dear heaven!" she cried as she jumped back and lifted her hand to her throat.

When he stepped forward into the dim light leaking from the window, she released a breath. "Blast it, Rhys, you gave me a start! I didn't realize you were here."

"I ..." He trailed off, uncertain how to explain his eavesdropping. Instead he changed the subject. "Who's the boy?"

She looked confused a moment before her face cleared. "Oh, you mean Evan. He's the son of one of your tenant farmers, Thomas Newcome."

He nodded. "I remember Thomas. A bit of a hothead, isn't he?"

"Aye. And he doesn't at all understand the value of an education."

" 'Tis common for a farmer to feel that lessons are a waste of time."

"I know. But Evan isn't merely a farmer's son. He's exceptionally bright. Before I started tutoring him, he didn't read and write at all, and spoke only Welsh. But in the four years since then, he has not only learned to read and write Welsh, but English and French as well. And he has begun to learn Greek."

"Greek?" he said in astonishment. "And French, too? My God, how old is the boy?"

"Twelve. It's amazing, isn't it? He has this facility for languages that's nothing short of fantastic." She wrung her hands. "And it's all wasted, thanks to that father of his."

Rhys rubbed his chin. "Perhaps we should find a way to convince Mr. Newcome that his son would benefit from schooling. Surely we can come up with something that won't get the boy into trouble."

She regarded him warily. "You would do that?"

"Of course. It's to my advantage to have my tenants as well educated as possible."

He was rewarded for that statement with a brilliant smile that took him back to the first time he'd seen her smiling at him from the audience at the Sons of Wales meeting. God, but the woman had a rich, enticing smile.

"If you could get Evan into school, 'twould mean a great deal to me," she was saying, her eyes bright with enthusiasm.

"I can see that. The boy is important to you. Do you mind if I ask why?"

"Evan has been my special charge ever since the gardener caught him stealing plums from the orchard. The gardener brought him to me here for a reprimand." She laughed as she began to stroll about the study. "Instead, we ended up talking about all the books in your library. He was terribly impressed. So I told him that his 'punishment' was to come every day for a month for a lesson in reading. After that ... well, he's been coming here a few days a week ever since. I pay him a small sum to help me in the garden, and then I spend much of the time teaching him. His father is pleased to have his son working for 'her ladyship,' and Evan gets an education, spotty though it is."

He drew in a heavy breath. This Juliana bore no resemblance to the timid, fickle woman he'd despised all these years. "That was very generous of you."

At the soft timbre of his voice, she stopped short near one of the bookshelves as a flush of pleasure lit her face. But she wouldn't look at him. "Not at all. As you said, 'twas to my advantage to have the tenants well educated."

"Was it also to your advantage to run my estate with care and efficiency?"

The change of subject seemed to startle her. Nervously, she ran her gloved finger along one of the bookshelves as if testing it for cleanliness. "What do you mean?"

"Why did you work so hard to maintain Llynwydd? I've been over the books. I've talked at length with Mrs. Roberts and your agent, Geoffrey Newns, and they both made it clear that you've succeeded in reversing the trend my father began. Why?"

A bitter smile tipped up her lips as she faced him. "It's my dower estate, isn't it? I had to keep it in prime condition for my husband-to-be, didn't I?"

"I thought of that." When a mutinous look crossed her face, he added, "But you could have done it from afar through Newns, and you didn't." His eyes never leaving hers, he gestured toward the bookshelves that contained his books. "You certainly didn't have to gather my belongings at Morgan's house and bring them here. Yet you did. Why?"

In the fading light, her skin was like softly burnished ivory and her hair the color of fine cherry wood as she held his gaze boldly, almost defiantly. "You know why. You simply don't want to believe the evidence of your eyes."

As he stood there, uncertain how to respond to that, she dragged her gaze from his and went to the door. "I'll see you at dinner," she murmured without turning to look at him.

Then she was gone, leaving him with nothing but an ache in his chest and a hundred new questions.

None of which were liable to have answers.

Feeling as jittery as a girl at her coming out, Juliana waited in the dining room for Rhys to appear. She paced to one end of the table, straightening a silver fork here, a china plate there. Everything looked perfect.

She'd been uncertain what to do about dinner. Serve him a dinner to remember, the kind an exile would enjoy? Or serve him gruel in a petty attempt to repay him for his distrust of her? In the end, her craving for peace and her pride in Llynwydd won out over her more vindictive instincts. Why not let him see how wonderful it would be when all was in harmony? Then if he kept baiting and tormenting her, he'd know what he was missing when she retaliated.

She and Mrs. Roberts had picked each item of the evening's menu to include as many native Welsh dishes as possible, since Cook, a holdover from the old staff, had said, "Master Rhys always did like his *caws pobi* and his *cawl*." The table was set with the finest china and silver and a lace cloth. She'd instructed the staff to be on their best behavior, to prove themselves as competent as she'd told Rhys they were.

She'd even dressed with particular care, the way Darcy had insisted they dress for dinner at Northcliffe, instead of the casual way she usually dressed at Llynwydd. Accordingly, she was wearing her periwinkle gown of Jacquard striped silk and her best embroidered stomacher. She'd even had one of the maids put up her hair, something she rarely did.

With a smile, she touched her hand to her hair. She would show Rhys she could be a proper wife when she wanted.

But what if he didn't care? What if he were surly and critical? Or what if she'd misjudged everything and he didn't want Welsh fare? She glanced around the room. What if he didn't approve of the way she'd refurbished the dining room?

If he didn't, that was his loss, she told herself, squaring her shoulders. If he couldn't appreciate all her efforts for this dinner, then he truly was a boorish, unmannerly beast and there'd never be peace between them.

A grim smile crossed her face. If that happened, she'd serve the gruel.

But it wouldn't happen, would it? This afternoon he'd shown he could be fair when he wanted. In fact, their encounter in the library had cheered her a great deal. There did seem to be a rational man beneath that unreasoning exterior. A man whose pride was suffering, true. Yet he did seem to be trying to make sense out of what had happened, instead of blindly believing Darcy's lies. Perhaps peace between them wasn't so impossible after all.

"I'm not too late, am I?" rumbled a voice from the doorway.

Her heart fluttered. He was here. Clamping down on her sudden nervousness, she faced him with a smile, determined to set a tone of pleasant cordiality.

Her obvious congeniality seemed to startle him, but then he responded with the same devastating smile that had once captured her heart. "You look lovely this evening," he murmured as he walked toward her. "That color suits you."

Embarrassed by the unexpected compliment, she ducked her head. He stopped close to her and then, to her surprise, took her hand and kissed the back of it.

But he didn't release her hand right away. Instead, he turned it to brush his firm lips along the inside of her wrist, making her quiver to her toes.

"Very lovely," he added as he lifted his head.

She forced herself to meet his eyes and instantly regretted it, for his gaze seared her with a heat that started a fire in her belly. Oh, bother, she thought. Why does he do this to me?

"Y-you look very well yourself," she stammered, completely unnerved.

" 'Well'?" He raised an eyebrow. "You'll make me vain with such extravagant praise."

His flirtatious words reminded her of the old Rhys, the one who'd teased her the first time they'd met. And he still hadn't released her hand.

"Then I'd best watch my compliments, hadn't I?" she said lightly. "We must keep you modest. We can't have you strutting about in fuchsia breeches like those fops in the Macaroni Club."

He laughed. Lacing her fingers through his, he drew her to her seat at the end of the table. After seating her, he strode back to his place at the head of the table as she watched him, fascinated.

For the first time since last night, he looked entirely relaxed. And her comment about his dress had truly done him no justice. He'd changed into evening dress much like he'd worn the night before at her engagement party, and now, as then, the tight satin breeches and perfectly tailored coat accentuated his muscular thighs and shoulders. His years of hard labor at sea had reshaped his body, adding bulk to his chest and arms and legs, although they had thinned his face. Where once he'd been like a rapier, lean and deft, now he was a sword. Which probably explained why she found him so much more intimidating than before.

And yet more handsome, too. The lines etched in his face took away whatever hints of youthful indecision had been there before, and his hair gleamed blue-black in the candlelight. It was his own hair tied back in a queue, and she couldn't help being glad that he eschewed the fashion that would have had him wear a powdered wig and redden his cheeks with rouge.

A Macaroni he could never be, thank heaven.

"The Americans have a song about the Macaronis, you know," he said as he reached his seat. "It's called 'Yankee Doodle Dandy.' I heard it sung in a tavern once before a battle."

He rang the bell to signal it was time to serve dinner, then settled himself in his chair with a great deal of relish.

"How does it go?" she asked, wanting to keep him in this amiable mood. Besides, she was genuinely curious about America.

Eyes twinkling, he sang for her a song about a man on a pony, and as he sang, she could almost envision him in a colonial tavern, singing what was clearly a call to arms. Poor Rhys. Unable to sing about Wales, he'd been forced to sing about another country's quest for freedom. How had it felt to be exiled from his home, to be the pawn of first one people and then another, neither of them his own?

The thought of it disturbed her. Surely he had some right to feel angry at her for the crimes committed against him, even if they'd been crimes of her brother's making. After all, if he hadn't met her, he wouldn't have been impressed. If he hadn't dared to love a woman above him, he'd never have known exile.

The door opened and the servant brought in the *cawl*, setting a bowl of the hot soup at each of their places as Rhys broke off his song.

After the servant whisked out of the room, Rhys looked down into the bowl, and his smile faded. He stared a long moment into the steamy liquid with the traditional blossoms of marigold floating in it.

Oh, dear, she thought, *he hates* cawl. *I should never have listened to Cook.*

Then he lifted his head. "Do you know how long it's been since I've had Cook's *cawl?*"

Trying not to show her relief, she kept her voice light. "Six years?"

"More. I was abroad for the Grand Tour, remember, when Llynwydd . . . changed hands."

She nodded.

He ate a spoonful while she held her breath. But she let it out in one long sigh when a blissful expression passed over his face. He swallowed, then flashed her a smile. "Double her wages. Give her whatever she wants, but make sure she serves *cawl* at every meal from now until doomsday."

Juliana couldn't keep the delight out of her laugh. She'd have to kiss Cook. Double her wages? It was worth that to see his face light up. And to hear him speak to her as a partner in their marriage, not a penitent.

"Am I to understand," she quipped, "that *cawl* was not a regular item on the menu in America?"

He tore off a piece of bread and dipped it in his soup. "Not in America *or* the navy." When her face fell, he seemed to regret his mention of the navy, for he added lightly, "But there were other interesting dishes in America."

"Oh?" She ate a spoonful of soup. "Like what?"

"Clam chowder, for one," he said between mouthfuls. " 'Tis merely clams in a cream soup, but the Americans add some sort of spice . . . anyway, when they get through with it, 'tis a delicious dish if the right cook does it."

She dropped her spoon, all thought of eating forgotten. "And who cooked it for you?" she asked, remembering all those women he'd said had shared his bed.

He seemed not to notice the sudden sharp tone in her voice. "My landlady most of the time. I lived in a boarding house when I wasn't at sea. That's how I saved so much of my money." He swallowed some *cawl,* then flashed her a grin. "You should have seen this terror of a woman. Gray-haired and pug-faced, she'd have made two of you, and if anyone entered her kitchen, she threw them out with one huge fist. Chambermaids, footmen, soldiers—they were all mincemeat once she got hold of them. But the woman did know how to cook. That I'll give her."

She relaxed. Somehow she couldn't see Rhys sharing a bed with an Amazon like that. "Tell me about your time in America. I've only read about the colonies, and I've always wondered if the truth is as intriguing as the stories."

He shot her an amused glance. "Are you serious? You really want to hear about America?"

"Aye. I want to hear it all."

He shrugged. "All right. What do you want to know?"

The next hour passed in a pleasant haze. Once she'd gotten him started, Rhys had been more than happy to tell her about the colonials. To her they sounded like a hodgepodge people—the English-speaking Dutch of the Hudson Valley, the Scots in North Carolina, the warring tribes of Indians, and the English themselves, some of whom were loyal to their mother country and some of whom hated it. He'd traveled up and down the coast of America in his privateering, and had seen more unusual things in his three years than she'd seen in a lifetime.

Courses came and went—lampreys in galantine, roast goose, boiled leeks with bacon, and preserved apricots—but she scarcely tasted a bite. Instead, she hung breathlessly on Rhys's every word about men who painted their bodies and went half-naked into battle, about wooden stockades and dense forests and rich fields tilled by slaves.

"It sounds so wild," she said as he finished his second serving of *caws pobi,* the toasted cheese on bread that the Welsh were so fond of. "How do people raise families and have peaceful lives with Indians whooping down about their heads?"

He chuckled as he wiped his mouth. "I'm afraid I've given you as distorted a look of America as the books. But 'tis your fault, you know. You were such a good audience that I was driven to exaggerate. Actually, 'tis only wild in the untamed forests that are well inland. Life in the coastal cities and along the plantations is quite civilized. People go to the theater and to church, children attend school every day ... it's not as different from Wales—or England—as you might think."

Just then the servant brought in an elaborate puff pastry that Juliana knew Cook had been working on ever since their arrival. Rhys gestured to it with a laugh. "Though I must say I've not seen a pastry as ornate as that in America. Obviously, Cook is still outdoing herself."

As the servant set the pastry down and began to cut servings, Rhys's expression grew serious. He settled back in his chair and drank deeply of his wine, looking very lordly in his fine clothes as his gaze lingered over her. For a brief instant, she was reminded of the night before when he'd thought to take her by force. But it was different tonight. Though he wore the arrogant expression of a man sure of what he owned, there was also invitation in his look tonight, invitation and promise.

He waited until they were both served, then set his wineglass down and leaned forward. "Cook wasn't the only one who outdid herself. This was truly a feast for an exile, Juliana. If I'd asked for every dish myself, I couldn't have chosen a better meal. You must have been preparing for this ever since we arrived."

His praise warmed her. Dropping her gaze to her plate, she said, "Believe it or not, I've been planning this meal for you ever since you left Wales. I thought surely that if ... when you returned, you would wish to have those dishes you'd been deprived of while you were ... abroad." She couldn't bring herself to mention the navy.

"Thank you." When she looked up, he added, in a gentle voice, "Thank you for caring that much. It wasn't what I ... actually, I didn't know what to expect."

He was being so truthful, she couldn't help saying, "After last night, I did consider serving you gruel, but Cook would have none of it. She wanted to amaze you with her talents."

With a laugh, he cut a bite of the pastry. But he didn't eat it. Instead he stared at her, his eyes growing thoughtful. "And you? Did you want to amaze me with your talents?"

She toyed with the piece of pastry puff on her plate. "Perhaps."

"I *am* suitably impressed, I assure you. But I was impressed before tonight, Juliana. With the house ... the furnishings ... the staff ... You've done well by me, even if it wasn't for me you were doing it."

She started to retort that it *had* been for him, that everything had been for him whether he believed it or not. Then she hesitated. Had it? Had it all been for him? Or had she done it to show her family she was more than some useless English noblewoman? Had she done it to prove her worth in a world where a woman was often only measured by her docility as a wife?

In truth, even before she'd been told he was dead, her pride in Llynwydd had ceased to be linked to her desire to make it thrive for him. As her hopes of seeing him again had faded, her thirst to improve Llynwydd had only increased. She'd truly found joy in making it a special place, both for her staff and the tenants. And none of that had anything to do with him.

Now, when she looked at him, it was with pride for what *she* had accomplished, what *she* had nurtured.

"For example," he said with a sweeping gesture that took in their surroundings, "I like what you've done to this room. 'Twas always far too dark for my tastes. With the lighter hangings and the paint, it's much cheerier than before. And less barren. It has more furniture, doesn't it?"

"Only that *cwpwrdd tridarn* there," she said, pointing to her pride and joy—a Welsh court cupboard made of mahogany with intricately carved doors.

He rose and went to stand beside it. "A fine piece of work. Where did you find it?"

"I commissioned it from a joiner in Carmarthen."

"It's very nice. I suppose you paid for it out of Llynwydd's profits?"

She shook her head. "Not exactly. I bought it before Llynwydd was doing very well, so I used my own allowance to pay for it."

Shifting his gaze to her, he looked at her as if she were a strange creature. "Your allowance? Did your father approve of that?"

"He didn't know. I used my portion on Llynwydd because *I* chose to do so."

"How much of your annual portion went to sustaining it?"

"Sometimes half. One year, two-thirds."

He moved toward her with a determined look on his face. "That was good of you, but it shall end now. You don't need to support Llynwydd anymore. I have ample money for that. I'd rather you spent your money on the usual things women buy—gowns, trinkets, jewelry—"

"I'd *rather* spend my money on Llynwydd." She rose from her chair. "There's still so much to be done, so much to buy."

"And I shall buy it. You needn't concern yourself with it anymore. If you want a piece of furniture, tell me, and I'll take care of it. Otherwise—"

"Otherwise, you'll do everything yourself, is that it?" Anger crept into her voice, despite her earlier vow to stay calm. "Why must you do it alone? I've proven I can take care of this estate without you, so surely you can allow me to do my part now. It's my estate, too. I won't sit in the drawing room and embroider all day when I could help you run Llynwydd."

His gaze darkened.

She forced herself to soften her tone. "I know you think to punish me by reducing me to a guest in my own home. But don't you see how foolish that is? Together we can do more good for our estate than you can do alone. And if we are to live as husband and wife—"

"Live as husband and wife?" He raised one eyebrow. "Ah, but therein lies the problem. You're my wife only when it suits you—in the study, in the kitchen. But not in the bedroom, eh?"

When she colored, his expression grew chilly for the first time that evening, and his voice became deceptively soft. "You directed the footmen this afternoon to move your belongings out of our bedchamber and into the Blue Room after I'd expressly forbidden it."

She stuck her trembling hands behind her back. She'd done that while he was touring the stables, and she'd instructed the footmen not to mention it to him. How had he known?

As if he'd heard her unspoken question, he said, "Remember, I told the servants to come to *me* when they had a question. They're not fools. They obeyed me.

They know who's master of this house. So they did as I told them and are moving your belongings right back as we speak."

Shaken by that, she started to turn from him, but he caught her arm, pulling her close until she stood mere inches away.

He bent his head until his lips almost touched her cheek. "So what's it to be, Juliana? You want the main privilege of a wife—to be mistress of her house. I'll admit you're good at it, and I'd find it intriguing to run this estate together. But only on one condition."

When he slid his arm about her waist and pressed a kiss to her hair, he made it completely clear what his condition would be. "Will you play the wife in every way to gain that privilege? Will you share my bed? Willingly?"

She ached to say yes, especially when he stood so close that she could easily remember what kissing him had felt like that morning. His breath against her cheek was warm and inviting and his hand at her waist rubbed enticingly along her ribs, tempting her to make the small shift of her body that would put her in his arms.

But she couldn't do it. If she let him buy her like this, she'd regret it, for it wasn't her he wanted, but her body. He wanted to treat her as a faithless betrayer at the same time he wanted to make love to her. If she gave in on this, she'd never make him see her worth.

"Nay," she whispered. "I won't share your bed until it means more than a conquest to you."

With a growl, he dropped her arm and whirled away from her. "Fine. Sleep wherever you like then. But prepare yourself for long days of embroidering and thumb-twiddling. Because you won't be mistress in this house until you're mistress to me."

And with that, he stormed out.

Chapter Fourteen

"All the old loves I followed once
Are now unfaithful found;
But a sweet sickness holds me yet
Of love that has no bound!"
—William Williams Pantycelyn,
"I gaze across the distant hills"

Darcy strode uneasily along the path to Lettice's cottage. After having received her note early today, he didn't know what to expect. She'd never asked him to come before. She'd always waited until his obsession got the better of him and he came to her. In fact, it was one of her most maddening, but appealing qualities—that she never needed him as badly as he needed her.

But today she'd summoned him, and instead of rushing over as he would have done if she'd ever summoned him before, he'd taken his time to respond.

Fear kept him from hastening to her. He could think of only a few reasons she might want to see him. None of them were good. Either Vaughan had spoken to her ... or brought some message from that scoundrel Pennant ... or ... He couldn't think about the last possibility. Morgan Pennant here in the flesh ... he wouldn't let himself even consider it.

As he picked his way up the winding path, now within sight of the lighted cottage windows, he wished he'd had more brandy before he'd come. He should have fortified himself better.

The place was ominously silent as he approached. Of course, Edgar would be in bed by now. But he could usually hear Lettice humming as she busied herself around the cottage. With his heart hammering in his chest, he walked up to the door and opened it, not bothering to knock.

The sight that greeted him struck him dumb. There was Lettice, *his* mistress, wrapped in the arms of another man. Darcy's stomach plummeted. He felt as if he'd come along a sunny walk and then stepped into a nightmare unprepared.

With a curse, he entered and slammed the door behind him. Instantly, Lettice jerked away from the other man, her eyes wide with guilt. A second passed before Darcy recognized the other man. Then rage scourged him. Pennant. A pox on him! He'd not only returned to Wales, he'd come straight to Lettice! And she'd welcomed him with open arms!

"Get out of my house!" he growled at Pennant. "Get out! You have no right to be here!"

Pennant blocked Lettice from his sight. "I have more right than you! 'Tis *my* woman and *my* son you've kept here with your lies!"

Darcy stood stunned into silence. *Edgar was Pennant's son? Why was the bastard saying that?*

Lettice thrust Pennant aside. "Be quiet, Morgan. I'll handle this in my own way."

"As you handled it before?" Pennant snapped. "Believing his lies and letting him take advantage of you? No. This won't go on any longer. There will be truth between us all now. I'll have it no other way."

He turned to fix Darcy with a fierce gaze. "Tell her the truth. She knows you had me impressed. Now tell her what you said about her six years ago. Tell her how you tried to destroy my love for her!"

Darcy cast about in his mind for some plausible tale, something that would keep her from hating him.

"Careful now," Pennant hissed. "If you lie, I swear I'll bring Vaughan into it. He was there. He heard everything you said, too, remember?"

Desperation clutched at Darcy. "Lettice, you mustn't listen to him. He and Vaughan have been spreading this mad tale that I—"

"Please, Darcy." Lettice stepped forward, tears shining in her eyes. "Please don't lie to me."

"You'd believe him over me? He wants you, damn him! He's always wanted you, and he doesn't care what he says if it'll bring you back to him!"

"Are you any different? You're lying to keep me, too."

He felt the room closing in on him. "Am I the only one who lied?" A painful pressure built in his chest. "You told me Edgar is mine. Pennant says the child is his. Which is the truth?"

She paled, and Pennant moved behind her, putting his arm about her shoulder. But she shook him off and moved to stand apart from both men.

"Is Edgar mine or not?" Darcy choked out. "You said you want the truth. I want the truth as well." When she hesitated, he added, "It won't make a difference to me either way, I swear it. I'll love the boy and care for him, no matter whose he is. But I want to know if he's mine!"

A pitying expression passed over her face, and he winced, feeling as if someone had just cleaved him in two. "He's not mine, is he?"

She shook her head. "I know I shouldn't have deceived you, but—"

"But you thought I was some stupid, lovesick fool who'd believe whatever you told me!" Anger made him want to hurt her. "You pretended to love me, didn't you, hoping all the while that one day your lover would return? Well, I pretended to help you, when it was me, yes, *me*, who sent your lover away!"

He stepped closer, unable to contain his rage. "Do you think I didn't see you pining for him when you thought I wasn't watching? Every time you asked if any mail had come for you at the house, I ached inside. I happily sent back the one letter that arrived from him. God, I hated him for having your heart! I despised him for it!"

"So you told me that she'd betrayed me," Pennant bit out. "You lied to me!"

"Yes, yes! I lied! I lied with great pleasure, seeing the love die a little in your eyes!"

When Lettice let out a sob, her face dark in her misery, he caught himself. God, he'd wanted to hurt her. But not destroy her. No matter what she'd done, he still loved her. She'd deceived him . . . she'd used him. And none of it mattered. He loved her.

He turned a pleading gaze on her. "You've got to understand, Lettice. I wanted you so badly. I—needed you. Yes, I lied, but it was a small lie, a necessary one. I knew he'd do anything to return unless he believed you unfaithful." His voice dropped to a whisper. "I know *I'd* have done anything."

"And did," she cried. "You told him horrible things about me, horrible, awful things!"

"Because I loved you! Because I wanted you for my own!"

"Yes," Pennant cut in, "but were those the only lies you told? You said a great many awful things about your sister as well, to separate her from Vaughan. You told Vaughan she'd gotten cold feet and backed out of the marriage, then urged you to have him taken by the press so she could be free of him."

Darcy groaned inwardly. *Deuce take the devil! Did he have to tell Lettice about that?*

Lettice looked stunned. "Did you truly say that? Did you lie like that?"

He dared not admit that he'd lied, for Pennant would go straight to Vaughan with it. And Vaughan wouldn't rest until he'd ruined the entire St. Albans family.

"Yes, I said that," he told them. "But it was the truth."

Lettice's eyes widened in shock. "Nay, I don't believe it! Your sister would never have done such a thing! Never!"

"This isn't your concern, Lettice." He prayed she wouldn't detect the shaking in his voice. "Juliana summoned me to the inn that night to rid herself of Vaughan, and I did so. That's what happened, whether you believe it or not."

Lettice shook her head, turning to Pennant. "She was so upset when she heard he'd been taken. She wasn't pretending. I know it! Don't believe his lies about this! Juliana would never do such an awful, terrible thing!"

Pennant stared at her, tenderness in his face. "If you say it, I believe you."

A painful knot tightened in Darcy's stomach. "Why? She lied to me about Edgar. She might be lying to you about this. It's not as if she's a complete innocent herself."

Lettice rounded on him, horror in her face. "And what do you mean by that?"

It tore at him to see her regard him as a traitor. He softened his tone. "I merely meant to point out that I haven't been taking care of you and Edgar without any reward. Pennant has come here, thinking to start again where the two of you left off six years ago, but he can't."

He turned to Pennant. "Lettice has shared my bed through six years of nights." He clenched his fists. "Through six years of days, she has looked to me for help, and I've cared for her. You won't erase that merely by whispering sweet promises in her ears."

Pennant's eyes blazed. "And what of your wife during those six years? What you shared with Lettice was only the crumbs of your life. I, on the other hand, want to share everything with her. I want to marry her and give her much more than you could."

That painful pressure in the chest came again. "She's mine. You can't have her!"

"She may have given you a great deal," Pennant continued, "but she never gave you her heart."

"You don't know that!"

Pennant opened his mouth to speak, but Lettice placed her hand on his arm, her face wet with tears. "Please, I can't bear this. You must leave, Morgan. I must speak to Darcy alone."

"Leave?" Pennant choked out.

"Yes, give me time to set things right."

Pennant clasped her hands. "How much time, Lettice? You said you'd be ready with your answer tonight."

"You've been here before?" Darcy roared, but the two of them ignored him.

"I won't give you up, if that's what you think," Pennant continued. "Not this time." He shot an angry glance at Darcy. "I won't let that bastard tear you from me again."

"Do you trust me?" Lettice asked.

Pennant didn't hesitate. "Yes."

"Then trust me to take care of this."

"I love you," he persisted, making Darcy grit his teeth. "Leave him and marry me."

She darted a glance at Darcy, another pitying glance. Then she turned back to Pennant. "I—I can't discuss it now. Please, return in the morning. I promise to give you my answer then."

Pennant hesitated, but when she drew her hands from his, he stalked toward the door. He hesitated in front of Darcy and held up his fist. "Listen to me, Northcliffe. If you harm her, if you do anything to her, I'll—"

"I'd never hurt her," Darcy retorted. "I love her. I wouldn't hurt her if my life depended on it."

"You hurt her once, by lying to me. But if you lie to her this time, if you try to turn her against me, I'll find you and choke the breath from you. Do you hear?"

"Get out," Darcy hissed. "Get out of my house!"

Pennant's eyes narrowed, but he said nothing. He merely turned to Lettice. "I'll be back for you tomorrow, love—for you and the boy."

"You can't have her!" Darcy cried out, but Pennant ignored him and left, slamming the door behind him.

Darcy whirled on Lettice. "You're not going to take up with him again, are you? Surely these years between us have meant something!"

She wrung her hands, her face pale and still in the firelight. "They meant a great deal. You know that."

He removed his coat, throwing it across a chair. Rubbing the bridge of his nose, he murmured, "I don't know what to believe. I thought Edgar was my son, and he isn't." He turned to stare at her. "Yet I told the truth when I said it doesn't matter. I want you, Lettice. No matter how you've lied to me, I want you and Edgar. Don't let Pennant destroy what it took us six years to build."

"You speak as if we're married, but Morgan's right. We're not married. You have a wife. And Morgan . . . has always had only me."

"My wife detests me! You know that!" He strode up to her, catching her arm when she turned from him. "Do you know that she hasn't once come to my bed unless I begged it of her? And I only begged because I need an heir." His throat tightened. "I would have made Edgar my heir. I would have acknowledged him as my son when he came of age." He tried to draw her close, but she resisted. "I *will* make him my heir, if you'll only stay with me. Oh, Christ, I need you! You can't leave me!"

He was desperate now. Desperation wasn't the way to keep her, but he couldn't help it. The thought of not having Lettice in his life was too painful to bear.

"Please, Darcy," she whispered, "you must understand—"

"I know I haven't been mistaken these past years." He clutched her by the shoulders, seeking some reassurance from her. "You felt real affection for me. I know you did."

Her eyes were deep with pity, and the pity made him ache. "I did feel a great deal of affection for you, Darcy. I know I lied to you about Edgar, but I truly thought of you as his father, for you've always been kind to him."

"That should count for something!"

"It does. But it doesn't excuse the way you've lied. About me. And about my lady."

"Leave Juliana out of this. She has nothing to do with it."

"But the lies you told about her do, don't you see?" She moved his hands off her shoulders. "I thought you were a generous man, a kind man. Instead I find you're a stranger, someone I never knew, a deceiver—"

"You deceived me, too."

"Yes, but I lied to protect my child from starvation. You . . ." Her voice dropped to a whisper. "You lied to gain something that didn't belong to you. 'Tis entirely different."

Her body stiff, she skittered away from him, and he could feel her withdrawing.

"I'll make it up to you," he said, reaching for her. "Let me make it up to you."

With a mournful shake of her head, she moved to the fireplace. "It's no use, Darcy. It could never be the same between us." She was silent a long moment, then sucked in a breath. "When Morgan comes tomorrow, I'm taking Edgar and going with him."

Her words shattered him so much, he scarcely planned what he said next. "And if I marry you?"

She pivoted to face him with shock on her face. "What in heaven's name are you talking about? You're already married."

"I'll divorce her." He strode toward her, his purpose firming as he got closer. "I'll divorce Elizabeth and marry you. I'll make Edgar my heir. I swear it."

"You're mad! An earl divorce his lady wife and marry a servant? If you did that, you'd lose every social advantage you've gained. You'd never risk that. You *shouldn't* risk it."

What she said was true, but he didn't know how else to keep her. "I'll risk anything to keep you with me."

She shook her head. "I couldn't accept such a sacrifice from you, Darcy." She paused, then straightened her shoulders. "Not when I love Morgan."

Those words drove into his brain, exploding shards of rage. He caught her in his arms, his hold hard and un-yielding, refusing to let her go when she pushed against his chest. "You don't love him. I can prove it!" He tried to kiss her, but she twisted her head away. "Let me make love to you, and I'll show you what still lies be-tween us."

"Don't." She fought him in earnest now.

Her fear of him only enraged him. He grabbed her chin, forcing her head still so he could kiss her on the mouth. But when he tried to force his tongue between her teeth, she bit him.

He jerked back from her, then slapped her—hard.

As soon as he'd done it, horror consumed him. He'd never struck her, not in all the time he'd known her. "Oh, God, Lettice . . . I'm sorry . . ." he began, reaching for her again.

But she pushed away from him, fleeing to the stairs. "Leave, Darcy," she choked out, holding her hand to the spot that bore the print of his hand. "Please . . . just leave."

He took a step toward the stairs.

She retreated farther. "You promised Morgan not to hurt me. Did you lie about that, too?"

Her words brought him to his senses. And slid deep into his gut like a well-honed blade. She feared him now, and rightfully so. He'd made her fear him.

He backed away, afraid of what he might do if he got any closer. Right now she had cause to fear him. But if he came near her again, he might give her cause to hate him.

"Please go," she repeated in a shaky voice.

He hesitated, feeling as if someone had wrenched his heart from his chest. But he had no choice. "Yes, all right. I'll leave."

With a sigh, he walked to the door and opened it,

then paused to look at her. "But even if you go with him, you'll come to your senses eventually. You'll see what you're too confused to see now—that you love me as I love you. He'll never be good enough for you."

He walked out, closing the door behind him. Then he stood there motionless a moment, able to hear her sobs even through the door.

Deuce take it, he'd lost her. Despite his brave words, he knew he'd lost her in a moment of blind stupidity.

How in God's name would he ever endure it?

Chapter Fifteen

"No profit, though near dead,
I've had of this white maid,
Save to love all entire
And languish with desire,
To praise her through the hills
Yet, solitary still,
To wish her at nightfall
Betwixt me and the wall."
              —Dafydd ap Gwilym,
                "The Grey Friar"

"And will dinner be at the usual time?" Mrs. Roberts asked Juliana. It was midafternoon, and they were standing in the hall.

"Yes." Juliana rolled her eyes. "That is, unless Squire Arrogance decrees otherwise."

Mrs. Roberts laughed. "Three days since you arrived, and he's still thinking he makes the rules around here? Ah, men are such fools."

Generally Juliana ignored Mrs. Roberts's thinly disguised attempts to find out what was going on between the master and the mistress, but today she was just angry enough to give the woman an earful. "Fools they may be, but they all stick together. I seem to have won a skirmish in the kitchen, but lost one in the stables."

"The groom refused to saddle you a horse again, eh?" Mrs. Roberts clucked sympathetically. "Well, milady, I'm sorry for it. I know you miss your daily ride. But you'll be at it again once the master realizes how foolish it is to keep you from it." She smoothed her apron with callused hands. "Well, then, I'd best get back to the kitchen. You know the kitchen maids—slaggards all if I don't hound them every moment."

As Juliana watched the woman bustle off down the hall, a dark frown creased her forehead. Over the past three days, the household had fallen into two distinct camps—the footmen, grooms, butler, and Newns on one side and the maids, the cook, and Mrs. Roberts on the other. It infuriated her.

All the wretched footmen and grooms were under Rhys's thumb. Some of them were newly hired, so their loyalty to him was understandable. But she herself had hired the blasted groom who'd thwarted her this morning. He'd hemmed and hawed and begged her pardon, but in the end, he'd escorted her from the stables.

The traitor! Like his male companions, he'd thrown in his lot with Rhys. Rhys had only to spin a few tales about his battles at sea and his experiences in America, and they were ready to die for "the brave master."

Her frown lessened. At least the women were on her side. They were too practical to be swayed by stories of adventure. Behind Rhys's back, they came to her for every instruction. Mrs. Roberts had been the most blatant about her insurrection, nodding and saying, "Yes, sir," to everything Rhys commanded, and then coming to Juliana to ask what *she* wanted done.

And Cook! Juliana chuckled aloud. Cook had baldly told Squire Arrogance that she wasn't so foolish as to take her orders from a man who hadn't the faintest idea what went on in a kitchen. He'd mildly hinted that he could dismiss her for such insubordination, but she'd told him he knew better than to dismiss the only woman who could cook a *cawl* fit for a king. She'd been right, of course.

So Juliana had gone on planning the meals, and Rhys had kept silent on that matter just as he'd acquiesced when she'd had the maids move her clothing and jewel cases to the Blue Room. But he'd asserted his authority everywhere else. He and Newns discussed all improvements without her. She was forbidden the stables. And any outing she took in the carriage had first to be approved by him, which invariably meant he went along.

It was most irritating, not to mention insulting. And she dared not complain, for his answer was always the same—"When you share my bed, then I'll share the estate." Since he accompanied the pronouncement with a sensuous look that always sent delightful shivers along her spine despite herself, she found it harder and harder to complain.

Instead she'd thrown herself into improving the squire hall. While he was surveying the tenant farms with an eye toward improvements, she clandestinely used her funds to order new drapes and linens. While he consulted with the estate blacksmith, carpenter, and gardener, she consulted with the housekeeper and oversaw the maids. It wasn't hard to keep busy, although many of her former duties had been taken from her. She used the time to catch up on tasks she'd put off before—cleaning out the attic ... taking stock of her wardrobe ... examining the books in the library for those that needed new bindings.

She rarely saw Rhys, and when she did, he was cordial but unrelenting in his determination to shut her out of the workings of the estate. Only at night, when they shared dinner, were they cordial to each other, as if an unspoken truce kept them from violating the dinner hour with their war. He continued to recount tales about America, and after some prodding from him, she'd begun relating all that had happened to the estate after he'd left.

But once dinner was over, she always excused herself before he could turn the full force of his seductive talents on her. Fleeing to the Blue Room, which was at the far end of the hall from the State Bedroom, she spent restless nights remembering every blazing look he'd given her at dinner, every brush of his hand against her waist as he led her to her place, every kiss he pressed to her cheek. As if he knew what his reticence did to her, he hadn't again tried to kiss her mouth or hold her. And he probably knew it was driving her insane.

"Milady?" said the butler, dragging her from her thoughts.

Oh, bother, she'd been standing here like a half-wit, staring into space. She forced her expression into some semblance of authority. "Yes, what is it?"

"Master Evan is here. He said you're expecting him for a lesson."

She groaned. "I completely forgot!" And she hadn't even gotten his paper ready yet! That's what all her woolgathering had done. "Send him to the kitchen and tell Cook to give him some tea and crumpets or something. He can take them up to the schoolroom if he likes. I'll be there shortly."

"Very good, my lady." The butler marched toward the kitchen to follow her commands as she hurried into the study and to the desk where she kept her supply of paper. Swiftly she drew ten sheets out of a drawer. Then she held the edges over the candle flame until they caught fire. After tilting the paper to make sure all the edges burned just a little, she blew out the flame, then waved the sheets in the air to dispel the smoke.

"What in God's name are you doing?" came a voice from the doorway.

She started, then whirled to face Rhys. "I swear, you have the most disturbing habit of sneaking up on a person."

A wry smile tipped up his mouth. "You have some peculiar habits yourself—destroying perfectly good paper, for example."

"I'm not destroying it, I'm merely ... ah ... dirtying it up."

"May I ask why?"

She shrugged as she pulled out ten more sheets. "It's for Evan."

He leaned against the door frame, tucking his hands in the pockets of his snuff-colored breeches. "Ah, yes. The boy who took the stained paper off your hands. I take it the 'staining' was no accident either."

"Of course not. But he won't take unspoiled paper from me, so I have to ... dirty it up for him some way."

"I see." He watched as she did the other sheets in the same fashion. "When do you bring this paper to him?"

"That's why I'm in such a hurry. He's here already, and I'd forgotten all about preparing his paper."

"May I come along?"

Her gaze shot to him, curious, speculative.

He met it. "May I?"

"Why?"

"Since I've agreed to do what I can to provide an education for your charge, I ought to be allowed to meet him. Don't you agree?"

"I suppose it wouldn't hurt," she mumbled, unable to

think of any good reason why he shouldn't. Except that it would mean spending time in his presence. And she couldn't very well give that as a reason without revealing what his presence did to her.

She gathered all the sheets and straightened them into a pile. "Evan's waiting in the schoolroom. I usually tutor him there."

He said nothing, but merely waited until she'd picked up the paper and walked toward the door. He shifted his position, moving out into the hall, but giving her not quite enough room to pass without touching him.

She slid into the hall, trying to keep the blackened edges of the paper from soiling her gown while at the same time trying not to touch him. It didn't matter. Even though she succeeded in passing him without so much as brushing against him, she could feel his eyes hot upon her. She almost imagined she felt his warm, enticing breath on her neck.

As soon as she was through the door and past him, she quickened her steps, but he fell easily into step beside her, settling his hand on her waist in that possessive gesture so common to men. Despite her attempt to keep calm, her breathing began an uneven rhythm that she could hardly hide.

Nor did it get any better as they climbed the stairs side by side, him with his hand riding on her waist as if to steady her when she knew he really did it to provoke her.

Unfortunately, it was working. She was overwhelmingly aware of the hard, lean body beside her, moving with the lithe, imperative grace of a thoroughbred racehorse as he climbed the stairs ... his thighs working beneath the glove-tight breeches ... his arm brushing her back every time she took a step . ... his fingers resting in the small of her back just inches above her hips. ...

Oh, bother, she thought peevishly. *He's a devil, he is. So what if he has a fine body? He's an untrusting, stubborn wretch, and totally unworthy of my attention.*

Too bad it did no good to tell herself that. By the time they'd reached the schoolroom, she was fit to be tied, her blood racing. It was with profound relief that she escaped from his side, moving into the room in a rush.

Seeing Evan sitting at the table took her mind thankfully off Rhys. As Rhys entered the room behind her, she watched Evan, a smile flitting over her face. He had apparently either refused the tea and crumpets or wolfed them down in record time, for he now sat engrossed in reading a book she'd only acquired yesterday—a copy of Daniel Defoe's *Robinson Crusoe*. He read quickly, oblivious to her and Rhys as he hunched over the book, eating up the pages. It never ceased to astonish her that he'd assimilated English so thoroughly that he could read at such a pace. For a twelve-year-old to read English, Welsh, and French with little prior schooling was nothing short of amazing.

"Sorry I kept you waiting," Juliana said gently.

Evan gave a start, his ruddy cheeks growing ruddier as he looked up to see her and Rhys standing inside the door. Shutting the book, he jumped to his feet and gave a bow. "Good day, my lady. I—I hope you don't mind. I saw the new book and—"

"Don't be silly." She smiled. "I'm glad you took the chance to look it over. How is it?"

He shrugged as he shot Rhys a curious glance. " 'Tis interesting."

And just the sort of adventurous tale a young boy loves, she thought, glad of her choice.

"I thought it might amuse you." She gestured for him to sit down again, but he didn't notice, his gaze turning to Rhys with his usual inquisitiveness. Sighing, she said, "Evan, allow me to introduce you to my husband, Squire Vaughan. He wants to observe the lesson today."

Evan's eyes grew full and brown like ripe chestnuts. " 'Tis a very great pleasure to meet you at last, sir. A pleasure and an honor."

"A pleasure for me as well," Rhys said, a hint of amusement in his voice.

Juliana took a seat at the table and barely gave time for Rhys and Evan to follow before she launched right into the lesson, eager to get this over with so she could escape her husband.

If Evan was surprised that she spent no time chatting with him about his mother or the farm, he didn't show it. Nor did he seem uncomfortable having Rhys watch him at his lessons. If anything, he showed off more—

conjugating French verbs with obvious pride, then reeling off a dozen new words he'd learned from the poem she'd assigned him to memorize.

"And what is Gruffyd's speaker lamenting here?" she prompted after he'd recited a particularly complicated line.

Evan thought a moment. "Is he saying he can't talk poetry while he's wandering?"

" 'Recite' poetry," she corrected. "But that's not it exactly. You see, he grieves for the old ways that are no longer valued. He says no one wants to hear Welsh verses recited anymore, so he must 'keep my poet's trade hidden in my despair.' "

Rhys spoke for the first time since they'd begun the lesson. "In Gruffyd's day there were few who would stand up to the English. The Welsh language was considered stupid and fruitless, and some Welshmen refused to use it anymore. So Gruffyd felt like a stranger in his own land, 'betrayed to wander the world in search of aid.' "

Without thinking, she lifted her eyes to Rhys's. He was watching her as if trying to fathom her thoughts. Gruffyd's poem had been one of their mutual favorites. She wondered if he remembered that. And had he guessed that she'd chosen it for Evan for that very reason?

If so, he gave no sign of it, though his gaze was soft as he stared at her.

Evan spoke up beside her, seemingly oblivious to the sudden current in the air. "Mr. Gruffyd is like you, Mr. Vaughan, isn't he?"

She turned to see admiration written all over Evan's earnest young face.

Rhys lifted one eyebrow. "How so?"

"Well, you had to wander the world, too, and give up your poet's trade."

With a groan, she dropped her gaze to the table, feeling rather than seeing Rhys turn to her for an explanation. She should have known that the very hero worship she'd instilled in Evan all these years would come out once he met Rhys. 'Twas her own stupid fault for telling him about Rhys in the first place. But in those six years, she'd needed someone to talk to, and Evan had been a willing listener.

She tried to sound nonchalant as she explained. "Evan has always been interested in your ... er ... situation."

"Oh, more than that, sir," Evan blurted out. "I think you're a great hero, to fight so nobly for the Welsh cause even when it meant being taken by the press-gangs. 'Tis a great man you are."

She could feel Rhys's eyes on her, probing her, but she wouldn't look at him. "I told Evan about how you were forced into the navy."

"She did." Evan warmed to his subject. "She told me how you said that we should speak Welsh if we like. And she told me about your poetry. I've read all your poems. Every one. And I don't even *like* poetry."

Rhys leaned forward to plant his elbows on the table. "How did you manage to read my poems? They were never published."

"Lady Juliana let me read them in the book you gave her. Oh, sir, they were wonderful."

"Really?" he said, his eyes narrowing as his gaze bore into her.

Juliana shifted in her chair.

"Aye." Evan smiled from ear to ear. "She told me all about you." He leaned forward confidentially. "She said you were very special."

" 'Special,' eh?" Rhys asked, his voice quiet.

Oh, why must Evan have such a talkative nature? Juliana thought. "Let's get on with the lesson, shall we?" she insisted.

"No, this is much more interesting," Rhys interjected in silky tones. "So, Evan, did she tell you what she meant by 'special'?"

Screwing up his face, Evan thought a moment. "I don't know. Like a hero. You know, like the man all the girls in the books fall in love with."

"And did she say she'd fallen in love with me?"

Evan's smile faded as he shot Juliana an uncertain glance. "Well, n-not exactly. But she talked about you like ... well, like girls talk about their true loves. You know. Like my sister Mary when she talks about that shopkeeper in town."

Rhys leaned back to cross his arms over his chest.

"Ah, but you're forgetting something. If I were her 'true love,' why did she go off to marry that other fellow?"

Juliana dropped her eyes to her skirts, fighting the blush that spread over her face. Dear heaven, he would never understand.

"That stuffy Englishman?" Evan waved his hand dismissively. "I told her not to do it." He drew himself up, chest full. "After all, why did she need a husband when she was managing quite well on her own?"

"Why indeed?" Rhys bit out.

Evan went on, oblivious to Rhys's comment. "She said t'weren't a husband she wanted, but children. And since you weren't here, and she thought you were never coming back—"

Rhys sat up straight. "Children? She would have married 'that stuffy Englishman' for children? Didn't she say anything about love?" The faintest hint of mockery was in his tone. "Didn't she say that he had become her 'true love'?"

Juliana's head shot up at that. How dare he ask such a question of poor Evan, who didn't understand half of what had gone on during the last six years? Rhys had never bothered to ask her if she'd been in love with Stephen, yet here he was, badgering a boy for his answers.

"My, but we've gone far afield of our lesson." She tried for a light tone. "Let's get back to it, shall we?"

Rhys's gaze locked with hers, full of burning intensity. "Evan hasn't answered my question. Come on, lad, tell me. Did Lady Juliana say she was in love with Lord Devon?"

"Not to me." Evan shifted uneasily in his chair. He'd finally begun to sense the tension in the air. "She wanted a husband who would give her children. That's all."

Incapable of looking away, she kept her eyes fixed on Rhys, whose mouth tightened into a thin line. "But I was already her husband. Did she tell you that?"

Juliana felt Evan glance from her to Rhys and back. "No." When Rhys frowned, Evan burst out, "But you mustn't blame her for not saying anything to anyone, sir."

"Oh? And why not?"

With a shrug, Evan said with perfect candor, "Well,

you did take an awfully long time to come back. She
thought you were dead. *Everyone* thought you were
dead."

The faintest smile hovered over Rhys's lips. "You do
have a point, Evan. I'll give you that."

"She used to cry about it," Evan persisted, determined
to defend Juliana. "I heard her sometimes, after we read
one of your poems. She cried in the garden."

"Did she?" Rhys's eyes burned all the brighter as they
stared into hers.

She wrenched her gaze from his. "That's enough,
Evan. We won't talk about this any longer. You've got
lessons to do and—"

"I think Evan has done so well today that he deserves
a rest from lessons," Rhys broke in, his voice like velvet-
encased steel. "Evan, why don't you go down to the
kitchen and tell Mrs. Roberts I said to give you a pork
pie?"

"But—" Evan began.

"Go on now. I need to talk to your teacher."

Evan looked to Juliana, and she sighed. There was no
point in trying to continue the lessons with Rhys asking
probing questions. In truth, she'd rather have Evan out
of it.

She flashed Evan what she hoped was a reassuring
smile. "Do as the squire says."

"Should I come back tomorrow?" Evan shot Rhys a
wary glance.

She nodded, her throat too tight for her to speak.

With his usual deference, he gave a small bow and
walked to the door. He had barely passed through it
when she glanced down and saw the charred paper still
in her hand.

She leapt to her feet. "Oh, dear, I forgot to give him
his paper—"

But Rhys was already beside her, staying her with one
hand. "You can give it to him tomorrow. Let him go."

They stood there in silence a moment, listening as
Evan's light footsteps on the steps grew faint. Rhys
rested one hand on her waist while with the other he
took the paper from her and laid it on the wooden table.

He was so close she could feel his breath on her hair,
hot and uneven. She couldn't look at him. She was afraid

to see what might be in his eyes. He was so unpredictable. No telling what he thought of Evan's revelations. He might even think she'd put Evan up to saying all of it. She couldn't bear it if he did.

"Tell me something, Juliana," he whispered. "Were you ... are you in love with Lord Devon?"

The question resonated in every part of her. Should she tell him the truth? Did he deserve to know the truth after everything he'd done to her?

While she hesitated, he raised his fingers to grasp her chin, turning her face toward him. She swallowed hard as she stared into his fathomless eyes. His back was to the window, and the late afternoon sunlight glanced off his thick, dark hair, giving him a halo of light.

Yet he was not an angel, but a man. A man who'd had heaven dangled in front of him, then snatched away one too many times. Even now he wore an expectant look, as if waiting for the push that would send him plummeting to earth. "Are you in love with Lord Devon?" he repeated, his tone sharper.

She could barely speak. "Nay. Once I thought I could grow to love him. But I know better now."

His eyes went wide. With relief? Hope? She wasn't sure. Whatever it was, it faded quickly from his face, as if he didn't dare believe in it.

But his fingers tightened on her chin as he turned her into his arms, pressing her against him. "Why did you tell Evan about me? Why did you let him read my poems?" His eyes blazed now. "Why did you cry for me after you tossed me aside so easily?"

She sighed. "You're such a fool, Rhys. Why do you think I cried? 'Twas just as I've told you all along. I loved you."

He ran his thumb over her lower lip as if testing its fullness. "You say that, but you kept our marriage a secret. Even from the boy. Why did you keep it a secret if you were in love with me? I have trouble understanding that."

"I kept it secret because I was scared, because ... because I was weak."

"Yes, but weak enough to have backed out of the marriage in the first place? That's what I can't decide."

"I didn't back out of the marriage! I swear it!"

His eyes scanned her face. "I no longer know what to believe. My mind tells me that none of your claims make any sense—that it couldn't have happened the way you say it did. And yet—"

"And yet you know the truth in your heart. You do know, if only you heed it."

He shook his head, his expression hinting at the confusion in him before he masked it. His gaze followed his thumb as it glided along her lips, tracing them with a touch as gentle as it was thrilling. "I only know one thing for certain. That I still want you, no matter what." He bent his head to press a kiss on her temple. "Oh, God, how I want you."

His lips moved to brush her cheek, and she dragged in a heavy breath, seduced by his touch into forgetting that he didn't believe her ... that he *wouldn't* believe her. No matter what he said, his heart knew the truth, and his heart was governing his actions now.

He skirted the edge of her cheekbone with his mouth, gliding over the skin, down along the curved line of her jaw. Her eyelids slid shut as he pressed an openmouthed kiss into the tender hollow of her neck.

His fingers no longer held her chin. He had slid them back to where a few tendrils escaped her cap. " 'Tis like the men who disappear into the fairy circle," he whispered against her ear as he tugged her cap loose to bring her hair down about her shoulders. "While they are in the enchantment, they know nothing of rational thought. Only when they leave the circle do they realize they've been seduced by a dream."

"Am I a dream then?" A half-smile played over her lips as she turned her face to him.

His lips hovered an inch from hers, their breaths mingling on a sigh as he stared down at her, eyes heavy-lidded with desire. "One of you must be a dream ... either the woman I fell in love with ... or the woman I hold in my arms now."

"Nay. They're one and the same, and no dream either. That I can prove." Then she lifted her mouth the scant distance it took to meet his.

With a groan, he covered her mouth with his, splaying his fingers on the back of her head to hold her still. Desire instantly jolted her. Too many nights had she lain awake remembering their last kiss. Too many years had she lain awake remembering their lovemaking. It would make a wanton of a nun, and she was no nun.

So when he swept his tongue along the crease of her lips, she opened her mouth with nary a thought to the consequences, allowing him to tangle his tongue with hers, teasing it with velvety strokes that made her blood race.

"By thunder," he murmured against her mouth, "you grow sweeter to the taste with each kiss. What sort of sorcery is this?"

"The best kind," she whispered back, the last word muffled when he renewed his assault. Only this time it truly was an assault, for his hand cupped her head as he drove his tongue into her mouth, delving for more sweetness even as he offered her a sweetness beyond compare.

When he had her completely limp under the seduction of his kisses, he released her head and wrapped his arms about her, molding her against him, his lean, muscled body straining against hers in an ancient fight for domination that she was at present only too happy to lose. Winding her arms about his waist, she dovetailed into him, unwittingly curving her body around his taut arousal.

"Ah, *cariad*," he whispered as he rubbed against her.

Then he lifted her onto the table, eliciting a gasp from her as he fitted himself between her legs. But before she could respond to that blatant act, he captured her mouth once more in a sense-stealing kiss.

Through a haze of voluptuous enjoyment, she felt his hand slip beneath her skirts and petticoats, whispering past her garter to the stretch of bare thigh, which he stroked with gossamer caresses. His other hand tugged loose her scarf, then inched her bodice down to free her breasts.

But he didn't touch them. Instead his mouth left hers to trail kisses along her chin, down the slope of her throat to the cleft between her breasts. Her head fell back, and he caught her about the waist, stretching her back until she was arched over his arm and suspended over the table, laid out for his pleasure.

And he took his pleasure with obvious delight, running his tongue all along the swell of her breast before he flicked it over her nipple, making her convulse against him.

At the same time, the hand not holding her inched higher between her legs until his fingers were stroking the swirl of hair that covered her most secret places. Before she knew what was happening, he'd slid his finger over the tiny nub nestled within her soft petals of flesh, rolling it beneath his thumb until she moaned deep in her throat.

At the sound, he plunged his finger into her slick, hot passage. While he slipped his finger in and out, he also drew her breast into his mouth, scraping the nipple lightly with his teeth until she thought she'd die from the delicious sensation of it. The assault on two different fronts was so titillating, she writhed against him, seeking more.

"Yes, *fy annwyl mhriod,*" he murmured against her breast. "Be the wanton for me again."

The wanton. She ought to protest that. She only became a wanton when he did these enticing things to her. Yet how could she protest when his silky tongue lapped and teased her nipple, sending a thousand little shocks of sensation through her? How could she protest his finger sliding so seductively inside her?

She opened her eyes to find him watching her, his blue eyes like sapphires glittering at the bottom of a dark, clear stream. His gaze, earnest yet confident, unnerved her so thoroughly she turned her face away, regretting that she'd let him go this far.

"Please ..." she whispered, not knowing what to beg for. Mercy? Forgiveness? He wasn't capable of either.

She tossed her body restlessly, thinking perhaps it wasn't too late to escape him. But he held her unbalanced, keeping her hovering over the table, her breasts raised for his mouth and her legs held open by his thighs. All she could do was cling to his shoulders and pray for the storm to pass.

"I won't hurt you," he murmured, as if sensing her sudden reluctance.

To prove it, he drew her up flush against him as he sought her mouth once more for a gentle, coaxing kiss. It was the kiss of a lover, not a conqueror. She could close her eyes and almost believe that it was the old

Rhys kissing her, the old Rhys whose fingers were working magic between her legs.

"Rhys ... oh, Rhys ..." she groaned as he increased the pace of his strokes until she felt she was climbing Icarus's path to the sun, willing to risk total destruction if only she could reach the heights. She scarcely noticed the sheen of sweat forming on his brow, nor the ravenous hunger with which he began to drive his tongue into her mouth in rhythm with the thrusts of his finger.

Her enjoyment blinded her to anything but Rhys, his body half-covering hers as he sought to make her part of him at every point—kissing, sucking, urging her into a glorious oblivion she'd never imagined.

Then a thousand sensations exploded in her at once, thrusting her into that sunlight she craved and feared. Uttering silent cries against his mouth, she dug her fingers into his shoulders and writhed against him, crushing her breasts against the scratchy wool of his waistcoat.

As her urgent need faded, replaced by a delicious warmth, he withdrew his hand from between her legs. Then he deepened his kiss to one of blatant need as he swiveled his hips against her, letting her feel the rigid member trapped inside his tight breeches.

The feel of wool against her soft skin yanked her from her sensual haze, and she wrenched her mouth from his with a gasp. What was she doing? They were in the middle of the schoolroom, for heaven's sake, with the door hanging wide open!

She felt him fumbling to open his breeches, and her head shot up. Wriggling her hips back, she tried to sit up on the table and right her balance. "Rhys, we can't do this here."

He lifted his face, eyes blazing. "But we *are* doing it here, *anwylyd*. And it's too late for regrets."

"I—I didn't mean ... It's not that. I do want you to ... to—"

"Make love to you?" A triumphant smile lit his features.

She wished she could say no. She wished she didn't have this unholy craving to join her body to his in the deepest union. But she couldn't deny that she wanted him. Desperately.

Without looking at him, she nodded. "But not here, where anyone might walk in and see us."

For a moment, he was so still, she thought she'd angered him. But when she glanced at him, he looked as if he were trying to marshal control over his body, his jaw taut with effort and his mouth thin.

"All right, my lady wife." He gave a pained smile. "I suppose I can make it to our bedchamber without devouring you."

With quick, sure movements, he refastened his breeches and helped her straighten her clothing. Then he clamped his arm about her waist and led her down the stairs at an almost alarming speed with single-minded purpose written all over his face.

They'd nearly reached the State Bedroom when a footman hurried from the other stairs, waving a piece of paper. "Mr. Vaughan! I've an urgent message for you, sir!"

Rhys spared the man only a glance as he opened the door to the master bedchamber. "Not now!"

"But it's from Mr. Pennant," the footman persisted. "His man is waiting outside to accompany you."

That made Rhys pause. Releasing Juliana, he motioned for her to enter the bedchamber, then took the piece of paper from the footman.

Motionless, Juliana watched as he read the note, then swore under his breath. Tucking it into his waistcoat pocket, he told the footman, "Tell Pennant's man I'll be right there."

The footman scurried off as Juliana went rigid. "What the devil? What do you mean, you'll be right there?"

Rhys turned to her, regret written across his face as he ushered her into the bedchamber and shut the door behind him. "I have to go," he said, his face set.

"Where? Why?" She shook her head in sheer disbelief. "What could possibly make you leave when we . . . before we . . ."

His gaze trailed down over her rumpled gown, as if marking all the curves he knew lay beneath. "I don't want to go, believe me," he said in a tight voice. "Especially not now. But I have to."

Drawing an aching breath through a hot, dry throat, she said, "At least tell me why. At least tell me where you're going."

"I can't." He stared at her a long moment, then moved about the room, gathering his gloves, his heavy riding boots, his cloak.

"You mean, you won't." She clutched her waist as a hollow pain gnawed at her gut. "You're quite happy to make love to me, but you still don't trust me with your business affairs."

He said nothing, drawing his gloves on with jerky movements.

And to think she'd almost allowed the bastard to touch her in the most intimate way of all! Her voice dropped to a whisper. "You call me your 'darling wife,' but you mean only your 'darling bedmate.' And you only want me for that when it's convenient."

A muscle tightened in his jaw. "Until now, you haven't wanted to be either a wife or a bedmate, so your anger is misplaced, don't you think? It's not my fault you waited so long to do your duty."

Your duty? It took all her control to bite back the hot retort that sprang to her lips. He always drew attention from a subject he didn't want to discuss by saying something he knew would inflame her temper. This time, she wouldn't let him get away with it. "So you're not going to tell me anything about where you're going or why."

"That's right." He sat down on the bed and pulled off his shoes with the faked nonchalance of a man who knows he's wrong and refuses to admit it.

Whirling away from him, she strode for the door.

"Where are you going?" He dropped his boots on the floor as he jumped to his feet.

"You're finished with me, aren't you? So I'm returning to my other wifely 'duties.' "

He was across the room before she could even get the door open all the way. Slamming the door, he dragged her around to face him. "Ah, but you're wrong," he said in a voice dangerously soft. "I'm not finished with you. Not now, not ever. My journey out is merely an interruption. But when I return late this evening, I expect to continue exactly where we left off."

When he raked her with a knowing glance, the heat rose again in her body despite all her anger. But as his gaze snapped back up to her face, she showed no sign of how his desire found an echo in her.

"That's what you expect, is it?" She put as much acid into her voice as possible. "Me here, warm and willing? And what will you give me in return?"

His eyes narrowed to slits. "What do you mean?"

"You want me to sell you my soul—to be a docile, dutiful wife outside the bedchamber and a wanton inside the bedchamber. You want me not to ask questions when you leave me to go on God knows what fool's errand for Morgan."

He stiffened, but she went on relentlessly, "In return you offer me only the ashes of your mistrust. Unfortunately, my price is higher than that."

"Price? You can't ask a price for what is mine by right—what you gave me and then took back." She opened her mouth to retort, but he cut her off, his voice harsh. "However, if I *did* decide to give you something in return, what would be your price? Complete run of the house? Me trailing obediently after you like that lapdog fiancé of yours?"

The thought of Rhys trailing obediently after *anyone* brought a bitter smile to her lips. "Nay. Nothing so strange as that. I only want one thing. Your trust."

Fury gleamed in his eyes. "You're right. Your price is high. Too high."

Casting her one last glare, he thrust away from the door and strode to the bed, where he sat down and yanked his boots on as if he couldn't do it fast enough.

She watched him a second, her hopes faltering. How foolish she'd been to think he might be softening, that he might one day come to trust her. The navy had sucked the essence of trust out of him, leaving his heart to calcify until it was so hardened even she couldn't soften it.

With a sigh, she opened the door and stepped into the doorway. But she hesitated on the threshold, turning to face him. "Then don't expect me to be waiting in this bedchamber for you when you return."

His head shot up, disbelief warring with rage in his features, but she only glimpsed it before she slammed the door between them and fled down the stairs.

Let him make his demands, she told herself as she ran. She heard the door open above her, heard him roar her name as he strode into the hall, but she didn't stop running. *Let him do what he will. But he won't have me in his bed until he shows me some faith.*

Chapter Sixteen

"Find her, if you can, and bring
My sighs to her, my mourning.
You of the glorious Zodiac,
Tell her bounty of my lack."
—Dafydd ap Gwilym,
"The Wind"

Rhys stood in the hallway, torn between finding Juliana so he could pick up exactly where they'd left off a few minutes ago or doing what he knew he must.

Gritting his teeth, he drew out the crumpled piece of paper Morgan had sent him and read it once more.

John Myddelton, the current holder of the seat for M.P. of the borough, is dead. Northcliffe is attempting to force through his own candidate tonight at the council meeting, so the Sons of Wales are preparing to storm Common Hall. They're already roused to fury over what Northcliffe did to you and me, and now they're determined to rout him. If they go tonight, I fear there will be bloodshed. But they'll listen to you. They're meeting in the basement of Gentlemen's Bookshop as usual. You must come help me stop them before it's too late.

Crushing the note in his hand, he stared out the window at the rapidly sinking sun. Carmarthen was two hours' hard ride from here. The council meeting probably still began around eight p.m. as it always had. if he left now and drove his horse to the limit, he could probably get there in time.

But if he left now, he'd lose any advantage he'd gained in his struggle to make Juliana his wife in every way.

He swore vilely, stuffing the wad of paper into his pocket. Why now? Why had Myddelton had to die now? The M.P. had been a moderate Whig respected by both sides, but if Northcliffe were to replace him with his own man . . .

Rhys sighed. He had no choice but to act.

Six years ago, he'd have enjoyed being in the thick of them urging on the fight, ready to cudgel freedom into the thick skulls of the Carmarthen burgesses. But war had made him more cautious. This wasn't the way to go about effecting change. Not in Wales. His experience in America had taught him that.

The American colonists had a number of advantages in their rebellion that the Welsh didn't have—distance from their oppressors, an extensive militia and navy, a great deal of wealth. If the Sons of Wales thought they could rid themselves of English rule simply by trouncing a few burgesses, they were destined to be disappointed, and possibly fatally so.

Morgan was his friend and so were the Sons of Wales. He was partly responsible for their current anger, and he couldn't let them suffer for their zeal to avenge him.

Juliana would simply have to accept that.

Perhaps she would if you told her, his conscience murmured. *But you didn't tell her.*

By thunder, I can't help that! he protested as he strode out the door. If he told her what was going on, she might send a messenger to warn Northcliffe of what the Sons of Wales were up to before Rhys could get to the men and convince them to choose another path of action. Then there would be bloodshed regardless of what happened at the council meeting.

She'd betrayed him and his friends once. She could easily betray them again.

She's not a betrayer, his conscience clamored as he mounted his horse. *You know better than that.*

Nodding to Morgan's man, he nudged the horse into a gallop, craving the speed that would take him out of his thoughts. But thundering along the road toward Carmarthen wasn't enough to draw his mind from Juliana. The Juliana who taught Welsh children in their own language. Who claimed the loyalty of her Welsh servants

with just the flick of a finger—who proclaimed her innocence with righteous indignation and pride.

He could still hear Evan recounting how she'd cried
over him. Oh, and her face when Evan had said she'd
called him "very special" ... it had been a too accurate
mirror of her emotions.

The muscles in his stomach bunched into a painful
knot. What if he'd been wrong about her? What if he'd
been totally wrong? If she were innocent, his every refusal to trust her must be like a slap in the face. She
might be growing to hate him by the moment.

After this afternoon, he couldn't bear having her hate
him. This afternoon. Oh, God, he grew hard just thinking about her wanton response to him, the arch of her
back as she'd pressed into him, the way she'd felt as
she clamped herself around his fingers—all tight and wet
and warm.

"Uffern-dân!" he growled, spurring his horse on. He
couldn't go on tormenting himself over this. He'd done
the right thing by not telling her everything.

After all, innocent or not, she'd taken great pride in
thwarting him these last few days, so she might have
enjoyed thwarting his plans this night if he'd given her
the chance. The damned woman had been going behind
his back to make the servants do as she pleased, treating
him with defiance ... refusing to share his bed.

With a snarl, he tightened his grip on the reins. That
at least would stop after tonight. He wouldn't let her do
it anymore. Tonight if she weren't in his bed, he'd drag
her there. He'd make her forget all her foolish defiance.
He'd stroke that exquisite body until she moaned and
writhed, wanting his touch as thoroughly as she had
this afternoon.

It would be easy. After this afternoon he was certain
of that. Although she hadn't been sharing his bedchamber, she hadn't been locking her door against him either.
He knew that because one night he'd slipped inside to
watch her sleep, torn between his craving for her and
his determination that she come to him of her own will.
He'd resisted the urge to seduce her when she was
half asleep.

Tonight he wouldn't resist the urge.

First, however, he must take care of this problem with the Sons of Wales.

Another low curse escaped his lips. God, how he wished they hadn't taken on his cause. He didn't need a group of wet-behind-the-ears radicals to uphold his honor. For God's sake, half of them were family men with children! They shouldn't be taunting a power like Northcliffe without considering what could happen to them.

He shifted uneasily, then bent lower in the saddle, forcing Morgan's man to increase his pace as well to keep up. They must get there in time. He didn't want the foolishness of all those men on his head. And judging from the tone of Morgan's letter, the printer felt the same way.

But what would he do when he got there? The Sons of Wales, hotheaded though they might be, were right. Northcliffe mustn't be allowed to put his man into the seat without a fight. Rhys knew how easily it could be done—all Northcliffe had to do was convince the burgesses that there wasn't enough time for a proper election and have them move up the election day to make it impossible for any other candidate to campaign. Contested elections were frightfully expensive and divisive, so elections in Carmarthen were generally settled beforehand. But if it were settled for Northcliffe's candidate . . .

He couldn't let that happen. Rhys's brow furrowed as he contemplated a number of possibilities . . . ones that didn't involve bloodshed. Then an idea came to him, and he brightened. Ah, yes, that might work. It just might work.

By the time he and Morgan's messenger had reached the bookshop basement exactly two hours later, he'd formulated a plan. And judging from the noise spilling out from the bookshop into the street, he'd come none too soon.

'Tis a wonder the watch hasn't arrested the lot of them, Rhys thought grimly as he strode down the stairs into the basement, his cloak billowing out behind him.

When he entered, Morgan was on the platform, trying to make himself heard. But the crowd was too aroused to listen to his words. At the other end of the platform was a fiery young laborer inciting them to riot and garnering all their attention.

The familiar smells of book paste, dust, and sweat jolted Rhys back six years to when he'd been the young man on the platform. It had been the first—and last—time he'd shouted revolution. 'Twas the same crowd, the same discontented tradesmen's sons and farmers and Dissidents as had come to hear him that night.

Except that these men were carrying weapons. Swarthy young men armed with hammers and truncheons jostled against work-worn older men carrying picks and axes, and all were echoing the young radical's cries for justice.

Justice, Rhys thought bitterly as he pushed his way to the front of the room. He wanted justice, too, but he was learning it was damned hard to get.

Morgan suddenly caught sight of him from his vantage point on the platform. Relief flooded the printer's face as Rhys climbed up on the platform.

"How long have they been at this?" Rhys shouted to Morgan as he faced the crowd.

Morgan went to his side. "An hour. The council meeting is in half an hour, and they want to remove Northcliffe's candidate forcibly. It's been done before, you know, intimidating a candidate into relinquishing his campaign."

"Aye. And the last time it happened, five of the men who did it were arrested and sentenced to service in the navy." Rhys gestured toward the young radical. "Who's he?"

"His name's Tom Ebbrell. That's all I know."

"Listen to me!" Rhys shouted at the crowd from the platform, but he couldn't make himself heard. Searching the crowd, he caught sight of a man waving an oak cudgel within a foot of his face.

Before the man knew what was happening, Rhys wrenched the cudgel from the man's fist. Grasping it tightly, he smashed the nearest chair with one fell swoop.

That got the crowd's attention. One by one they quieted, until even the man named Ebbrell was gawking at him.

He wasted no time in taking advantage of the quiet. "For those of you who don't remember me, I'm Rhys Vaughan," he said in Welsh. "I'm the one Northcliffe had impressed."

There was a murmur throughout the crowd. Then Ebbrell moved along the platform toward Rhys, extending his hand. "I've heard much about you, sir. I read your pamphlets when I was but a stripling lad, and 'twas them that made me learn about the blindness of Wales. 'Twas them that awakened my heart to our plight."

After a second's hesitation, Rhys shook the man's hand. "Those pamphlets gained me a long stint in the English navy," he said, loud enough for the crowd to hear.

Ebbrell released his hand. " 'Twasn't the pamphlets that did it, but that devil Northcliffe. Ever since his father's death, he's been casting about for a man he can own, and he thinks he's found one in Sir Davies. We'll show him otherwise, won't we, lads?"

That brought a roar of assent from the crowd, but when Rhys held up his hand, they went silent.

" 'Tis a noble fight you're choosing." He put all the force of his old revolutionary zeal into his voice. It had been so long since he'd commanded men in Welsh that he feared his words creaked with the rust of misuse, but he forged on, trying to make up in fervor for what he lacked in eloquence. "You *should* thwart Northcliffe's attempt if you can."

He held the cudgel aloft. "But this is not the way to do it—with truncheons and axes. 'Twill only make the burgesses dismiss you as an ungoverned mass of wild men whose opinions can be ignored."

Angry mutters rippled through the crowd, and Tom Ebbrell's face reflected outrage. "How can you say this?" Ebbrell asked. "Don't you want to see justice done, to see Northcliffe suffer? What happened to all your words about making Wales free?"

Rhys turned to the crowd. "Freedom comes at a price, and sometimes that price means acting with forethought instead of rumbling forth like a herd of bulls."

Rhys stared into the faces of furious, tired men and found himself inexplicably thinking of their wives and children. How many other wives tonight had protested their husband's activities? Six years ago, he'd scarcely cared when Lettice had protested their actions. But tonight, he couldn't help seeing Evan's face—and Juli-

ana's—as the boy had described how Juliana had cried
when Rhys left.

In ringing tones, he said, "The colonies resorted to
battle only when they couldn't have representation. Yet
we *have* been given the right to representation—"

"Aye!" shouted a voice near him. "We have Northcliffe's puppet for representation!"

A swell of disgruntled voices filled the room.

"If you pull down Northcliffe's man," Rhys called out,
"he will only find another. And you will be branded as
rough, unschooled Welshmen bent on violence. You will
find yourselves impressed as I was, made to serve the
very men you detest, and all for nothing but to vent
your spleen!"

A man in the crowd stepped up onto a chair. "Why
are we listening to this coward? Northcliffe sentenced
him to a fate worse than death, yet he has returned to
make Northcliffe's sister his wife! He has gone over to
the enemy—"

The crowd took up the cry. "The enemy! He's the
enemy!"

Fury exploded in Rhys, and he darted forward, determined to make mincemeat of the man who accused him
of cowardice. But Morgan caught his arm and jerked
him back, reminding him of what he was here for.

Rhys nodded grimly at Morgan, then pounded the
cudgel against the floor until he got their attention once
more. "I want Northcliffe's hide as much as you do!
Perhaps more so, for he sought to keep me from my
wife, who is sympathetic to our cause and a Welsh
scholar besides!"

He realized as he said the words that they were at
least partly true. No matter what whim had made Juliana
reject their marriage, it hadn't been a hatred of the
Welsh. Of that, he was sure. As for Northcliffe's part in
it, the man *had* been the instrument of her distress, and
it wouldn't hurt Rhys's case if they thought Juliana was
her brother's victim. Nobody loved a romantic tale of
star-crossed lovers more than the Welsh.

When they quieted, treating him with a wary regard,
he took quick advantage of the temporary silence. "If
I've learned one thing abroad, 'tis that the only way to
free Wales is to gain a voice in Parliament. Tonight you

are planning to keep one voice—a pro-English voice—out of Parliament, but all that does is delay the inevitable."

" 'Tis true," Ebbrell said. "But what else can we do? Lay down our weapons and trot off like sheep to the slaughter?"

"Nay," Rhys told the young man. Then he turned back to the crowd. "I have a better idea than either raising your weapons or laying them down." He paused, letting his gaze sweep over the expectant faces of men who'd long been oppressed by landholders with no care for their needs. "I say put forth your own candidate. Tonight. Then you'll have your voice. And that's the first step to freedom."

The crowd fell into a stunned silence so complete that Rhys thought he could hear the collective beating of their hearts.

Then Tom Ebbrell cleared his throat. " 'Tis impossible. Although I daresay many on the council dislike Northcliffe as much as we do, they're afraid of him. And we have no candidate to match his in wealth and influence." Men began to nod their assent. "You, sir, are the only one with that kind of wealth and influence, but you're not of this borough. While that hasn't always been an issue, Northcliffe will surely use it now to protest your candidacy."

Rhys nodded. "That's why I'm not putting myself forth as a candidate." He shot Morgan a quick glance, relieved when the man nodded. "But I am offering to put all my influence . . . and my wealth behind someone else. And the man I suggest *is* of this borough and does have some wealth of his own. He also has influence in London, as well as the popular support of many freeholders in this city." He turned to put his arm around Morgan's shoulders. "Morgan Pennant."

Another silence, this one very short, and then the crowd broke into cheers. Morgan had always been a favorite with the Sons of Wales, and Rhys didn't think anyone begrudged him the money he'd made in the colonies. Morgan was also better educated than many of them, yet as Welsh as the triple-harp and the *eisteddfodau*. No one could question his suitability. Thank God.

"You don't object, my friend?" Rhys said in a low voice meant only for Morgan's ears.

Morgan's face was solemn. "Nay. I have a score to settle with Northcliffe. And I suspect a beating will not hurt him near as much as this challenge will."

"Is it agreed then?" Rhys called out to the crowd. "Will you lay down your arms and instead put forth Morgan Pennant as a candidate? If we produce a suitable candidate, the council will be forced to allow an election and give time for the campaign. What do you say? Will you go with me to the meeting to serve the writ for Morgan, then join me in a campaign that will shame Northcliffe forever?"

"Aye!" said Tom Ebbrell, wreathed in smiles as he stepped forward to clap his arm about Morgan's shoulder as well.

"Aye!" the crowd echoed.

Rhys flashed them all a triumphant smile as he tossed his cudgel aside, then raised his fist. "To Morgan!" he shouted.

There was a thunderous noise of weapons being dropped. "To Morgan!" they cried.

And to Wales, Rhys thought, feeling the old zeal swell in him again.

This time he'd be smart, however. This time he'd fight the battle with the Englishman's weapons. And this time, not even his wife's brother would keep him from gaining his share of freedom for his country.

Three hours later, Rhys cast Morgan an amused glance as they rode away from Common Hall at a leisurely pace. "Well, Morgan? How does it feel to be a candidate for Member of Parliament?"

With a laugh, Morgan shifted his weight in the saddle. "Ask me tomorrow. I suspect I'll have a more sober view of it in the morning."

"No doubt," Rhys said wryly.

"You know that tonight was only a minor victory. 'Tis easy to serve a writ, especially when the council is sorely tired of dealing with pompous English noblemen like Northcliffe. But to put a man like me into office is not so easy."

"Still, 'tis worth a try."

"Aye. But this plan of yours could wring you dry. Disputed elections for a seat in Parliament nearly always devastate the loser financially. And sometimes the winner as well. There are the banquets to pay for and the palms to grease and—"

"I know." Rhys stared ahead at the moonlit road. "I know only too well. Father considered running for M.P. of the shire once and decided against it when he counted the potential cost." He rubbed his weary neck. "But I am not my father. Nor are you, for that matter. We are both far more responsible." A trace of bitterness entered his voice. "And far less likely to gamble our funds away before they can be used to good purpose. Between us, I think we can pull it off."

Morgan ran an idle hand over his horse's mane. "I hope so." He grinned. "Did you see Northcliffe's face after you agreed to donate enough money to refurbish Common Hall? I thought his eyes would pop out of his head. He's no fool. He knows 'tis easy to buy the votes of the burgesses. Worse yet, you're buying them for me. To have me steal the election from him after I've already stolen his mistress is the worst indignity of all."

"His mistress?" Rhys flashed Morgan an uneasy glance. "We haven't had much chance to speak this evening. Does this mean Lettice has come to live with you?"

"Aye. And as soon as the banns are read, she'll be marrying me." A thread of steel entered Morgan's voice. "She and Edgar are my family now."

"I see." Rhys couldn't quite hide the envy in his tone. Family. He and Juliana could be a family. If he let it happen. If he could see his way through to trusting her.

Morgan cast him a look of pity. "From what you said earlier, I thought perhaps you'd changed your mind about Lady Juliana and Lettice and their part in our impressment. I take it you and your wife are still at odds."

The saddle creaked as Rhys shifted in it. "At odds? Sometimes I think we'll always be at odds."

"So you still distrust her?"

"I don't know, Morgan. I don't know what to think anymore. To tell you the truth, the woman is driving me mad." He gave a grim laugh. "The night of the damned engagement party at Northcliffe Hall, she threatened to make my life hell if I continued to distrust her. I thought she meant she'd be a shrew or do some petty nonsense like throw tantrums and defy me. I could handle that."

He thought of this afternoon, when she'd made him want her with a fierceness he'd never known, then had told him, "Don't expect me to be waiting when you return." A groan escaped his lips. "But I've discovered there are other kinds of hell."

"That I can well imagine," Morgan said with a laugh.

Rhys gritted his teeth. "I can't believe I'm so bedeviled by one small Englishwoman. 'Tis enough to make me doubt my own sanity."

Morgan sobered. "Lettice says Juliana was Northcliffe's victim. She's convinced the girl would never have done what Northcliffe claims. Lettice even told Northcliffe that to his face."

Five days ago, Rhys had argued vehemently with Morgan over the absurd idea that Juliana might be innocent. Now the idea seemed much less absurd. "And what did he say?"

Morgan's heavy sigh sounded loud in the still night air. "He kept insisting he hadn't lied. Unfortunately, there seems to be no way of knowing the truth if the innkeeper and the St. Albans brothers stick to their story. Even Lettice has no real proof of her innocence."

"So Lettice admits that it's possible Juliana betrayed us."

"Nay. I think Lady Juliana would have to confess it under oath before Lettice would believe ill of her."

Rhys suppressed a curse. No one believed ill of Juliana. It was becoming irritating to see how the maids at Llynwydd deferred to her wishes no matter what he said. Then they looked upon him as a wolf preying on the poor lamb.

Poor lamb, indeed! That poor lamb was rapidly twisting everyone in the household about her little finger. Before long, he'd find even his own valet taking her side.

"One thing you should know, however," Morgan went on. "Northcliffe did admit to keeping my letter from Lettice, which means it's likely he did the same with yours to Lady Juliana."

"Yes, it's likely. It's even likely that Northcliffe lied.

But how do you explain the time discrepancy and the fact that *someone* told Northcliffe where to find us? And why did Juliana hide her marriage from everyone from the very beginning?"

"What reason does she give?"

"Youth . . . fear . . . weakness—"

"All valid reasons—"

"And all reasons for her backing out of the marriage. Can't you see? She must have kept it hidden because she didn't want it. And if she didn't want it, then she betrayed me."

"Perhaps it's not as simple as all that."

"I don't know. I can't even think straight anymore. I want to trust her even though I know she must be lying."

"Maybe you *are* thinking straight when you want to trust her." Morgan remained silent several moments, then spoke hesitantly. "Has it occurred to you that you may be choosing not to trust her for reasons other than the evidence before you?"

"What in God's name do you mean by that?"

Morgan shrugged. "I mean, if you accept she didn't betray you, then you can't in good conscience force her to stay in the marriage against her will, can you? You'd have to let her choose between marriage to you or freedom. You'd have to take the chance of losing her, as I took the chance of losing Lettice to Darcy by letting her choose. And you won't risk that, will you?"

Rhys fisted his hands on his reins. There was too much truth in Morgan's words, far too much truth. And indeed, if Juliana *were* innocent . . .

If she were innocent, he'd been so unfair, so callous. And to think of how he'd treated her this afternoon, walking away and not trusting her with something she couldn't have done anything about anyway! Damn it all, if she were innocent—

He wouldn't think of that. He couldn't. He made himself sound convinced, although that was far from what he felt. "She's not innocent. She can't be."

Morgan shrugged. "Only you can know, I suppose."

Rhys chafed at the reproof latent in Morgan's noncommittal words. Thankfully, they were approaching the road to Llynwydd, and he could escape his companion.

As he turned in that direction, Morgan halted his

horse. "You're not staying at your own town house tonight? 'Tis near midnight and with the moon setting early, you may not have much light to ride by."

Rhys thought of Juliana lying awake in bed. She'd said she wouldn't be waiting for him, but he couldn't take the chance. This afternoon's encounter had sharpened the keen edge of his hunger for her to a fine point, and he wouldn't be able to sleep until he'd satisfied that hunger.

"No, I'm going home. I think I can make it with no trouble." He drew his horse toward the road. "I'll come to town in a few days so we can plan the campaign."

"Fine," Morgan called out behind him. Then inexplicably he added, *"Lwc dda."*

Good luck. Rhys groaned as he rode off toward Llynwydd. He would need luck tonight.

Juliana jerked up straight in her bed, cocking her head in the dark to listen. There it was again. The sound of metal jangling. The latch on the door! Someone was trying to open her door, which she'd latched shut tonight.

When she heard a low curse muttered from beyond the door, she groaned. Only one person would be trying to enter her bedchamber in the middle of the night.

Blast the man! Hadn't he heard a word she said before he left? Had he really expected her to be waiting in his bed, warm and willing?

The crack of a fist slamming against the door sent her shrinking back against the headboard, clutching the damask counterpane instinctively to her chest. "Go away!" she called out.

"Juliana, open this door," he commanded in a low-thrumming voice. "I must talk to you."

Oh, is that the new term for seduction? she wanted to ask, but didn't dare bring up *that.* She was already too willing to let him in, to take him in her arms and forget what he thought of her . . . just lose herself in the mindless pleasure he offered.

Mindless. That's what he wanted of her. A mindless union to satisfy their mutual urges. But she wanted far more. And giving in now wouldn't bring her that.

"Juliana?" His fist hit the door again. "Open . . . this . . . door! Now!"

"No." She forced a steadiness into her voice that she didn't feel. "I told you before. I won't share your bed until you show some faith in me."

There was a long silence on the other side of the door. "Open the door and I'll tell you where I was tonight," he said at last. "Please, Juliana."

The "please" nearly shattered her resolve. She left the bed and moved to the door, then paused, her hand on the latch. Was this simply another of his tricks to bring her close enough so he could seduce her? After this afternoon, he was bound to know that all he had to do was kiss her and she turned into wax in his hands. She sighed and drew her hand away from the bolt.

"I was at a Sons of Wales meeting," he said from the other side of the door. "The men were threatening to riot at the council meeting, and Morgan asked me to come and stop them."

Her heart lurched in her chest. Not again. He wasn't going to get involved with them again, was he? She couldn't bear to see him lost to her a second time. "And you went? Without telling me why? Without stopping to think about how dangerous and how stupid and—"

"I had to go." He gave a heavy sigh. "Please, Juliana, open up, so I can explain."

She slumped against the door. What he meant was, *Open the door so I can take you in my arms and make you forget that I don't trust you with anything.*

Closing her eyes, she said, "You can explain just as well from out there as in here."

"I've told you what you wanted to know." Irritation crept back into his voice. "Isn't that enough?"

"Why didn't you tell me before you left?"

Another long pause ensued. "Because ... your brother was going to be there at the council meeting and ... well ..."

When he trailed off awkwardly, everything fell into place. Darcy had mentioned that he would be putting forth his candidate at the upcoming council meeting. Apparently, the Sons of Wales hadn't wanted that, and Rhys had been only too happy to help them thwart his enemy. Even when it meant leaving her to rush off to Carmarthen.

"You thought I might warn him, didn't you?" she whispered.

"I didn't want you to worry—"

"Don't! Don't lie to me. You know that's not why you went off without a word. You didn't want me to warn Darcy ... as if I could do so when you won't even let me saddle a horse from my own stables or call for the carriage or ..." She broke off, realizing she was dangerously close to tears.

"Damn it all, I'm sorry," She could almost hear him weighing his words. When he spoke again, his voice sounded strangled. "I was wrong to run out without any explanation. It was an instinctive reaction. I didn't stop to think ... I just—"

"Didn't trust me." She bit her lip viciously, determined not to cry, afraid he would hear it.

He didn't even try to deny her words. "Let me make it up to you." His rumbling voice made it absolutely clear how he intended to make it up to her. "Open the door, *cariad,* and let me show you I'm sorry."

She tensed, her whole body racked with the need to respond to his call for her. Why not? For a moment, she indulged the dream of what it would be like to have him make love to her again, fusing his naked body to hers, driving himself deep inside her. Her knees went weak, and she nearly threw caution to the winds and unlatched the door.

But she knew too well what would happen afterward. He would do the same thing tomorrow. And the next day. And the next. He would keep pushing her away with his shield of distrust even while he made love to her.

And that would hurt far more than this absence of him.

"Go away, Rhys," she whispered through a raw throat. "Go back to your radical companions and leave me in peace."

The door shook against her back as he pounded his fists into it. *"Uffern-dân!"* he exploded, then lowered his voice to a murmur she could hear even through the door. "I know you want me, *fy mhriod.* You cannot deny it."

She held her breath, irrationally hoping that if she

stayed very still, he would leave her alone. And when the silence stretched out for several seconds, she actually thought he had.

Then she heard a weary sigh come from the other side.

"You're such a little coward," he muttered. "You're willing to spar with me when the servants are around, but take them away, and all your bravery disappears."

"That's right," she blurted out, feeling an overwhelming urge to strike back at him. "I don't want you to hurt me. I'm afraid of you, Rhys, and if that's cowardice, then so be it."

"Nay." His voice sounded so close to her ear, she had to remind herself of the stout oak door between them. "You're not afraid of me, *cariad.* You're afraid of yourself. That's why you haven't started locking your door until tonight—because you know that this afternoon you almost gave in. And you're terrified that you might do it again if you unlatch the door."

"I'm not ... I won't ..."

He gave a bitter laugh. "Good night, *cariad.* I won't make a liar of you tonight." He dropped his tone to a satiny caress. "But you can't stay in there forever. And the next time I catch you alone ..."

She heard his footsteps echo down the hall as he strolled off without finishing the sentence. But he didn't need to finish it. She knew exactly what he meant.

Blast the man. It was only a matter of time before he took complete advantage of her weakness for him. She could only hope that by that time, his weakness for her would be just as great.

Chapter Seventeen

"Sea on the shore no longer
Stays than this outlaw in care.
So I'm bound with pain, shackled
Straitly, and my breast is nailed.
Scarcely, beneath her goldhead,
Shall I have my wise young maid."
—Dafydd ap Gwilym,
"His Affliction"

Already midmorning and the laggard was still asleep, Lettice thought as she stopped at the bedroom to check on Morgan. A smile drifted over her face to see him sprawled across the mattress like a conquering hero. Ah, well, it was Sunday after all, and he'd had a late night in town.

She still could scarcely believe he was hers. All these years of missing him, aching for him in secret when Darcy came to her . . . and now he was hers in body and soul. Forever. Soon to be bound by vows that even the mighty Lord Northcliffe couldn't break.

As she studied the familiar face still tanned from months at sea and the long, smooth scar that divided his bristly cheek into two distinct halves, her smile faded. "My poor love," she whispered. Would she and he ever be able to put those six years behind them? Could he ever completely forget that she'd spent that time with another man . . . his very enemy?

As if Morgan felt her presence, he slowly opened his eyes, swiping back a hank of dark, unruly hair. A smile spread over his face when he saw her watching him. "Good morning, sweetheart," he said in a husky voice, patting the bed and shifting to his side to give her room to sit down.

She slipped into the room and sat beside him. "Good morning, my candidate for Parliament."

He laughed. "So you actually heard all that muddle I told you last night when I stole into bed. Your 'hm' and 'um' sounded suspiciously like someone talking in her sleep."

Punching his arm playfully, she tossed her head. "Oh, I heard all right. Besides that, while you've been sleeping the day away, you and Rhys have been the talk of the town."

"Have we?" Without warning, he pulled her atop him, settling her against the length of his body. "And what are they saying?"

"They're boasting that you'll be a 'force to be reckoned with' and other such nonsense."

"Oh? And are they saying what clever devils we are to rout Northcliffe at his own game?"

When her smile faltered, so did his.

"A pox upon't it, I'm sorry, love," he muttered. "I didn't mean to bring him up—"

She bent her head to kiss him. "It's all right. We can hardly avoid it. It's not as if we can erase what happened by not talking about it."

Clasping her arms in his hands, he began to knead them absently. "I suppose you're right. But I wish I *could* erase what happened." His voice turned grim. "I wish I could blot the devil completely from your mind . . . and your memory."

"You've nothing to worry about. Those years were like wandering through the mist to me. These few days with you have been more real than all my years with Darcy."

His eyes searched hers. "Still, it must bother you to hear me speak of him with venom."

"Nay." She toyed with a lock of his hair. "I understand why you wish to see him pay for what he did. But you can't expect me to feel the same urge. I've already made him suffer by leaving him. Nothing more I could do would punish him further."

When she saw understanding in his face, she lowered her head and rested it against his chest. Morgan stroked her hair and twined one of her curls about his finger. "You know, if he hadn't done what he did, I could almost like the man. His father was a stupid noble who let his holdings fall into disrepair, but Northcliffe turned that around and made it all profitable in a short time. He's got a good mind. 'Tis a shame he uses it only to gain power."

She nodded, then shifted her head to rest her chin on his chest, forcing a smile to her face. "Yes, but he won't be doing that much longer. With Rhys's money and influence behind you, we'll soon be putting M.P. after your name, and that will put an end to Darcy's power, I suspect." She kissed his scruffy chin. "I'm only hoping you don't grow a big head once you're an M.P. I won't countenance that."

He chuckled, then thrust his hips up against her suggestively. "I'm already growing a big ... something, my love. Do you think you can 'countenance' that?" With a leering grin, he reached for her skirts, dragging them up her thighs.

"Morgan!" she protested. "Edgar might come in and see us!"

He clamped his hand on one of her buttocks and squeezed it. "Then he'll learn a thing or two from his old da, won't he?"

"Morgan Pennant!" she said, eyes wide with outrage. His fingers slid between her legs, and she said his name again, but this time it was more a sigh than a protest. "Let me at least close the door," she whispered as he lifted his mouth to hers. "Really, Morgan—"

A sound from the doorway made her look up, and there stood Edgar, round-eyed and bewildered. In a thrice, she jerked down her skirts and scrambled from the bed, hearing Morgan groan behind her.

"What are you doing with Father?" Edgar asked, shoving his thumb into his mouth.

It was amazing how it had taken only a day for Edgar to accept that Morgan was his father, Lettice thought as she went to the door. Apparently, he thought boys' fathers appeared magically from the sea every day.

She stooped down beside him and wiped a smidgen of flummery from his cheek. "Mother and Father are ... er ... playing a game, dear. Why don't you finish eating your flummery and then play with the toy ship Father bought you yesterday?"

She glanced back at Morgan, who was regarding her with frank male appreciation, one eyebrow raised as he trailed his gaze over her body. "Mother and Father will be ... through in just a bit, and then we'll do something fun. Does that sound good?"

He nodded solemnly, then turned and walked off. She shut the door, but before she could even flip the latch, she heard a timid knock on it.

"What is it, son?" Morgan barked.

There was a pause, then Edgar murmured, "Can Mr. St. Albans have some flummery, too?"

Lettice swung the door open so fast, she made Edgar step back. "Mr. St. Albans?"

Edgar nodded. "He's in the kitchen. He's come to see you and Father. He asked me to fetch you, but I can tell him you're playing a game. Only he might want some flummery, too, and—"

"It's all right," she muttered, hastily straightening her skirts and smoothing her hair. "I'll come out and talk to Overton."

Over her shoulder, she cast Morgan a helpless glance, but he was already out of the bed, pulling on his drawers and hunting for a shirt.

When the three of them entered the kitchen, Overton was sitting at the table, staring into Edgar's bowl of flummery as if hoping to find the secret to some puzzle in the depths of the hot mixture of oatmeal flour and milk.

"Do you want some flummery?" Edgar chirped as he went to sit beside the man.

Overton's head shot up. He looked warily at Morgan, who returned his stare with an equally wary one of his own. "I—I'm not hungry," he said to Edgar. "Listen, my boy, I need to talk to your ... parents. Do you think you could go play in the garden for a bit?"

With a disappointed shrug, Edgar said, "I suppose so." Then he brightened. "But only if you'll let me feed your horse later. Last time you came, you said I could."

"Of course." Overton watched as Edgar skipped out to the garden. "He's awfully fond of horses, isn't he?"

"Yes, my *son* is fond of a lot of things," Morgan gritted out. "Of course, I'm only now learning what those things are."

When Overton went beet red, Lettice laid a gentle hand on Morgan's arm. "It's all right. Overton has always been a friend to me and Edgar."

She could feel Morgan's muscles tense beneath her fingers, but he thankfully said nothing.

Overton rose from his chair, thrusting his hands behind his back to clasp them together. "I haven't always been a friend. Darcy didn't send Mr. Pennant and Mr. Vaughan to the press-gangs alone, you know. I had a part in that. I should have told you the truth about it from the beginning, but Darcy . . ."

He trailed off, but she didn't have to hear more. She knew what Darcy was like. And she knew what Overton was like. If Darcy asked his brother to go to sea in a leaky coracle, Overton would do it. That's how loyal he was to his brother.

"All that matters is that I know the truth now," she said reassuringly, ignoring Morgan's stiff stance at her side. "Darcy has already admitted to what you and he did."

"Well . . . as long as you know," Overton muttered. "Actually, that's not why I've come."

"Why *have* you come?" Morgan growled.

He met Morgan's gaze with a steady one of his own. "Because I need your help." His voice grew taut. "I—I'm worried about Juliana, out there alone at that estate with . . . that bloody crazy Vaughan."

"He's not crazy," Morgan bit out.

"Isn't he? I heard what he did last night at the council meeting, showing up with those radicals to . . . to . . ."

"Put me forth as his candidate?" Morgan finished for him.

Overton nodded. "I don't care about that. 'Tis all a bunch of bloody politics. I don't give a damn about who's M.P., as long as it's not me." He jutted his chin out, though it quivered. "But I heard that Vaughan is going to put all his money into your campaign. That's proof enough that he's crazy. He'll lose everything trying to fight my brother."

"I think he's willing to risk that," Morgan retorted dryly. "And I'm not sure what concern it is of yours."

"My brother hates Ebbrell and all his lot. He couldn't wait to have them come to the council meeting with cudgels in hand, so he could have them all arrested. And now that you've thwarted him—"

"Wait a minute." Morgan held up his hand. "How did your brother know that the Sons of Wales had planned to riot?"

"Because . . . well . . ." Overton cast Lettice an uncertain glance.

She smiled. "Go on. My husband may be gruff, but he won't hurt you."

"Don't be so sure of that," Morgan muttered, but she pinched his arm, and he added, "Just tell me the truth. I'm a reasonable man."

Overton set his jaw. "Darcy has a spy among the Sons of Wales."

Lettice saw Morgan clench his fists, and she stepped between the two men. "Hear him out, Morgan, before you lose your temper." The dark fire in Morgan's face truly alarmed her.

"I want to know who the wretch is," Morgan ground out.

"I—I thought you might." Without hesitation, Overton gave a name Lettice recognized. " 'Twas he who revealed that you and Vaughan printed those pamphlets six years ago. That's how Darcy justified handing you over to the press. "

Morgan stared at Overton, eyes going wide. "You mean . . . it had nothing at all to do with . . . with Lettice and Juliana?"

Overton shook his head. "No, except that he overheard you and Lettice speaking in the forest one night. That's when he first heard of it. Then he paid one of the men to give him more information, so he could convince the press to take you without letting you ransom yourselves as is sometimes done."

Paling, Morgan dropped into a chair.

Lettice moved to stand beside him, resting her hand on his shoulder. "Doesn't that also mean my lady was faithful to Rhys? She didn't betray him, did she?"

Overton ran a finger beneath his collar. "Nay. She knew nothing of it until after Vaughan and Pennant were well away."

Lettice smiled. She and Morgan had argued at length about this, for Morgan couldn't decide whether or not to believe Lady Juliana. But Lettice had always known she was blameless, even though the evidence to the contrary was great.

"How did you find her and Rhys then?" Morgan asked. "If she didn't tell you where to go—"

"The innkeeper recognized her and sent for us at once."

"The innkeeper?" Lettice asked. All she'd been told was that Rhys had been captured at the inn where he'd been with Juliana, but now she wondered . . . "What inn was it?"

"Didn't you know? The White Oak."

Now it was her turn to sink into a chair. The White Oak, with that bastard innkeeper—

"He said he recognized her because he'd courted you once," Overton added.

Morgan flashed her a quizzical glance, and she nodded.

With a muttered curse, Morgan shot up from the chair. "The innkeeper helped you two that night, and he's been lying about it ever since, hasn't he?"

"Aye." Overton gave a great sigh. "Darcy paid him well."

Morgan paced the floor. "Devil take it, we've got to tell Rhys! He still thinks she betrayed him."

"I know." Overton's face grew wan. "That's why I've come. I want to ride out to Llynwydd and tell him everything, but I don't dare go alone. He might bar the gates to me. But he'll let you in and maybe me with you."

"Why didn't you tell the truth before?" Lettice whispered, thinking of all Juliana must have suffered, living with a man who thought the worst of her. "Why has Darcy continued to insist that she wanted to escape from the marriage? She's his sister, for heaven's sake! And your sister, too."

Overton wrung his hands. " 'Tis a bloody mess, I know. I didn't want Darcy to do any of it, but he wanted a better husband for Juliana than a Welsh squire. I—I just went along, because I thought he might be right. Also, he threatened to cut off my income if I didn't."

"Yes, but what about at the engagement party?" Morgan asked. "Why did he keep lying?"

"He's afraid Vaughan will turn his wrath—and his

newfound influence—on him. Besides, Darcy thinks Vaughan is bewitched enough by Juliana that he won't hurt her. So he won't risk his empire for her."

"And you?" Lettice asked. "What do you think?"

Overton's voice shook. "I'm afraid Vaughan will turn his wrath on all of us if I *don't* tell him the truth. Last night he proved that not knowing the truth won't keep him from destroying Darcy. I don't want him to destroy poor innocent Juliana, too."

Lettice smiled reassuringly. "I truly don't think Rhys would—"

"There's no telling what a man like Rhys might do when he's angry," Morgan interjected, casting her a warning glance.

She frowned and opened her mouth to retort. Then she realized what Morgan was up to. If Overton were reassured about his sister, he might not be so eager to tell the truth. And right now, it was important that Rhys know. Even if, as Morgan had said last night in his rambling, Rhys was bedeviled by his wife, he wouldn't trust her until he was sure of her. Rhys was too cautious a man to throw in his lot with a woman he thought had once betrayed him.

"So." Overton leveled his gaze on Morgan. "Will you go with me to Llynwydd?"

"Of course we'll go," Lettice exclaimed.

Morgan shook his head at her. "*I* will go, love, but not you. Rhys isn't kindly disposed to you either, for he still believes you had a part in the whole thing. 'Twill be better if I go." He faced Overton. " 'Twill be better if I go alone."

Overton shook his head vehemently. "I have to see my sister. I must make certain that she's well." Pain slashed across his face. "And I must explain why we've wronged her so. You're not going without me."

Morgan nodded. "As you wish. Give me a moment to dress, and we'll be off."

When he disappeared into the other room, Lettice went up to Overton and took his hand. "Don't worry about Juliana. It will all come right in the end. I'm sure of it."

Gripping her hand, Overton ventured a smile. "I hope you're right."

They stood awkwardly like that a moment.

Then Lettice gazed up at Overton. "How's Darcy?"

Overton's face clouded as he released her hand. "As well as can be expected, considering that the light has gone out of his life."

Reluctant sympathy made her frown. "He's not taking it well then?"

"Nay."

"I'm so sorry."

"It's not your fault. He was the fool, to toy with your life and then expect you not to hate him for it."

She sighed. "I don't hate him. I just pity him."

Overton stared at her. "You know something, Lettice? When Darcy first became obsessed with you, I didn't understand it. He had a rich, beautiful fiancée and was heir to an earldom. I thought he was mad to dally with a lady's maid."

"He *was* mad," she said, attempting a laugh.

Overton shook his head solemnly. "Nay. In the past few years that I've come to know you, I think he should have done more than make you his mistress. He should have married you."

"Don't be silly," she murmured, but couldn't deny the way his words warmed her. As Darcy's mistress, she'd always received the brunt of Carmarthen's disapproval. No one had chastised him for keeping a mistress, but everyone had criticized her for being his kept woman.

Sometimes she'd even believed they were right to disapprove. And telling herself that she'd had no choice didn't lessen the pain or self-doubt. After a while, she'd almost begun to believe she didn't deserve to be a wife ... that in taking Morgan away, God had deemed her unworthy of it.

Morgan entered the room, and she faced him, a brilliant smile on her face. Time had proven her wrong, thank heavens. Time had brought Morgan back to her.

And now Morgan must bring Rhys back to Juliana.

It was noon, and the house was as quiet as a tavern at dawn, but Juliana still couldn't concentrate on the task before her—examining the larder inventory to assess what items couldn't be provided by the estate and so must be purchased in Carmarthen. Every time she set her mind to reading the list, her mind ignored her wishes and wandered elsewhere.

And always to the same subject. Rhys, still asleep down the hall, but bound to emerge sooner or later. She'd instructed his valet not to awaken him, but not entirely out of consideration for him.

Nay, it had been as much to protect herself as anything—to put off the inevitable. When he'd said last night that he'd soon catch her alone, the blasted man had known exactly what his words would do to her. Now all she could do was wonder when it would happen ... where ... how.... Such thoughts inevitably led to memories of heated kisses and tempting caresses.

Oh, bother, she thought as she set the list aside. She should lock him in the State Bedroom. Then she wouldn't have to worry anymore about when he'd catch her unawares ... or what she'd do when he did.

Lock him in, eh? A smile touched her lips. That would be a change, wouldn't it? Of course, some wretched footman would let him out at once, but still it was lovely to think of him helpless and at her mercy, forced to follow *her* whims for a change.

"Milady?" said a voice at the door to the salon, jarring her from her pleasantly malicious thoughts.

She turned to find Mrs. Roberts in the doorway. "Yes?"

"The master has visitors. I told them he was asleep, but they're being very insistent."

"Who are they?"

"Your brother. The younger one. And a man named Pennant."

Her eyes went wide as she settled back against the caffoy upholstery. Overton had come here to see Rhys? Pennant's appearance she could understand after what Rhys had told her last night, but why was Overton here? The betraying wretch, how dare he visit, as if nothing had happened!

"Send them up here," she choked out. "I'll speak with them." *Oh, yes, I'll speak with my brother,* she thought. *And this time, he'll have to listen to my anger.*

Mrs. Roberts nodded and left, returning a few minutes later with Overton and Morgan.

Juliana rose from the chair as Mrs. Roberts ushered

them into the salon, then left, closing the door. For a moment, Juliana could only stare at her brother, her throat thickening with tears. He wouldn't meet her eyes as he shifted from foot to foot.

"I can't believe you have the audacity to come here after what you've done." Her voice was low and bitter. "Have you come to tell Rhys more lies about me?"

Overton shook his head violently as his gaze snapped up to hers. "I've come to tell him the truth."

"Don't you think it's a little late for that?" Her shoulders shook with a sudden urge to throttle him.

The torment in her voice seemed to alarm him. "He hasn't hurt you, has he?" His gaze roamed over her, looking for signs of physical injury.

She deliberately kept quiet a moment, watching him grow more anxious. *Let him worry,* she thought. *He's done little enough of it until now.*

"Has he hurt you?" Overton repeated, his fists clenching. "If he has, I'll murder him, I'll—"

"Nay," she hastened to tell him. The last thing she needed was for Overton to engage Rhys in fisticuffs. She sighed. "Not physically anyway."

Overton clearly didn't know what to make of that, although Morgan's eyes narrowed.

Somehow she managed a smile. She didn't want to give the wrong impression, and she found herself suddenly loath to share with anyone the details of her stormy relationship with Rhys. "I'm well." She swept her hand about the room. "As you can see, I have the run of the house and . . ." Her voice faltered at the half-truth, then she went on coldly, "Anyway, you needn't worry."

"But I *do* worry," Overton protested.

"Do you? When did this change of heart occur? After all, less than a week ago, you publicly proclaimed me a heartless witch and a betrayer. You lied about me to my husband, who already had good enough reason to resent me. It must have occurred to you then that your lies would turn a tormented man into an unreasonable tyrant."

Terror mixed with self-deprecation in his face. "I'm sorry, Juliana. Oh, God, I'm so bloody sorry. I'm sorry I let Darcy convince me to lie to you in the first place all those years ago. I'm sorry I kept secret what he'd told your husband. And I'm desperately sorry I didn't speak the truth at your engagement party, but Darcy—"

"Darcy this and Darcy that," she cried. "Is it all his doing? What kind of secret hatred must he bear for me that he'd lie so?"

"Not hatred." Overton's distress made his shoulders tremble. "Truly not. You must understand—Darcy thought Vaughan had married you to regain Llynwydd. He thought he was saving you when he had your husband impressed."

She closed her eyes, trying to shut out Overton's woeful expression. What right had he to be sad? He hadn't suffered from his lies. *She* had.

"When Vaughan returned," Overton went on, "Darcy thought he could rescue you by maintaining his tale. He thought Vaughan would want to be rid of you once he was convinced you'd betrayed him."

Behind Overton, Morgan snorted. "Obviously your brother had no idea of how strongly Rhys feels about your sister."

Her eyes shot open to stare at Morgan, but Overton continued as if Morgan hadn't spoken. "Once he realized that Vaughan was serious about revenge, he got scared. He ... he was afraid Vaughan would destroy him."

"And of course, it didn't matter at all that Rhys might destroy me, did it?" she whispered.

Overton paled. "What has he done to you? Don't lie to me, Juliana. If he has abused you or—"

"He hasn't. I—I merely meant that Darcy gave permission to Rhys to do with me as he wished."

She turned away from him to hide the sudden surge of emotions in her. Rhys hadn't abused her ... not in the sense Overton meant. But he'd been tightening his hold on her emotions as each day passed. Soon it wouldn't matter to her that he thought her a witch. Soon he'd have her heart in his hand, while he kept his heart quite safely protected. Was that abuse? She didn't know.

"Where is Rhys now?" Morgan asked.

"Asleep." She faced him. "But surely that doesn't surprise you, Mr. Pennant. He had a late night, since he went out at *your* behest to take on Darcy. I suppose you and my husband are trying to get yourselves impressed all over again."

Morgan's voice was very quiet. "I think Northcliffe knows better than to try that now."

A sudden fear gripped her. She knew only too well how desperate Darcy got when he was cornered. And now that she knew he'd sacrificed her well-being out of fear . . . "He could try something more drastic. Darcy isn't going to take all of this lying down. He'll strike out at Rhys somehow."

"Don't tell me you're worried about your 'unreasonable tyrant' of a husband?" Morgan asked.

Her gaze flew to meet his. He was watching her with the faintest hint of a smirk on his face, but she didn't care. She had to make him understand the treacherous path Rhys had embarked on. "Of course I'm worried. I don't want to lose Rhys again."

Apparently she'd revealed far too much in that one statement. Relief spread over Morgan's face.

And Overton looked hopeful for the first time since he'd entered the study. "So things are going well with you and your husband? Truly?"

"I'm sure things will go much better once you tell him the truth about that night," Morgan said with satisfaction. "I'm sure when you explain how you knew where to find her and—"

"Yes, how did you know?" she interrupted. "That's the one thing I haven't been able to figure out."

Overton shifted from foot to foot. "The innkeeper recognized you and sent word."

She sucked in a breath as everything clicked into place. Yes, she'd thought the innkeeper looked familiar. So that was how they'd known. If she'd only asked the man if she knew him . . . if she'd only thought to ask . . .

"Once we explain about the innkeeper," Overton said, "how Darcy paid to make him lie and how you were blameless, surely Vaughan will realize that you had nothing to do with any of it."

His statement brought her up short. She'd been too busy chastising Overton to realize the full implications of his visit. He'd come to tell the truth. To vindicate her totally to her husband. At last.

Hope swelled in her. Finally, someone would reveal

to Rhys what had really happened that night. And then he'd be suitably chastened and beg her forgiveness. All would be well, and they could put this terrible time behind them.

Until the next time.

Abruptly her hope faded as anger surged in her. This wasn't the first time Rhys had let circumstances convince him to believe the worst of her. Six years ago he'd falsely accused her of spying on the Sons of Wales, only to realize his mistake when her father had threatened to cane her.

Each time she told him she was innocent he refused to believe her. Only when he had external evidence to the contrary did he trust her. Despite all she'd done for Llynwydd and all her explanations for why she'd hidden the marriage, he continued to believe the illusion Darcy had created that night.

And now Overton wanted to prance in here and tell Rhys everything, to act as if none of her suffering had occurred. Overton thought to wipe away the years with a few words.

Worst of all, Rhys would probably believe Overton. Rhys wouldn't believe her, but he'd believe her treacherous brother. She clenched her fists. Then Rhys, too, would act as if none of it had happened, as if she hadn't been publicly maligned and betrayed by them all.

A pox on him! And on them, too! How dare they think they could simply trot in here and make it all right with a few simple words! Well, she wouldn't give them that, nor him either. Not this time. She'd told him she was innocent. It was time he decided if he believed her or not.

She'd done everything in her power to convince him, and still he distrusted her. How could she and he go on if he were always assuming the worst about her, always believing everyone else's perceptions? The distrust would never end.

No, she thought. Much as she ached to have them vindicate her to Rhys, it would only be a temporary solution to a permanent problem. Marriage had to be built on trust. And no one else could provide that trust to him. He must find it in himself.

"I don't want you to tell him the truth," she stated.

Morgan and Overton both stared at her as if she'd just spoken some pagan curse.

Stiffening her spine, she gave them a mutinous glare. "I don't want you to say anything to him. Just go, before he awakens."

"Why the bloody hell would you want that?" Overton exploded.

Morgan was regarding her with a strange expression, but he said nothing.

She drew herself up. "He'll probably believe the two of you if you tell him the truth," she said, the pain of it eating at her. "The trouble is, I want him to believe *me*. I want him to learn to trust *me*. And if you tell him the truth now, he won't learn that."

"But Juliana—" Overton began.

Morgan placed a hand on his shoulder. "She's right. 'Twould be better if Rhys accepted the truth on his own." He cast her an enigmatic glance. "But do you realize what you're asking of him? He suffered much on the H.M.S. *Nightmark,* far more than I did. They battered his pride, stole his dignity, reduced him to an animal. And he's lived six years believing that you helped put him there. Even before that, he'd not had many in his life he could trust. You're asking him to ignore his entire past. Speaking as his friend and one who thinks highly of him, I don't know if he can do that."

Tilting her chin up, she said in a choked voice, "He'd better learn to do it, hadn't he? You seem to forget, he's not the only one who suffered through this. I may not have spent six years in exile nor endured floggings, but I had to live in a perpetual limbo, never knowing if I was widow or wife, never knowing what had happened to him. I even went through the agony of grieving for him after that investigator falsely told me he was dead. And then, when Rhys returned to me, he treated me with a contempt I didn't deserve."

"Yes, but if we tell him—" Overton began.

"If you tell him, he'll say he's sorry, and it will all be better, right? Men! You think a few apologies will wipe away the heartache you've caused by your own stubborn refusal to see a woman's true character!" She fixed her brother with an intent gaze. "Well, I won't let you assuage your guilt this easy way, Overton ... not at the cost to my marriage. Either Rhys learns to trust me or he lives with the consequences of his distrust. But I will not give him this easy solution."

Tears threatened to spill down her cheeks, but she suppressed them. "I *can't* give him the easy solution, not if I want our marriage to last."

They were all silent a moment, the two men watching her as she tried to look convinced about the rightness of her decision. Unfortunately, she wasn't at all convinced. Morgan was right about Rhys's reluctance to trust. She was taking a big chance.

But she had to take it.

"You love him, don't you?" Overton muttered. "You still love that bloody Welshman, or you wouldn't care if your marriage lasted."

She hesitated as the painful truth hit her. Oh, yes, she did love him. Despite everything, she loved him still. She'd always loved him, even after he'd appeared at Northcliffe Hall making those dreadful accusations.

A heavy sigh escaped her lips. "Unfortunately, I do love him. Foolish as it is, I do."

Overton got a sudden sheepish look on his face. "Then I suppose that takes care of my other reason for coming."

Morgan's head shot around. "What other reason?"

With an apologetic glance at Morgan, Overton drew a folded sheet of paper out of his waistcoat pocket along with a sealed envelope. "Well ... you see ... I didn't think I should tell you, Pennant, since I knew you wouldn't approve. But I promised to bring this to Juliana."

As Morgan looked on in bewilderment, Overton gave the paper and the sealed envelope to her. She unfolded the paper. Instantly she recognized the crest at the top. And the signature at the bottom.

Her face drained of color as she dropped into the chair and read it, then opened the sealed envelope and read its contents, too.

"What the devil is it?" Morgan snapped when she lifted her head to stare into space.

"Apparently," she announced in a strained voice, "Lord Devon has decided he wants to resume our betrothal."

Chapter Eighteen

"I'm her true lover always
While the quick life in me stays.
Without her, I go lovelorn—
If it's true she's not foresworn."
—Dafydd ap Gwilym,
"The Wind"

Something tickled Rhys's nose, waking him slowly from a dreamless sleep. He groaned, thinking of Juliana as he tightened his arms about a soft form.

Too soft. Curious, he opened his eyes to find himself clutching a pillow to his face and staring down a feather that had poked through the ticking.

Muttering a curse, he tossed the pillow aside and sat up against the headboard, pushing the hair out of his eyes. Opposite him was a lush tapestry depicting cherubs cavorting with nymphs, one of his father's excesses of interior decoration. Rhys had been staring at those damned curvaceous nymphs for four nights now and thinking of Juliana. No wonder he'd been reduced to hugging pillows.

He groaned as he surveyed the massive state bed with its ivory embroidered silk hangings. It was big enough for three people his size.

Too bad he slept in it alone.

Alone. A sudden gut-deep yearning assailed him, so strong he clenched his fists in his lap. He hadn't thought this far when he'd planned his vengeance, when he'd decided to make Juliana pay for her youthful betrayal. He hadn't considered what it would be like to live with a stranger whom he'd taught to despise him.

He hadn't thought of what it would be like to be so heart-wrenchingly alone.

Nor to have the answer to his loneliness so close, and yet beyond his reach, tantalizing him constantly with possibilities. He craved her more each day, no matter how he battled it or blocked her out of his activities. And it wasn't just the pleasures of her body he craved either. It was the way she startled whenever he entered a room, the smile that broke over her face when he told a funny tale, her endearing turns of phrase and her quick wit.

Not that he'd been deprived entirely of all that. She'd doled smiles and small talk out to him in just enough portions to whet his appetite.

What would it be like to have her be his wife entirely? To have her not only share his bed, but his thoughts, his plans, his hopes for the future?

An ache settled in his belly as he stared around the room so obviously meant to be a place of union for a man and wife, with its matching walnut chests of drawers and its cavernous bed. What would it be like to wake up beside her in the morning? To have her rub his feet? To help her dress, letting his fingers linger over her back as he fastened all those tiny buttons he'd unfastened the night before?

He could only imagine, since he'd never lived with her like that . . . never spent more than one night in the same room with her. But his imagination painted a picture too tempting to be borne.

Sitting up, he threw his legs over the side of the bed. This was insane, this constant, tormenting craving. If he wanted Juliana to be his wife in every way, he could have her.

She was willing. She only required one thing of him before she'd agree to be his wife in more than name. His trust. His faith in her.

Yesterday, he'd said he couldn't pay her price. Today, he wondered why not. True, she'd betrayed him once, but that was a long time ago. Had she betrayed him since his return?

Nay. She'd defied him, but that was different. Her household rebellions commanded his respect, not his distrust. She hadn't tried to rouse her brothers against him . . . she hadn't tried to run away. She'd endured his petty tyrannies with grace and forbearance.

Would it be so impossible to give her what she asked?

Musing over that, he dressed. He glanced at the clock and got a start. God, it was almost one o'clock. She must have ordered the servants to let him sleep. Despite the fact that he'd rushed off last night without telling her where he was going, she was letting him rest today.

A faint smile passed over his face. No doubt she had some other reason for letting him sleep. After last night, his recalcitrant wife was probably plotting a major upheaval ... arming the footmen against him or ordering the cook to feed him gruel so he'd have no strength to seduce her. With Juliana, there was no telling.

The urge to see her grew so great, he hastened to finish dressing, not bothering to don a coat. He went out into the hall, trying to guess where she might be at this hour of the day. Then he heard voices coming from the salon and strode in that direction. She must be in there consulting with Mrs. Roberts, although he couldn't fathom why she would have closed the door. Perhaps to keep from waking him.

The closer he got, however, the more distinct—and unfamiliar—the voices became. He picked out Juliana's at once, but the other voices with her weren't those of Mrs. Roberts or even Mr. Newns.

There were two voices. Two male voices. He walked more briskly toward the salon and just as he reached the door, picked out a faintly familiar voice that made him stop in his tracks and frown. Who in God's name was in there?

"So what do you want me to tell him, Juliana?" the voice said. "You've read the letter. Lord Devon insists that you meet with him, and he's appealing to me and Darcy to arrange it. I have to tell him *something*."

It was St. Albans, he realized in a flash. St. Albans, come to wrest his wife from him.

Fury ripped through him as he swung the door open with such force that it crashed against the outer wall. Both St. Albans and Juliana whirled around. He didn't need to see the guilty flush start in Juliana's face or the terror leap into St. Albans's eyes to know he'd stumbled onto a discussion he hadn't been meant to hear.

"*Uffernol diawl!*" he ground out. In two quick strides, he was across the room and drawing his brother-in-law

up by the collar before either St. Albans or Juliana could
stop him. "You tell that bastard Devon that *my wife* is
no longer his to command!" He twisted the collar until
it tightened about St. Albans's neck. "And if I ever find
you bringing letters to Juliana from him again, I swear
I'll bind you hand and foot and sink you in the Towy!"

"Rhys!" Juliana cried, hurrying to his side and jerking
at his arm. "Let him go! Please!"

"What's he doing here?" Rhys snapped at her. He
shook St. Albans, who was starting to turn blue. "What
in God's name is he doing bringing letters to you from
Devon?"

"Let him go, Rhys," penetrated another voice through
the fiery haze of his anger. It took a few seconds for the
voice to register, but when it did, he released St. Albans
out of sheer shock and turned to find Morgan standing
there.

"Morgan? What are you doing—" He broke off and
turned to look at St. Albans, who was pulling at his
collar, gasping for breath. "Surely the two of you didn't
come here together. . . ."

But obviously they had.

He stood in disbelieving silence, his gaze going from
Morgan to his wife, not sure how to grasp what was
going on.

It was Morgan who finally broke the silence. "St. Albans wanted to make sure Juliana was all right, and I
accompanied him because he was afraid you wouldn't
let him see her."

"I certainly wouldn't have!" Rhys bit out. "Especially
if I'd known he was playing messenger for that damned
marquess! How could you bring him here to coax my
own wife away from me? What kind of friend are you?"

"I didn't know he had letters from Devon with him—"
Morgan began.

"Be quiet, the lot of you!" Juliana turned on Rhys,
eyes flashing. "How dare you dictate from whom I can
and can't receive letters? Overton brought a letter addressed to *me*, and I had every right to read it."

His control snapped as he bore down on her. "How
many letters like this has he delivered? How many times
has he sneaked in here behind my back to help you carry
on a clandestine correspondence with your ex-fiancé?"

"Don't be absurd!" she hissed. "As if anyone could sneak in here with the footmen and butler and maids running about. This is the first time Overton's been here, and I assure you I didn't know he was bringing letters from Stephen."

Letters, he thought. *More than one.* That, plus her use of Devon's Christian name, sent him over the edge. "Well, it's the *last* time he's coming here. And there will be no more letters from your precious 'Stephen,' if I have to lock you into your bedchamber to ensure it!"

"Juliana!" came St. Albans's shocked voice behind Rhys. "You must let me tell Vaughan what—"

"No!" she shouted, her eyes never leaving Rhys's. "Go home, Overton. I thank you for coming. I thank you for your offer earlier. But I'll handle this my own way."

"Yes, go home, St. Albans," Rhys echoed as he glared at her. "And don't come back!"

Juliana settled her hands on her hips. "Pay no attention to my husband. He becomes irrational whenever Lord Devon's name is mentioned."

"Irrational!" Rhys growled. "Irrational? Because I take umbrage at having my wife—"

"Go home, Overton!" Juliana ordered. Briefly she turned her gaze to the two men behind Rhys. "Morgan, take him out of here and go. Both of you! Please!"

"Come on, lad," Rhys heard Morgan say behind him.

"I can't leave her here with this madman!" St. Albans protested, but when Rhys turned to fix him with a murderous gaze, the man paled and let Morgan drag him from the room.

As soon as they were gone, Rhys strode to the door and closed it. "The letters," he commanded, holding out his hand as he returned to where his wife stood. He snapped his fingers. "Give me the letters he brought you!"

A mutinous expression crossed her face. "You have no right to read my letters!"

"I'm your husband! I have every right!"

She looked as if she were about to refuse. Then she muttered, "Oh, you blasted stupid fool!" She picked up two sheets of paper lying on a lacquered table and threw them at him. "Here, have them. Read my 'clandestine' correspondence if you wish! I don't give a damn!"

He snatched them up from where they'd drifted to the floor and began to read them. Both were from Lord Devon. The first was addressed to Lord Northcliffe and St. Albans, asking them in cordial terms to arrange a meeting between him and Juliana, so they could settle affairs between them.

But the other one was addressed to "Lady Juliana, my one true love." Full of effusive apologies and warm compliments, it stated Lord Devon's desire to renew his courtship of her if she could divorce her husband.

The letter would have enraged him even further, except for one fact. It was clearly the first, and it didn't appear to have been solicited by Juliana.

Yet that only slightly mollified him. "So your titled ex-fiancé wants a meeting, does he?" Rhys balled up the letters and tossed them into the fire. "Well, he's not having one."

She watched as the paper burst into flame. "Rhys, I know this is upsetting, but you must let me explain to Stephen that—"

"He's had his explanation!" The thought of her meeting with Lord Devon struck him with such fear and jealousy, he didn't bother to govern his words. "I'm forbidding you to see him, to write to him, to communicate with him in any way, and I will hold firm on this, Juliana!"

"Why are you being so pigheaded? I've already told you I don't love him. What would it hurt for me to write him a letter explaining that ... that ..."

"That what?" His jealousy rode him too hard for him to hold back. "That your cruel husband won't allow you a divorce? He knows that. Or will you offer him an alternative ... an affair perhaps, to give him what you deny your husband!"

The horror in her eyes dashed cold water on his anger, and too late he realized he'd gone too far. "Oh, God, I'm sorry, Juliana. I didn't mean—"

"Yes, you did." She backed away from him, her shoulders shaking uncontrollably. "No matter what I do, you still think I'm some ... despicable creature who would deceive and betray you at every turn."

All he'd meant to do before he came in here was tell her that he cared, that he wanted to change things between them. Instead, he'd let his jealousy get the better of him. "Nay—" he began.

"You won't be happy until I've received my just deserts for what I supposedly did to you ... and for what I really did by stupidly keeping our marriage secret." Tears welled in her eyes as her voice dropped to an aching whisper. "I—it's not enough to make me a prisoner in my own home or cut me off from my family or refuse my help in caring for the estate. Nay, you must have more, mustn't you? You must remind me at every turn of your distrust. You must punish me and torment me!"

He shook his head, but she looked at him with a wild light in her eyes. "Perhaps I should help you, so we can be done with this once and for all!"

Without warning, she flew past him to open the door, and he turned, poised to run after her, but she surprised him by calling the housekeeper in a shaky voice.

"What the devil—" he said as he strode toward her.

Mrs. Roberts had apparently been listening at doors again, for she appeared in the doorway almost instantly. "Yes, milady?"

Juliana drew a ragged breath. "I've decided on the marketing list. You won't find most of the items in the market, but I'm sure Simms can get them from one of the warships in Carmarthen Bay. I'll need hardtack, the oldest and most maggot-ridden you can find ... some salt beef ... and ... and grog ... let's not forget grog."

"Juliana!" he said sharply, but she ignored him, her voice rising as she recited several of the foods she'd apparently learned were served on navy warships.

"But milady," Mrs. Roberts protested, "why would you and the master want—"

"Oh, not for the master." Her voice had reached a hysterical pitch. "This is to be *my* diet. The master will eat his usual fare, but for the next ... oh ... three years or so, I'll be wanting—"

"That's enough!" He grasped her arm, alarmed by what she was saying ... and the more frightening fact that she was apparently serious.

He pulled her back into the room, then turned to the

startled housekeeper, whose mouth was opening and closing in bewilderment like a beached carp. "Your mistress has had some upsetting news. Ignore what she just said. She's overwrought and—"

"Don't you dare ignore that order, Mrs. Roberts!" Juliana cried as he attempted to thrust her behind him.

"Ignore that order and go away!" He shut the door in Mrs. Roberts's face.

As he turned back to Juliana, he noted with distress the torment in her eyes.

"I should have realized that wouldn't be harsh enough for you," she whispered in a reedy voice as she backed away from him. "It doesn't entirely live up to what *you* suffered, does it? I—I mean, I couldn't hope to satisfy your desire for punishment with mere food deprivation."

"Don't be ridiculous, I don't want you punished." He fought to stay calm when all he felt was growing fear at the strange, lost look on her face.

She didn't even seem to have heard him. She was wringing her hands, her gaze darting this way and that. "Perhaps a few floggings would satisfy you. It might be difficult to find a servant who'd agree to flog me regularly, but maybe one of the farmers—"

"Juliana, calm down," he said, truly disturbed by the panic creeping into her voice. He edged toward her.

But she darted behind the sofa, now rubbing her hands in a frenzy up and down her arms. "Then again, even a few floggings wouldn't take care of those years you spent in America, would they?" Her voice had taken on a plaintive, pitiful note that clutched at his heart. "You were wounded and cut off from your home and—"

"For God's sake, Juliana—"

"I—I'm not sure what I could do about that." She stopped moving, as if that would help her think, her eyes wide and frightened as a doe's.

In a flash, he was around the sofa and had her in his arms.

As she struggled against him, he held her close, feeling her body shake. "Hush, *cariad*," he whispered in sheer desperation. He'd never seen her like this. Never. Damn it all, he'd driven her to this with his foolish accusations. "Hush. I don't want to hurt you."

Her breath came in quick, short gasps as she flailed against him. Tears coursed down her cheeks. "Y-you must help me think of a suitable punishment, Rhys. Tell me what you require . . . as penance, so I can . . . do it and be done with it."

"I don't want a penance," he insisted, having the devil's own time keeping her in his arms. "God knows I don't want you to suffer any of what I suffered. I swear it!"

"Oh, but you *do*!" she protested, though the hysterical note in her voice was weakening. "You want to strip me of everything . . . to make me your slave. . . ."

He groaned and tightened his arms around her. "Nay. Not so."

She went still, then lifted her tear-stained face to his. "What do you want of me then?" She clutched his waistcoat with trembling fingers. "Tell me what you want of me!"

"I want you to be my wife. Nothing more than that." When she stared at him blankly, he plunged on, "I want you to share my life with me. I want to put the past behind us and go on."

Her absolute quiet made him fear he'd gone too far, but he kept talking anyway. "You remember how you said we should find peace together? I want to do that, Juliana. I want peace. With you. Here at Llynwydd."

" 'Tis too late." She shook her head. "You don't want anything but my body, and you certainly don't want peace. You told me you don't even know what it is. And now I believe you."

She averted her face from his with a look of such desolation, he felt fear claw at him. This acquiescence worried him more than all her anger.

He released her only to catch her head between his hands, forcing her to look at him. "You said you'd teach me to find peace, *fy annwyl mhriod*. I'm holding you to that promise."

She closed her eyes, hiding from him as she whispered, "I—I can't. . . ."

"You *can*." He rubbed one of her tears away with his thumb.

"You'll only hurt me again—"

"Nay!" He sought for something, anything that would

pull her out of this hopelessness. "Don't tell me you're giving up on me. If you give up on me ... I'll ... I'll turn into a beast such as you've never seen. I'll terrorize my tenants and run roughshod over the servants."

She shuddered, but said only, "It doesn't matter."

He made his voice deliberately provoking. "You don't care? Then I'll throw your precious *cwpwrdd tridarn* out in the rain and I'll ..." God, she was limp in his arms as if she truly didn't care what he did anymore. He forced steel into his voice. "I'll cut off Evan's lessons. I'll not even give him the paper you had for him yesterday—"

That did it, he thought as her eyes shot open.

"You wouldn't dare! Why, the poor boy never did a body wrong in his whole life! I won't let you—" She broke off as she saw relief in his face. "You wouldn't hurt him, would you?"

Encouraged that her expression had lost some of its bleakness, he murmured, "Who knows what I'd do without you? I can be a monster, you know."

"I know." She stared at him a long moment. Then she gave a shuddering breath. When she spoke again, her tone was more pointed. "How well I know."

He couldn't resist a smile. The desperate creature of a moment ago seemed to have fled, leaving *his* Juliana, full of stubborn rebelliousness. Thank God.

He dropped his hands from her face, but only so he could clasp her shoulders and draw her to him. "Then tame the monster. You're the only one who can."

"I haven't had much success with that to date. I've obviously been going about it all wrong."

He bent to nuzzle her temple, then pressed a kiss against the pulse, feeling it quicken beneath his lingering lips. "Nay. You've been driving me mad with wanting you, and surely that's the first step in taming a monster."

She glanced uncertainly at him, her eyes green as the meadows surrounding Llynwydd. "I don't know. I think you're worse when you want me. You ... you become so jealous and—"

"And I say stupid, foolish things," he finished. "Yes, I know. I shouldn't have said what I did about you and Devon. I went a little insane at the thought of him trying to get back into your life. But 'tis only because I want you so very much, and my wanting hasn't been satisfied." He wound a lock of her hair loosely about his hand, relishing the spun silk texture of it, before he lifted it to his lips and kissed it. " 'Tis only because I've spent endless hours remembering the feel of your hair and the taste of your mouth."

She drew a ragged breath as she tried to push away from him. "You say these lovely things one minute and then the next—"

"I know, but I'll turn over a new leaf." Slowly, he wound her hair tighter around his hand until his fingers were against the back of her neck. Cradling her head in his hand, he held her still as he lowered his head. "I promise to be a monster no more ... if you'll only satisfy this craving that's eating me up." He brushed her cheek with his lips. "This hunger that can only be assuaged by you." He closed his mouth over hers, fearful that she wouldn't respond, that he had driven her out of his reach.

But although she froze a fraction of a second, stiffening in his arms, it only took a moment for her lips to soften. He lingered over them, drinking in her hot little breaths until he could stand the beckoning heat no more. Then he plunged his tongue inside her wet, warm mouth, feeling her tongue dance away, only to come back and tentatively touch his.

By thunder, she was wonderful. And she was his. All his, whether she admitted it or not.

Taking his time, he explored the hot satin of her mouth, the slide of her tongue around his. He left her not a moment to think about what she was doing. And when she slipped her arms about his waist and pressed against him heedlessly, he took the invitation to grow bolder. He rubbed the heel of his palm over her breast, groaning when she arched into his hand.

"That's it, darling," he whispered against her parted lips, then trailed kisses along her smooth, damp cheek, and up to her delicate ear. "That's the way to tame the monster."

"You're not acting tame," she grumbled. But when he ran his tongue along the exquisite rim of her ear, she gasped and dug her fingers into his waist, curving her body against his like a cat.

"Neither are you." He ran his hands along the front of her dress and found the hooks that held her bodice together.

"Rhys!" she protested when he worked them loose. "For God's sake, 'tis daylight and we're in the middle of the salon!"

"Aye, and after yesterday, that's where we'll stay. I'll not lose you on the way to the bedroom again."

"But Rhys—"

He stopped her mouth with a kiss, a hearty one that left her clinging to him. Peeling open her bodice and drawing down the neck of her shift, he filled his hands with her soft breasts, which were thrust high by her corset. Then he thumbed her nipples, feeling them draw tight until they were as hard as cherry stones—hard and sweet and driving him utterly mad.

By thunder, he wanted to tear the clothes off her, to devour those luscious breasts as he thrust into her delectable body over and over and . . .

Mustn't do that . . . mustn't scare her, he thought in a jumble as even his mind became thick and slow with need. *Must make her want me. As she used to.*

He skimmed his hands over her gown, unlacing and unpinning what he could, desperate to have her naked so he could touch her and caress her and make her desire him. But it had been too damned long since he'd undressed a woman, and Juliana was wearing far too many clothes.

Despite what he'd told her, he'd only had relations with a few other women in America. All of them had been scantily dressed, the kind of women who spread their legs for a fee, even when the customer was drunk and called another woman's name as he found his release. He'd scarcely even been conscious during those couplings.

Not like this time. This time he was unbearably conscious and ready to explode with wanting her. He fumbled with the corset laces, cursing when he couldn't unknot them.

His ineptness touched Juliana. "Let me," she whispered and began to work loose the knots of the front-laced corset she'd taken to wearing.

She felt almost as much urgency as he, and that terrified her. After his fury this afternoon, she didn't want to need him so much. Why did she have to need him more than he needed her?

"Take it off," he said hoarsely—and unnecessarily—as she undid the last knot of her corset.

She did as he asked, but a shiver passed through her, for his words echoed those of their first night together after his return . . . when he'd commanded her so cruelly.

Yet as he lifted his hands to push the shift from her shoulders, dragging it down her arms with aching slowness, she knew this was not at all like that night. His eyes were still that intense blue, raking hotly over her bared breasts and belly, and his brow was still furrowed with concentration.

But when he grazed his fingers over her skin, it was with a gentleness near to reverence. "How can you have grown only more beautiful in six years?" he whispered as he traced the outline of one breast.

He'd never denied that he found her beautiful. Still, his words gratified some ancient female urge in her to be admired, and she found herself smiling in feline satisfaction.

With a look that scorched her, he dragged his finger down her belly to the waistband of her skirt.

"Take the rest of it off," he said in a husky voice. "I want to see all of you, *cariad*."

She started to obey, then paused. "Only if you remove your waistcoat."

A flicker of surprise passed over his face at her sudden boldness, but he quickly acquiesced, then went one step further and removed his shirt.

"Well?" He tugged at the waistband of her gown. "I'm waiting, *anwylyd*."

Suddenly shy, she removed her gown and then her petticoats, hiding her blushing face from him as her shift slid to the floor last of all, leaving her naked.

She heard his quick indrawn breath, felt the heat of his gaze on her. She shrank back, overwhelmed by her own emotions, afraid of how easily he could take her will from her.

But he caught her up in his arms and strode to the sofa. Laying her down upon the caffoy upholstery, he knelt beside her and cupped her chin in his hand to force her to look at him. She trembled when she saw the desire whirling like a thousand flames in the depths of his eyes.

He ran his thumb over her lips. "You have nothing to fear from me, *cariad*. I want only to please you."

"And not yourself?"

With a smile, he bent to brush his mouth against hers. "Aye, and that, too. Surely you won't deny me that. I've spent too many nights longing to touch your 'sweet body that from faith can guile.' "

The poetic words jarred her. Then she recognized the lines from Robin Ddu's poem. "That's not fair. You know I can't resist when you quote poetry to me."

His low, seductive chuckle echoed down deep in her loins. "I know." He kissed her brow. " 'Your brow like a daisy bright.' " He swept her hair back off her shoulder to fan out on the upholstery. " 'Your hair like a tongue of gold.' "

Then he touched his lips to the hollow of her throat, before running his tongue down the slope of her breast to curl it about her nipple. " 'Your throat's upright growth,/Your breasts, full spheres both.' "

He tugged at her nipple with his teeth, shooting such sparks through her that she whimpered and clutched his shoulders. But he didn't linger there. His mouth inched lower as he trailed his tongue in a line down her belly to her navel, dipping it there before sliding lower.

"Your belly like a ripened peach," he intoned, then sucked the skin lightly into his mouth, making her squirm beneath him.

"Those aren't ... Ddu's words," she choked out as his lips brushed the edges of her silky triangle of hair.

"Nay, those are mine," he whispered. He skirted the throbbing place between her legs. Instead he pressed a kiss into the silky skin of her thigh. "Your thighs smooth as polished beech."

"Th-that's enough," she choked out as his tongue spiraled higher and higher toward the spot no man had ever kissed.

"Enough what? Poetry?" he rasped. "Or this?"

But he didn't wait for her answer. Using his fingers to part the delicate folds of skin, he darted his tongue over the tiny nub he found there, and she thought she'd die.

It was like being stroked by lightning, courted by sunshine, and caressed by moonlight all at once. The heat of it made her buck beneath him, trying to get more, yet afraid she'd never get enough to satiate the tension he was building between her legs with each flick of his tongue.

He shifted position until he was crouched over the sofa, his tongue licking up at her like flame, laving her, teasing her. She thrust against his hot mouth, wanting something she couldn't fathom, feeling the tension lengthen and stretch and grow tauter by the second.

"Oh ... Rhys ... Rhys."

His mouth suddenly left her and she moaned, undulating against the sofa in a fruitless attempt to ease the craving in her loins.

"I can't ... wait ... any longer," he ground out.

She opened her eyes to find him standing beside the sofa, tearing off his breeches, then his drawers. And before she could turn away, she was looking at his long, hard shaft.

Her mouth went round as she stared at it in blatant fascination. Her first night with Rhys, she'd been too shy, too naive to really look at the part of him that had thrust up inside her. But six years of remembering had made her curious.

Pushing up onto one elbow, she reached out and touched him, stroking the smooth, firm skin. When he groaned, she glanced at his face, at the dark red flush spreading over him from the neck down as he tried to stay still.

But he couldn't help thrusting against her hand, and instinctively she encircled him with her fingers. Instantly he cursed and clasped her wrist in an iron grip.

"Nay," he moaned. "If you touch me like that, I'll explode." Then he knelt on the sofa. "And I want to explode inside you."

Inside me, she thought, growing warm again. *That's what I want. Rhys inside me.*

Quickly he covered her, nudging her legs apart with his knee. "I need you, Juliana," he whispered as he pressed up against the juncture of her thighs. "God, how I need you."

A brief pang hit her. The first time they'd made love, he'd said, "I love you."

Then he eased into her, making her forget everything but the present. "Christ, you're tight as a virgin." A quick flash of satisfaction crossed his face. "Tight as that first time . . ."

For heaven's sake, had he actually thought she might have done this with someone else? He'd accused her of it before, but she hadn't thought he really believed it. The bastard! She writhed angrily against him, but that only planted him deeper, stretching her, urging her untutored body to accommodate him.

"You've been the only one to touch me," she moaned, half in distress, half in pleasure as he began to move in slow, enticing strokes.

"And I will always be the only one to touch you, *fy annwyl mhriod,* for I'll let no one else have you," he vowed, his face dark and tight as he quickened his thrusts. "Oh, God . . . Juliana . . . it's been so long. . . ."

The sense of invasion began to lessen as his movements drew the silken tension tight in her again. With a choked gasp, she strained against him, clutching at his buttocks to anchor him between her thighs. She felt his muscles flex and grow tight as he lunged against her, inside her, filling her so fully she cried out with the pleasure of it.

"That's it, my darling," Rhys whispered as he plunged his hard length to the very heart of her. "If you only knew how incredible you feel. . . ."

She knew how incredible he felt, driving into her like thunder, bringing her closer and closer to some dark explosion she sensed lay waiting. Each time their bodies came together, she went a little insane, twisting beneath him like an ensnared tigress as she tried to seal herself more tightly to him.

He bent his head to taste her mouth, and when she nipped at his lower lip, he growled, then caught her open mouth, stabbing his tongue into her in perfect rhythm with the thrusts of his hips. She met every kiss with her own wild hunger as raw, sheer need made her want to devour him, to entrap him in her heart so he could never doubt her again.

The words "I love you" burned the back of her throat,

but pride kept her from saying them. Instead she yielded up her body completely to him, sure that one day she'd be able to give him the words, too.

When the explosion hit her, she wasn't prepared for the pure, white heat of it ... the power that hurtled through her, shattering all her control. She gasped and surged up, feeling her body pulse against his as she held on tight and let the force shudder through her, in her, around her.

"Jesus!" he cried out, then drove into her one last time, his body convulsing as he spilled his seed inside her. "By thunder, Juliana ... *cariad* ... mine ... all mine ..."

He trailed off into muttered Welsh endearments as he collapsed atop her, burying his face in the crook of her shoulder.

She felt totally spent, drained of both her will and her strength. Yet it wasn't an unpleasant feeling. There was something deeply satisfying about lying in the arms of her handsome husband, knowing that she'd just pleasured him ... and found a pleasure of her own in the process. Even his weight upon her gave her contentment.

After several moments of lying there with limbs entangled as their heartbeats slowed to normal, Rhys pressed a kiss against her neck. "Now *that*, my darling, was the way to tame a monster."

"Mm," she murmured, running her fingers over his sweat-sheened back. "I shall have to try it more often."

He drew back, a mischievous smile on his lips. "Yes, a great deal more often. In fact ..." He ground up against her.

To her shock, she realized he was growing hard again. "Rhys!" she whispered. Dear heaven, was it normal for a man to be so lusty again so soon after lovemaking?

His gaze burned into hers. "Six years is a long time, *anwylyd*. And contrary to those hateful words I said to you our first night together, you were the only woman I truly wanted in all that time, the only woman I craved."

Something unknotted inside her at his confession. It had driven her mad thinking of all the women who must have pleasured him in America.

"So you see, I have six years of hunger for you stored up inside. And it'll take me at least six more years to reduce my hunger to a manageable level." He slid off of her, stretching out his hand. "But this sofa is uncomfortable, and what I wish to do with you requires a more comfortable setting."

She blushed as she took his hand and sat up. "You don't mean—"

"I do," he said, raking her with a lascivious glance before he threw her gown at her. "Come on, wife. Let's continue this in our bedchamber. We've got all day . . . and all night . . . and I intend to use very minute of it."

She had to admit the thought of spending the day in bed with Rhys made her heart pound all over again. Eagerly, she rose from the sofa.

They drew on the minimum of clothing amid myriad quick kisses. When they left the salon, they found no one around, but as soon as they took a few steps, Mrs. Roberts rushed up the stairs. She'd obviously been listening and waiting in the hall below.

"Milady, are you all right?" the housekeeper asked in alarm as she noted Juliana's dishabille.

Any other time Juliana might have welcomed the housekeeper's concern, but not at the moment. "I'm fine," she answered, unable to repress the lilt in her voice as she gazed up at Rhys. "Go back to the kitchen, Mrs. Roberts. Everything is fine."

The housekeeper hesitated as Rhys and Juliana swept past her, then watched uncertainly as they began to stride down the hall arm-in-arm. As they reached the door to their bedchamber, Juliana paused. "Oh, and Mrs. Roberts, tell the servants that I will personally dismiss anyone who ventures up here in the next few hours."

Rhys chuckled as he drew Juliana into their room. "Aren't you worried about what the servants will think, my lady wife?"

She gazed up at him with a shining face. "They'll think I've decided to share a bed with my husband," she said, purposely echoing his words of a few days past. "I should hope they'd realize that."

With a crow of triumph, he caught her up in his arms. And she didn't protest when he carried her to the bed.

Chapter Nineteen

"Three things are reckoned wealth:
A woman—sunshine—health—
And in the heaven's dower
(Save God) a maid's the flower."
—Dafydd ap Gwilym,
"The Grey Friar"

Juliana tucked a loose tendril of hair beneath her cap as she stared up at the threatening clouds massing in the sky. Just what they didn't need for the hay harvest. A thunderstorm. She could only hope that since it was near dusk, the men were close to being finished.

With sharp commands, she ordered the footmen to hurry as they loaded the carts with the harvest feast that the farmers expected the squire to provide as reward for their work. But her mind wasn't on what she was doing.

It had been two weeks since Rhys had carried her into their bedchamber and, as he'd promised, made love to her for hours. Since that day, much had changed between them. True to his word, Rhys had treated her as his wife from the moment she'd come to his bed. He'd given her all the freedom and privileges a wife deserved and more, for he'd made her his equal partner in running the estate.

Their days were busy and full. She usually rose before Rhys and attended to breakfast. Then they went their separate ways for the most part, having found the tasks that suited them best and appropriated them accordingly. Sometimes they lunched together, sometimes not. And they took the occasional ride in the late afternoon.

It wasn't until evening that they truly had any time for themselves. Dinner was leisurely. Then they played backgammon or chess. Sometimes they read. And afterward . . .

Her cheeks flushed as she helped a footman slide a large pan on top of another and secure it in place. Oh, yes, afterward, she and Rhys went to bed in the great state bed. He often made love to her. Some nights he peeled her gown slowly from her, lavishing kisses over every inch he bared, then lingering over her body for what seemed like hours as he brought her to the heights of pleasure. Other nights, they tore off each other's clothes and came together like animals, writhing and straining in their haste to join their bodies in complete union.

She'd grown to know every inch of him . . . every scar, every small blemish, every well-shaped muscle. She loved the way he clutched his pillow in sleep. She loved how he stretched his legs and groaned when he awakened in the morning, then opened his eyes with a slow, sensuous smile meant only for her.

She loved everything about him. She loved him, period.

A splinter of wood pricked her finger, and with a frown she sucked off the droplet of blood that beaded on the skin. She still didn't know if Rhys loved her, however. He often said that he needed her. And that he desired her.

Still, he never said he loved her. It wouldn't have bothered her so much if not for one other thing—they never spoke of what had happened six years ago. The one time she'd brought it up, he'd refused to talk about it. He'd insisted that he wanted to put the past behind him, that it didn't matter what had happened.

But it did matter. She could feel it sometimes in the way he watched her, his brow furrowed and his eyes tormented. She could feel it in the sudden shuttering of his expression whenever his impressment was mentioned. He needed her and he wanted her, but he couldn't bring himself to trust her. And he still couldn't love her.

Nonetheless, she told herself as she helped a footman spread an oilcloth over the cart, she *had* made progress. Why, she'd accidentally mentioned Stephen yesterday, and although Rhys had flinched, he hadn't exploded or baited her with questions about what had gone on in the course of Lord Devon's courtship of her.

Yes, she was definitely making progress. And in time—

Two hands closed over her eyes. She dropped the oil-cloth with a shriek.

"Good evening, my lady," murmured a husky voice in her ear.

"Rhys Vaughan!" she scolded as she wriggled away from him. "I swear, if you don't stop creeping up and frightening the life out of me, I'll—"

The rest of her words were muffled by his kiss, a long, probing one calculated to rouse her blood. His face was grimy and he smelled of hay, and they were surrounded by curious footmen, but she responded nonetheless.

When he drew back after several long moments, his eyes were laughing. "What were you saying, darling?"

She blushed as she glanced around to find all the foot-men smirking as they went on about their work. "You're the most infuriating man I've ever known," she whispered, but he merely chuckled.

She rolled her eyes in disgust. The man was certainly sure of her. With a little sniff, she strode down to the last cart, which the footmen were already covering with oilcloth. "What are you doing here anyway? I thought you were overseeing the hay harvest. Surely they're not finished."

He fell into step beside her. "Almost. We worked fast to make sure we beat the rain."

"How did it go?"

"Very well. The farmers were pleased that I joined them, since they're used to having Newns oversee every-thing. But I've come back to fetch the harvest feast. And to fetch you to join us."

She looked down at her dirt-stained gingham gown and touched a hand to her flushed face. "Like this?"

He laughed. "Believe me, you look a lot better than the rest of us."

"I'm sure. But they won't expect me to attend. There's so much to do and . . ." Gesturing to the sky that threat-ened rain, she added, "I don't know if I want to be caught in that."

"It'll hold off a while longer. Besides, I have my rea-sons for wanting you there this evening. I need your help."

"For what?"

"I'll tell you on the way. Come on." Without warning, he lifted her onto the perch of the cart. Going to his horse, he took off a burlap bag that was slung over the saddle, then returned to throw it onto the seat next to her before climbing up to sit on the other side of the bag. With a click of his tongue, he started the horses into a walk as the liveried footmen scurried to take their places on the carts and then moved into position behind Rhys's cart.

She crossed her arms over her chest. "Now, Squire Arrogance, if you'll tell me why you're dragging me off to the fields—"

"Thomas Newcome helped us bring in the hay harvest today," he said, his eyes on the road.

"Of course. He always does."

"And Evan was there, too."

She remained silent, eyes narrowing as she waited for Rhys to get to the point.

"You told me you wanted to see the boy in school."

"Yes, but—" She bit her lip. "Rhys, if you're thinking of talking to Mr. Newcome about Evan this evening, you must abandon that idea. Evan is terrified of what his father might do if either of us speak to him." She caught her breath. "You know, sometimes I worry that . . . that he beats the boy. He's a stern man given to harsh punishments."

"I imagine you're right about that." He urged the horses into a faster pace as they cleared the entrance gates. "I gather that he's also a very proud man. But I don't intend to talk to him. Not at first. I have a better method of convincing him to let his son go to school."

"Oh?" She laid her hand on the seat beside her, only to feel the burlap bag he'd placed there. It squirmed under her hand, and she shrieked, yanking her hand back. "What in heaven's name—"

"It's all right. It's just a garden snake, perfectly harmless."

"A snake! A snake?" She scooted as far away from the bag as she could manage. "Why on earth are you carrying a snake about?"

He grinned at her. "Well, my darling, it's like this. . . ."

Fifteen minutes later, when they'd arrived at the hay

field, Juliana was grinning as widely as Rhys. Only Rhys could come up with a plan so devious. She eyed the squirming bag nervously, then glanced up at the dark sky. She only hoped it would work and that the rain would hold up long enough for them to pull it off.

As soon as the men saw the carts driving up the road, they let out a cheer. Rhys had been right. Only a small spot at one end of the field was left uncleared and the workers took scant moments to finish it and load the wagons that were carrying the hay to the barns. As the wagons lumbered off, Rhys's carts lumbered up to the field, and the workers fell into step beside them. There were women among the workers, stout farmer's wives who'd obviously shared in the work. The faces of every man and woman were caked in dust and sweat, and their clothes were all of one color—hay brown.

As she and Rhys pulled to the side of the road, she spotted Evan standing with his father, his young face flushed and his thin, bare shoulders smeared with hay dust, and she was glad she'd come.

Rhys stood up in the cart and raised his hands. "*Noswaith dda, ffrindiau!*"

"*Noswaith dda,*" the workers echoed as they smiled, clearly pleased to hear the squire greet them as friends.

Rhys continued to speak in Welsh. "You've all worked very hard. You've done well by me and my wife today. Now it's my turn to do well by you." He turned and gestured to the carts behind him. "There's mutton with potatoes and arage and pottage as well as pudding, cheese, spiced fruit cakes, and light ale, compliments of my wife and her efficient kitchen."

Cheers rose up all around. Sometimes the harvest feast was nothing more than barley bread and salt pork with *glasdwr*, watered-down buttermilk, to drink. So a dinner of mutton stew and cheese washed down with *diod fain* was generous indeed, especially since both mutton and cheese were very dear.

Juliana smiled. It was just the feast for a squire to offer who wanted to endear himself to his tenants. Rhys was nothing if not canny in the ways a laborer's mind worked. Later they'd be saying what a "good fellow" the squire was, "not one of those stingy men who spend all their time in London, but someone who knows how to fill a body's stomach."

Juliana swelled with pride. Rhys made a wonderful squire. But she'd known he would.

He grinned as he handed her down from the cart, but soon they were too engrossed in serving out the meal to even speak to each other. He cut slabs of the stiff rice pudding as she doled out stew into earthenware basins, then cut hunks of Resurrection cheese, a popular local cheese so named because it was pressed between the fallen gravestones of a ruined church.

As she worked, she kept a wary eye on the burlap bag she'd tucked up under her cloak. Rhys had said the blasted snake only *looked* like a poisonous adder and wasn't dangerous at all, but she wasn't taking any chances.

When everyone had gotten their food and gone to sit in groups about the field, Rhys came to her side. The light was rapidly failing, and a contented quiet filled the chilling air as some of the workers ate and others built a fire in the center of the field, surrounding it with stones that had been bared in the reaping.

"Let's do it now, before the light is completely gone," Rhys murmured under his breath, then slipped his arm about her waist.

Nodding, she walked beside him across the field to where Evan and his father sat alone. As she and Rhys approached, she flashed both Newcomes a wide smile.

"Good evening," she said brightly, ignoring the way Thomas Newcome scowled at her. "I hope the meal is good."

The father merely grunted, but Evan mumbled, "Very good, my lady," shooting his father an anxious glance.

"I'm so glad you're here, Evan. I have some plums I wanted to send back to your mother. If you'll accompany me to the wagon, I'll give you the plums and you can bring them home with you."

Evan looked at his father, who shrugged. "Go on, then. Your ma would like a plum or two, I'll wager."

Obediently, Evan stood up and began to walk with her. As soon as she heard Rhys saying, "I need to have a word with you about the barley harvest, Mr. Newcome," she grabbed Evan's arm, pulling him up close.

"What is it, my lady?" he whispered as they strolled toward the cart.

"Do you want to go to school, Evan?"

"You know I do, but Father—"

"Never mind him. Do exactly as I say, and I think your father will be willing to send you to school."

She murmured instructions as they walked, and as soon as they'd skirted the men, she made sure they moved as close to the abandoned scythes and as far from the workers as they could while still looking as if they were headed for the cart. Then she reached under her cloak for the burlap bag.

Glancing around, she found no one watching her. Quickly she emptied the snake onto the ground, then stepped back and let out a bloodcurdling scream.

Every man and woman around jumped to their feet. Despite the fact that Evan had been told to expect the scream, he recoiled as if he'd been stung, then stood there frozen.

"A snake, a snake!" she cried as she shot Evan a stern glance.

Shaking off his surprise, he ran toward one of the scythes.

The blasted snake started to crawl off in the opposite direction, and she had to do some quick maneuvering to make it look as if it were headed for her.

On cue, Rhys started running from across the field. But before anyone else could react, Evan had returned with the scythe. Just as Rhys reached her, Evan chopped downward, cutting the head off the snake.

Forcing tears to her eyes, she collapsed into Rhys's arms. "It was coming for me . . . oh, Rhys, it was dreadful. . . ."

"My God, 'tis an adder," Rhys said as he held her against him and stared at the dead snake in the rapidly failing light.

"An adder," murmured the voices of the men, crowding in around her.

"You might have been killed," Rhys exclaimed, holding her tightly against him. Then he looked up and stared at Evan. "You saved my wife's life, Evan."

Evan beamed, thoroughly caught up in the deception.

"What?" said Thomas Newcome as he reached them. "What has happened?"

"Your son has saved my wife's life," Rhys repeated as Juliana continued to shake, her trembling real this time. The most important part was still to come.

Mr. Newcome stared at the snake. "God have mercy. A snake! Did my boy kill it?"

Juliana dug her fingers into Rhys's arm.

"Yes," Rhys said. "Thank God. Otherwise it would have killed my wife. It's an adder, the kind that lives in tall grasses like these. We probably flushed him out today with our reaping." Releasing her, he bent to point out some faint markings on the snake's head. "You see? There's the markings."

Mr. Newcome nodded his head as if he knew exactly what Rhys was talking about, though it was doubtful he did. Vipers were rare enough in Wales, and he'd probably never seen one before. Besides, she thought, in the dying light, he wouldn't have been able to tell much anyway.

" 'Tis an adder, all right," piped up another man in front, who bent to examine the snake. "One bite from this and milady would have been dead in an instant."

Juliana felt a little guilty at the man's tone of assurance, but told herself that their trick was for a good cause.

Rhys made that plain with his next words to Mr. Newcome. "For this, your son deserves a reward." He straightened.

Mr. Newcome straightened, too, his face brightening. "He does?"

"Of course." Rhys flashed her a smile. "I am forever in his debt for saving my beloved wife."

Stepping forward, he clapped his arm about Evan's shoulder. "Juliana tells me you're an intelligent boy, son. She says you could make your mark in any school. How would you like to go to Eton in the fall? That is, if your father would allow it."

The stunned expression on Mr. Newcome's face was matched by the one on Juliana's. Eton? Rhys had promised to send Evan to school, but Eton? That was exceedingly generous and far better than she'd dreamed.

Evan was staring up at Rhys in wonder. "You'd send me to school, sir? Do you mean it?"

"Aye. 'Tis the least I can do."

"But isn't Eton in England? Isn't it the grand school that Lady Juliana told me about, the one you went to that's for the sons of rich men and lords?"

Rhys nodded.

Evan's face clouded. "Are you sure I could manage at such a fine school?"

Rhys glanced at Juliana, and she nodded, still speechless. Turning his attention back to Evan, Rhys said, "If Lady Juliana thinks you're ready, I'm sure you are. But if you're worried, my wife would no doubt be willing to tutor you for the rest of the summer, so that you won't be lacking."

"Hold on here," Mr. Newcome burst out, having finally found his voice. "The rest of the summer? Send him away to this Eton place? The boy has to work the farm. He can't be going off to some bloody English school!"

The gaze Rhys leveled on Mr. Newcome was so frosty and aristocratic, it would have made any English nobleman proud. "Are you refusing to let me repay your son for what he has just done?"

Mr. Newcome paled. "N-no, sir," he stammered, "but . . . but what about my farm?"

"You have another son, don't you? Surely you can spare the younger one."

The other men were whispering, and it was clear from the scornful looks they cast Mr. Newcome's way that they thought he was a fool for not immediately snapping up the squire's offer.

"Or perhaps the way I've chosen to show my gratitude is not to your liking," Rhys added coldly. "I'm sorry. I didn't realize you wouldn't want your son to be educated. Wait, I'll just send someone back to the house for my purse and—"

"N-no, of course not, sir," Mr. Newcome broke in as the men around him began to grumble about "stupid fools" and "men who looked a gift horse in the mouth." "Whatever you see fit to do is . . . is fine. I'm very grateful that you would honor my son this way."

Evan and Juliana both let out a breath at the same time.

"Good," Rhys said. "Then Evan shall start spending half a day at the house until time for the fall session. I will, of course, pay for all his expenses at Eton." He softened his tone. "And you might consider, Mr. Newcome, that if your son succeeds at school, he'll one day bring into the family a far greater income than he could ever bring you as a farmhand."

Mr. Newcome looked startled. He glanced at Juliana. "Do you think he's really all that bright, milady? That he could make something of himself at a fine school for lords?"

She smiled. "I think Evan is the most brilliant child I've ever seen. He would do you proud at any school."

"So it's settled." Rhys thrust his hand out to the older Welshman.

Mr. Newcome hesitated only a moment before taking it. "Aye, sir. It's settled."

The poor man was wearing a look of dazed confusion, as if someone had just thrown a viper at *him* and forced him to deal with it. Tomorrow, she thought, he'd be much more unhappy about all this. But if he was as proud as he'd always seemed to be, he wouldn't go back on the agreement he'd made before all of his neighbors.

As Rhys led the man off to discuss the details of their arrangement, she hastened to Evan's side. He was looking a bit perplexed himself, and she wondered if perhaps they should have given him more warning about what they intended to do instead of springing it on him.

"You do *want* to go to Eton, don't you, Evan?" she asked softly as she laid her hand on his shoulder.

He seemed to shake himself out of his daze. "More than anything."

"You know that it means you'll be living away from home during most of the year."

"Aye. I don't know how Father will manage—"

"Don't worry. Let Rhys take care of your father. I suspect he doesn't need you as much at the farm as he contends." She tipped up his chin. "And don't forget what I told you. If you ever need me for anything"— she drew a sharp breath—"if your father should . . . try to punish you for this, you tell me, all right?"

He lifted his face to her, his smile hesitant at first before it broadened into a grin.

"After all," she added with a laugh, " 'tis the least I owe to the boy who saved my life."

His smile faded, replaced by a solemn expression. " 'Tis you who have saved *me,* my lady. You and the squire. And I will always remember that."

"Evan!" came a shout from a short distance away. "Come on, m'boy, we're going home. You can talk to milady another time."

"Go on," she murmured, chucking him under the chin.

As he walked off, a grin spreading over his face, she called out, "I'll give you a day's respite, but I expect you to be ready to go right to work the day after, you hear?"

"Aye, my lady!" he called back to her.

Rhys walked back to her as the father and son left together. He stopped to pick up the snake with a stick and toss it into one of the fires, then came to her side. "We don't want anyone examining that snake too closely, do we?"

"I suppose not." She laughed, then slid her arm about his waist and rested her head on his shoulder. "That was wonderful, what you did just now."

He crooked his arm about her shoulders. "I told you I'd take care of it."

"Yes, but Eton?" She stared up at him as he began to lead her back to the cart. "Aside from the expense, I'm surprised you chose an English school for him."

He was silent a long moment. Behind them, someone had brought out a fiddle and was playing a dance as couples rose to their feet, flushed with ale and ready to extend the celebration into the night.

When he spoke, he had to raise his voice over the music. "Much as I hate to admit it, there are no schools in Wales that can prepare someone as gifted as Evan. Not yet, anyway. But perhaps one day . . ."

He trailed off, turning to look back at the dancing men and women, whose fire-lit shadows made them look larger than life. "Yes, perhaps one day."

She stood with him, watching a man caper here, a woman twirl there, their bodies extensions of the leaping flames. " 'Tis better for him to go to England anyway. At least there his father won't be able to hurt him."

Rhys looked pensive. "There are worse things than physical pain," he murmured, and she knew he was remembering six years of separation from his home.

Then he shook off his sudden melancholy, turning to her with a faint smile. "Well, wife, now that you've been saved from certain death, shall we celebrate the harvest with our friends?"

She grinned. "I'd like that. Nothing builds a woman's hunger and thirst quite so much as playing the damsel in distress."

Chapter Twenty

"My breast is pained with passion,
    Pining for love of a girl."
                —Sion Phylip,
                "The Seagull"

The celebration at the field ended abruptly an hour later when the rain finally came, the torrent taking them all by surprise. Amid laughter and shouting, Rhys grabbed Juliana and dashed to the cart. With rain half blinding them, he drove as quickly as possible to the squire hall.

By the time he pulled up under the eaves of the stable, they were both soaked to the skin. But he didn't feel the least bit cold, having drunk just enough ale to fend off any chill brought on by a summer rain.

Rhys jumped down, then lifted Juliana out, letting his hands linger on her waist as the groom emerged and led the cart into the stables. They stood there a moment, for the rain was still pounding the ground and it was a long dash to the house, but it was warm and dry under the eaves. Rhys bent to kiss Juliana's hair, damp and rich with the scent of rain and lavender.

"Rhys," she murmured as he drew back.

"Hm?" He tightened his hold on her waist.

Her eyes glimmered, mysterious as the sea. "Thank you for what you did for Evan. You've saved him from a cruel father. I'm sure of it."

He hesitated, wondering if she should tell her that life at Eton would probably be harder for Evan than it had ever been at home—canings and other harsh punishments were still routinely given, although Rhys had been told it was better than in his day.

But he couldn't bear to tell her of that. It would still be much better for a brilliant child like Evan to be at Eton than serving a wasted life as farm help.

"Also," she continued, seeming not to notice his hesitation, "thank you for taking me tonight. I enjoyed it very much."

"You're very welcome," he said as he dropped a kiss on her forehead. The mere touch of her smooth skin against his lips made desire bolt through him, swift as lightning and just as devastating.

She ducked her head, toying with the buttons on his waistcoat. "I only hope I didn't make a complete fool of myself, dancing out there with the others like a ten-year-old girl."

He thought of how she'd looked when she'd been whirling with the other dancers in the circle . . . her hair a nimbus of fire and her green eyes glowing like cut jade.

There it was again—that clutching burst of desire that made him want to devour her. "Nay, not a fool at all." He tipped up her chin. "You were wonderful." He moved his forefinger over her mouth, coaxing the wine red lips open. "Only one thing could make this night more enjoyable."

"Oh? And what might that be?" She caught his finger in her teeth, swirling her tongue around it with a mischievous smile.

He pressed her against the stable wall, letting her feel the hard ridge of flesh in his breeches. "I'll give you three guesses," he murmured as he drew his wet finger out of her mouth and ran it down her collarbone into the hollow between her breasts.

"Mm. A nice hot cup of tea by the fireplace?"

"No." He slid his finger beneath her sodden bodice until he found one pearly nipple.

Her chest rose and fell more quickly as he rubbed the nub that was already hard from the cold rain.

"Perhaps a . . . a quiet game of chess?" she choked out.

"Definitely not." He pushed the wet gingham material of her bodice down to free her breast, then lowered his head to suck at the damp skin.

"Rhys!" she protested weakly, pushing his head away. "We can't do this here! What if someone should come along?"

His eyes gleamed. "Wouldn't they get a show?"

With a mock stern gaze, she drew up her bodice and

shoved him away from her. "*Not here,* my lusty husband."

The rain was still coming down in sheets, but she ran out into it laughing. She raced toward the house, dancing up the wide staircase as he followed at a more leisurely pace behind, letting the rain beat the grime of a day's work from him. At the top of the stairs, she paused to blow him a kiss, then opened the door and slipped inside, giggling as she closed it between them.

"God save me from teasing wenches," he grumbled as he shoved the wet hair from his face and stalked the rest of the way up the stairs. If it was a game she wanted, she'd best make it quick. That one taste of her had not been near enough.

But when he opened the door and walked in, she was standing in the hall and all the humor had completely vanished from her face. She was holding a sealed envelope in her hand. And Mrs. Roberts was at her side.

Mrs. Roberts glanced up at him. "Oh, there you are, sir. Don't you look a sight, the two of you. I was telling milady that you'd best get out of those wet clothes at once before you catch a chill and—"

"Who's the letter from?" Rhys interrupted, alarmed by Juliana's wan cheeks.

"Oh," said Mrs. Roberts, "it came from Northcliffe Hall while you were both at the harvest."

Northcliffe Hall. His gaze flew to the envelope as a sudden fear clamped down on his heart. The last time someone had brought a message from Northcliffe Hall ...

"Darcy sent it," Juliana whispered, and he felt the fear clamp tighter.

"How do you know?"

" 'Tis his handwriting." She hesitated a moment more, staring at the envelope as if to decide what to do with it. Then she ripped it open and drew out a letter. She read it quickly, her mouth forming a small "O." Her hand dropped to her side as she looked up and stared into space.

"What does it say?" Rhys asked, fighting the urge to snatch the letter from her and toss it into the nearest fire.

She shook her head as if to clear it. Nodding toward

the housekeeper, she said, "Thank you, Mrs. Roberts. That will be all this evening."

As Mrs. Roberts walked off, her eyes bright with curiosity, Juliana handed him the letter, then began to walk toward the stairs.

He started reading. The letter was addressed to Juliana and indeed bore Northcliffe's signature. Apparently, Northcliffe and Devon had been involved in some investment project together, and now Lord Devon was threatening to back out if Northcliffe or his brother didn't arrange a meeting between him and Juliana. "One final meeting," it said, "to satisfy Lord Devon that Vaughan is not holding you in the marriage against your will."

Against your will. That phrase made him curse aloud. Damn them all! How dare they?

Worse yet, Northcliffe had apparently responded to Lord Devon's blackmail by setting up the meeting. The letter said that Lord Devon was invited for dinner at Northcliffe Hall two days hence, and Northcliffe was asking, no, commanding his sister to attend.

It didn't help that the bastard included Rhys in the invitation. It didn't help at all.

Diawl! Rhys thought as he balled the letter up and shoved it in his pocket. *The audacity of the man!*

Juliana was already halfway up the stairs now, and he hurried after her, falling into step at her side. "For God's sake, Juliana, where are you going? We must talk about this."

"Yes, but not here." Juliana nodded toward the door that led to the basement and the servant hall.

He gritted his teeth as he followed her the rest of the way up the stairs to their bedchamber. She was right. This was definitely *not* something to be discussed in front of the servants.

Because he suspected that she planned to go.

And there was no way in hell he'd allow it.

As soon as they'd passed through the door to their bedchamber, he slammed the door behind them and tore off his drenched coat, tossing it over a chair. "You want to go, don't you?"

"No, I don't *want* to go," she said as she undressed, letting her wet clothes fall into a puddle on the floor.

With a shiver, she drew a dry chemise and her silk wrapper off a hook, then put them on. "But I have to. I have to settle this matter once and for all."

He dug his fingers into his palms. "It was settled the night of your engagement party. I told Devon you were married, he bowed out of the engagement, and that was that. He has no damned right to come back asking for you. None!"

Releasing a shuddering breath, she went to sit on the edge of the bed. "Are you ordering me not to go, Rhys?"

He clenched his fists tighter, fighting down the fear that twisted inside him. "I don't think it's a good idea." He held his breath, waiting for her to explode, knowing that his words would make her do so. He could deal with anger. He could fight her when she was shouting at him, much better than he could battle this quiet acquiescence that increased his fear.

But she lifted a calm face to his, as if she knew where he was weakest. "Why? What are you afraid will happen?"

Her rational question took him aback. He raked his fingers through his hair in extreme agitation. "*Uffern-dân*, Juliana, that should be obvious. I don't want you anywhere near that damned marquess."

"I can see that, but that's not what I asked. What do you think will happen if I go 'near that damned marquess'?"

You'll leave me, came the words instantly to his mind. *You'll realize what you're missing and you'll run away from me, as you did before.* But he didn't dare say those words.

Instead he concentrated on peeling off his own wet clothes, wanting to do something ... anything ... that would keep his fear from making him say things he'd regret later.

As he jerked on a pair of dry woolen drawers and his dressing gown, Juliana rose from the bed and came toward him. "What are you afraid Stephen will do? Kidnap me and carry me off to his estate? I hardly think even my brothers would allow that. Present proof of his legal claim to me? We both know he *can't* do that, for there is none. So what is turning you into a beast at the very idea of my joining him over dinner? There will be other guests present ... you, for one, since you were invited."

"I was present at your engagement party, too," he gritted out, the words dragged out of him by her solemn gaze. "Yet that didn't prevent you from choosing him over me. If I'd released you from your vows that night, you'd have gone with him. You wanted a divorce then. You said so."

She flinched and turned away, rubbing her arms as if to restore the warmth to her body. "Yes ... I did, that's true. I was very angry that night." She tilted her chin up. "I think I had a right to be angry. But since then, a great deal has changed between us. Surely you realize I've been more than content to be your wife these past two weeks."

"If you're so content, then why must you see Lord Devon again?" he snapped.

She faced him, laying her hand on his chest. "Can't you understand how *he* must feel? To have his fiancée leave him at his own engagement party and not know what has happened to her?"

"He can't feel any worse than I did to have my wife leave me on my wedding night!"

She whitened and dropped her hand from his chest. "You ... you still haven't gotten past that night, have you? You still believe I betrayed you then. That's why you're so afraid now. You're worried I'll run off with Lord Devon and betray you again."

Her voice sounded so distant that the terror churned in him even more fiercely. "Nay," he protested. "Nay." Thunder cracked the air outside, as if to echo his terror.

But she was oblivious to the terror as she looked at him, her eyes glimmering with the beginning of tears. "If you trusted me, you wouldn't be afraid to let me go to this dinner. You'd have faith in me to handle whatever Lord Devon requests."

He closed his eyes. She was being too rational about this. She didn't understand the wholly irrational clutch of fear in his heart at the very thought of her speaking with Lord Devon. He'd nearly lost her to the bastard, and only by force had he gained her back. God, how could he endure losing her for good?

On the other hand, would he lose her if he refused to trust her?

"It's not that simple." He turned away from her, unable to see the pure, honest question in her eyes ... *Do you trust me? Do you trust me?*

"Yes, it is." She came up behind him, encircling his waist as she laid her head against his back. "It's as simple as deciding to trust me or not."

He could feel the damp in her hair soaking through his dressing gown, could look down and see her small hands linked together over his stomach. Two weeks ago, she wouldn't have held him so easily, nor touched him with the casual intimacy of a wife.

He didn't want to lose that. "It's not you I don't trust," he said, striving for a calm tone. "It's those treacherous brothers of yours ... and Lord Devon."

She sighed. "They can't do anything to me without my permission. What are they going to do? Have *me* impressed?" Her voice dropped a fraction. "If you're so worried about what will happen, come with me. As I pointed out before, the invitation included you."

With a snarl, he twisted around to face her. "Aye, it did, and doesn't that surprise you? Your brother is furious at me for what I did at the council meeting. So why has he invited me to his home?" He paused. "This could be a trap, you know. Perhaps your brother has done this on purpose, using Lord Devon to lure you—and therefore me—to Northcliffe Hall, so he can ... can ..."

"Can what? What can he do to you, Rhys? He can't have you impressed again, for your friends would protest and he'd find himself in trouble. He certainly won't kill you. If he'd wanted to do that, he'd have done it before now. These are all just excuses, and you know it."

He did know it, but how else could he keep her away from her *uffernol* ex-fiancé and her devious brothers?

"Rhys, listen to me." She lifted her hand to his cheek, her fingers stroking the stubbled skin with a tenderness that made him ache. "I told you I didn't love Lord Devon." His eyes met hers, and she dragged in a deep breath. "I love *you*. So why would I toss aside a marriage with the man I love for a man I don't?"

He froze. *I love you.* Damn it all, he'd waited so long for her to say those words to him again. He'd yearned for them even when he'd been unwilling to say them himself, to allow her that hold on his heart.

But her saying them now renewed his terror threefold. What if she were saying them only because she wanted him to give in to her request?

He caught her hand, holding it still on his cheek. "If you love me, you won't go. You'll stay here with me and not give those bastards the chance to separate us again."

He knew he'd said the wrong thing when Juliana went ice white, then snatched her hand from him with a shudder. "I bare my heart to you, and that's all you can say? That's all you can do, use my love as a lever to get what you want?"

"My God, Juliana," he whispered, closing his hands on her shoulders. "You don't know what you're asking of me."

"I do know." Her face was drawn now. "I'm asking you to trust me. And it's clear that you can't."

The air in the room grew arctic, despite the closed window and the fire blazing in the hearth. The rain pounded so loudly against the windows that it seemed to stretch its chill into the room until it froze Juliana's face into such a mask of pain, it drove icicles through his heart.

As if the mere sight of him might shatter her, she averted her eyes from him. Damn it all, he was losing her ... he could feel it. Despite everything he was losing her.

And he simply couldn't. "I do trust you, *cariad*. I do."

Her silence spoke her disbelief.

He stumbled for words and could only come up with the ones he'd spoken years before. "And ... and I love you."

Her gaze shot to his, wild and luminous in the firelight, but her expression was skeptical.

As it should be. He could scarcely believe he'd said the words himself. Yet he had to admit he felt them. In the past two weeks, the beauty of what they'd had before had echoed in what they had now. He'd come to realize that he loved her now as much as he'd loved her then ... perhaps more. It didn't matter if she'd betrayed him or not. Nothing mattered but her.

"Yes, I do love you," he went on, feeling like a youth

with his first woman. This was every bit as important to
him as the first time he'd declared his heart to her, if
not more so. "I love you so much. I've loved you from
the day I saw you at that lecture. I never stopped loving
you, even during all those years at sea and in America."

When she said nothing, he sucked in a harsh breath.
"That's why it nearly killed me to think you'd betrayed
me. And then to see you with that damned English lord
..." He broke off with a choked groan.

"He doesn't mean anything to me anymore, I swear
it." There was frustration in her voice. "Not a blasted
thing. 'Tis you I love."

He caught her hand, lifting it to kiss the palm. "Show
me then." With a sudden movement that took her off
guard, he hauled her into his arms. "Show me. Make
love to me, darling."

"But Rhys—"

He didn't let her finish, but covered her mouth with
his, possessing it, urging her to respond. At first she resisted, but when he swept her lips with his tongue, she
groaned and her mouth opened like a flower. With a
moan, he drove into her mouth, wanting to strike deep
into the heart of her, to find that place she held separate
from him and make it his.

She wrenched away from him. "Rhys, this won't solve
anything ... we have to talk about this—"

He touched his fingers to her lips. The savage need to
make her forget everything and everyone but him was
so strong, it clawed at him. "I need you. By thunder, I
need you and I love you ... more than breath ... more
than life. I have to know you need me as much. I have
to know you love me."

"I do."

"Then make love to me," he said hoarsely. "Show me
that Lord Devon means nothing to you."

When she hesitated, her face tortured, he drew her
hands to the belt of his dressing gown. "Please," he
whispered through a throat taut with fear. If she rejected
him now, he didn't know how he'd live through it.

Her eyes met his, then she glanced down at her fingers
on the cloth belt. And she seemed to realize—and to
accept—what he wanted of her, for she undid the knot.

He said nothing, made no move to touch her as she

peeled off his dressing gown, baring him from the waist up. She seemed to have settled something in her mind, for her movements became more purposeful. Without a word, she shed her wrapper, her eyes on him as she let it slip to the floor. When she shimmied out of her chemise, he caught his breath, drinking in the sight of her finely sculpted form—all feminine lines and curves and smooth, tempting surfaces.

With a sensuous look, she drew his hands to her waist, then stretched up on tiptoe to fit her mouth to his. He shuddered all over from the exquisite pleasure of having her body against his.

Hard as tiny pebbles, her nipples pressed into his bare chest, and he wrapped his arms about her to hold her tighter as he opened his mouth over hers. His shaft grew even more hard, if that were possible, straining against his too snug drawers, and he fought the arousal, not wanting to spill his seed before he could even be inside her.

But when she darted her tongue into his mouth, hesitant, seeking, he thought he'd lose his mind. She was doing exactly as he'd asked, yet he'd had no idea what it would do to him to have her initiating everything. She ran her small tongue along the sensitive skin lining his lips, then teased his tongue with sweet, coaxing thrusts.

With a growl, he plunged his tongue into her mouth, deeper and deeper, intoxicated by the faint taste of spiced fruit cakes on her breath. But before he could fully satisfy his craving to taste her, she'd drawn back and begun to kiss down his throat to his shoulders and then in a crooked line down his chest.

"Damn it all," he muttered as she stopped to tug at his nipple, then ran her tongue down along the furrow of dark hair on his chest, scorching him everywhere she touched. When her tongue delved into his navel, a shock of pleasure shot through him that was so intense, he clasped her head, burying his fingers in her lush mass of hair to hold her still a moment.

But she wasn't finished with him. Her fingers began working loose the buttons of his drawers, and as soon as she had them free, she tugged them down, freeing his aching shaft. She was kneeling now, and he suddenly realized through a haze of shock and excitement what she was intending to do.

"No," he muttered thickly. Lightning split the sky, illuminating the room with its quick flash, and when she touched her hot mouth to the tip of him, then swirled her tongue over the tight, aching skin, he thought the lightning had surely struck him. He gave a choked curse and pushed her head away. "No . . . no, 'tis too much."

Jerking back from her, he kicked aside his drawers, then dragged her up into his arms. "You're a seductress, you know that?" he growled as he scattered rough kisses over her rounded cheek . . . her damp, tangled hair . . . her wide, flawless brow.

"I'm merely doing what you asked," she said in a throaty voice, rubbing up against him, against his arousal full to bursting.

"I said, make love to me, not drive me to distraction." With a savage growl, he bent to suck her breast, drawing hard on the flesh.

She pushed him from her, then slowly circled him until she stood at his back. He could feel her breath on his tense muscles as she glided her hands down his back. Without warning, she cupped his buttocks, then smoothed and squeezed them in her deft hands.

He flung his head back, his eyes sliding shut. "Damn it all," he muttered hoarsely as she grabbed his shoulders and molded herself to him.

He could feel her triangle of hair against his rear, the dewy fleece crushed against him. That was titillation enough, but when she anchored him to her by clasping his thighs so that her fingers were inches away from the part of him that ached to be buried inside her, his eyes shot open.

"Is this to be my punishment for all my demands on you?" he said hoarsely. "Are you deliberately tormenting me?"

She went still. "Do you really think I would do that to you, Rhys?"

"I don't know."

"Don't you?" she asked, her voice slightly muffled against his back. "Surely you know by now that I could never hurt you. Do you so doubt my love?"

Glancing up, he saw their images reflected in the wide

pier glass that hung next to the bed—her arms curved
around his hips, her hands on his thighs, the top of her
head showing above his shoulders. Clasping her hand,
he drew her to stand beside him.

He nodded his head toward the gilded mirror. "Look
there." He touched their clasped hands first to her
creamy shoulder and then his own scarred one. "While
you're as sweet and smooth and lovely as your skin, I'm
grievously marred and angry and dark. Since my return,
I've tormented you and deliberately sought to hurt you,
even when you met my anger with kindness. *Uffern-dân,*
if I doubt your love, 'tis only because I can't believe
you'd love me when there's so little in me to love."

She turned to face him, her eyes glowing with desire.
"So little to love? You blind fool."

As he watched in the glass, she slipped her hands up
to his shoulders, running her fingers along the scars at
the top. "For surviving this, I love you," she whispered
as she stroked each one. She brushed aside his hair to
finger the scar at his temple. "For turning my brother's
punishments into a triumph, I love you."

A faint smile tipped up her lips. "For giving Evan a
new life, I love you."

Her smile faded as she reached up to bracket his face
in her small hands. "Most of all, for putting aside your
vengeance so you could be my husband completely, I
love you. For that, I will always love you. Don't you see,
I can't help but love you? As long as I have life or
breath, there will never be anyone else for me but you."

With a growl that was part endearment, part curse, he
lifted her into his arms and strode to the bed with her,
laying her down, then covering her with his body. "I
don't deserve you, but I don't care. I love you, and I
want you so badly, I'm drowning in it."

"Then take me," she murmured, spreading her legs to
fit him against her.

His control broke. With a guttural moan, he sheathed
himself in her, in the warmth he needed so badly. She
was glove-tight and wet, and when she began to move
under him, undulating to create the friction he craved,
he thought he'd go mad.

"Juliana . . . sweet Juliana . . ." he said hoarsely
against her neck as he joined her motion, sinking himself

into her, wanting to lose his soul in her, to bury his fears in her welcoming body.

Her breasts were crushed against him, and she smelled of rain and smoke and lavender. He wanted to devour her or have her devour him ... to be so much a part of her that she could never leave him ... not ever again.

Rain pounded against the roof in time to the pounding of his heart as he thrust into her over and over. She was making enticing little cries and moans, and her body wriggled against him, seeking its own fulfillment. He wanted her to find it ... to find it in him, so he struggled to hold back his release until she could find hers as well. Lowering his mouth to her breast, he drew hard on the plump flesh and nipped at the pebbled tip until he felt her writhe beneath him urgently.

Raw tension built in him as he ground his hips against hers. *Not much longer,* he thought as her head fell back, and her movements grew frantic.

"That's it, *anwylyd*," he growled in her ear. "That's it."

As if responding to his words, she strained suddenly against him, shudders overtaking her. "Oh, Rhys ... *fy melys phriod*!"

It was the first time she'd called him "husband," and it sent him over the edge with her. He erupted in her hot silken body with a harsh moan, her sweet spasms wringing him dry.

"Christ in Heaven," he groaned as he collapsed on her, feeling her shake beneath him with the aftershocks of her pleasure. Never had he known this with any woman. Never with anyone but Juliana. He was awestruck that making love to her could be so entirely satisfying.

Outside, the thunder and lightning still rampaged, but here in the cocoon of their bedchamber, with the fire blazing and the light of the candles reflecting off the creamy bed linens, he felt secure. Her body beneath him was warm and yielding. He wished he could wrap it around him forever. This was what marriage was meant to be, wasn't it? The security of being locked away with one's love, not needing the rest of the world.

It wasn't distrust that made him want her to stay here with him, he told himself as rolled off her, tugging her up against him until they lay spoon-fashion. It was love, only love. He nuzzled the drying ends of her hair aside so he could kiss her shoulder. "I love you."

"I love you, too," she whispered.

He lifted himself on one elbow to see her face better. Her eyes were closed, and her breathing seemed to have evened out. "Juliana?"

"Hm?" she said dreamily.

"You like being here with me, don't you?"

"Mm," she murmured, snuggling against him. "It's nice."

"And you understand why I can't bear to let you go to Carmarthen for this dinner, don't you? You'll stay here with me. You won't leave me."

Her only answer was to shift her body more comfortably against his, and after she remained silent a moment longer, her breathing slow and deep, he realized she was asleep.

No matter, he thought as he drew the counterpane up over them and sank back against the pillow. After tonight, she must understand how he felt. And surely in the morning, when they could discuss it more rationally, she'd agree with him.

Let her sleep, he told himself.

But Juliana wasn't sleeping as she lay with her body curved into his, fighting hard to keep her breathing even.

Just as she'd told him, making love had changed nothing. Not for him. But it had changed a great deal for her. She couldn't go on with him like this. The truth of what had happened six years ago had to be faced. Judging from his overwhelming jealousy and fear of letting her out of his sight, he still hadn't come to accept that she hadn't betrayed him.

Obviously, that hadn't prevented him from recognizing that he loved her. No doubt he accepted his love for her by telling himself she was different now, that her betrayal no longer mattered, that it was all in the past.

But nothing was ever completely in the past. Like a deeply buried thorn that festered if it wasn't removed, his doubts about her would eat away at him—and at his love for her—if he didn't face them.

So she must make him face them, and she could think of only one way to do that. Go to the dinner, with or without him. Leave tonight, before he could make it impossible for her to leave. Then pray that he followed ... or that he didn't spurn her when she returned.

The storm seemed to have finally subsided, and the rain had dropped to a gentle drizzle. She didn't relish the thought of riding in a drizzle, but if she didn't leave tonight, she'd never get away from him tomorrow.

Shifting to her back, she stole a peek at him. He was asleep now, his breath even and his eyelids shut. She stared at the full lips half parted in sleep, the angular jaw shadowed with his evening growth of whiskers, and the two dark slashes of eyebrows straight and even in the comfort of sleep. The fear and anger had fled from his face, and he wore an expression of peace that clutched at her heart.

She turned her face away. What if she took this bold step, and it proved too much for the fragile portion of trust he'd begun to feel for her? What if it shattered everything between them?

She chewed on her lip. And if she didn't do this? How long before the fear of betrayal devoured him until he couldn't let her out of his sight? How long before she struck out against his unreasonable demands and destroyed whatever lay between them?

No, she thought, *I have to do this. He must find that he loves me enough to brave his fears. Or there's no chance for us.*

Her decision made, she slipped out of bed and began to gather clothing for a trip to Carmarthen.

Chapter Twenty-one

"Sad outlaw, I've no ransom,
  Shut out from her town and home.
  She to her outlaw's bosom
  Sent but longing, bitter doom."
                    —Dafydd ap Gwilym,
                       "His Affliction"

"What do you mean, one of the horses is missing?" Rhys demanded of the young man before him.

It was early morning. Rhys stood in the entrance hall with his groom. The quaking servant had met him at the bottom of the stairs as soon as Rhys had stalked down them.

Rhys had awakened early to find Juliana already gone from his bed. At the time, he'd merely wondered how Juliana had risen so early without his noticing, and he'd hastened downstairs to find her.

But the knowledge of a missing horse shed an entirely different light on matters. Juliana was missing. A horse was missing. Not a good picture at all.

"Which horse is gone?" he asked, fearing the answer.

The groom crushed his hat in his hands as he dropped his gaze to his toes. "Milady's, sir. Her saddle, too."

"Damn it all!" Rhys ground his teeth together. She couldn't have left him. She wouldn't have. Not after last night. "Can you hazard a guess as to when it was taken?"

"Aye. There were no tracks in the mud outside the stable, so she must have left in the middle of the night, while it was still raining. I suspect she's been gone a good while."

"She?" Rhys snapped.

"Er . . . milady."

"You're sure it was my wife who took the horse?"

"N-nay, but 'twas her mount, so I—I assumed—"

That she left me, he thought grimly. "Don't assume anything. Go see what else you can discover, while I try to get to the bottom of this."

As the groom scurried out the door, Rhys swung around, feeling like a madman destined to wander through the airless halls of an asylum. Despite what he'd told the groom, he knew the truth.

Gone. She was gone. Who else would have taken her horse and saddle?

His heart pounding, he turned back to the stairs and took them two at a time. Perhaps the groom had been mistaken about what time the horse had left. Perhaps Juliana had merely gone for a ride. She did that sometimes in the early morning.

But not without telling me. Not without asking me to join her.

Fear battered him as he hastened to their bedchamber. When he entered, he stood motionless, wondering what he ought to look for. He scanned the room blindly, and that's when he saw the note propped up against the pier glass. When he'd awakened, he'd been in such a rush to find Juliana that he hadn't noticed it.

In a half-trance, he walked toward the mirror. As he drew closer, he saw that the folded sheet of paper bore his name on the outside. He reached for it with trembling hands. He hesitated, holding it clutched in his hand, afraid to read the words she'd left for him.

Then, fear hollowing out his insides, he opened the note and read.

Dear Rhys,

I have gone to Northcliffe Hall. I know how you feel about my attendance at this dinner, but I had to go. If you search your heart, you'll understand that I must settle matters between me and Lord Devon. I also wish to be reconciled with my brothers, devious though they have proven to be.

I know you don't see matters as I do and you will be furious at me for leaving in this manner. I realize that my hasty, furtive departure may only increase your distrust of me, but you left me no choice. I only

pray that you can find some measure of forgiveness in
your heart.

You told me two weeks ago that you wanted me to
be your wife, to share your life in every way. I agreed
to that. Now I'm asking you to be my husband. Put
aside your fears and come to me at Northcliffe Hall.
Come sit at my side when I face Lord Devon. Show
that you trust me to do the right thing.

I know well what a great thing I ask of you. If you
cannot do it, I will understand. In either case, know
this. You will always have my love.

Juliana

The ache in his heart grew nearly unbearable. He
could hear the words in her voice as if she stood beside
him, entreating him. And every word was like a poniard
driven into his breast.

He read the letter through three times, trying to
fathom her thoughts as he read it, but each time only
tormented him more. He ought to take comfort in the
fact that she promised him her love forever.

But all he could think was that she hadn't said when
she would return ... *if* she would return. Worst of all,
she hadn't said what she would do if he didn't come,
but he feared he knew the answer to that. If he refused
to be husband to her in this, then wouldn't she have the
right to refuse to be wife to him?

*Put aside your fears and come to me at Northcliffe
Hall.*

With a savage curse, he balled up the note in his fist
and threw it at the pier glass where their images had
been linked last night. *Uffern-dân,* had it been only last
night that she'd opened herself to him so passionately?

And then had slipped out of their bed without so
much as a word ... just this foul note asking him to sell
his soul for her! Devil take the woman! Was this her
way of repaying him for all his misuse of her? She said
she knew what she was asking of him, but obviously she
didn't know at all or she wouldn't ask it.

Go to the house of his enemy? Break bread with him?
And as if that weren't enough, watch her greet Lord
Devon, a man who'd once sworn to marry her, and pre-
tend it didn't ravage him to witness it?

She had no right to ask this. No right at all. Her brothers had sent him into certain death, and Lord Devon had meant to enjoy the fruits of that betrayal. Damn the lot of them! How dare she expect him to go there, to pretend civility when he detested them? If she loved him, she wouldn't ask this of him.

He wouldn't go. Damn her, too, if she thought she could twist him like this, bend him to her will. She'd disobeyed his direct order ... she had left him, and she thought to force his hand by doing so.

Well, he was not so easily manipulated. Let her sup with her foppish suitor and her *uffernol* family. He would not come to heel like some sad hound trailing after the master. Nay, he would not!

And if she couldn't accept his terms, then that was her loss. He would not force her to remain in a marriage she found too binding.

At that thought, such pain tore through him that he swore and swept her dressing table clean with one fist. He watched with bitter satisfaction as perfume bottles shattered on the floor and the jewelry she kept in several small chests went flying. His anger only a little abated, he stalked toward the door, his boots crunching over the broken glass as the stench of mingled perfumes assailed him.

Then he nearly slipped as his shoe came down on something bigger than shards of glass. His weight snapped it in two. He kicked it aside, then froze as he saw what it was.

A love-spoon. And if memory served him right, it was the love-spoon he'd given Juliana on the night he proposed.

His throat tightened as he crouched to pick up the two halves. Aye, it was the love-spoon he'd carved for her. He looked around for where it had come from. Quickly he spotted the jeweled case she'd apparently kept it in, for the cloth, worn and yellowed with age, that he'd used to wrap it in was lying in the case.

He stared at the case, perfectly made to fit the love-spoon, and then at the two pieces of the spoon itself. By thunder, she'd kept his gift all these years. And in a special place created solely for it. She hadn't hidden it or thrown it away. She might have kept their marriage secret from the world, but here was proof that she'd remembered it in private.

He closed his fingers around the ancient totem, the emblem of Welsh marriages for centuries . . . the emblem that he'd broken, as surely as his refusal to go to Northcliffe would break his marriage.

"Ah, Juliana, my love," he whispered hoarsely as he tightened his hand about the two pieces of the lovespoon. "What have you done to me?"

How foolish had been his plans when he'd stormed into Northcliffe Hall a few weeks ago. He'd thought to make her suffer. Yet once again, she'd played him for a fool.

It didn't matter how much he railed against her. It didn't matter that he'd lived without her once and ought to be able to live without her again. He couldn't. If she left him, there would be nothing in his life of worth.

The worst of it was, while last time he'd had no choice in the matter, this time the choice was wholly his. She was forcing him to choose whether to live with her or without her.

And if he chose wrongly, he'd have no one to blame but himself.

It was the hour when breakfast was served at Northcliffe Hall, and Juliana sat at the table awaiting her family. No one yet knew she was here. Since she'd arrived in the middle of the night, she'd urged the housekeeper not to awaken anyone, but had merely gone to bed in her old bedchamber.

Unfortunately, she'd slept little. How could she sleep when all she could think of was Rhys's face when he'd touched their joined hands to his scars? He'd been so unsure of her, so afraid, and now she'd given him new cause to doubt her loyalty and her love.

But she couldn't have acted in any other way. She was certain of that. Besides, it was done. By now, he'd read her note and realized what she intended.

What would he do? Would he come? Or worst yet, would he follow her here today in a fury, ready to drag her back to Llynwydd? That would devastate her, for it would show that he still lacked regard for her needs and wants.

Of course, if he didn't come, it would devastate her, too. How could she bear it if he refused to give her this proof of his trust?

"The housekeeper said you were here," came a voice from the doorway. "Thank God you've come."

Darcy. Her heart suddenly pounding, she turned to face her brother, who'd also become her nemesis. But when she caught sight of him, her anger instantly lessened.

It had been three weeks since she'd seen him, but the changes wrought in him made it seem like a lifetime. His face was as gaunt and chalky as a death mask, but his eyes glittered like a man too much alive, too aware of the pain being visited on him. His clothes hung on him, and his entrance into the room was marked by an uncharacteristic lack of energy.

Despite all he'd done to her, she pitied him. "Good morning, Darcy," she said, more softly than she'd intended.

He seemed taken aback by her gentle greeting. "I—I was afraid you'd ignore my summons. You had every right to do so after what I've done to you."

"Darcy, I—"

He held up his hand. "Please, Juliana, don't say anything yet. There's nothing you could say that would be crueler than the words I've said to myself."

With shaky fingers, he drew forth his snuff box and sniffed a pinch of snuff, then shoved the box back in his pocket as he began to pace beside the table. "After Overton came back from Llynwydd and told me how Vaughan spoke to you, how much he distrusted you, I thought I'd go mad. I wanted to rush there myself and bring you back, to force you from the bastard's hands, but Overton wouldn't let me. He said you wouldn't wish it."

"Yes, that's what I told him."

Darcy halted, fixing her with a panicky gaze. "But here you are. I'm not sure what to make of it. Did you come to stay? I can't believe Vaughan would allow you to come." His voice grew bitter. "Not after he made his grand gesture at the council meeting and effectively ruined all my future in politics by nominating Morgan, who'll probably win the election. Vaughan made it quite clear then that he's not through tormenting me."

"Rhys knows I'm here. He may join me tomorrow evening, although I'll admit that we were both surprised you invited him."

Abruptly, Darcy dropped into a chair. "I didn't want to, but Overton insisted. He said it was time we treated you as husband and wife, as family."

"Ah, yes," she thought, a wry smile flitting over her lips. She should have known Overton would be the one to act humanely. Darcy never would.

When had Darcy changed from an over-protective brother into an obsessed politician? The night he'd betrayed her and Rhys? Or before that?

And was his present self-deprecating air an act? Her fingers tightened on the napkin in her lap. Perhaps not, judging from his obvious distress. Still, she had to know one thing. "Did Lord Devon really threaten to pull out of your mining project, or was that something you invented to get me to come back here so you could throw me at Stephen?"

Darcy looked stricken. "It's the truth, I swear it. The man's totally besotted with you, and ever since he found out from Overton the kind of life your husband intended for you, he's been racked by worry." He dropped his voice. "Especially once he learned my part in all that happened six years ago. Only by promising to arrange this meeting did I keep him from bowing out of our investment venture entirely."

"If nothing else, Stephen is a man of character." Bitterness boiled up in her throat. "You should be grateful he didn't call you out. 'Tis what you deserved."

"I know. I know too well." He leaned forward. "Juliana, I can't excuse what I did back then. I can only say this—if I'd known how unhappy it would make you, I'd never have done it."

" 'Tis a pity that's not true," she said, her face stony.

"But it is!" His face wore a pleading expression. "I know it's no excuse, but I only did it to protect you from that ... that scoundrel!"

"I was in love with that scoundrel." She leveled an accusing gaze on him. "And that wasn't the only reason you wanted me separated from him, was it?"

Darcy paled and averted his gaze from her.

"You were appalled to find me married to a penniless Welsh radical. Letting me stay married to him would have been disastrous to all your plans for political gain."

He didn't try to deny it, although his brow clouded with pain. "If you still hate me so much for what I did, why did you come at my summons?"

She dropped her eyes to her plate. "I have my own reasons."

When she said nothing else, his face fell as if he realized that things could never be the same between them. She could never trust him again—not as she had before—and that was something he'd have to live with.

He drew a deep breath. "Whatever your reasons, I'm grateful you've come. It will help me a great deal if you can meet with Lord Devon tomorrow night and put his mind at ease."

She regarded him warily. "If putting his mind at ease means reassuring him that I'm content with my marriage, then yes, I am happy to put him at ease."

"I suppose it was too much to hope that Vaughan would let you go if you wished to leave him." He stared into space, his face drawn.

She couldn't help but smile at the disappointment in his voice. Darcy would never change, would he? "I don't want to leave him, Darcy. I love him, and he loves me, despite everything you did to part us." Her smile faded. Rhys loved her, but she had yet to see if he trusted her.

With a nod, Darcy shifted his gaze to hers. "He . . . he treats you well, then?"

"Yes. He treats me very well."

He said nothing for a long time, merely trailing his eyes over her as if to assess the truth of her statement. Then he sighed. "If that is true, then perhaps all has not been lost."

Not yet, anyway, she thought without rancor. Although Darcy had set all the events in motion, it had long ago stopped having anything to do with him. Rhys's decisions were now governed by other things. She could only pray his love for her won out over everything else.

"Juliana?" Darcy said, drawing her from her worrisome thoughts.

"Yes, Darcy?"

"Do you think you could ever forgive me for what I did?" When she pursed her lips and frowned, he hastened to add, "I now know what it is to suffer as you did six years ago. I have lost the woman I loved, for Lettice has left me for that Pennant fellow. As if that weren't enough, I've lost my position in the community and my wife."

She glanced at him in surprise. "Your wife?"

"Elizabeth is leaving me." He tried for a nonchalant shrug, but looked whipped instead. "Not legally, of course. Neither of us could tolerate the scandal of a divorce. But we are separating. She intends to live apart from me. Since we have no children ... she thinks it's best."

"Oh, Darcy, I am sorry," she said with genuine feeling.

A faint smile hovered over his lips. "Don't be. We were never well-suited for each other. And in truth, we never could be, although Lettice no longer stands between us." He left his seat to come sit beside her, taking her hands in his. "But you see, if I lost you, too, I'd have nothing left. Even Overton can scarcely bear to speak to me anymore. Please, Juliana. Say that you won't always hate me for what I did."

Something in his face triggered all her memories of when they were both children and she'd begged him for his help. He'd always given it. Only this time, it was him begging. And try as she might, she couldn't find it in her heart to refuse him.

"I don't hate you," she murmured. "I can't forget what you did, but I'll try to forgive you for it. In time, perhaps we can put it behind us."

He caught her hand up and kissed it gratefully, but her mind was already somewhere else, on another man who said he wanted to put the past behind him.

Would he? And if he didn't, how would she ever endure it?

Chapter Twenty-two

> "I'm but an ailing poet,
> I cannot keep it secret:
> My voice grows faint for her fair face."
> —Salbri Powel,
> "The Lover's Hope"

Evan stood in Llynwydd's entrance hall two days after the harvest, his hands shoved in his pockets to still their nervousness. He waited, just as the housekeeper had bid him, but couldn't help thinking that something was wrong. Everyone was acting funny, all sad and quiet. And here it was morning, but the house was so still. There were no maids chattering in the hall. Everyone seemed to be walking about in a hush.

A murmur of low voices came from the room to his left, and he strained to hear what they said. Without quite meaning to, he edged closer to the door until he could make out the words.

"The poor man won't eat. I'd swear he hasn't touched food since she left yesterday."

It was Mrs. Roberts's voice. Evan wondered who she was talking about. Some relative of hers most likely.

"He said she'd gone to visit her family. Is that all there is to it or is there more?" That voice belonged to Mr. Newns.

"There's more to it, to be sure," Mrs. Roberts said with confidence. "They quarreled." The voice lowered so that Evan had to strain to hear the words. "You should have seen what I had to clean up in their bedchamber. Broken bottles and a stink of lavender water everywhere. The master said not a word about it, just 'clean up this mess,' but he's been brooding every hour since, closing himself up in that study and drinking himself into sickness. 'Tis a crying shame, that's what it is."

The master? Surely she wasn't talking about the squire and Lady Juliana. Why, only two days ago, he'd seen them dancing in the fields, cooing together like pigeons.

"Good morning, Evan," came a voice from behind him.

Evan whirled around to come face to face with the squire himself. The blood rose guiltily in his face. Oh, God, to be caught listening at doors. The squire would surely think he was awful.

But the squire didn't seem to notice what he was doing. He came toward Evan with a distracted expression on his dark face, the blue eyes odd and glittering.

Now that the man was close, Evan could see great changes in him from two days ago. The squire looked as if he hadn't shaved since then, and he was wearing no coat or neckcloth. His waistcoat was buttoned wrong, as if he hand't even paid attention while putting it on, and his shirt was opened at the throat like a common laborer's. What's more, Evan could smell the brandy on him. Instantly, the words of the housekeeper came back to him.

"G-good morning, sir," Evan stammered. "I—I came because Lady Juliana said I was to start my lessons today."

"Aye, I know." Pain slashed over Mr. Vaughan's face. "We need to speak about that." He gestured toward the drawing room, then stalked off.

His curiosity growing, Evan followed Mr. Vaughan. When the squire gestured to a chair, Evan sat on the edge of it gingerly, schooling his face to show nothing. Years of living with his father had made him good at that. Not showing emotion had often saved him from his father's quick tongue and even quicker fist.

The squire stood with his arms folded over his chest, his face blank and distant. "Lady Juliana is not here right now, so she won't be able to tutor you today."

His heart sank. This wasn't good. Not at all. "Where is she?"

A muscle worked in Mr. Vaughan's jaw. "In Carmarthen, visiting her brothers."

Once again, he thought of what the housekeeper had said. They had quarreled, she'd said. "If I may ask, sir, how long will she be gone?"

"She may return tomorrow." The squire swallowed convulsively. "Or it may be longer. I don't know. She has gone to speak with the man she'd planned to marry before I returned." He tensed, as if he'd suddenly realized that he'd revealed too much.

Ah, the poor man. He was suffering with his lady gone. Evan could tell that. He knew it wasn't his place to speak of such things, but the squire looked so bereft, Evan couldn't help reassuring him. "I'm sure she'll be back soon, sir. She doesn't care for that other fellow at all. Not like she cares for you."

Evan's words seemed to startle the squire. Then the man averted his gaze with a frown. "I wish I could share your certainty."

"Oh, but you should," Evan protested, unable to govern his tongue when it came to Lady Juliana. "Anyone can see that she wants no one for husband but you."

The squire went to stand by the fireplace, staring into the flickering flames with his thumbs tucked in his pockets. "She hasn't always felt that way, you know. She wanted to spurn me upon my return." His voice fell to a hoarse whisper. "And 'twas said that she had a part in sending me into the navy."

Evan's mouth dropped open. "Who said that? Whoever it was is a bloody liar, sir, if I may say so. Why, my lady never spoke of you without saying how wise you were and how beautiful and how kind. Surely she wouldn't have sent such a man to suffer."

At the man's continued silence, Evan jumped to his feet. He couldn't let the squire think such awful things about sweet Lady Juliana! "I could never believe that of her when she has been nothing but kind to me. And to everyone on this estate." He drew himself up stiffly. "I don't understand how you can believe it either."

The squire turned to look at him, a wan smile crossing his face for the first time that morning. "You're very fond of my wife, aren't you?"

A tight knot formed in Evan's throat. He remembered the first time he'd met her, when the gardener had dragged him into her study and shamed him by telling her of his thievery. She could have ordered any punishment for him, and his father would certainly have approved.

Instead she'd opened up the world for him.

"Aye," he said thickly. "I think she is the finest woman in all of Wales."

Mr. Vaughan stared at him soberly a moment. "She is indeed." He raked his fingers through his unkempt hair. Clearly, he'd done it several times in the past two days. "No doubt you're right, and she'll be coming home soon. Why don't you return tomorrow, eh? I'm afraid there won't be any tutoring for you today."

Evan nodded. He knew when he was being dismissed, and wasn't fool enough to question it. He could only hope he had eased the squire's worries in some way. With a murmured "good day," he turned and left the room.

Rhys watched the boy go with a painful tightness in his chest. What a strangely perceptive child Evan was. And what had possessed Rhys to confide in him?

Simple. Rhys had felt this sudden overwhelming desire to have someone counter all the bitter doubts and fears he'd wrestled with since yesterday. His instinct had told him that Evan would do so.

And so the boy had. Rhys smiled faintly. Evan was so sure of Juliana, so very stout in his defense of her character. It made a mockery of his own attitude toward his wife.

Yesterday, Rhys had been sure of his decision to stay at Llynwydd. He'd told himself that his anger at Juliana was justified, that it did *not* signal a lack of trust in her, but merely his refusal to be involved with her treacherous brothers.

But Evan's visit, coming on the heels of Rhys's one ghastly night spent alone in their bed, had forced him to admit the truth. She had known the truth better than he. She had known what ate at him, what made him hesitate to place his full faith in her, and it did indeed come down to a refusal to trust her.

It was worse than she knew, however. For his deepest, most secret fear was more despicable than that. He feared that the dinner, the meeting with Lord Devon, all of it was merely another setup for betrayal. He was terrified that he would go to Carmarthen only to find her once more willingly allied with Lord Devon as her brothers protected her. So it was easier not to face it, to wait here like a coward and see if she'd spoken truly of how she felt for him.

Shudders racked his body. Evan was right. How could he think such terrible things of her? These past two weeks, she'd been everything he could dream of in a wife. To believe that she would betray him again would be to ignore the many demonstrations of her affection that she'd given him from the day of his return.

And to believe that she'd ever betrayed him was to ignore her true character.

His head pounding, he dropped into the nearest chair. Perhaps it was time he faced the issue he'd been avoiding for the past few weeks. Had she betrayed him all those years ago? Or was it as she claimed, that her brothers manipulated everything to paint her the villainess?

He stared into the fire, wishing the hot flames could incinerate his fears, his doubts. *Uffern-dân,* what had happened on that night six years ago? If it had been as she had said, her brothers had somehow found out about the marriage on their own and had taken steps to prevent it.

Was that so impossible to believe? Nay. Her brothers were certainly deceitful enough to do such a thing. Whereas everything he'd seen of her since his return had shown him a woman of responsible character, who wouldn't ignore a vow as holy as that of matrimony, especially for the reasons Northcliffe had provided.

And what had been the reasons Northcliffe had given for her betrayal, which had seemed so convincing at the time?

Reason one: dislike of his Welsh blood. Rhys drew in a deep breath. Could the woman who'd danced freely with Welsh laborers, who'd endured holding a snake under her skirts so she could help a Welsh boy receive schooling be ashamed of his Welshness? Not likely.

Reason two: a desire for wealth. That one made him smile. If living with Juliana had taught him anything, it was that she was careful with money, but not overly concerned about the luxuries it brought. Though he'd made all his wealth available to her, she had yet to order expensive gowns or pressure him to buy frivolities for her.

The next reason took his smile away: his lack of a title. That one he couldn't be entirely sure of, but she didn't seem to care about such matters. Her concern for her fiancé had revolved around the man's feelings, not his status as a marquess. She didn't seem to care that she'd lost her one chance to be a marchioness. Obviously it didn't matter to her.

Burying his face in his hands, he came to the last one, the one that had been the most convincing. Reason four: her fear that Rhys was marrying her for her property.

It was true that if Juliana had believed he was doing such a thing, she would have rejected him. She had put much store by having a husband who wanted her for herself.

Rhys lifted his head. But he hadn't known that Llynwydd had been deeded to her, and he felt certain she'd realized that. Besides, she'd asked him once if he was marrying her to strengthen his claim on Llynwydd, and when he'd denied it, she'd seemed to believe him.

A curse escaped his lips. Truly, now that he considered it all together, none of Northcliffe's reasons were that convincing. Faced with everything he knew of her now, Rhys couldn't believe she'd have thrown him aside so ruthlessly.

But what about the innkeeper? What about the fact that no one could have known where to find them without her help? What about all that Northcliffe had claimed to learn about the Sons of Wales from her? And why had her brothers continued to insist that she'd betrayed him, even after he'd returned?

She'd given him no reason for that. There was no good reason.

Yet there must be. And like her reasons for hiding the marriage, which, though they rankled, were sound, there must be a good explanation for everything that had happened. Perhaps if he hadn't been so busy convincing himself that she'd betrayed him, he might have taken the time to examine more thoroughly what had happened. Even now, if he asked the right questions, he could probably find answers.

But he didn't need to find answers anymore. He couldn't believe that she'd betrayed him, no matter what the innkeeper or her brothers said. Her brothers had lied, the innkeeper had lied ... damn it all, the whole world had lied. She was innocent. He would swear it. And he'd known it for some time.

So what was holding him back? If he knew in his heart she was innocent, what was preventing him from putting all his faith in his lovely wife, who, in Evan's words, was "the finest woman in all of Wales"?

The words Morgan had spoken to him two weeks ago now hit him full force. *You may be choosing not to trust her for reasons other than the evidence before you. If you accept that she didn't betray you, then you can't in good conscience force her to stay in the marriage against her will, can you? You'd have to let her choose between marriage to you or freedom. You'd have to take the chance of losing her. And you won't risk that, will you?*

With a low moan, Rhys jumped to his feet and began to pace. Morgan was right. At the root of his distrust of her was a horrible fear—that given the choice, she would not choose him. That he was not worthy of being chosen.

He drove his fist into his palm. How *could* she choose him? He'd refused to have faith in her when she had waited for him until all hope was gone. Upon his return, he'd publicly maligned her, humiliated her before her family, carried her off like a pirate with his booty, and nearly raped her.

And here she was a sweet, generous woman whom he shouldn't even be allowed to touch! Why had he mistreated her so?

Stopping short, he thought back to when he'd first met her and discovered her real identity. He'd been angry then, too, angry that he couldn't have the English earl's daughter, so he'd tried to bring her down to his level by accusing her of being a spy.

He'd mistreated her because he was afraid, terrified that she would find herself too good for him. In a strange way, it was like what the navy men had done to him. Each time they'd lashed him to that spar, each time they'd brought the cat down to tear the skin from his back, they'd told him he was miserable and worthless, a puny Welsh landsman not good for anything but fishbait. But what they'd really meant is, *You damned squire's son with your education and your proper manners— you're too smart and too strong-willed for the navy and we hate you for it.* And so they'd sought to chain him to the navy by making him like them—scared and stupefied by grog.

And he'd tried to chain her to him, too. He'd bullied her and then when that hadn't worked, seduced her to stay, all the while trying to tell her that *she* was the betrayer, that she wasn't worthy of him, when he knew in his heart that *he* was the one who was unworthy. Worst of all, he'd never given her the choice of staying. Not once.

He stopped short before a gilt-edged mirror, staring at his ravaged features. How could he have given her a choice? She wouldn't choose this despicable creature who'd been nothing but a torment to her, would she? How could she?

And yet ... The image of them standing together before the mirror two nights ago flickered into his mind. She'd listened to him say, *I can't believe you'd love me, when there's so little in me to love.*

How had she answered? By calling him a blind fool and quoting all the ways he had pleased her. And by saying, with fervent reverence, *Don't you see, I can't help but love you? As long as I have life or breath, there will never be anyone else for me but you.*

With a tortured sigh, he shoved his hands in his pockets, his fingers closing on the two pieces of the lovespoon that he'd carried around with him ever since he'd found them yesterday.

It made no sense that she would love him, that she'd choose him over a wealthy English nobleman. His mind told him it couldn't be true. But for once he had to believe what his heart said.

And his heart said she loved him and would never betray him. His heart said to trust her.

He clenched his fist on the broken love-spoon. Then trust her, he must. For there was no other way he would find peace and keep her love.

He now knew that for a certainty.

Chapter Twenty-three

> "I have my choice, beauty bright as a wave,
> Wise in your riches, your graceful Welsh.
> I have chosen you."
>
> —Hywell ab Owain Gwynedd,
> "Hwyel's Choice"

By midafternoon of her second day at Northcliffe Hall, Juliana had decided that Rhys wasn't coming. If he'd intended to come, surely he'd have come sooner. She'd half expected him to arrive yesterday, furious and determined to bear her away from the lion's den. But he hadn't. Nor had he sent word or in any way acknowledged that she'd left.

A keen pain sliced through her. If he didn't come, what would she do? How could she face him again, knowing how low in his esteem he held her?

As she sat brooding in the drawing room, a footman entered.

"A messenger has brought this for you, my lady," he said as he handed her a package.

There was no card outside the expensively wrapped box. She opened it to find a purse of intricately worked lace tracery. She looked inside the purse itself and found a slip of paper bearing only one sentence—*Everything I own is yours.*

Rhys! she thought, leaping to her feet. "Where is the man who brought this?"

" 'Twasn't a man, my lady, but a boy. And he's gone."

She sank into the chair, disappointment clutching her chest as she stared at the slip of paper. She knew it was from Rhys. She recognized his handwriting. But what did it mean?

"Did the boy say who the gift was from?"

"Nay, my lady. I'm sorry, but he wouldn't say."

She tamped down the first stirring of hope in her breast. Rhys had sent a gift, but he had not come himself. There was no cause yet for joy.

Two hours passed, and then a second gift arrived—a gold heart-shaped locket in a Celtic design. This time the slip of paper inside the box read, *My heart is yours.*

She smiled at the sweetness of that, but her smile quickly faded. Why was he doing this? She wanted *him*, not his gifts, dear as they might be.

By the time the third gift, a slender volume of ballads by Dafydd Jones entitled *Bloedeugerdd Cymry,* arrived two hours after the second, she could almost not bear to open it, to find another note that told her nothing of what he intended to do. But she opened it anyway to find inscribed on the frontispiece the words, *My soul is yours.*

Oh, my darling, my soul is yours, too. But if you give me your soul, you must give me your trust. So where are you?

She fretted for an hour, finally taking her mind off everything by dressing for dinner. Despite her misgivings about whether Rhys would come, she put on her best gown, the one she'd brought from Llynwydd in her mad flight. She knew the emerald satin made her green eyes sparkle and her skin glow like cream, but it didn't matter how she looked if Rhys didn't come. Nothing mattered anymore if he refused to be here with her.

With a sigh, she went down to the drawing room and spread his gifts out on a writing table. What was he trying to tell her? If he was asking her forgiveness, he had certainly chosen a dramatic way to do it. But then, Rhys had always been dramatic. 'Twas one of the things she loved about him. He knew how to hold an audience.

The trouble was, she wanted more from him than gifts and sweet words this time. And she feared she wouldn't get it. What if he was plying her with gifts to make her overlook the fact that he hadn't come to join her at Llynwydd? It would be so like him to do that. He'd brought her poetry before when he'd come to beg for forgiveness.

Her head drooped. But he'd brought himself then, too. And this time he hadn't.

Well, if this was his attempt to make amends, it would all be for naught. He knew what she wanted of him, and it wasn't his gifts.

This afternoon, in the midst of all her speculation and turmoil, she'd come to one irrevocable conclusion—if he couldn't do this for her, if he couldn't give her this demonstration of his love and trust, then he was indeed not the man she wanted. She couldn't bear to live with him anymore, knowing that he couldn't have even a little faith in her.

And no amount of gifts—lovely and thoughtful as they were—would change her mind about that.

She glanced at the clock. The time they'd set for Lord Devon's arrival was only fifteen minutes away. Mother, Darcy, and Overton were still upstairs. She'd asked them not to come down until she summoned them, so she could greet Stephen alone and talk to him privately before dinner even began.

At the thought of the coming confrontation, she grimaced. She didn't want to talk to Stephen. She didn't want to eat dinner with him or even with her family. She wanted to eat dinner with Rhys. And it didn't look as if that were going to happen.

Suddenly the footman appeared at the door to the drawing room. "My lady? Another gift has arrived, and the bearer of it wishes to speak to you."

She nodded, her heart sinking. This could only mean one thing. Rhys had refused to come to dinner. Instead, he'd sent yet another gift, hoping to smooth the way for the person he'd sent to make his excuses. The miserable coward! Why was this so difficult for him?

In numb silence, she followed the footman into the hall, wishing she could simply tear out her heart and not have to suffer this dreadful pain.

And there, standing in the middle of the entrance hall and staring at her with a solemn gaze, stood her husband.

She caught her breath, a flurry of hope rising in her chest. Rhys was splendidly bedecked in a cobalt coat and breeches of shot silk that made his blue eyes burn bright in the candlelight. His embroidered waistcoat was the best one he owned, his neckcloth was immaculately tied, and his shirt sparkled white against the dark blue of his coat.

He looked like any gentleman arriving for dinner with an earl and a marquess. But she could see from the pallor of his skin and the tautness about his mouth that this wasn't easy for him. There was no smile hidden anywhere in his face, nor any hint of softness in his stance. He was an arrogant man being forced to bend his will to another, and he obviously disliked it intensely.

Which made his coming all the more wonderful to her.

"Leave us," he said curtly to the footman, who at once did as he commanded.

She bit back a smile. Not all of his arrogance was gone, that was certain. But he had come to join her, and that was the only thing that mattered.

It was all she could do not to throw herself into his arms and cover him with kisses the moment the footman had left the room, but something in his expression made her restrain the urge. Slowly she walked toward him, her breath quickening as he followed her steps with a hungry, ardent gaze.

As she reached him, he held out a jeweled case. "I've brought you something else," he murmured, his voice hoarse.

His hands trembled as she took the case from him. She recognized it instantly. So he had found where she kept the love-spoon, had he? How beautiful of him to give it to her again.

But when she opened the case and spread the cloth aside, she found the love-spoon broken cleanly in two. Her heart leapt into her throat. Dear heaven, what did it mean? Surely he wasn't saying . . .

Her gaze shot to his as she held her breath.

His eyes darkened to blue slate. "In my thoughtless anger and foolishness, I've broken it." He took the case from her and removed the two pieces of spoon before setting the case on a nearby table. Then he took her hand and closed it around the pieces, covering her hands with his own. "Now I need you to help me mend it, my love. For I cannot live in peace until it is whole again. And I only hope I have not left the repair until too late."

Suddenly, she knew he was no longer talking about the love-spoon. He was speaking of their marriage, of the way he'd torn it apart with his distrust. Now he was asking her to help him put together what her brothers had torn asunder. And what he had spurned so recklessly.

She met his gaze, so full of uncertainty, so tense and worried, so fearful, and her heart swelled with love for him, that he could take his pride in his hands and come to her like this.

He was not an easy man to live with. His years at sea had made him more impatient and more quick to find fault. But he was fair and truthful, even in his arrogance. And he did love her. That, she could see in his eyes.

"It's not too late," she told him joyously. "It's never too late."

At her words, all the fear seemed to drain from his face. With a choked cry, he dragged her into his arms, covering her face with kisses before he settled his mouth on hers. The kiss they shared then was so gentle, so loving, she knew she'd cherish it in memory for the rest of her life.

"Never leave me again," he whispered when he drew back. He held her face cupped in his hands. "Ask me to do anything, and I shall do it. Ask me to give you anything, and I shall give it. But never leave me."

She pressed a soft kiss to his mouth. "Don't worry, I have no intention of leaving you, not now, not ever."

When she would have drawn back, he clasped her tight, burying his face in her neck. "Good," he murmured as he kissed her throat. "These past two days have been sheer torture. If you'd wanted to punish me, you couldn't have found a better way."

"I didn't want to punish you, but make you see what we could have if you'd only trust me."

"And I do," he swore. "I've found that if I don't have faith in you, I can't have faith in anything in this world, for you are the only one I dare trust ... even more than myself."

"Oh, Rhys," she said, melting. "I have waited so long to hear you say that." And this time, she was the one to scatter kisses over his face, pressing them to his wan cheeks, the fragile skin of his closed eyelids, the tip of his arrogant nose.

When she drew back, she wore a smile. "But there's

one thing I don't understand, my love. Why did you send me all those gifts? I was afraid they were in lieu of your coming, but obviously I was wrong."

He brushed her forehead with his lips. "Perhaps the poet in me hasn't died yet. I wanted to reveal my heart to you, but I was so afraid to just show up on your doorstep with my heart in my hands. I thought you might be so angry at me for waiting so late to come here that you wouldn't even speak to me. The gifts were to soften you up."

She grinned. "So you offered me everything you own, eh?" Her grin faded. "But I am much happier to have your heart and soul, as you have mine. And your trust. At long last."

He rested his forehead against hers. "I've been a fool, my love. There are so many ways I've been a fool that I scarcely know where to begin apologizing for them, but—"

A knock at the door behind him gave them both a start. It took them a moment to come back to earth, to realize they were standing in the entrance hall of Northcliffe Hall.

Then she sucked in a heavy breath and gave him a wan smile. "I hate to interrupt your lovely confession, dear husband. But that is probably Lord Devon."

To Rhys's credit, he managed to keep an even expression.

"I must let him in, you know," she added.

He gave a long sigh. "Yes. I suppose you must."

She lifted her face imploringly to his. "And it would probably be best if I greeted him alone first."

"As you wish. I came here because I understand what you feel you must do." He scowled. "But you can't expect me to like it."

"I'd worry about you if you did." She handed him the pieces of the love-spoon he'd given her, then pointed to the entrance to the dining room. "Go in there and wait for me. I promise I'll speak to him only a few moments."

He nodded, but as she slid past him, headed toward the door, he caught her about the waist and bent her over his arm to give her a long, draining kiss, driving his tongue into her mouth with possessive strokes.

When he let her up, her head was spinning.

"Wh-what was that for?" she stammered.

A faint smile flitted over his face. "To give you something to remember while you're speaking to your *ex*-fiancé." Then he strolled off toward the dining room, looking markedly more sure of himself.

She laughed and shook her head, then hastened toward the door as another knock rang out, and a footman scurried out into the hall.

Motioning the footman away, she opened the entrance door.

It was indeed Stephen who stood on the other side. He looked startled to have her answer the door, but he quickly recovered. "Good evening, Juliana."

Taking the gloved hand she proffered, he lifted it to his mouth to brush a kiss across it. Although the gesture filled her with friendly affection, that was all it was.

"Good evening, Stephen. Won't you come in?"

He entered the house, giving his greatcoat and hat to the footman. His eyes were fixed on her, as if by watching her he could fathom what she was feeling.

She couldn't meet his eyes. Guilt had overtaken her, and she was finding it hard even to speak to him. But speak to him she must, and the sooner the better. "The others haven't come downstairs yet. Shall we wait for them in the drawing room?"

With a flicker of resignation, he shrugged. "Whatever you wish."

As soon as they'd gone into the drawing room, she closed the door. Now that she was face-to-face with him, it was hard to know exactly what to say. His erect posture and air of aloof dignity made him look so terribly noble that she wasn't certain how to approach him. Had she once thought to live with this man, to share a bed with him and bear his children? No doubt they would have had a tolerable marriage. But next to what she had with Rhys, it would have been a pale substitute.

As if he sensed her discomfort, he spoke first. "Seeing you here at least answers one of my questions. Vaughan is obviously not keeping you a prisoner at Llynwydd."

"No, he is not." She managed a faint smile as she twisted her hands together. "Actually, Stephen, I'm at Llynwydd because I choose to be. I'm happy there."

He raised his chin and leveled on her a skeptical gaze.

"With him? I know you always loved Llynwydd and preferred to live there, but are you pleased to be living with him? I would hate to think he is treating you with the same contempt he showed you the night of our engagement party."

It was hard for her to even remember *that* Rhys. He'd changed so much since then. "That was a difficult time, I'll admit. But things have gotten better. We have found that we suit each other very well."

"Yes, but is that enough?" Stephen's pretense of dispassionate interest faded abruptly. He stalked forward and clasped her arm. "Tell me the truth, Juliana. Does he make you happy?"

He looked so forlorn, so lonely, as he stared at her that she wished she could comfort him. But she could find no way to soften the words. "Aye, he makes you very happy. We have found again what we once had before."

Releasing her arm, Stephen pursed his lips, then turned away from her. "I see."

"Stephen, I can't tell you how sorry I am for the way I deceived you. If I'd had any inkling he was still alive, I would never have accepted your offer. But I truly believed he must be dead to stay away for so long. I know I should have told you that I'd been married once, but Darcy was adamant that I keep it a secret, 'to protect the family name,' he said."

He nodded, his eyes distant. "Yes. Overton has told me something of what happened six years ago, and how you dealt with it. I take it your brothers were largely to blame for separating you from your husband. And for keeping the marriage secret from me."

"Aye," she said, surprised that he knew so much. Perhaps that had been what prompted him to threaten to pull out of the mining project. "You mustn't blame them, you know. They thought they were acting in my best interests."

He shot her a skeptical glance. "Perhaps Overton was, but Darcy had only one thing on his mind, as always. His own interests."

"Aye, 'tis true." She couldn't very well defend her brother, when she half agreed with Stephen. Still, she didn't want Stephen to strike out at Darcy on her ac-

count. Darcy had suffered quite a bit for his mislaid ambition. "But Darcy's machinations wouldn't have caused
nearly as much havoc if Rhys hadn't believed his lies. If
Rhys had fought harder to notify me ... if he'd sent a
messenger earlier, I would never have considered marrying you."

She averted her gaze. "And I played my own part in
the mess, by keeping my previous marriage secret from
you. I should never have let you court me when I knew
my heart belonged to Rhys. So any quarrel you have
with the St. Albanses must be with me first."

He said nothing.

She sighed. "I know you won't believe this, but it was
probably best that Rhys returned when he did. If you
and I had married, I don't think I ever could have been
yours entirely. And you are too wonderful to have a
wife who doesn't love you."

He winced at that. "I would have been happy to have
you in any case."

"Nay, you wouldn't have. Trust me, Stephen, marriage
is much more satisfying when you love your spouse."

He fixed her with a keen-edged gaze. "And do you
love your spouse, Juliana?"

"Aye, I love him. And he loves me."

A shudder passed over him before he mastered himself. "Well, then, I suppose it's pointless for me to stay
for dinner, isn't it? You've made your position clear, and
there's nothing left for me to do but accept it."

Relief swept through her. At least she wouldn't have
to bear an entire dinner with Rhys and Stephen glaring
at each other. Still, she hated to see Stephen go, looking
so tragic.

"I hope someday you can forgive me," she murmured.
Oh, bother, now she was echoing poor Darcy's words.
Truly, she had no right to ask Stephen's forgiveness.
She'd behaved abominably toward the poor man.

He flashed her a woeful smile, then sighed. "It would
be fruitless to do otherwise, wouldn't it? Bad blood between us would serve no purpose at all."

Briefly, she thought how different he was from Rhys.
Stephen would never let his emotions push him to do
anything impractical, while Rhys had to fight to keep his
emotions from consuming him. Perhaps one day Stephen

would meet someone who could truly capture his heart, who could rouse him to act on his emotions. But whether he realized it or not, she hadn't been the one for that.

She swallowed. There was still another matter she had to take care of. "I hesitate to mention this, but I promised Darcy I'd speak to you about the project."

"It's all right," he said tersely. "I told your brother I wouldn't pull out of the project if he arranged to have you meet with me, and he kept his part of the bargain." He lowered his voice. "But surely you won't blame me if I sever the relationship in every other way."

"Nay. I doubt even Darcy would blame you for that."

Silence fell between them, awkward and uncomfortable.

"Come, I'll see you out," she said, opening the door.

"Yes, that would be wise." He followed her out the door.

As soon as they reached the entrance hall, she rang for the footman. But as the servant emerged from one door, Rhys emerged from the other. He strolled toward her with affected nonchalance, but his expression was hooded as he halted beside her.

"His lordship is leaving," she mumbled to the servant. "Fetch his coat and hat."

As the footman scurried off, Lord Devon steadily met Rhys's dark gaze.

"You're not staying for dinner, Devon?" Rhys asked, tension in his voice.

Stephen's gaze flicked briefly to her, then back to Rhys. "Nay. It seems I've been mistaken in some of my assumptions."

She could almost feel the tension ebb from Rhys.

"At least you're good enough to admit it," Rhys said, the faintest hint of respect in his voice.

"Goodness has nothing to do with it," Stephen said in clipped tones. The footman had brought him his things, and he donned his coat and hat with quick, jerky movements. "And you should know one thing, Vaughan. If I ever suspect that you are treating Juliana as harshly as you did the night you took her from me, I promise I'll do my best to steal her back from you."

Juliana stared at Stephen in surprise. Perhaps there

was some depth of feeling in him, after all. Maybe it wouldn't be so long before some woman captured his heart.

Rhys slid his arm about her waist in a blatantly possessive gesture. "I shall never give you a reason to try it. Rest assured that I know the worth of what I have."

Stephen smiled for the first time since his arrival. "Then I wish you both luck. So few of us learn the worth of what we have until it is beyond our reach."

And with that, he left.

As soon as the door closed behind him, Rhys turned her in his arms, relief evident in every line of his face. "I hope you know that I've suffered a thousand deaths in the last ten minutes."

She couldn't help but tease him. "You deserved it for the way you made me suffer the past two days, making me wonder if you would come or no."

"It couldn't have been more than I suffered." He drew her close. "The servants at Llynwydd will tell you how I became a monster of epic proportions once you were gone."

"And you must suffer a while longer, I'm afraid." She pushed away from him and went to pull the cord for the bell that would ring upstairs, summoning the family to dinner. "There's still my brothers to endure."

He groaned. "You do know how to torment me, don't you?"

"Aye." She grinned, then stretched up on tiptoe to kiss his forehead. "But if you're very, very good, and not too much of a monster, I promise that this damsel in distress will give you a reward to remember."

"I'll hold you to that promise, *fy anwylaf mhriod,*" he muttered as he slid his hand over her rear, his eyes gleaming brightly. "You can be sure of it."

With Juliana's hand tucked in the crook of his arm, Rhys watched Northcliffe descend the stairs, accompanied by his mother and followed closely by Overton St. Albans. Briefly Rhys wondered where Northcliffe's wife was, but he put that thought from his head as Northcliffe's eyes met his.

They hadn't seen each other since the night of the council meeting, and Rhys was shocked to see the change wrought in the man in so short a time. His air of cocksure arrogance seemed to have disappeared, and his posture was almost stooped. He'd lost weight, it appeared, and his skin bore an unhealthy pallor.

Still, he managed to fix a haughty expression on his face as he held Rhys's gaze. "Good to see you, Vaughan."

Rhys bit back a retort to that blatant lie. For Juliana's sake, he must be civil. "Good evening, Northcliffe."

After briefly assessing Rhys, Northcliffe turned to his sister. "Where is Lord Devon?"

"He left," Juliana said. When Northcliffe went white, she hastened to add, "Oh, don't worry. He said he wouldn't withdraw from the project."

Overton came down the last two steps ahead of his brother. Approaching Rhys, he thrust out his hand. "I'm glad you've come, Vaughan." His gaze flickered to Juliana, and Rhys briefly wondered how much she'd confided in her brother about her marriage. Then Overton met his gaze again, smiling broadly. "Yes, we're very glad to have you here."

"You look well, sir," said the dowager countess as she looked down her nose at him. "My daughter has told me that Llynwydd thrives under your care."

Rhys cast Juliana a quizzical glance. "Has she indeed?" He had a quick moment of fear. What else had she told her mother about him, about their marriage?

Ducking her head, Juliana said, "I'm afraid Mother was concerned that you might not be able to support me in a style fitting for an earl's daughter, but I put her fears to rest on that account."

In that one sentence, spoken with resignation and a hint of regret, Juliana had completely summed up her relationship with her mother. No, she couldn't have told her mother much. The dowager countess was obviously not the kind of woman Juliana could confide in.

A quick stab of pity went through him. It was a miracle that his lovely wife had *not* turned into a spoiled noblewoman when she'd had such selfish creatures for parents.

"Let's go in to dinner," her mother said. "By now, the servants are probably all buzzing with gossip about us, and we'd best squelch it by making an appearance in the dining room."

Northcliffe patted his mother's hand. "Yes, why don't you take Juliana and Overton in to dinner? Vaughan and I will be along shortly. First I'd like a word with him in private."

Juliana tightened her fingers on Rhys's arm. "Not without me present."

"And me, too," Overton added.

Northcliffe stiffened. "Very well. Let us all go into the study then. Mother?"

Their mother rolled her eyes. "Since the three of you are determined to foment speculation among the staff, I suppose it's left to me to squelch the rumors. I shall be in the dining room when you are ready." With a regal sniff, she lifted her skirts and walked off.

Northcliffe led the way to the study. Rhys was fairly certain of what the earl intended to tell him, so as soon as they entered the room and Northcliffe closed the doors, Rhys announced, "Before you say anything, Northcliffe, I have something to say myself."

Three pairs of eyes fixed on him. He was struck by the uncomfortable realization that the St. Albans siblings bore a remarkable resemblance to one another. Juliana might be superior in character to her brothers, but no one could mistake that they were her family. Unfortunately.

He dragged in a deep breath. "I think that you lied to me about my wife's part in the impressment. I think you lied to me twice—on the night you took me from her and on the night I took her back. And now I want to know why."

Northcliffe's gaze shot to Overton.

"Truly, I didn't tell him," Overton protested. "Although I would have if Juliana had let me."

It was Rhys's turn to be surprised. He turned to his wife in blank astonishment.

She wouldn't look at him. "That's the main reason Overton came to Llynwydd two weeks ago. To tell you everything. To explain that the innkeeper, who'd once courted Lettice, had recognized me and that's how they knew to come after you. To tell you about the spy in the Sons of Wales. That's why Morgan agreed to accom-

pany him, so he could help Overton tell you what had
really happened."

"But she wouldn't let us say anything," Overton
interjected.

Rhys covered her hand with his. "Why? If they had
told me—"

"You would have believed them. I know. But as I said
to them then, I didn't want you to believe them. I
wanted you to believe me. And I was willing to wait
until you could say you trusted me despite all the damning evidence."

As he remembered that day in the salon, a wave of
self-hatred swept over him so intense he nearly reeled
from it. *Uffern-dân*, after she'd made such a sacrifice
for their marriage, he'd responded by accusing her of
infidelity. No wonder she'd been so hysterical and angry.
Damn it all, he'd deserved that and more from her.

Instead she'd given him her body. And her heart,
though he hadn't realized it at the time.

Full of shame, he averted his gaze from her. "I have
been more of a monster than I realized. How can you
ever forgive me?"

"How can I not?" She squeezed his arm. "No matter
what the truth was, you *thought* that I had betrayed you,
that I'd sentenced you to a living hell. And that day in
the salon, you forgave me everything to make me your
wife. I could hardly do otherwise."

His gaze locked with hers, and something passed between them more profound, more awe-inspiring than
anything he'd ever known. Suddenly, he knew he would
barter his soul to keep the glow on her face and the
smile in her eyes, to keep her staring at him as if he
were the most wondrous creature in the world. For without her beside him, life was nothing but one empty step
after another, and all of them leading into a void.

Northcliffe broke the silence. "I can see my confession
would be somewhat anticlimactic now."

Rhys swung his head around to fix Northcliffe with an
angry gaze. "Not entirely. Juliana explained how it all
happened, how you could succeed in convincing me of
her betrayal. But I still don't understand why you did it.
I mean, I can guess why you wanted me away from
Juliana in the first place. You had bigger plans for her.

But why lie to me that night? And why keep lying later?"

With a tortured sigh, Northcliffe turned from them all to face the fire, his hands clenched together behind his back. "I lied the first time in what I see now was a futile attempt to keep you from wanting to return."

"And after I came back?"

"I thought that if you believed her to be a betrayer, you would grant the annulment."

Rhys tried to remember all that had happened that night. "Yes, but I made it clear that I wouldn't, and you still kept lying. Why did you lie after you knew that I would regain your sister at any cost?"

Northcliffe's entire body stiffened. "The reason for that is so contemptible, I'm not sure I can speak it."

Juliana dug her fingers into Rhys's arm. "He was afraid of what you might do to him if you knew it was all his doing," she said in a hard, cold voice. "After you told him how much influence and wealth you'd gained, he was afraid you'd use it to destroy him. So he let me stand between you and him. He let me take the brunt of your anger."

Shocked to the core, Rhys stared first at the rigid profile of her brother and then at her pain-filled face. Oh, God, what she had suffered! What kind of brother hid behind his sister's skirts and made her face a tormented man alone? Northcliffe ought to be shot . . . no, flogged as terribly as Rhys had been flogged, and *then* shot.

Of course, Northcliffe wouldn't have been successful if Rhys hadn't believed him. Rhys remembered how firm he'd been about what he'd do to Northcliffe if the man thwarted him, not knowing how he was sealing Juliana's doom.

No, the events of that night hadn't been entirely Northcliffe's fault. If Rhys had been less angry and more determined to ferret out the truth that night, he could have saved them both so much heartache. Instead, he'd let Northcliffe use her as a shield, because he'd been too jealous to hear the truth, too furious over finding her betrothed to another.

"I am so sorry, my love," he whispered. "Sorry for all that you have been through. We have truly made your life hell for quite some time, haven't we?"

She touched her hand to his cheek. "It hasn't been so bad. And I must take the blame for some of it, too. If I hadn't let Darcy talk me into keeping the marriage a secret, none of it might have happened."

Northcliffe had turned to face them. "Nay, 'tis still mostly my doing. I toyed with people's lives and coerced Overton into doing the same. And for that I can only offer my deepest apologies."

Juliana's head snapped around. "Apologies? You think your apologies will wipe out all that my husband suffered because of you? You think that it will bring back the six years of marriage that we lost, the times I wept for Rhys while he withstood flogging after flogging? How dare you offer something as meager as apologies!"

When Northcliffe stepped back as if stricken, Rhys lifted Juliana's hand to his lips. "It's all right, love. I appreciate your fury . . . and I share it. But I have a more productive response to your brother's offer."

He leveled a solemn gaze on Northcliffe. "While you and St. Albans can do nothing to repay Juliana and me for those six years, you can do something to show your remorse. At Llynwydd, there's a Welsh boy whose genius is being wasted, thanks to the shortsightedness of his father and the refusal of your countrymen to provide for his education. I am sending him to Eton, because there is nowhere here in Wales for him to find such an education.

"But there are other children who haven't found a champion, who yearn for schooling and have no chance of it. So do this. Give the Welsh something other than your English ambition. Take some of that money and influence you've gained by walking over the backs of others and turn it toward opening a school as respected and prestigious as Eton, where Welsh children can go to learn about their own country's glories."

He glanced at Juliana, who nodded, then he returned his gaze to the St. Albans brothers. "That would satisfy us far more than any apology, I assure you. And you may find in years to come that it will satisfy you more as well."

"It will be done," Overton vowed at once.

Northcliffe hesitated only a fraction of a second, before he bowed his head. "Aye. I will see that it is done."

Rhys smiled. At present he felt charitable toward the whole world, even Juliana's family. His wife was at his side, full of love and hope for the future, which at the moment appeared rosy. They had Llynwydd and each other. And one day soon perhaps, they would have children.

Indeed, life was good.

Overton stepped forward, his face showing his relief. "And now, my friends, let us seal the agreement with dinner. I fear that if we linger here much longer, Mother will wash her hands of us entirely."

With a murmur of agreement, Northcliffe turned to the door and Juliana started to follow her brothers.

But Rhys caught her arm. "We'll be there in a moment," he said to the two men, "but I'd like a word with my wife in private."

The two brothers shot knowing glances at each other, but did as he asked.

As soon as they were gone, Rhys slipped his arms about her waist and bent his head to kiss her, reveling in the softness of her mouth as she opened it beneath his.

She let him kiss her for one long, aching moment, then drew back, laughing. "I thought you wanted 'a word' with me? It appears to me, my impatient husband, you wanted to do something else with your mouth. But now is not the time or the place for that."

He thought of the whole family awaiting them at the dinner table, of the servants speculating about his appearance and Lord Devon's abrupt disappearance. He thought of the long two hours ahead of them at dinner before they could even think of politely excusing themselves. Then he grinned and walked to the door. After everything her family had made him suffer, they could wait a while longer to watch him play the dutiful in-law.

He shut the door and turned the key in the lock.

"Rhys!" Juliana scolded.

Yet her eyes smoldered with the beginnings of desire as he stalked back to her. He hauled her into his arms once more, sliding his hands down to cup her bottom and pull her up against his aching loins.

She gave him a mock stern look. "My life on't, you're a wicked man, Rhys Vaughan!"

Bending his head to nip at her ear, he began to undo

the hooks at the back of her gown. "Aye, *cariad*. Very wicked. But no more wicked than my wife, I suspect. Shall we find out?"

Her breath was already quickening, and he could feel her resistance melt as she slipped her hands about his waist. "Well . . . I suppose we can always join the family for breakfast. . . ."

Then she smothered his laugh with her kiss.

Epilogue

"And though in the desert night
I've wandered many a year
And often had to drink
Of the bitter cup, despair;
The yoke I suffered was my gain
And not for nothing came that pain."
—William Williams Pantycelyn,
"Fair Weather"

"Mother, I want to go home!" five-year-old Owen announced as he threw himself across the bed in Northcliffe Hall's nursery. Enveloped from head to toe in a flannel nightshirt, he tossed his auburn curls and crossed his arms, looking for all the world like an imperious lord.

"Sh!" Juliana cautioned with a glance at his little sister. "You'll wake the baby, and I had a wretched time getting her to sleep tonight."

Thankfully, Margaret merely turned over and chewed on the corner of her blanket before settling down once more.

Owen lowered his voice to a stage whisper. "I'm not sleepy. Can't I stay up?" A wily look crossed his face. "You *must* let me stay up. Mrs. Pennant is letting Edgar come over to see Uncle Overton tonight. Uncle Overton is going to let Edgar look at his French pictures, and I want to see them, too!"

Juliana rolled her eyes as she pulled the covers up around Owen. Much as she loved her brother, he was a bachelor through and through. French pictures, indeed! She could only imagine what was in those pictures. Lettice would be appalled to know her son was being corrupted by Overton while Morgan was away. It made Lettice uneasy to have her son at Northcliffe Hall, even though Darcy spent little time here now and was in London at present.

"No, you may not stay up, and certainly not to look at Overton's pictures. Tomorrow your father will be back, and there will be plenty of things to do, not to mention the ride to Llynwydd. So be a good boy and go to sleep." She blew out the candles in the sconce by the bed.

"But I'm not sleepy," he protested. Immediately afterward, he yawned wide enough to swallow a small cat. He settled against the pillow, his eyes drooping closed. "I'm ... not ..."

She stood there a moment looking at him. Although he'd gotten his auburn hair and green eyes from her, he was like his father in every other way—cocky and confident and arrogant.

And utterly lovable. With a sigh, she tucked the covers around him. "Sleep well, *cariad*," she murmured. Then she picked up the brace of candles and went to her own bedchamber a few doors down.

Only one more day until Rhys returned. Although she was glad that he'd won a seat in parliament as M.P. for the shire, thus joining Morgan as M.P. for the borough, she hated the long absences when Parliament was in session.

It had been a good idea to come to Northcliffe for part of the session, since it provided a change for the children and allowed her to visit with her family. Besides, it was always nice to see Lettice and trade stories about their children. Between Lettice's son and daughter and Juliana's own two, there was plenty to talk about. But like Owen, she too was eager to return to Llynwydd, to go to work acquiring sufficient stores for winter.

And to spend her nights once more in her husband's arms. Even after six years with him, she could never get enough of his lovemaking. She smiled secretively. Her mother would be shocked if she knew just how "impure" Juliana's blood had become.

With a sigh, Juliana entered her bedchamber and set the brace of candles on the dresser. Slowly, she began to disrobe. It was still early, she knew, but she didn't feel like dealing with her family tonight. She wanted to lie in bed and read. And dream about tomorrow.

Suddenly, a noise at the window startled her. It sounded like ... like ...

She whirled toward the window, her heart jumping into her throat as she saw Rhys perched on the branch outside, a rakish grin on his face as he tossed pebbles at the glass.

Quickly, she flew to open the windows. "Rhys! You're here!" Then she looked down at the hard ground below and her delight abruptly faded. "Are you mad? You could fall and break your neck, you blasted—"

"I'm coming in," he warned as he stood up on the branch. He gave her only a second to back away from the window before he stepped onto the sill and down into the room.

Before she could scold him further, he caught her about the waist and bent his head to kiss her soundly on the mouth. "I missed you," he murmured. "God, how I missed you."

Pleasure at seeing him surged in her, and she covered his face with kisses. "I missed you, too, you big fool. But if you'd broken your neck coming in that window—"

He laughed. "I swear it's the last time. I'll leave the tree climbing to Owen from now on. But I couldn't resist it tonight. I saw the light in your window, and I knew if I came in downstairs, I'd have to endure an hour of Overton's questions and your mother trying to force food on me, before I could finally get you alone." His voice dropped to a husky murmur. "And I very much wanted to get you alone, *cariad*."

A knowing smile spread across his face as he began to loosen the ties of her nightrail, then slid it off her shoulders.

"Why are you back so soon?" she whispered. "We weren't expecting you until tomorrow."

Quickly he shed his own clothing. "The session ended early. And now I am yours for the next year." His eyes gleamed as he jerked down his drawers. "All yours." Then he caught her up in his arms and carried her to the bed.

Much, much later, she lay beside him, sated and content. Their bodies were curved together spoon-fashion. His legs were draped over hers, and he was pressing soft kisses into her shoulder.

"Juliana?" he whispered.

"Hm?"

He splayed his hand across her belly. "Do you realize

that it's been almost exactly six years since I returned to Wales?"

"I suppose you're right."

"Yet we've been married twelve years," he said softly. He nuzzled her neck. "Have you ever wondered what might have happened if the coach hadn't been late? If we'd been able to leave together as we'd planned?"

She covered his hand with hers. "We'd have had six more years together. Sometimes I hate Darcy for taking those years away from us."

"Me, too." He paused, lacing his fingers with hers. "But other times I wonder if our six years apart are what has made our marriage strong. Perhaps we wouldn't have cherished each other as much if we'd had that time. Perhaps we wouldn't have known the depths of our love without our separation."

She turned to face him, looking up into his serious face. "An interesting thought, my love. You are either the wisest man I know ... or utterly mad. I'd have rather had the six years with you and saved us some pain."

His rich, deep chuckle filled the room. "Yes, well, I thought I should find some silver lining in the cloud Darcy created, since he's established not one but several schools in our names." He grew sober once more. "But really, *fy annwyl mhriod,* don't you think our marriage might have faltered if we'd been left to our own devices? We were so young and foolish, who knows what might have happened?"

She stared up at the man she loved more than life itself. Was he right? Was it possible that their marriage might not have been so full and rich if they'd thrown themselves recklessly into marriage from the beginning? If they hadn't been forced to overcome so many obstacles to be together?

Perhaps. Or perhaps not. "I think, my dearest husband, that time and place have always had little bearing on our love. If we'd spent one hour apart or an eternity, I know I would have always loved you. We were meant to be together always. Compared to that, six years apart means nothing, don't you think?"

He smiled as he pulled her into his embrace. "Aye, my love," he murmured. "Nothing at all."

Deborah Martin
continues to deliver bestsellers
for Topaz with her next
enthralling romance novel,

Windswept

on sale in the summer of 1996.
Here is a tantalizing glimpse . . .

As Mrs. Williams, the innkeeper's wife, trotted off up the stairs, Evan Newcome leaned back and mused on what she'd told him. Catrin Price, the woman he knew as the Lady of Black Mountain, had been to London, which meant she'd certainly been the one to meet with his friend Justin the night of Justin's murder.

Still, Mrs. Williams seemed to think she'd returned empty-handed, without the chalice that she'd been supposedly buying from Justin. That may or may not have been the case—the chalice, though large, was still something she could pack in her bag if she wanted. Nonetheless, the bit about the hundred pounds intrigued him. It had been the exact amount she'd offered in the letter Justin had shown Evan. How odd that she'd sold a painting to raise the funds for the purchase. After all, why make such a sacrifice if she were planning to have some hireling steal the chalice back and the money, too?

For the first time since he'd set off from London with the urge for vengeance burning in his chest, he stopped to reconsider his suspicions. Until now he'd postulated that Mrs. Price might have lured Justin to the inn with the aim of gaining the chalice, then reclaiming her money by setting hirelings upon him.

Now he wasn't so sure. The woman Mrs. Williams described wasn't the type to engineer such a scheme. Obviously, she'd wanted the chalice. Yet that wasn't suspicious for a woman who specialized in studying such things.

On the other hand, why hadn't she written to Justin in a forthright manner, stating her real name? Why hadn't she met him at his home, for God's sake? And what about the missing letter and all the lies she'd told him yesterday about her identity? That was all very suspicious.

"Good morning, Mr. Newcome," said a low, melodic voice from the doorway, jerking him from his thoughts.

He glanced up to find the very object of his ruminations entering the inn. He watched as Mrs. Price came across the room with a solemn expression on her face.

Inexplicably his pulse quickened. She looked not at all as she had yesterday, when he'd come upon her swimming at the lake. She was dressed fashionably, the very picture of a woman paying a formal call—all white muslin and pearls. Seeing her clothed had nearly as profound an effect on him as seeing her in her wet chemise, for with the swell of her breasts and her sweet throat rising from amidst a froth of lace, she resembled nothing so much as a delicious confection. And he wanted to devour her.

He shook his head to clear it. What was he thinking? No matter how enticing the woman looked, she still could have been the one to lead Justin to his death. She was also still the woman who'd made a fool of him yesterday, spinning tales about a nonexistent recluse.

Remembering how she'd led him about by the nose, he stiffened. "Good morning," he quipped as she approached his table. "I trust you've recovered from your illness?"

A quick flush of embarrassment stained her cheeks, though she continued to hold his gaze. "I suppose I deserve that, don't I? I behaved very badly yesterday."

He regarded her with a cold gaze. "Yes, you did."

Only the barest flicker in her blue eyes betrayed that

he'd scored a hit. She jutted out her chin, her hands tightening on her reticule. "I've come to apologize."

"I see. I trust you received your shawl?" *The one I left at your estate to show you I knew who you were?* he added to himself.

Her cheeks grew pink once more. "Yes." She gestured to the chair Mrs. Williams had recently vacated. "May I join you?"

"Certainly, Mrs. Price." He stood, remaining standing until she was seated, then settled back into his chair. "I do have the name correct, don't I?"

This time she flashed him an irritated glance. "Don't you think you've rubbed it in quite enough?"

"Oh, I don't know. You haven't apologized yet."

"You haven't given me the chance."

"True. But then I don't have to, do I? I'm the one who was lied to, who was misled and then turned away on your whim. I don't have to talk to you at all."

She dragged in a heavy breath, the faint tightening of her lips showing her distress. "Why are you making this so difficult for me?"

He leaned back in his chair, wondering the same thing. The truth was, he was enjoying watching her get flustered. Besides, flustered women often said things they didn't mean to. "I'm afraid I become very cantankerous when I'm lied to."

"Will explaining why I lied make you less cantankerous?" she asked in a small voice.

"Perhaps."

"Very well." She tipped up her chin. "It so happens that I'm . . . well, I'm shy. When you asked for directions to my estate, I . . . I panicked and said a lot of nonsense to put you off."

He could tell from the way her eyes wouldn't meet his that she was lying. Again. He lowered his voice to a silent murmur. "Why? I wouldn't have guessed it from the way you came up out of the lake wearing nothing but your chemise."

Never had he seen a woman grow so red. "B-but that's just it," she stammered. "A-after you'd seen me like that . . . I-I knew I could never face you again."

"So what are you doing here now?"

She met his gaze, looking miserably humiliated. "I realized later how badly I'd behaved, and I wanted to rectify my error."

"That's a bald-faced lie. You wouldn't be here at all if I hadn't left your shawl at Plas Niwl to show that I knew who you were."

And if I hadn't left my name, he thought with a little stab of anger.

She stood abruptly, her chin trembling. "I am so ... so very sorry. Obviously I underestimated how much I offended you yesterday. It's clear that no apology can excuse my abominable actions."

When she turned away from the table, he jumped to his feet. "Wait!"

She halted, her back to him.

He forced a conciliatory note into his voice. He would get nowhere with the woman if he drove her away. "Please, Mrs. Price. Sit down. I promise I'm finished being a beast about yesterday."

Still she hesitated. "You have every right to be a beast. It wasn't hospitable of me to take advantage of your having confused me with Grandmother. I should have set you straight from the beginning."

"Enough, please. You've made your apology, and I accept it. All right?"

When she turned to look at me, her eyes misty with tears, he felt a stab of guilt. Dear God, but she knew how to play a man, didn't she? After one look in those eyes, Justin must have left the inn floating on a cloud. No wonder he had been so easily taken off guard by those thieves.

Evan thrust that thought from his mind. "Won't you join me for some tea or something?"

She hesitated a moment, then pulled out the chair and sat down, folding her hands primly on the table.

"I'll just fetch Mrs. Williams and order us a pot of tea," he murmured.

"That's not necessary. I just breakfasted. I don't need anything."

He shrugged and took his seat. When she stared down at her hands, obviously uncertain how to go on, he said, "I hope you're not going to be 'shy' again. After all, we have much to talk about. You write essays on Welsh folklore, and I'm contemplating a book on the subject. We have a great deal in common, don't we?"

For the first time since she'd entered the White Hart, she smiled. "Not as much as you think. I've only begun to scratch the surface of Welsh literature and the oral tradition, whereas you have mastered it."

The hint of awe that had crept into her voice struck him with surprise. "So you did recognize my name."

"Instantly. I've read many of your essays and three of your books. I even have my own copy of *The Development of Celtic Languages*."

Despite himself, he smiled. "I'm flattered."

"No, 'tis I who am flattered, nay, astonished that you even know my name." She flashed him a shy glance. "When Bos said that you told him you'd read my essays ... well, I could hardly believe it."

Her essays. Oh, damn. He'd only read one of them

His smile grew forced. "Actually, I have a confession to make. I'm not as familiar with your essays as I implied."

Instantly, that wariness she'd shown at the lake entered her expression. "But you told Bos—"

"I wanted to see you."

"Why?" Her voice was the barest whisper.

"You're going to laugh when I tell you."

She remained silent.

"I did come up here to do research for my book on folk tales. But as I told you before, I stopped in Carmarthen to visit my friends, the Vaughans, and they told me this intriguing tale—"

"The Vaughans?" Her face had lost its wariness. "You know Lady Juliana?"

"Yes. She and her husband are the ones who sponsored me at Eton and then at Oxford. They've been my patrons for some time." For some reason he couldn't bring himself to tell her the whole truth—that his father had been one of Rhys's tenant farmers.

"They're wonderful people, aren't they?" she said with a broad smile.

"Yes." Then he added in a dry tone, "Of course, they were the ones who misled me about you in the first place."

"Oh?"

"We began talking about legends of the region, and Lady Juliana mentioned the Lady of Black Mountain. I'd heard of the Lady of Black Mountain all my life, so I made some comment about the old woman. Juliana got this peculiar look on her face and began going on and on about your advanced age. I should have guessed then that she was jesting with me, but I didn't. And she never set me straight."

"That's awful!" Mrs. Price exclaimed. "Why on earth would she do such a thing?"

He shook his head. "There's no telling. In any case, she told me about your writing, and I remembered that I'd read an essay of yours. She also suggested that I see the lake. So I thought, why not take a jaunt up to Llanddeusant and see this old woman for myself? Maybe I'll put her in my book about Welsh legends. Then when Sir Jenkins told me *you* were the Lady of Black Mountain—"

"You became angry at me for having let you continue in your misconception," she said, lowering her gaze from his.

"Not entirely. I also became interested. You're an intriguing woman, Mrs. Price."

She lifted her head, and her eyes met his. Something passed between them—a frisson of awareness that he felt clear to his bones. Despite himself, he wondered what it would be like to have those eyes on him all the time, to feel that luscious mouth soften under his—

With an inward oath he beat down his lascivious urges. He wasn't here to seduce the woman, after all. He was here to find out what happened the night of Justin's murder.

"So you didn't really want my help with your book," she said, disappointment evident in her voice.

He felt an instant desire to wipe away that disappointment. "Actually, last night I thought about it and realized it would be a good idea. You know the area. You know the superstitions and local tales. Perhaps you wouldn't mind showing me around and helping me collect information." Yes, he thought, pleased at his own brilliance. What a perfect excuse for getting to know Mrs. Price.

A smile lit her face. "Oh, I would like that so much.

and I have done a little work myself in that area, so I think I can help you."

"Catrin!" exclaimed a voice behind Evan.

Both he and Mrs. Price turned to see Mrs. Williams hurrying down the stairs. They both instantly stood.

Mrs. Price's face was wreathed in smiles. "Good day, Annie. How are things with you?"

"Fine, fine." Mrs. Williams hurried to Mrs. Price's side, and the two women embraced. Then Mrs. Williams held Mrs. Price out at arm's length. "You're looking well." She cast Evan a sideways glance. "She's looking well, isn't she, Mr. Newcome?"

"Quite well," he said, relishing the blush that briefly touched Mrs. Price's cheeks. "Quite well indeed."

"I saw you come in, Catrin," Mrs. Williams said, "and I thought I'd best warn you that Huw Aberdare might be here any moment. He promised to come by this morning and show me the verse he's going to recite for the wedding."

Instantly a change came over Mrs. Price. "Thank you for telling me, Annie," she said, but though her voice was steady and calm, he could tell from the trembling of her hands and the way she twisted the strap of her reticule that she was agitated.

"I thought you'd want to know," Mrs. Williams repeated, then with a glance in Evan's direction, she hurried back up the stairs.

"Who's Huw Aberdare?" Evan asked when Mrs. Price continued to stand there, looking uncertain.

"The schoolmaster," she murmured, casting a nervous glance at the entrance to the inn. "Actually, Mr. Newcome, I must be going. I'll see you tomorrow morning." She turned toward the door.

"He must be a dreadful man to make you run off so quickly," Evan remarked as he followed behind her.

She stopped short and turned to him, a forced smile on her face. "He's not dreadful at all. Unfortunately." She sucked in a heavy breath. "If you'd be so good as not to tell him I was here, I'd appreciate it."

This was growing more and more curious. "May I know why?"

She frowned. "It's a personal matter. You understand."

Though he wanted to ask more, he didn't. This wasn't the time to alarm her with prying.

Then her frown faded, replaced by a soft smile. "It's been lovely meeting you. Good day, Mr. Newcome."

"Evan," he corrected.

"What?"

"Call me Evan. If we're to be working together, there's no point in standing on formality."

She cast him a searching glance. "Then you must call me Catrin, of course."

"Good day, Catrin," he said, but before she could get away, he took her gloved hand and pressed a kiss to it.

When he released her hand, she stood there, the color rising in her cheeks. Then she mumbled, "Good day, Evan," and left.

He went to the window and stared after her, wondering at the perverse impulse that had made him kiss her hand. It had been a long time since he'd felt such intense hunger for a woman. He wondered what it would be like to kiss her for all she was worth. How would she react? Would she slap him and tell him that he was being entirely too forward, as his former fiancée had done the first time he'd kissed her? Or would she blush prettily and return his kiss?

Much as he wanted to find out, he knew he wouldn't ever try it. Despite her excuses for her behavior yesterday, she still hadn't sufficiently explained why she'd lied to him. She was hiding something, and she thought he couldn't tell.

But he wasn't that much a fool. He fully intended to find out everything about her trip to London, no matter what defenses she put up. And he wouldn't let his attraction to her stand in the way of that either!